Echo in Emerald

ECHO IN EMERALD

SHARON SHINN

Where to find Sharon Shinn:
Website: www.sharonshinn.net
Facebook: https://www.facebook.com/sharonshinnbooks/
Amazon: https://www.amazon.com/s?k=Sharon+Shinn&ref=dp_byline_sr_all_1

THE KINGDOM OF THE
SEVEN JEWELS

The Kingdom of
The Seven Jewels

CAST OF CHARACTERS

PROFESSIONALS & WORKING CLASS FOLKS

Chessie: a young woman who lives in the "Sweetwater" district of the royal city

Red and Scar: her echoes

Morrissey: one of Chessie's professional acquaintances

JoJo: Morrissey's partner

Dallie: a server at a tavern called Packrat

Jackal: a dangerous man who trades in information

Bertie: a man who works for Jackal

Pippa: a woman who works for Jackal

Halloran: Jackal's chief rival

Trout: JoJo's brother, a thug for hire

Covak: Trout's partner

Orrin: Morrissey's nephew

Malachi Burken: the king's inquisitor

Nico Burken: Malachi's nephew and apprentice inquisitor

Nadine Burken: Nico's mother

Brianna: Nico's fiancée, a seamstress

Angela: the former governess who raised Chessie

Lourdes: head housekeeper at the royal palace

Gina: a purveyor of recreational drugs

Eva Candleback: a jeweler

Curtis: one of her clerks

Ronin: another jeweler

Mallory: a priestess at a small temple in Alberta

NOBLES AND ROYALS
Leffert: a low noble who was found murdered in the royal city
Wimble: a low noble who throws notorious parties
Trev, Jordie, Barton: lords who attend Wimble's parties

Harold: the king
Tabitha Devenetta: the queen, Harold's second wife, the mother of his daughter
Cormac: the king's oldest legitimate son and heir
Jordan: the king's second legitimate son
Annery: Harold and Tabitha's daughter
Jamison: Harold's bastard son

Edwin of Thelleron: the first king of the Seven Jewels (long dead)
Amanda: the first queen

CHAPTER ONE

It's always a bad sign when someone wants to meet you at midnight under a bridge in a dicey part of town. I'd only agreed to the meeting because Morrissey and I had a long history, and he'd been more or less honest in all our past dealings. The last job I'd done for him hadn't gone so well, but I figured everybody should be allowed at least one mistake. Certainly I'd made more than one in my own dubious career.

I got to the rendezvous an hour ahead of time, trailed as always by Red and Scar. I left them lurking in the shadows of a noisy tavern while I went to investigate the terrain. We were on the easternmost corner of Camarria, in a part of town generally known as Sweetwater in honor of the foul trenches of offal that used to line half the streets back when this area was home to most of the city's slaughterhouses. Every third building was locked up or abandoned, but the ones that were occupied were doing a lively business as they offered every form of after-hours entertainment. I had glanced through the doors of the bars and brothels and gambling halls as we slipped through the city, and nobody had seemed to notice us at all. That was pretty much always my goal.

The bridge Morrissey had specified was a crumbling structure of wood and plaster that arched over a long-dry drainage canal. At one time it had probably allowed farmers coming up from Banchura to drive their carts over the trenches without splashing through the blood and entrails, but it had been unstable and unused for as long as I had been in the royal city.

Well, unused except as a meeting spot for people who didn't particularly want to be seen.

I poked around, but there weren't many hiding places where I could install Scar and Red to make sure this meeting didn't suddenly get ugly. The shallow drainage ditch stretched out for a quarter of a mile in either direction from the crossing point of the bridge, and it was entirely empty except for the accumulated trash of a decade and the occasional slick of ice. Not only that, a three-quarter moon rained down a watery light that illuminated anything that wasn't standing in the shade of something else. There were no buildings crouched along the stony banks of the canal, at least none that were close enough to provide cover for my backup team. I would have to rely on shadows if I wanted to keep my echoes nearby.

I retraced my steps to the tavern to fetch Scar and Red. As far as I could tell, I was the only person in Sweetwater who had echoes—creatures who looked like me, exact replicas down to my moles and fingernails—though they had no real volition of their own. I could direct them from short distances, making them turn or wave or smile even when I was doing something else. I could maintain the illusion that we were three separate people. That was critical to my survival. Here in Sweetwater, it never did anybody any good to be out of the ordinary, and I didn't want to be the only girl in this part of town with echoes. And the only person with echoes who had a few other tricks, too—again, as far as I knew.

I hid Scar on the opposite side of the ditch, directly under the overhang of the bridge, hunkered down close enough to the ground to almost disappear into darkness. Red carefully climbed the broken scaffold of the bridge to take her place directly above the meeting point. My hope was that, if I needed her, she could swing down with a few quick swoops. Then I settled into an easy crouch to await Morrissey's arrival, placing myself so that I was vis-ible from the street but could quickly dive into the shadows if it sounded like trouble was on the way.

The view from down there was utterly tedious, so I shifted my consciousness into Red's body and looked around. I liked this vantage point better. I could see flickering lights and moving silhouettes as people milled past windows and doorways in the nearby neighborhood. For a while I watched a tumbling ball of flying limbs and torsos—a barroom fight that had spilled out onto the street, it seemed, taking half the patrons with it. The wind, which had been tame all day, developed a rebel streak and whistled past my shoulders, causing me to draw my jacket a little tighter. Here at the border of autumn and winter, I probably should have been wearing a wool coat already, but I didn't like the way the heavier garment restricted my movements. I'd endure the cold if it meant I was free to fight.

A moment later, my eyes caught the rhythm of purposeful movement as two shapes headed my way. The smaller one was probably Morrissey. The bigger one—a hulking body at least a head taller than Morrissey—was likely to be JoJo, a broad bull of a man who was usually trailing Morrissey to make sure everyone listened to what his smaller friend had to say. Morrissey had told me we should both come alone, and I'd agreed, but obviously we'd both been lying.

Still in Red's body, I drew myself almost flat with the splintered floor of the bridge, so neither of them would see me even if they glanced up. Then I cast myself back into Chessie's body and angled my head up toward the neighborhood behind me. When it seemed reasonable that I might hear footsteps, I came to a standing position and turned to face the street. The pose of someone waiting.

Morrissey must have ditched JoJo somewhere nearby because he was alone as he skidded down the shallow, rocky bank of the canal. I waited till he came to a halt and found his footing about two yards away. Close enough for me to hear him, too far for him to make a sudden lunge for my throat. I studied him in the frosty moonlight. He wasn't much taller than I was, scrawny, with wild hair and nervous hands. His patched overcoat looked much warmer than mine.

He nodded. "Chessie."

"Morrissey."

"You looking for work?"

"Depends on the job."

"I need something returned to me."

I cocked my head. "Something that actually belongs to you?"

"That's not fair," he said sharply.

I shrugged. "Last time you asked me to fetch something for you, it wasn't yours."

"It was. Halloran never paid me, so it was mine."

"I don't know how many times I have to tell you. I'm not a thief. I'll run errands, I'll make deliveries, I'll find out anything you need to know, but I won't steal."

"I'm not asking you to steal. This job is perfectly legal."

"So what is it?"

"I need something picked up for me. From Empara."

"Empara! That's a week's journey away!"

"What do you care? I'd pay you by the day, or the mile. Whichever you prefer."

"What would I be picking up?"

"Do you want the job?"

"Not if I don't know what I'd be carrying."

"Accompanying," he said.

It took me a second to digest that. "It's alive? It's a *person*?"

"A child."

Now I could only stare at him in the silvered dark. He was always twitchy, but he seemed even more nervous than usual, fidgeting with something in his pocket, twisting around to look over his shoulder, scuffing at the rocks with his toe. "*Your* child?" I demanded.

"No. My sister's son. She can't keep him anymore."

Is she injured? Is she dead? Has she run out of money for food? Or is he so wild she can't control him? I couldn't imagine any person in any province within the Seven Jewels considering Morrissey a better alternative to any situation that the boy might currently be in. "I don't think I'm the person for this job," was all I said.

"Think about it," he urged. "I told her it would be a month or two before I had my living situation straightened out. She's not in a hurry. But it's got to be done."

"How old is he?"

"Thirteen."

Almost, I was curious enough to ask for the rest of the details. Almost, I was sympathetic enough to agree. For reasons Morrissey couldn't possibly know, I was undoubtedly the perfect person for this job. Ten years ago, at the exact same age, I'd made that identical trip from Empara to the royal city, though I hadn't had someone even as pathetic as Morrissey waiting for me at journey's end. I could probably give the boy some useful advice, prepare him for how very different life in Camarria would be from the existence he was used to, reassure him that the world hadn't entirely ended and might actually become a place he liked again one day.

But I had exactly zero interest in returning to Empara, on my behalf or anybody else's.

"I don't need to think about it," I said. "I don't want the job. Ask somebody else."

"I will," he said. "But I'll keep asking you, too. You might change your mind."

I shrugged. Then I gestured at the bridge overhead. "So why the secrecy? Why meet me here? I could have joined you at the tavern some night to hear about a job like this."

He glanced over his shoulder again. "Well, yeah, that's part of the living situation I have to take care of," he said. "I didn't—maybe there are a couple of other debts that haven't been settled—"

Almost as if his nervousness had summoned them, three men suddenly came pelting down the bank of the canal. Four, because I saw JoJo's oversized shape charging after them, a step or two behind. Morrissey and I cursed in unison and backed toward the imperfect shelter of the bridge. I could do the math here—one of the ruffians would go for Morrissey, one would tussle with JoJo, and one of them would come for me.

Which was exactly what happened.

I had a knife, of course, and it was instantly in my hand, but the man who bore down on me was wearing a thick leather vest that might turn back my slim blade. I feinted—right, left—as he swung his arms in my direction, trying to connect a fist with my face or grab me in a hold that would squeeze the breath out of my lungs. He chopped at my wrist so hard that my knife went flying. Grunting in satisfaction, he lunged forward and wrapped his fingers around my throat.

I let Chessie go limp as I threw my soul into Scar, who shot up from concealment and flew across the canal. In Scar's body, I leapt onto the assailant's back and started gouging his cheeks while clamping my legs around his waist hard enough to make him struggle for air. Loosening his grip on Chessie, he clawed at my knuckles and tried to throw punches over his shoulder. From Scar's pocket, I pulled another knife and began stabbing into his meaty flesh just below the collarbone. He yowled in pain and tried to shake me off his back. From this angle—if he hadn't been flailing about so violently—I probably could have sliced his jugular. But the only thing I wanted more than to survive the night was to not kill a man, so I didn't do it.

I shoved the point of the knife deeper into his shoulder, and he shouted again, capering around like a madman. I locked my other hand around his wrist, tightened my legs, and tried to simply tie myself onto his body in such a way that I could hold on without any particular concentrated thought. Then I skipped back into Chessie's shape where it lay almost motionless on the ground. Just for a moment—just long enough to roll to my knees, grab hold of the bruiser's ankles, and pull him to the ground in a noisy crash. Then I flung myself up, into Red's body, and scrambled down over the side of the bridge, giving Scar and Chessie just enough time to roll out of the way. When I was dangling over the bully's writhing form, I dropped down, landing on his belly with both feet. He *oofed* with pain, doubling up with the force of my weight; as his head jerked up off the ground, I punched him on the chin. He grunted again, fell back to the ground, and lay still.

I looked around quickly. JoJo's assailant was already lying in the ditch, moaning, and JoJo was hauling on the shoulders of the man who was hammering at Morrissey's face. Morrissey had his arms up in a feeble attempt at self-defense, but it was clear that JoJo would take care of things and everybody knew it. I allowed myself to come down off my state of high alert. With a shrug and a shake of my head, I flowed back into Chessie's body and jumped to my feet. Scar stood up more slowly, then edged closer to Red. They were both ranged behind me when JoJo grabbed the third man by the waist and sent him crashing into the dry ditch.

Morrissey gasped and staggered sideways, and then for a moment, we all just stood there, waiting to see what might happen next. The three attackers all lay on the ground in various stages of immobility, but none of them looked eager to leap up and reenter the fray. They were all alive, of course. The king's inquisitor took a very dim view of murder, and even in Sweetwater, killings were rare because justice was so drastic.

Breathing hard, Morrissey stepped past one of the groaning bodies and came my way. He nodded at Scar and Red. "You said you'd come alone."

I didn't even bother pointing at JoJo. "So did you."

"So you'll think about the job?"

I almost laughed. "I don't want to go to Empara to bring back a boy to come live with *you!* Who are these men, anyway? What have you done now?"

"It's a misunderstanding. It'll get straightened out. But I need you to make the trip."

I just shook my head. "I'm going home now. You can solve this problem without me."

He might have replied, but I was walking away, Scar and Red at my heels. Usually when we travel through the city, I let them trail farther behind, so far that it often looks like we aren't even together, but the little incident under the bridge had spooked me. So I kept them close, though I didn't have them synchronize their movements with mine. Even at night, even in a largely inebriated part of town, that would have been too noticeable. And so we walked together like a tight band of friends constantly looking out for trouble.

Pretty soon we were out of the questionable part of town and in the working-class neighborhood where I had my small lodgings.

The advantage was that the streets were quieter and safer; the disadvantage was that all the respectable people were already asleep, so there was very little light from doorways and windows to supplement the moon's ghostly glow. Technically, the neighborhood was a level above my station, since most people who met me would have assigned me to the lowest category of society: the persistent poor. But I was quiet, well groomed, paid my rent on time and never caused trouble, so my landlady was glad enough to keep me as a tenant. I was sure she wondered at the precise relationship between my roommates and me, but she never asked questions and never interfered in my business, and so we got along just fine.

My apartment was on the second floor of a squat two-level building, and we all climbed the steps as noiselessly as cats. Once we were inside, I made a quick pass through the two rooms to make sure no one was lying in wait. Despite the fact that no one I was acquainted with even knew where I lived, despite that fact that I'd never witnessed any violence in this district, I couldn't seem to break my habits of caution. Then again, I knew better than most that even home could turn from a haven to a hell in a matter of minutes.

But for tonight, at any rate, all was well. Nothing disturbed, no one lurking in the shadows. I made sure the curtains were closed, then lit a couple of lamps. Red and Scar were already sprawled on the large, lumpy sofa, one of the six pieces of furniture I owned— the others being two chairs, a table, a bed, and a tall chest of drawers. Anyone who walked in would think the echoes were sleeping, but I knew better. Once we were inside, I had wholly withdrawn my consciousness from them, setting them aside like a pair of shoes I'd kicked off. They wouldn't move again until I fixed dinner and made sure we all got ready for bed.

I'd never had a chance to talk to anyone else with echoes, so I didn't know how it worked for other people. Sure, I'd seen plenty of high nobles riding by in their carriages or strolling through the pricey shopping districts, followed by one or two or three shadow creatures who looked just like them. But from what I'd observed, all of those other echoes absolutely, unswervingly, replicated the actions of their originals. They all dressed alike, they all moved and gestured and smiled in unison—so much so that you wouldn't have been able to tell them apart if there wasn't something just slightly different about the echoes themselves. They were all paler than their human counterparts, more diffuse, with eyes that were vacant and voices that never materialized. Reflections, if you will. Nothing more.

It had been like that at the beginning with my echoes and me, but by the time I was a teenager, I could move between the three bodies as easily as I could turn my head to look over my shoulder. And anytime I was in one body, I could maintain minimal control over the other two, enough to let them walk independently or maneuver around obstacles and other people. I never let them get too far away from me, though; any distance greater than a hundred yards and I started getting nervous.

I thought this ability to jump between bodies might make me unique among originals with echoes, but I had no way of finding out. Generally speaking, the only people with echoes were high nobles, and maybe the occasional low noble who had married into the uppermost level of society. Not illegitimate street girls like me. Even asking the question—*How is it with you and your echoes?*—would bring me so much attention that I would rather never know the answer.

I also went to some trouble to make sure nobody realized what Scar and Red really were. To that end, I took pains to make us look as different as possible. I always dressed Scar in a young man's clothes, baggy and nondescript. I darkened her auburn hair, kept it cropped short, and usually covered it with a soft-billed cap. I also played up the faint scar that ran across her left eyebrow, using grease paint to redden it every morning. When I was in her body and had to have a conversation, I kept my voice pitched low and my mannerisms brusque. I'd lost track of the people who had later made a point of saying to Chessie, "Your friend Scar isn't very sociable."

By contrast, Red was all woman. I'd let her hair grow out almost to her waist and deepened the auburn color with a rinse that I faithfully reapplied every week. Even on outings like the one we'd been on tonight, I made sure she was dressed in more feminine attire, with low-cut shirts that hugged her bosom and skirts or trousers that emphasized her backside. She got made up every morning, too, but the scar that we all shared was powdered over on her face. Instead, I emphasized her eyes and painted her cheeks and lips in rosy shades. When I was in Red's body, I was always smiling. Sometimes I thought she might be the only one of my incarnations that remembered how to do that.

Chessie's look fell somewhere between the two. I made no effort to hide her shape, so everyone could tell Chessie was female, but her clothes were almost as nondescript as Scar's and her face nearly as plain. Her hair was longer than Scar's, shorter than Red's, and left to be its natural color. All three of us had brown eyes, and there wasn't much I could do about that. Fortunately, brown eyes were common and no one seemed to notice that ours were all shaped exactly the same.

While I could spend hours in any one of the three forms and not think twice about it, Chessie's was the body that I thought of as being *me*. If I didn't have a reason to act as Red or Scar, I tended to return to Chessie. As I had tonight.

I rummaged through the small eating area to put together a late meal, then I roused the echoes so we could all eat. These were the times—at the end of a long day, when I was almost too tired to think—that I was most likely to put the echoes completely under my control. It was just simpler and less wearisome to follow one set of commands—*lift fork, open mouth, chew food*—than it was to try to orchestrate actions for three different bodies.

Similarly, once we'd eaten, I got us all ready for bed with one coordinated effort, and we climbed under the covers at the same time. Sleeping was the easiest thing the echoes and I did together; we all dropped off at the same time, turned restlessly with the exact same movements, and woke up at the same instant.

I did wonder, sometimes, if we all had the same dreams. We had to, didn't we? Even though Scar and Red moved independently from Chessie, they moved at Chessie's direction. I never surprised unfamiliar thoughts in their brains when I flung my consciousness from one body to the next. Sometimes I looked—sometimes I thought wistfully how much I would like the echoes to be friends, or sisters, whole and separate creatures with whom I could share my hopes and secrets. But I never found anyone except myself inside their heads.

So I had to believe that their dreams were my dreams—though tonight, at least, it didn't matter. I didn't dream at all.

CHAPTER TWO

In the morning I took on Red's body and dressed with special care, adding a braid to the luxuriant hair and wearing my most flattering black blouse. I worked several days a month at a tavern called Packrat that was located in a neighborhood only slightly less disreputable than the one I'd been in last night. I liked having the steady income to supplement the money I brought in from my more lucrative but less reliable pursuits. And I liked the bits of knowledge I often picked up from the less discreet customers who tended to patronize this establishment.

It was noon when I arrived for my shift. As usual, I left Scar and Chessie across the street in a scrubby patch of greenery that passed for a city park. In reality, it was a place where a whole range of people loitered looking to make connections for generally illegal transactions. Few people lingered long enough to realize that Scar and Chessie were there all day. Whenever I got the sense that their presence had drawn attention, I called them into the tavern, sat them at one of my tables, and served them a meal. They could sit there a couple of hours pretending to talk and play cards. The bartender and the regular patrons knew them as friends of mine. No one paid them much attention. Or at least, no one asked questions.

But then, Packrat wasn't a place people tended to ask—or answer—too many questions.

Today the weather was chilly but sunny, so I figured the echoes would be fine outdoors at least until nightfall. I settled them on the broken remains of a park bench and stepped through the front door into the tavern. I was instantly enveloped by the friendly smells of beer, bread, onions, and smoke. There were probably a dozen people already there, scattered among the twenty tables. Five or six greeted me by name and a few others nodded in my direction. One of the other servers, Dallie, greeted me in relief as she passed by with a loaded platter. "I could kiss you," she said.

"Overworked already?" I asked as I headed toward the kitchen to get an apron.

She jerked her head to a table of four shoved into the darkest corner of the room. "Jackal's been here for an hour already. He keeps asking when you're going to show up."

"I'll have to see what I can do to keep him happy."

She snorted and kept moving. I went to the back, said hello to the cook, put on my apron, and picked up a tray of food to carry out to Jackal and his friends.

The four people sitting at the table all greeted me in their own ways. One of the men and the lone woman said, "Hey, Red," as I set down the tray. Jackal patted my wrist. The fourth one, the only stranger, slapped me on the buttocks. I nodded at the first three and coolly unloaded all my plates before I spun around and tucked a short blade right under the stranger's chin, digging it in just enough to let him feel the edge. He goggled up at me, paralyzed with surprise.

"Don't touch my ass," I said in a pleasant voice, "or I'll cut your hand off."

Jackal and the other two laughed uproariously. "She'll do it, too," Bertie said gleefully, as if watching a dismemberment was his favorite pastime.

"Oughta cut his balls off," Pippa said.

"I would, but it's easier to reach his hand," I said, still pleasantly, still staring calmly down at the stranger. He was thin and a little weaselly, but wiry and probably stronger than he looked. He wouldn't be easy to overcome if he really went after me, but I'd learned that a show of force early on usually discouraged bullies from making additional attempts.

"Don't scare the piss out of him, Reddy-girl," Jackal said, touching my arm again. "I might need him."

I slipped my knife back in its sheath on my forearm and turned to give Jackal the attention he deserved. He was a bit of a rake, a bit of a ruffian, with curly dark blond hair, a ruddy complexion, and a permanently inquisitive expression. Built like a brawler, with big hands and strong arms and a swaggering stance that suggested he thought a fight was the best way to settle a disagreement. He was only ten or twelve years older than I was, but a sharp brain and an utter lack of fear had turned him into one of the savviest players in the criminal network of Camarria. Everyone knew Jackal. If there was a job you needed done, but you weren't sure who could do it, Jackal could make the introductions. If something had happened but you didn't know the details, Jackal could fill you in. He generally didn't bother taking direct action, but he knew how all the game pieces were deployed in the less legitimate enterprises of the city.

He was my friend, my mentor, and my sometime lover, but he didn't know I had two echoes. I always assumed he had secrets equally as big. I always assumed everybody had secrets.

I shook Jackal's hand off, to show that *nobody* could paw me without my permission, but then I leaned over to give him a quick kiss on the mouth. Because he was dangerous as hell, but still one of my favorite people. "I'll be good if he will," I said.

Jackal nodded at one of the empty tables nearby. "Grab a chair and sit with us for a while."

"Can't. I just got here. I have to work."

"Well, we'll be here for a few hours," he said. "Whenever you want to take a break, come over and join us."

"All right." I looked around at the others. Bertie and Pippa were already tearing into their sandwiches, but the stranger was just poking at his, still sulking at my treatment. "Anyone need anything else?"

"Good for right now," Pippa said. "Check back later."

I nodded to them, then headed to the kitchen. Looked like it was going to be an interesting day.

And it was, in fact, an interesting day, though long and tiring. The sunshine lured people out of their homes and away from their shops, so we were kept busy serving beer and food. A tableful of drunk young men got a little rowdy and had to be ousted by the bartender and the cook, with Dallie following behind armed with a poker to enforce order if necessary. A young couple who were fondling each other in a booth were interrupted by a furious woman who came charging into the tavern, screaming about cheaters and whores. She picked up a mug of beer from someone else's table and dashed it into the other girl's face, so then there was more screaming and some broken glassware. One of the inquisitor's men dropped by and took a stool at the bar, nursing a drink for an hour as he attempted to overhear what the patrons might be saying about any nefarious plans they were cooking up. Of course, everyone recognized him as one of the inquisitor's spies, so no one discussed anything more exciting than horse racing while he was on the premises.

Jackal stayed at the same table all day long, though the roster of people who sat with him changed every couple of hours. He was doing deals, no doubt, collecting and sharing information. He even went over and exchanged a few words with the inquisitor's man, who seemed to know him. Everyone else smirked into their beer as they watched that conversation.

I took my second break of the evening a few minutes later. It was an hour or two before midnight and I was tired, but still game for the rest of my shift. Scar and Chessie had come in from the night chill and taken a small table near the back. I'd given them each a beer and let them be.

Now I dropped down next to Jackal, took a sip from his glass, and nodded at Bertie and Pippa, who had returned about an hour earlier. For the moment, there was no one else at their table.

"Look at you," said Bertie. "Still look fresh and pretty as a flower."

"I don't feel fresh and pretty."

"You don't need to be pretty," Pippa said in her usual bored drawl. "You just need to be good at what you do."

Jackal reached over and rubbed the back of my neck, putting some force into it to knead away the tension. "How was your day?" he asked.

"Long," I answered. "But entertaining."

"That woman," Bertie said, delighted as always at drama. "Screaming her head off. Do you think that was her husband? She's got to shorten his leash."

Pippa made a sound of disgust. "Man like that, she'd be better off just to let him go."

I ignored them. "Best part was watching *you* make nice with an inquisitor," I said to Jackal. "You about to turn us all in to Malachi?"

Jackal grinned. "Now that *would* be an interesting day," he said. "I bet he pays better for information than all the rest of these lowlifes."

Malachi—the king's head inquisitor—did pay well and everybody knew it. Stories were legion of would-be conspirators betraying their fellows for the reward money Malachi handed out so liberally. You couldn't trust your brother, your lover, your best friend not to supply information to the inquisitor if the price was good enough.

It was one of the reasons Jackal was so popular, and so successful. He would never sell anyone out—at least, not to Malachi. His hatred for Malachi was a pure and beautiful thing, completely free of the possibility of corruption. His brother had died at the inquisitor's hands; Jackal had witnessed the execution, and there was nothing in the world that he wanted more than to see Malachi suffer. He didn't have the means to hurt Malachi in any significant way, but he took any chance he could find to throw an obstacle in the inquisitor's path. He would hustle informants out of the city, feed false information to Malachi's spies, erase evidence that some careless criminal might have left behind. It was the thing I loved about him most, since I was probably the one person in Camarria who hated Malachi even more than Jackal.

Though Jackal didn't know that about me, either.

Didn't know that Malachi was my father. Didn't know that I'd spent the first eleven years of my life hearing stories of his faithlessness and cruelty. Didn't know that I sidled around the streets of Camarria, always on the lookout for the inquisitor, always afraid of encountering him unexpectedly around some busy corner. Didn't know that I wondered, almost every day, *Would Malachi know me if he saw me? Would he remember my face?*

I didn't imagine I'd ever have a reason to tell Jackal all that.

"So what did he want here? The inquisitor's man?" I asked.

"He didn't specify." Jackal took his glass back from my hand and took a slow sip. "But I'm thinking it had to do with the assassination attempt. Malachi's been investigating that for close to eight weeks now. Must bother him that he hasn't found anything out."

Now we all nodded. Two months ago, someone had tried to kill Prince Cormac, who was next in line to lead the Kingdom of the Seven Jewels. The prince had been unharmed, but the incident had shaken everyone in the city—because just a couple of weeks before that, Cormac's illegitimate brother Jamison really *had* been killed. A young noblewoman and her echoes had been publicly executed for Jamison's murder, but this second attempt had gotten everyone talking. Was someone intent on slaying each of the king's three sons? Was Prince Jordan also in danger? What about the young princess?

So far there had been no answers. As Jackal said, Malachi's investigation had turned up nothing. Jackal himself swore he had no idea who was behind the attempted assassination, which would be the first time something had happened in the whole city that remained a mystery to him. I had to wonder what the mood was like at the palace: Were Cormac and Jordan nervous and on edge? Were King Harold and Queen Tabitha furious at the inquisitor's ineffectiveness so far? Was Malachi himself full of rage and fear at the notion that he could not protect his royal charges? Maybe he would even lose his job over this failure.

That would be the best day I had had since…since I could remember counting up good days.

"From what I hear, Malachi's got all his men working on that one case," said Bertie.

Jackal nodded. "That's right. You want to kill anyone else in Camarria? Now's the time to do it because Malachi doesn't have the resources to come hunt you down."

Pippa gave him one slow, level look. She was a sleek, long-limbed woman who didn't waste words or motions, and I'd always considered her the most lethal person in the room next to Jackal. "Well, I *don't* want to kill anyone in Camarria," she said at last. "You saying you do? That would be a first."

It would be a first for most of the petty criminals in Sweetwater. There was plenty of illegal activity in Camarria, but most of it was minor: smuggling, robbery, gambling, prostitution. Murder was rare, violence tended to be short-lived and personal, and the good behavior of the citizens could largely be attributed to the implacable presence of the king's inquisitor. Everyone feared Malachi, even Jackal, and Malachi was unswervingly loyal to the crown.

"*I* don't want to kill anybody," Jackal said, "but somebody did. And from what I can tell, the inquisitor isn't looking into that murder at all."

I had to think about it a minute to realize what he was talking about. Maybe two weeks ago, a man's body had been found a few blocks over from where I'd met Morrissey and JoJo. It was pretty clear how he died because there was a deep gash across his neck and his clothes were covered in blood. Everyone in Sweetwater knew not to touch a murder victim until an inquisitor came to haul him off, so someone sent a message to the palace while a ring of curious onlookers gathered around the corpse, simply staring. The way I heard the story, the first officials to arrive on the scene were a couple of priestesses from the temple of the triple goddess, dressed in white for mercy and saying prayers over the dead man. But it wasn't long before some of Malachi's men appeared. They commandeered a cart and quickly took the dead man away. That was the last I'd heard about him.

"There's been no investigation?" I asked, surprised. "Do they even know who the poor soul was?"

"As far as I'm aware, the answer to both questions is no," said Jackal. "But I've heard a couple of rumors."

Of course he had. "What kind of rumors?" I said.

"That the dead man was a lord. Low noble—but still noble."

That made all of us stare at him in shock. You might expect Malachi to ignore the death of a career drunk or a working girl, but a noble? I couldn't see the inquisitor—or the king—letting such an outrage go unpunished.

"That doesn't seem right," Bertie said. "A man gets his throat cut, he has a right to expect someone will try to find out why."

"Apparently the king agrees with you," said Jackal. "Because he's appointed someone he's calling a 'special investigator' to work with the inquisitor to solve the crime."

"I bet Malachi doesn't like that much," Bertie said with satisfaction.

"He's acting like it was his idea," Jackal replied. "But I agree with you. I bet he doesn't like it at all."

"So who is this investigator?" Pippa asked. "An inquisitor from one of the other provinces?"

"That's what you might expect," said Jackal. "But no. He's a lord himself. A friend of Cormac's named Dezmen. He's from Pandrea."

"Gorsey," Bertie said, using the workingman's corruption of *goddess have mercy on my soul.* Anyone who uttered it sounded like an uneducated provincial, but it sounded entirely appropriate at the moment.

Pandreans were rare in this corner of the world. Pandrea was the southernmost of the seven provinces that made up the Kingdom of the Seven Jewels. It wasn't as wealthy as Banchura or as strategic as Orenza, but it was unique in its own way, in that most of the people who lived there were dark-skinned and dark-haired. Each of the seven regions had a certain traditional "look." Those from Banchura were frequently blond-haired and blue-eyed, for instance, while those from Alberta tended to have porcelain-white skin and rich black hair—though, of course, there was great variation among appearances, helped along by the constant

19

intermingling among the provinces. But if you spotted a blond woman with huge cornflower eyes and you said, "I bet you're from Banchura," seven times out of ten you'd be right. In fact, Camarria was overrun with these fair-colored folks, because Banchura was so close to the royal city.

But people from the more distant provinces didn't travel here quite so often. The city of Camarria was located in the province of Sammerly, at the northeast tip of the kingdom, so it took a little effort to get there. Pandrea, for instance, was half the width of the country away, and a Pandrean man would have to have a powerful incentive to make the trip. Folks from Alberta and Orenza were even less likely to be found in the royal city—partially because they were even farther away, and partially because the western provinces were in a state of constant rebellion against the eastern ones. Pandrea had a reputation for being loyal to the crown, but even so it had managed to maintain good relations with the governors of all the other provinces, even the fractious ones.

That might have been the reason, come to think of it, the king had chosen a Pandrean man to look into this mysterious murder.

"Maybe the king thinks the lord was killed by someone from Alberta or Orenza or Empara, so he has to proceed with caution," I said slowly.

"I had the same thought," Jackal agreed. "He thinks if the crown makes an accusation, it will be just one more reason for the western provinces to rise up in rebellion."

Bertie heaved himself to his feet. "Well, let me know if the country goes to war," he said through a yawn. "Until then, I'm going to get some sleep. I'll see you in the morning."

"Hang on," Pippa said, grabbing her coat. "I'll walk out with you."

In a few moments, they were gone. I glanced around the tavern once, checking to see if I should cut my break short, but there were only a few drowsy customers sitting at three other tables, and Dallie didn't look too pressed to keep up with them. She wouldn't even bother checking on Scar and Chessie, because she knew I'd take care of them.

I brought my attention back to Jackal. "Well, come on, out with it," I said.

He showed me a face of innocence. You wouldn't think he could pull it off, but he can. "With what?"

"Come on. I know you better than that. You had some reason to be talking about this dead lord and this Pandrean noble."

He grinned. "I did. I'm interested in Lord Dezmen of Pandrea. I want to know what he's found out. *I* keep coming up against blank walls, and this is my city. How can *he* discover anything?"

"Maybe he's smarter than you are."

His grin deepened. "Well, anything is possible. But is he also more careful than I am?"

"What's that supposed to mean?"

Jackal drummed his fingers on the table. "Seems like Lord Dezmen has already poked his nose into a couple of places where he wasn't wanted. Asked a few questions about Halloran, and Halloran didn't like it."

Halloran was Jackal's chief rival on the east side. I'd never had any personal dealings with him, but, of course, I knew all about him. He was probably twice Jackal's age, a tall, fine-looking, white-haired autocrat who owned half the property in Sweetwater and had no end of enemies. But he also had money, power, loyal supporters, and—some said—a direct connection with the king's inquisitor. He was probably the person Jackal hated second most in the world.

I opened my eyes as wide as they would go. "You think Halloran would do something to the Pandrean man? A friend of the king's? That seems a lot riskier than killing off some anonymous lord that nobody seems to recognize."

"It does. But I heard a rumor today. A pretty specific one. It mentioned a time and a place and the number of men you'd need if you wanted to kill all three."

"Three?"

"Lord Dezmen has two echoes."

I felt an odd pain arrow through my heart at the thought of anyone killing an echo. I didn't even know the man, but I had a sudden, sharp sympathy for him. I pushed it aside, as being a use-less emotion. "Do you believe it?"

Jackal waggled his head back and forth. "I don't know. Halloran's a rogue, but he hasn't been mixed up in murder before, at least not that I've ever heard. Maybe I'm linking two separate stories that don't go together at all. But I know Halloran doesn't like the questions the Pandrean is asking. And I know that someone has hatched a plan to do some harm to the Pandrean. Seems to me those two things might be related."

"Well, then, I hope the Pandrean man is careful," I said. "Maybe he's smart enough to bring a few guards with him the next time he starts asking people questions."

Jackal fixed me with a sudden, unnervingly direct stare. "I need to warn him."

"That his life is in danger? That's kind of you."

He responded with a half-smile. "Not entirely. If Halloran wants him dead and I can keep him alive, then Halloran's unhappy. And that makes *me* happy."

I laughed. "Good enough for me."

"Will you help me?"

"What?"

"Take a message to Lord Dezmen. Let him know he's in danger. I'll give you all the particulars I've been able to pick up."

"No."

"Why not?"

It had been an instinctive reaction; I didn't have a good reason to say no, except that the request was so odd. Warn a high noble that his life might be in danger? Why would he listen to me? "He'll think I'm a lunatic."

Jackal shrugged. "Why do you care? I'll pay you. It's a job. That's what you do, isn't it?"

"I wait tables," I grumbled. "*Chessie* carries information."

"Then I'll hire her. Send her on over."

I sighed theatrically but pushed myself to my feet. "All right, then. I'll have her come talk to you."

"That's my girl," he said with a smile. "Now give me a kiss."

I complied, then headed over to the table where the echoes sat. This was just a little tricky since I had to shift bodies while anyone could be watching. I also had to send Red out of the room for the duration of my conversation with Jackal, because I didn't have the focus to carry on a conversation with one person while mixing drinks and making change for any number of other people. So Red exchanged a few words with Chessie, then slipped out the back as if getting some fresh air. Instantly I was in Chessie's head and sauntering over to Jackal's table.

"You've got an assignment for me?"

"Take a seat."

I settled across from him and propped my chin in my hand. In part, trying to change my mannerisms from Red's to Chessie's. In part, trying to cover at least some of my face. The bar was dark, I was wearing a cap and a lot less makeup, but Chessie's face was identical to Red's and Jackal had just been looking at Red. I didn't want him to start noticing resemblances.

"Tomorrow afternoon, in the botanical gardens, a man will be waiting by the statue of King Edwin," he said. "You know it?"

"Sure."

"He'll be meeting someone who might be bringing him information. Don't interrupt the conversation, but once he's free, go up to him. Tell him that there will be some men waiting for him by the entrance. It's not clear if they want to kill him or if they just want to scare him, but they're planning to do some level of damage. I want you to show him another exit."

I feigned surprise. "There's another way out of the gardens?"

He gave me a stern look. "Don't pretend to be dumb. Or uninformed."

I grinned. "All right. I'll show him the way out. Then what?"

"That's it. If you want to guide him back to the palace or wherever he's staying, that's up to you. I just want you to warn him." He pushed a small bag of coins across the table. "Payment in advance."

It was a heavy bag for such a small job. But Jackal always paid Chessie well—because of his fondness for Red, I'd always thought. I slipped the bag in my pocket. "How will I recognize him? There could be more than one man standing around admiring that stupid statue."

"He's Pandrean. And he has two echoes. Should be easy to spot him."

"Sounds good. You want me to come report to you afterward?"

Jackal smiled. "Don't bother. If he turns up dead, I'm sure I'll hear about it. I'll know something happened to keep you from making contact."

The threat was unspoken but perfectly clear. Jackal would most definitely learn the news if a Pandrean high lord was killed in the public gardens. And he would most definitely want an explanation from me. I unhurriedly stood up. "If that happens, I'll make sure I give your money back."

Jackal laughed soundlessly. "That you will. But I don't foresee any problems, do you?"

I shook my head. "None at all. Thanks for the work." I nodded confidently and strolled back to my table. A moment later, Red reappeared and I went back to waiting on tables. The final hour of the night flew by. When my shift was over and I collected Chessie and Scar, I glanced over at Jackal's table one last time. But he was already gone.

CHAPTER THREE

I wanted to look a little less like an urchin for my encounter with a high noble, so the following day I dressed myself with more care than usual. As Chessie, I usually wore pants and oversized jackets, and I wasn't about to don one of Red's flashy dresses, but I didn't want to look like a sewer rat, either. So I put on a pretty white blouse with floral embroidery around the high scoop neck, a pair of tailored black trousers that flattered my figure, and a pair of black boots that could almost be called fashionable. I couldn't do much to style my short hair, but I made sure it was clean and well brushed. The lightest touch of cosmetics gave me a slightly more feminine air. When I studied myself in the mirror, I thought I looked respectable enough—certainly like a working-class woman, maybe even a merchant's daughter. Almost good enough to address a high noble in public.

I dressed the echoes with a bit more care, too—toning down Red's usual bright attire, and smartening up Scar's—even though I didn't expect them to be anywhere that the lord might notice them. Still. The rich and titled tended to promenade around the botanical gardens. I didn't want to be embarrassed by my own appearance.

As was my habit, I got to the meeting spot more than an hour in advance and spent the time familiarizing myself with the locality. The gardens were one of the loveliest spots in Camarria, and every time I visited them, I wondered why I didn't go more often. They had to encompass seventy or eighty acres of flower beds and stands of ornamental trees, all tied together with winding paths and delightful low bridges arching over man-made streams. This late in the season, there wasn't much left in bloom, but most of the trees and shrubs were still green. Here and there unexpected bursts of glorious color could be found as hardy rosebushes defied the onset of cold weather.

The whole park was bounded by a latticework metal wall close to ten feet tall and tipped by decorative spear-point finials. Easy enough to climb, of course, and I had to imagine that vandals made their way in over the top on a regular basis. But most people came in through the formal entrance, which consisted of a sweeping stone archway large enough to admit a carriage. Two young women sold tickets and flirted with the soldiers who stood nearby to make sure everyone paid their way.

I paid the entry fee for the three of us, then set off on a slow circuit of the whole park, keeping mostly to the formal pathways. I let Scar and Red fall a discreet distance behind, walking hand in hand like lovers. The day was cold and somewhat overcast, so there weren't too many others in the garden admiring the flowers, the water features, and the scattered statuary. We made the loop a second time, stopping at a point almost exactly halfway around. Here the metal of the wall was woven with ivy and clematis, the leaves and vines so thickly interlaced that you couldn't see the lattice underneath. The ground between the path and the wall was carpeted with more ivy and other creeping plants that I couldn't identify, all of them so old and well established that the vines were almost as thick as my wrist.

Leaving Scar and Red on a wrought-iron bench, I investigated more closely, wading through the ivy so I could put my hand on the fence. My fingers closed on a mesh of metal and greenery. I gave the bars a shake, but this section was solid.

Somewhere, there was supposed to be a marker. My hand still on the fence, I looked around. On the other side of the path, I could see a bronze statue of an archer pulling back his bow, but his arrow looked like it would shoot straight toward the grand entrance. I noticed an ornamental bridge, but it lay parallel to the wall, so I couldn't cross it in the hopes that it would deliver me to the right spot. But there. A few yards away from where I stood, half covered in ivy and green with moss, was a small bronze sundial with a triangular wedge of metal set on its circular rim. If I considered the wedge its own kind of arrow, I could tell it was pointing straight toward a specific section of the fence.

I tripped through the heavy ground cover, paused to make sure I was aligned with the sundial, and poked my fingers through the ivy on the wall again. Instantly I could feel the break in the integrity of the fence as it wobbled under the pressure of my hand. I pushed harder, and a narrow door opened in the greenery. It only swung out about two feet, but I figured that would be wide enough even for a big man to squeeze through, if he was desperate.

It was certainly wide enough for me. I slipped through, wrestled the gate almost entirely back in place, and tore a rip in the ivy curtain so I'd be able to find the spot again. Then I hiked quickly around the outside of the wall, back toward the formal entrance.

I could feel the absence of the echoes tugging at me with every step I took. It was as if we were connected by long, thin, springy bands that had a certain amount of give; I had a sense that if I got too far away, those bands would abruptly tighten and practically yank me back to that hidden door in the garden wall. I just had to hope my sortie didn't take me quite that distance away.

As I passed the grand entrance, I glanced quickly at the soldiers posted by the gates. They would undoubtedly spring into action if they saw a Pandrean lord fall under attack, so whoever was lying in wait for Lord Dezmen would be stationed out of their line of sight. Still, the attackers would have to be close enough to keep the entrance in view so they could fall in step behind the noble and follow him to a less visible spot.

There weren't that many places a couple of ruffians could loiter near the entrance without drawing attention. To my left was a small stand of vendors selling food and beer to tired tourists; to my right was a squat structure, about head high, that might be a water reservoir. Would-be attackers could be lurking behind either. But my first guess was a tiny city park straight ahead of the entrance, featuring a patch of greenery, a simple fountain, and four benches. As I headed that way, striding along as if I was on an important errand, I could see that two of the benches were occupied. One of them held three woman and four squirming children; they seemed unlikely agents of violence.

Two men slouched on the other bench, facing away from each other as if they were strangers who had just happened to take seats there at the same time. From what I could see from the corner of my eye, both were big and predictably burly; both wore oversized coats designed to hide any number of weapons. They exuded an air of indefinable menace, and I wasn't surprised to see the three women gathering their things as they prepared to make a hasty exit.

I'd only gone a few yards past the park when I stopped suddenly, threw my hands in the air, and reversed course as if I'd just remembered something I'd forgotten to bring with me. I took one more quick glance at the two men on the bench, wondering if I might recognize them. One looked vaguely familiar, and I thought he might be JoJo's brother, Trout, but I couldn't be certain.

Still. If I'd had to put money down, I'd have bet that these were the men hired to assault Lord Dezmen. That was all I really needed to know.

I made my way briskly back around the garden fence, feeling my heart lighten with every step that brought me closer to my echoes. My small disturbances in the fall of ivy made it easy for me to locate the door again, and I was quickly back on the other side of the wall. Scar and Red were just as I'd left them, apparently undisturbed. I reset the door, smoothed down the heart-shaped leaves, and stepped onto the path. Scar and Red were on their feet and following me as I made my way back toward the middle section of the garden. Time to get in place and wait for Lord Dezmen's arrival.

The bronze statue of King Edwin was about dead center in the garden. It was taller than life size and mounted on a marble block, so you had to gaze up at it in humble adoration. It was set at one of the short ends of a long reflecting pool that was ringed with a varying border of shrubs. The shrubs had apparently been chosen based on when they came into flower, from the earliest bloomers to the latest, because there was almost always some kind of color to be had in that shrine to the nation's first king. Today, every third bush sported a few scarlet roses shivering in the chilly air. I wanted to pluck one and tuck it in Red's hair, but I was pretty sure visitors were supposed to leave the flowers alone.

We made one circle around the pool, looking for resting spots. I left Red sitting on a slatted wooden bench situated in front of what might be an herb garden in better weather. Scar skulked in the shadow of a gazebo on the other side of the pool. I found my own waiting spot, just behind a massive metal armillary sphere. I could see right through its collection of arrows and rings to the base of King Edwin's statue. I settled in to wait.

Probably another fifteen minutes passed before we saw any action. But then—finally—I spotted three men striding purposefully toward the sculpture. Or, no. Not three men. One man and two echoes. I peered around one curved surface of the sphere to get a better look.

The man was somewhat over medium height and dressed in expensive, fashionable clothing and polished leather boots. From this distance, I could make out his dark skin tone and closely curled black hair, though not the color of his eyes. He came to a halt precisely at the base of the statue, glanced up once at the king's aristocratic face, and then fell into a pose that I could only describe as relaxed waiting—his feet slightly apart, his hands folded behind his back, his demeanor one of infinite patience.

Behind him, side by side, his two identical echoes took identical stances. They were all in profile to me, so I couldn't make out the expressions on their faces, but I had to suppose those all matched as well. When Lord Dezmen casually turned his head, following the flight of a questing bird, they mimicked the motion exactly. When he dropped his gaze to study the shine on his boots, they engaged in similar contemplation. It was eerie and mesmerizing to watch.

They had been standing there maybe five minutes, and I had been staring at them the whole time, when they were approached by a much less sophisticated-looking figure. It wasn't a man I recognized, though I knew the type—thin and edgy, surviving primarily on luck and nerves. I tried to commit his features to memory so I could describe him to Jackal.

Whoever he was, he didn't bring the information Dezmen had hoped for because their conversation was brief and the lord shook his head repeatedly in disagreement or disappointment. But *some* part of the encounter went as planned because the noble handed over a sum of money, and the other man didn't bother to protest. A few more words, and then the local man slunk off, melting away as if he had never been there.

Dezmen took a moment to frown at the reflecting pool as if considering what he'd learned and not liking his conclusions. Then he straightened his shoulders and spun smartly on one heel to head for the exit. His echoes followed.

I was already on the move, and I intercepted him before he'd taken ten steps. He pulled up sharply, his echoes similarly reeling back, and I offered him what I hoped was a disarming smile.

"Lord Dezmen," I said. "Good afternoon."

This close up I could see that his eyes were light brown, almost the shade of amber, a decidedly attractive effect against the deeper color of his skin. He didn't seem disconcerted that I'd called him by name. Rather, his face took on an expression of intense curiosity, and he looked me over with great interest.

"That's right. Who are you?"

"My name's Chessie. I have information for you."

For a moment, I thought he might laugh. "You do? And what will it cost me?"

"I've been paid in advance. By someone who has your interests at heart."

That was definitely a smile on his face. "I didn't know there was anyone like that in the whole city of Camarria."

For some reason, his amusement annoyed me, though I tried to speak in a dispassionate tone. "It's true even so. It seems that someone doesn't like your investigation, and as soon as you leave the gardens, you're going to be attacked. My role is simply to warn you to be careful."

He raised his fine eyebrows. "Who wants to assault me? Who wants to protect me?"

"As for the attacks, just rumors. As for the protection—" I shrugged. "Someone who has a grudge against the person who might hurt you."

He was smiling again. "This is all very murky."

"That tends to be the way of information you get from Sweetwater. I'm sure your last informant wasn't very forthcoming, either."

That made his bright eyes brighten even more as he scanned my face. "Ah. So you've been spying on me."

I was annoyed again. "Just for the past few minutes. Just while I waited for a chance to talk to you."

He waved vaguely in the direction of the main gates. His echoes repeated the gesture. "So if someone is planted at the entrance, waiting to attack me, how would you suggest I leave here safely?"

"I can show you a different way out of the gardens."

"A different way out! Of course! Because that's where *your* men are stationed to kill me."

"Goddess have mercy on my soul," I muttered. I took a deep breath and once again made a special effort to speak in a neutral tone. "I'm just here to warn you that someone in the city doesn't like your investigation. If I were you, I would watch my back—or start going around with a hired guard within call." I indicated his echoes. "I don't think *they* will do much to defend you if someone tries to cut your throat."

"No, they're not very effective fighters," he agreed. "But the advice about a personal guard is very good. What makes you think I haven't already secured one?"

I couldn't hide my surprise. "You have?"

"Well, no, not yet. But now maybe I'll have to. Is there anyone you'd recommend? You seem to know all kinds of interesting people."

I felt fresh irritation well up, and again I strangled it. "I don't know anyone who does that kind of work, but Jackal could probably give you a few names."

"'Jackal'? You're seriously suggesting I turn for help to someone named *Jackal*? This encounter is becoming more entertaining by the minute."

I was ready to just stalk off and leave him to his fate, but introducing Jackal's name to the conversation reminded me of what the man had said just last night. *If he turns up dead, I'm sure I'll hear about it.* None of Jackal's fondness for Red would keep him from blaming Chessie if something terrible happened to Lord Dezmen. I tried to gather the shreds of my patience. "I can see you don't believe me. I can see you think *I'm* the one who wants to put you in harm's way. I don't know how to convince you that I'm serious, that you're at risk, and that I'm not the one who might harm you."

"You could start by being a little more forthcoming. Who *are* you?"

"I'm just a messenger. People hire me to carry information and goods across the city."

"So who hired you to warn me to be careful?"

"Jackal."

"And who is he exactly?"

"Someone who trades in information. Everyone in the Sweetwater district knows him. Everybody trusts him—until they've crossed him. And I already told you why Jackal wanted to warn you. He doesn't like the person who wants to harm you. It's no more complicated than that."

"It's so much more complicated than you seem to realize," Dezmen said. For the first time since I'd greeted him, he actually sounded serious. He appeared to be thinking something over. "Do you think he'd have information for me? This Jackal? If I asked him some very specific questions? And paid him, of course."

"He might. Though as far as I know, he has no idea who killed that lord two weeks ago."

Dezmen smiled again, but this time he didn't seem so amused. "Ah. But he does know exactly what crime I'm investigating."

I let a shrug be my answer.

"Maybe he'll know something else that would be useful to me."

"Well, if Jackal doesn't have the answers, he'll know someone who does."

"Then will you take me to meet him?"

I hesitated a moment, but it didn't take much thought to realize Jackal would probably love to meet the Pandrean man. A new source of information! Jackal would be as eager as a cat in a cow barn. Still, I couldn't just lead Dezmen down to the Packrat without providing some advance warning. "I'll ask him if he's willing to meet you. On some neutral ground. When's good for you?"

He spread his hands; so did the echoes. "I have no other occupation, so I am free whenever he is."

"I'll talk to him as soon as I can. How can I reach you to let you know what he says?"

"Do you know where Amanda Plaza is?"

"Everybody knows where Amanda Plaza is. It's the most famous place in the city." I left the *you idiot* unspoken, but he obviously heard it because he actually laughed.

"All right, then meet me there tomorrow morning by the statue of the goddesses, and you can tell me what Jackal says."

"How about the day after tomorrow? I might not be able to track him down today."

"Of course. Someone named Jackal would necessarily be elusive. The day after tomorrow."

I glared at him. It was getting harder to keep my irritation in check. "*Of course,* you might not be around to meet me if you don't take my advice today and slip out a back exit. Where I do *not* have men stationed to murder you."

He smiled again. "No, I am starting to realize you—" Abruptly his smile faded, and he focused all his attention on a point over my left shoulder. "No, I am starting to realize you've been telling the truth from the beginning," he said in a hard voice.

It took all of my willpower not to spin around, but I knew better than to let the predator know that the prey had spotted him. I let Chessie fall into a tense, listening stance while I flung my consciousness into Scar's body, where I had a wide-angle view of the reflecting pool. Sure enough, Trout (if it was Trout) was approaching at what he clearly thought was a stealthy angle, jogging in the grass just outside of the path to take advantage of the cover offered by the trees and flower beds. I looked around, but I didn't see his companion. Where would *he* be stationed to do maximum damage?

I slipped back into Chessie's head. "When I reconnoitered earlier, I saw two men," I said in a quiet voice, still not looking over my shoulder. "How many are coming this way?"

"Just one that I can see."

"Then his buddy is somewhere else inside the garden—or waiting outside to catch you when you run."

"Outside," Dezmen guessed. "Wouldn't want to pay the entrance fee."

Despite myself, I had to choke back a laugh because that actually made sense. "You any good in a fight?"

"Well," he said. "I've had some training. I'm sure I'm not as good as someone who brawls for a living."

I nodded, as if he'd just offered me a deal and I was accepting it. We were trying to act as though we were still in the middle of an ordinary conversation, not straining every nerve to catch the sounds of danger. "All right. I'll walk away as if I'm leaving the garden, but I'll circle back to see if you need help."

Despite the very real peril he was in, Dezmen paused to give me one comprehensive look—as if, for the first time, registering that I was a woman, and a not very large one at that. "Are *you* any good in a fight?"

Damned if I could stop the smile. "Well," I said modestly, "I manage to keep myself alive."

"Then I'll be glad to see you come to the rescue."

"All right. Nod or something like we've just come to an agreement, and I'll be on my way."

He pulled his features into a serious expression and nodded twice. I touched my fingers to my cap in a show of deference, then tucked my hands into my back pockets and strolled off down the path as if I didn't have a worry in the world. The only way I could have appeared more carefree was if I'd started whistling. I left Scar and Red where they were since I'd be coming right back.

Trout was a big, dumb guy, so I figured he would scarcely wait till I was out of sight before he made his move. As soon as I was a reasonable distance away, I stepped off the path, hid myself behind a tree, and slipped into Scar's head to see what was happening back at the Edwin statue.

And goddess have mercy on my soul, I was almost too late. Trout must have rushed Dezmen the minute I stepped away, the force of his momentum carrying both of them into the reflecting pool. The water was shallow, but deep enough to drown a man if someone was holding him down by sitting on top of his head. I could see three sets of legs thrashing up spray as three shapes went under—the noble lord, who was being kept down by brute force, and the two echoes who were so tied to the actions of their master that they *held themselves beneath the water* and struggled to breathe.

No time to call Chessie's body back. As Scar, I leapt out of the gazebo and raced across the lawn to launch myself at Trout's bulky shape. He yelped in surprise as I knocked him away from Dezmen and sent him splashing headfirst into the pool. Dezmen and his echoes shot up, gurgling for breath, but I couldn't spare them any attention. I punched Trout hard in the face, my fist connecting with his cheekbone just as he was surfacing, and he went under again. His hands scrabbled for a purchase in the air and I saw his mouth making gulping motions under the water. When he came up a second time, I punched him again, and back down he went.

I didn't want to drown him, of course, so I watched closely, but he was far from done for. This time, when he came up, he was on his hands and knees and charged at me like a wounded animal. Neither of us was expecting Dezmen's wet body to slam into him so hard the force of it carried both of them to the edge of the pool.

The echoes hit the wall a second later. I heard Trout's head make a sickening *thud* against the decorative stone lip, and the big man grunted with pain. He put his hand to his skull and, still lying half in and half out of the water, he stared up at us, blinking in confusion.

Good. Disabled but not dead. Just the way I liked to leave my opponents.

"Time for us to leave," I said, getting to my feet with a great deal of splashing.

Dezmen and his echoes rose from the water more gracefully, all of them staring at me. "Who are *you?*" Dezmen demanded.

"Friend of Chessie's," I said in a low, raspy voice. "I'm Scar." I gestured over my shoulder, where the other echo hung back a cautious distance away. "That's Red."

He glanced between us. His clothes were streaming with water, and his curls were plastered to his head. He should have looked ridiculous, but even in this situation he retained a sort of aristocratic poise. "And you've both been here this whole time?"

"Chessie doesn't like to take chances with her safety," I said. "We usually follow her around when she's doing something dangerous."

"Then my thanks to all of you."

Now that the adrenaline of the fight was wearing off, I was starting to feel seriously cold through my soaked clothes. "Come on," I said. "Let's go find her and get out of here."

We clambered out of the pool, spared one last look for Trout but decided he would be able to help himself out, and then took off in the direction Chessie had gone. Dezmen seemed interested in learning more about Scar, but I didn't want him getting too comfortable with anyone but Chessie, so when he looked like he was going to ask me a question, I pointed a little farther down the path. When he glanced that way, I flung myself back into Chessie's body, which was already headed toward us on a run. I let Scar and Red fall a little behind Dezmen's echoes as Chessie came close enough to speak.

"I'm sorry! One of the soldiers came walking through and started asking me questions and I couldn't just leave him." I let my eyes take in the sight of his wet clothing before I glanced at his echoes and Scar, who were just as wet. "But maybe I should have. He'd have followed me and then we both could have helped you. What *happened?*"

Dezmen gestured in the direction from which Chessie had just come. "I think we'd better keep moving, because if there's a second man waiting for us outside the entrance, he might start wondering why his companion is taking so long to dispose of me. You said there's a back way out?"

I nodded, and turned toward the path that led to the hidden door. Dezmen fell into step beside me, followed by his echoes, followed by mine. Practically a parade. I had to swallow a somewhat hysterical giggle. "This way. So? He tried to drown you, I take it?"

"Pretty smart, I thought. Would have taken much less effort than beating me to death. And when the guards found me, they might have thought I'd just fallen into the water."

"Less suspicious than drawing a knife across your throat," I agreed.

Dezmen pointed over his shoulder. "Your friend Scar saved my life."

I turned to look behind me and gave a thumbs-up to my echoes. "He's a good man in a fight. Red's not bad, either. She's better with a knife than a punch, though." Oddly, that was really true.

"You should have told me they were with you."

I shrugged. "I never give away information unless I have to. Force of habit."

"Well, I'm glad he was there." Dezmen glanced over at me. He was taller than I was but only by a few inches, which I liked much better than the way Jackal towered over me. "Maybe I don't have to meet this Jackal character after all. I can hire *you* to be my bodyguard. You and your friends."

I laughed. "Trust me, we're not nearly as effective as some of the people Jackal would recommend."

"Think about it anyway."

I didn't answer him because we'd arrived at the back wall of the garden and my eyes were tracing the path from the sundial to the secret exit. "This way," I said, plunging off the path into the sea of ivy. Dezmen followed, the four echoes right behind him. The hidden door opened even more easily this time, and we were all through in moments. Dezmen helped me wrangle it back in place.

"Do you want to go get a look at your second assailant, just so you'll know him if you see him again, or are you ready to be done with this adventure?" I asked as we began working our way around the outer perimeter.

"Since the whole point of sneaking out the back way was to avoid him, I think we should just head home," he said. "I hope that doesn't make you think I'm a coward."

"It makes me think you have some sense in your noble head," I said, amused. I was actually starting to like him, though I couldn't have said why. Maybe because he didn't seem to mind being defended by a woman. Maybe because, even though he was rather hopeless in a fight, he didn't just sit back and let others take care of him; when he had the opening, he threw his own punch. Maybe because I liked his natural air of curiosity. It was different from Jackal's obsessive quest to know everything. Dezmen seemed intrigued by everything he encountered in the world around him and interested in learning more.

It would make him a good friend, I thought, unless you were someone with secrets.

And, really. Who didn't have secrets?

He laughed as he navigated his way around a protruding tree root. "Sensible is a word that has often been applied to me," he answered. "Though I admit to a little recklessness now and then— when the situation calls for it—I try to strike a balance between being too cautious and being too cocky."

"I try to strike a balance between keeping myself fed and ending up dead," I retorted. "I suppose it's the same thing."

He gave me quick sideways glance. Probably my imagination that I could feel the eyes of both his echoes also turning my way. "It doesn't sound like the same thing at all," he said seriously.

By now, we were clear of the landscaping that surrounded the gardens and back on a city street, a couple of blocks from the formal entrance. I wondered how quickly Trout's buddy would go looking for him, and what he would do when he realized Dezmen had slipped the net. Would he come looking for his quarry? It seemed prudent to move to another part of the city as quickly as possible.

"Well, in the interests of *not* ending up dead, we should probably get out of here," I said. "Do you know where you are, or do you need me to escort you back to the palace?"

He glanced around, as if orienting himself. "I know where I am, but I— Aren't you hungry? I'm starving all of a sudden. Would you want to go somewhere and get something to eat?"

"I'm always hungry after a fight," I agreed. Then I gestured at him, sweeping my arm back to indicate both of his echoes and one of mine. "But four of you are still soaking wet. Aren't you cold? Don't you just want to go home and change clothes?"

"I'm cold, but I'm even hungrier," he said. "Do you think there's any café where they'd let us come inside with our damp clothes?"

I eyed him for a moment in silence. A Pandrean lord who had just escaped a violent attempt on his life wanted to go have a civilized meal with a roguish band of strangers? This fell so far outside of my experience I wasn't quite sure how to answer. Finally I said, "Maybe the cafés wouldn't let us in, but I know where we can go. Come on."

CHAPTER FOUR

Lord Dezmen fell in step beside me as I cut across the street and angled in a southeasterly direction. "I feel like I'm going to get a chance to see the more exotic neighborhoods of Camarria," he said.

I laughed. "You'll be safe. I won't take you to the east side. You might wait till you've hired one of Jackal's friends before you explore Sweetwater."

We only had to cross two bridges to get to our destination, a big open plaza in the middle of a wealthy merchants' neighborhood. It was about as respectable and safe as a place could be, patrolled by watchmen and frequented primarily by mothers and children out for their daily walks. There was a simple fountain in the middle, a handful of vendors around the perimeter, and—at this time of year—seven or eight big braziers set up to provide warmth to the citizens who weren't quite ready to give up their afternoon promenades. Each brazier was ringed by benches, and about half of the benches were already full.

"Isn't *this* delightful?" said Dezmen, looking around with appreciation. "I feel warmer already."

A flock of mothers and children was just now vacating a set of benches on the far edge of the plaza. "Quick—over here," I said, hurrying past the fountain to stake our claim. The others sprinted after me, and pretty soon we had commandeered a whole section of seating. Scar and Red took one bench, Dezmen's echoes a second one, and Dezmen himself settled on a third one. He held his palms out to the fire and I noticed that he wore a large opal ring on his left hand. It glowed with its own buried blaze, looking particularly brilliant against his dark skin. That was when I remembered that opals were the traditional jewels claimed by the people of Pandrea, though if you'd asked me the question ten seconds ago, I wouldn't have been able to name it.

"I am, for the moment, suffused with bliss," he said, smiling up at me. "What simple things it takes to keep us happy."

"That's been my experience, but sometimes it takes big disasters to make us appreciate the little joys."

"And food. That's a little joy I'm anticipating. What are our choices?"

"All of you half-drowned creatures stay here," I directed. "Red and I will go see what's available."

"Do you need money?"

My expression was derisive, but I thought it was nice of him to offer. "The food here isn't very expensive. I think I can absorb the cost."

Red followed me over to the circle of vendors and we investigated the options. Roasted nuts, sweet cakes, and hot cider seemed to be the best items on offer, and one of the vendors even lent me a tray to carry the six mugs on. We returned to our companions and distributed the food, then Red dropped down next to Scar and I took a seat on the bench next to Dezmen. We were half turned toward each other, our bags of food spread out between us, stuffing our mouths as fast as we could.

"I don't think I've enjoyed a meal at the palace as much as this one," Dezmen declared when there was nothing left but crumbs.

"Do you want more? I could get another bag of nuts."

"No. In fact, I *am* dining at the palace tonight, so I should probably save some of my appetite for that."

Abruptly I remembered that he was a noble lord and I was a street urchin, and although we had shared a breathless adventure, we were hardly equals. But I didn't want to suddenly act all obsequious and shy, so I merely sat back on the bench a little and said, "The palace. What's that like?"

He gave a slight shrug, as if it was impossible to convey the information to someone who was so ignorant she had to ask the question. "Big. Full of people. There are rules for every type of behavior, and you don't want to transgress because you don't want to offend the king. Every time I turn around, there seems to be a servant coming down some hallway or out of a room I thought was empty. There's a housekeeper. Lourdes. I swear she never sleeps. She is *everywhere* in that palace. At every hour of the night or day."

The answer made me relax again. And laugh. I'd dealt with Lourdes a number of times and I had noticed her unfailing ubiquity. "Maybe she has echoes," I suggested. "You think it's her, but it's one of her shadows."

He laughed. "Interesting theory, but that's not really how it works with echoes. I think it's more likely she has a twin and she just hasn't bothered to mention the fact."

"So what's the mood at the palace these days?" I asked curiously. "The past two months have been very…" I searched for the right word. *Violent* was accurate, but didn't seem politic. I settled on: "Eventful."

"That they have," he said. "Starting with Jamison's death, and culminating with the attempt on Cormac's life two months ago."

"So one of the king's sons is dead and another one *could* have been dead," I pointed out. "Does that make anyone suspect that someone is trying to kill *all* the royal heirs?"

"Believe me, that notion has been discussed endlessly at the palace. But Lady Marguerite confessed to killing Jamison and she was executed before Cormac was attacked. It seems unlikely the two crimes are related."

"Does anyone have any idea who tried to kill Cormac?"

"Not yet," he said. "But it's the question the inquisitor is working night and day to solve."

"How about this other lord who showed up dead? Does anyone know who killed *him*?"

"Not so far," Dezmen said. "We're still trying to discover who he is. We know he's noble, but we haven't learned much else."

"If you don't know who he is, how can you be sure he's noble?"

"His clothes, for one thing."

I shrugged. "There are a lot of places in the city where you can buy cast-off clothing that's as fine as it was the day it left the shop. Clothing doesn't mean anything."

"You're good at this," he said in an admiring voice. "You ask the right questions and everything makes you suspicious."

I tried not to be pleased. "Well, but clothing is the easiest thing in the world to fake."

"I made the same point as soon as I was asked to work on the case. But there's another reason we believe he's noble. He had been seen a few days prior at a function at the royal palace. No one remembers inviting him, no one could identify him, but several people interacted with him, and found his deportment flawless. So either he *is* a lord—at least a low noble—or he knows how to play the part because it occurred to no one that he didn't belong."

"Better evidence," I agreed. "But not conclusive. He could have been an actor."

"An actor usually has specific lines, and he can deliver those convincingly. But to move through a crowd of royals and nobles and never once say the wrong thing? That sounds like the work of someone born to the part."

"So these people who talked to him that night. They don't remember anything about him that would be helpful?"

"Only one thing—that he was wearing an amethyst ring. So he's probably from Alberta, where amethyst is the traditional jewel."

"Or he wanted you to *think* he was from Alberta."

Dezmen laughed so loudly that people on nearby benches looked over at us, smiling in response. Even his echoes looked amused, and they hadn't shown much emotion so far. "Or he was hired by some-one from Alberta, or he was hired by someone from Thelleron who wanted us to *think* he was hired by someone in Alberta," he rattled off. "Yes. All those things have occurred to me as well."

"But you still think he's from Alberta."

Dezmen tilted his head. His echoes copied the motion. "There's been a lot of unrest in Alberta lately," he said at last. I had the feeling he was editing out wide swaths of information that I would probably have found very boring—except, the fact that he was concealing it made me want to know it all. "There are factions that want to ally with Empara and Orenza and secede from the Seven Jewels. There are factions that want to stay loyal to the crown. Marguerite's death has stirred up a great deal of resentment and even some violence in the three western provinces."

Well, that wasn't interesting after all, but I made an attempt to seem engaged. "Even if there are factions turning against each other in Alberta," I argued, "why would someone follow a lord to Camarria just to kill him? Why not kill him in Alberta?"

"Maybe the lord was carrying information to the king and whoever killed him was trying to prevent him from sharing that information. And the murderer just didn't catch up with him until he was in the royal city."

"That would make me a little nervous about doing deals with Alberta, if I was King Harold," I said. "Knowing people were going around trying to kill off all my messengers."

"Indeed, and I think it *does* make him nervous, but he is determined to maintain good relations with Alberta—if he can. That's why Prince Jordan might be compelled to marry Lady Elyssa of Alberta, even though he can't stand her. To strengthen the bonds between Alberta and Sammerly."

"That makes me glad I'm not a noble," I observed. "I wouldn't want to marry someone just for the good of the kingdom—especially someone I hated."

Dezmen grinned and leaned back against the bench, stretching his feet out toward the brazier. His clothes looked like they were almost dry, and he appeared utterly relaxed. I thought it had to have been a strange day for him, since I didn't imagine a high noble often had the chance to consort with criminals and nearly get drowned by a malevolent stranger. But he seemed to be completely at ease. Enjoying himself, even.

"Well, sometimes arranged marriages work out very well," he said. "From all accounts, Harold had a very good relationship with his first queen—Cormac and Jordan's mother. But he hasn't been so fortunate with his second wife. He and Tabitha despise each other. They got married back when Empara was the most restless of the western provinces, and Harold thought a royal wedding would bring some stability to the realm. It seemed to work from a political standpoint, but from a personal one? Cormac says he never would have thought two people could hate each other so much."

"'Cormac says,'" I repeated. "You're friends with the prince?"

"Since we were children. My father and Harold were friends as well."

"Is that why they asked you to look into the death of that lord that you've decided is from Alberta?"

"Partly, I suppose. Partly because Pandrea and Sammerly have always had a special relationship. Pandrea has always been unswervingly loyal to the crown. In return, the crown relies on Pandrea when it has a problem it cannot solve on its own. My father served King Harold, and my grandfather served Harold's father, and there are stories that go back another five generations."

"So the king trusts you," I said. For the life of me, I couldn't keep the skepticism from my voice.

Dezmen tilted his head. "You say that as if you think he shouldn't."

I wrinkled my nose because there was no good way to explain. "It's just that I think it's so hard to ever really trust anybody."

"Not even this Jackal fellow you're going to introduce me to?"

"I *mostly* trust him," I said. "But I always keep a little doubt at the back of my mind. I remember that he knows a lot of people and he has a lot of business interests, and someday what's good for him might not be good for me. And I'm pretty sure he keeps that little bit of doubt about me, too."

Dezmen nodded past the brazier, to where Scar and Red were sitting quietly, holding hands. Red was resting her head on Scar's shoulder and appeared to be drowsing, while Scar looked around absently, smothering a yawn now and then. "How about those two? Do you trust them?"

Like I trust my hand or my foot. Like I trust my eyes and my lungs. Of course, I'd seen people betrayed by their bodies before, as their hearts gave out or their brains turned on them. "Mostly," I said again. "So far they've never let me down."

"So what's your story?" he said. "Who are you? Were you born in Camarria? How'd you end up doing—whatever it is you do?"

I blinked at him. It never would have occurred to me that he would be interested in the tale of my life. I didn't think even Jackal had ever inquired into my background.

"Not born here," I said. "Came here when I was a teenager. My parents died when I was young, so I was shuffled around to different people who took me in." Nothing I said was more than half true. "By the time I was seventeen, it was obvious I needed to be taking care of myself, so I found some friends—" I gestured at Red and Scar. "I found a place to live. And I started looking for work. I was lucky to meet Jackal early on. He lives pretty far outside the law, but he has a reputation for being fair. That's why he has so many people who'll work for him. He doesn't cheat."

"What is it you do for him, exactly?"

"I carry messages. I courier packages. I run errands. I don't just work for Jackal. Some of my clients are merchants and traders. I'm pretty well known in the business district."

"I'd guess the work they offer is a little more respectable."

I grinned. "Some of it. But you'd be surprised. There's a man who owns three shipping companies and might be as rich as King Harold. He hires me to escort his mistress across town to some new place where he's just taken rooms. That's not so respectable."

"Maybe I should have said less dangerous."

I shrugged. "Well, when you've got low nobles being murdered on the street, I guess you'd have to say everyone's life is dangerous. Most of the time I feel safe enough."

"So do you have any family left?"

"I do. A cousin who lives here in Camarria."

"Is she one of the people you ended up staying with when your parents died?"

Really, he was asking many more questions than I would have expected. I was having a hard time continuing to concoct replies that were true enough not to trip me up. "He. And no. He didn't live here until a couple of years ago."

"Are you close?"

I thought about that a moment. I could easily have added Nico to that short list of people I *mostly* trusted—even though Nico wasn't entirely convinced of the blood tie between us. But he was solid. He was reliable. He was a laughing man with a serious heart, and if ever I got into real trouble, I would count on him to help me to the full extent of his ability.

This despite the fact that he worked for the king's inquisitor. And that he was the inquisitor's nephew. And that the inquisitor would be very interested in knowing I was here in the city.

"We're getting closer," I said at last. "The longer we know each other."

"That's good," he said. "Makes you seem like less of a waif."

I laughed out loud. "You're feeling sorry for me? I think I like my life a lot better than I'd like yours. Answering to the king's bidding and being spied on by the servants. You don't make it sound like that much fun."

He laughed in return and sat forward to lean his elbows on his knees. I couldn't believe he was still sitting here talking to me. Didn't he have important business to return to? A report to make to the king, if nothing else? How could he possibly be so entertained by an uneducated street girl that he didn't want to leave the moment his clothes were dry? "Here I was, thinking you were envying me for my fine jacket and my elegant life," he said. "And my money, too, don't forget. Shouldn't you be jealous of me for that, at least?"

"So far, I earn plenty," I said, amused again. "And Scar and Red work, too. Between the three of us, we can afford a nice place and anything else we really want. So I wouldn't say I'm *jealous*." I looked beyond him to his echoes, who had just adopted his new pose. "Curious, though, maybe."

He glanced over his shoulder at his shadows, who naturally glanced over their *own* shoulders, before they all looked back at me. "Ah. You're wondering what life is like for a man with echoes."

"It seems like it would be very strange."

"Not to me. I can't remember a time I didn't have them. They showed up two days after I was born, so they've just always been part of my life."

"And they always do exactly what you do? All the time?"

He nodded. They nodded. "Sometimes there's the slightest variation. For instance, if we're walking down a street and there's a boulder in the way of one of my echoes, he'll swerve around it. But if *I* trip over a rock, even if there's no rock in their path, both of them will trip as well."

I simply couldn't imagine living that way. "Do they speak?"

"Not really. If they're in pain—which usually means if *I'm* in pain—they can make sounds. Moaning sounds, not real words. Sometimes if I'm laughing very loudly, you'll hear them make a noise that sounds like a laugh. But they have no conversation."

Stranger and stranger. "And they can't move independently on their own? At all?"

"Mine can't," he answered. "I know of a few nobles who can ... can *release* their echoes, as they've described it. So their echoes can sit or stand or walk in a slightly different direction. Though, as far as I know, they still stick very close to their originals. But that's rare. I can sometimes let my echoes fall into a quiet state that's almost like a trance, but I have to be sitting pretty still, so I don't do it often."

"Do you like having echoes?"

"I can't imagine life without them."

"They don't—get in the way? You don't bump into them accidentally? You don't wish they'd go away and give you privacy?"

"It's hard to describe to someone who doesn't have them," he said. "They're part of me. They're not something extra and cumbersome. They're just—me. I don't know how else to put it."

Well, *that* part sounded familiar, at least. But I would find it awfully limiting to be confined to one body. I wanted to ask how common it was for people to be able to move between shapes, but I didn't know how to phrase it in a way that wouldn't make him wonder how I even knew to pose the question. So instead I said, "Can they die?"

He nodded. "Yes, though it's horrible when they do. A person who's lost an echo feels that loss forever. I've heard it's like having a limb amputated—it still aches, even when it's gone. I hope I never have to find out."

"What happens to them if *you* die?"

"They die, too," he said simply. "If you were to stick a knife in my heart right now? If you killed me? They'd fall to the ground, dead, even though there wasn't a mark on them."

I stared at him a moment. "That's what always happens to echoes? That's terrible."

He smiled. "Well, I don't think you're going to stab me in the chest, so they should live another day, at least."

"They'll live another day if you're careful and don't let yourself get attacked by hired bullies."

"That's why I'm going to meet your friend Jackal. To keep us all safe."

"Speaking of Jackal—I need to go looking for him. I don't know how long it might take me to find him."

Dezmen nodded and pushed himself to a standing position. I came to my feet as well but left Scar and Red sitting there for a moment, just to reinforce the notion that they were *not* echoes. Though, given the way he'd just described his own, I was betting it would never occur to him that creatures who behaved as independently as Scar and Red did could be anything but ordinary human beings. Good.

"And I've got to get back to the palace and change clothes for dinner," he said.

"Do you know your way? Do you feel safe to go alone?"

He made a slow pivot, as if checking his surroundings for landmarks, and said, "I *think* I know where I am. But—"

"I'll walk you back. At least to Amanda Plaza. Come on."

We fell into our parade formation again, Dezmen and me in the lead, followed by his echoes, followed by mine. The minute we stepped away from the brazier, I realized how much the air had cooled down. We might be an hour from sunset and ten degrees from freezing.

"Brr," said Dezmen, setting off at a good pace. "I think my clothes are still a little damp, because that wind is *cold*."

The most direct route to Amanda Plaza lay over three bridges of wildly different construction—one all heavy stone, one brightly painted wood, one half-rusted metal. Dezmen looked askance at the last one until I convinced him that taking it over the abandoned stockyard would cut about fifteen minutes off our travel time, but he still clung to the railing for the entire passage.

"I've never seen a city with so many bridges," he complained once we were safely on the other side. "And some of them utterly pointless. There's no stream, there's no crevasse, there's nothing that needs to be *crossed*. And yet there's a bridge."

"Jackal told me it was something started by King Edwin. You know, the king who united the provinces?"

"I know who Edwin is, thank you very much."

"He was trying to make the point that we can overcome the things that divide us. So he wanted bridges throughout the city, every time a new road or neighborhood was built. And even though it's hundreds of years later, people still add bridges when they lay in new roads because now that's what Camarria is famous for."

"That's nice. All right, I won't be so annoyed about the bridges."

I laughed. "But then Jackal said that was probably just a pretty myth, and Edwin had them built because he liked to have high places where his inquisitors could stand and spy on the people below."

"Now *that* sounds like something Malachi would say."

"I would bet Malachi knows every bridge in the city."

A few minutes later we arrived at Amanda Plaza, which was, in many ways, the heart of Camarria. It was a big, open space in the middle of the financial district and was filled with people at almost any hour of the day—merchants' clerks rushing off on errands, visitors trying to take in all the sights, pickpockets looking to do a little business. It was the place people came when they wanted to hear the news or they wanted to join hands in public mourning; it was the place Lady Marguerite had been executed two months ago. One of its most famous features was a grouping of statues right in the middle of the plaza—three women, back to back to back, their arms held out at different angles. The triple goddess, offering her benedictions of mercy, justice, and joy. In the brickwork at their heels was a wide grate where people could toss in coins to pray for the goddess's favor.

The second most famous feature was an elegant bridge of pale yellow stone. It didn't lead anywhere except from one side of the plaza to the other, but it was constantly thronged with people. Newcomers who just wanted to gawk around, lovers pledging their vows, mothers tired of telling their children, *No, there's no reason to climb the bridge*. I tended to spend more of my time under the bridge than on it because it was a favorite meeting spot for people who wanted to commission someone to run a delicate errand.

"Another useless bridge for you," I said to Dezmen.

"At least it's a beautiful one."

I pointed at the goddess statues. "So. That's where I'll meet you the day after tomorrow. I'll still come, even if I haven't found Jackal yet, and we'll figure out what to do next."

"Sounds good," he said. He didn't just go striding off, but stood there a moment, looking at me, as if memorizing my features or just remembering something I'd said that he didn't want to forget. "I'm glad you were there today at the gardens, Chessie. I'm pretty certain you saved my life. I haven't thanked you for that, have I? So thank you."

"I was paid to do it," I said outrageously, just to make him laugh, which he did. "But I'm glad I was there, too. It's been more interesting to talk to you than I thought it might be talking to a high noble."

"Just think how interesting the next few days could be."

"They'd have to be pretty extraordinary to beat this one."

"Well," he said, turning in the direction of the palace, "we live in extraordinary times."

I nodded and turned in the opposite direction so I could head back to my lodgings. There was no reason to do it, but when I got to the goddess statues, I paused and pivoted just enough so I could watch him walk away. No one followed him but his echoes; no sinister shape detached itself from the crowd and slunk along behind him. He would certainly be just fine without my continued observation.

Still, I felt a little chill, a tiny shiver, and it made me draw my own echoes closer to me. Scar came up and put an arm around my shoulders; Red squeezed my hand in hers. I fished a coin out of my pocket and tossed it into the grate, but I didn't vocalize any particular prayer. I listened as the coin hit the metal of the grill and rattled down into some stone sewer below, then I shook my head and continued on toward home.

CHAPTER FIVE

Predictably, Jackal was delighted at the thought of meeting the lord. And he was all for accompanying me to the plaza to carry on his conversation there. Jackal tended to operate in two modes: extreme secrecy, so no one could overhear him, or total visibility, so no one could sneak up and catch him unaware.

"And if some of the inquisitor's men happen to see me talking to the Pandrean lord, well, let them wonder what we might be discussing," Jackal said. "It will do Malachi some good to know that Sweetwater is watching what the palace is doing."

"And you'll find him a bodyguard?"

"I will."

"Because if I hadn't been there yesterday, there's no way Dezmen could have fended off the man who came after him."

Jackal looked thoughtful. "Describe him to me again," he said. "Describe both of the men you saw."

I filled him in on the details as best as I could remember, but I hadn't registered much about the second assailant. As I spoke, Jackal's eyebrows drew into a small frown.

"You look puzzled," I said.

"I am. I know Trout—"

"It might not have been Trout. I wasn't sure."

Jackal nodded. "Well, it sounds like him, and it sounds like a man he often pairs up with—a fellow named Covak—but I've never known either one to hire out to Halloran."

I shrugged. "Maybe that's why Halloran picked them. So you wouldn't think he was the one who'd sent them."

"Maybe...but that's a little subtle for Halloran. He tends to want you to know he's paying attention."

"Well, if they don't work for Halloran, who *would* be paying them?"

Jackal drummed his fingers on the table. "That's the problem. People like that tend to be closemouthed about their employers—because their jobs tend to be dirty."

"Give me an example."

His smile was strained. "I don't want to fill your mind with ugly pictures. But there was a wealthy merchant who wanted to discourage a business rival. Trout and Covak left the man alive, but since then he's never been right in the head."

I digested that. "So they're not working for east siders like you. They're taking jobs from bankers and businessmen."

"And nobles," Jackal added softly.

"That'll make it harder to learn who hired them."

"It will. But I'll see if there's anything I can find out."

I got to my feet. "If you can't, nobody can. I'll see you in the plaza tomorrow." He nodded a goodbye, and I headed for the door.

I'd finally found Jackal in a smaller and much seedier tavern than Packrat, but it had taken me almost a day to do it. So there was a day's worth of wages lost, but honestly, he'd paid me well enough for meeting Dezmen the previous afternoon that I couldn't really complain. Nobody had mentioned paying me for setting up tomorrow's meeting, but that was the sort of thing Jackal usually remembered.

And I had become curious enough about the lord that I probably would have done it for free.

I could think of only one place I could go where I might be able to ask more questions about Lord Dezmen of Pandrea. So when I left Jackal, I headed straight to the flower markets.

It was close to dark by the time I arrived, so most of the vendors were packing up or already gone. During the day, even when it was winter, the place was an explosion of color and scent, with booth after booth crammed with blossoms of every variety. I rarely bothered with such small amenities and graces, but even I could rarely walk through the place without at least buying a daisy for my jacket or a rose for Red's hair.

But today I was looking for a person, not a flower, and I spotted her almost immediately. She was carefully putting her goods away in specially made carriers that looked like wire racks encased in leather shells. I went over to her at an angle, so she'd see me approaching, and said, "Need any help?"

"Hi, Chessie," she answered. She glanced behind me, looking for the echoes. She was the kind of person who never overlooked servants, so she certainly wasn't going to forget I was usually trailed by a couple of friends. "Red—Scar. Good to see you all."

Scar, the less sociable one, just waved, but Red smiled widely and stepped close enough to talk. I stilled Chessie's body into the pose of someone waiting while I slipped inside Red's mind. "Good evening, Brianna! Did you have a good day?"

Brianna glanced around at the fast-emptying market and nodded. "I did. Made about ten sales and had at least twenty people stop by and seem interested. I told them what days I'm usually here and that I accept commissions."

Back into Chessie's head. "When are you going to open your own shop?"

"I don't know. Nico and I talk about it all the time, but it's such an expense. But I've been having conversations with the wigmakers."

Now Red. "Wigmakers?"

Brianna nodded. "I figure, they're selling fake hair, right? Something that goes on top of a lady's head. So maybe they'd be interested in carrying my caps and veils and hairpieces."

Red again. "And are they?"

"We haven't finalized details, but I think they're going to take some stock on consignment. I'm pretty excited about it."

Chessie. "Sounds like it could be pretty profitable."

Red, teasing. "But what if you sell so much you can't keep up with all the orders?"

Brianna laughed. "That would be an wonderful problem to have!"

Chessie again. "But back to my original question. Do you need any help carrying stuff back to your place?"

"I can usually manage it on my own, but since you're here—and if you're going my way —" She lifted one of the leather cases and handed it to Red.

Who promptly turned around and handed it to Scar. "Here. Make yourself useful."

I slipped into Scar's body just long enough to make sure I had a good hold on the handle, then I bounced back to Chessie. "I wanted to see if there might be a time I could stop by and talk to Nico. Tonight or tomorrow or later in the week?"

Brianna handed Chessie the second case, then proceeded to fold up some cloths and papers and tuck them under her arm. "Come on," she said, setting off across the open space of the market in the direction of her lodgings. Red and I fell in step on either side of her, while the less chatty Scar lagged behind. Brianna said, "Nico's coming by for dinner tonight if you want to join us." She glanced at Red and then behind her at Scar. "You could all join us, if you want."

I was swiftly in Red's head. "Scar and I have errands we need to run, but thanks for the offer."

And back in Chessie's. "I'd be glad to come, though. Can I stop off somewhere and pick up something to bring?"

"Sure. I'm almost out of bread. There's a bakery down the street from me."

"I know exactly where it is. Great. We'll drop everything at your place and then I'll go shopping."

We carried out this excellent plan, although I, of course, did more than simply pick up bread at the bakery. I bought more bread and a round of cheese for the echoes, who otherwise might not get a chance to eat till midnight, and then found a place they could sit for a few hours, out of the wind and out of sight. Brianna lived in a quiet little working-class neighborhood where most of the two- and three-story buildings contained tiny two- and three-room apartments. There were no parks or cafés close by, so there were limited options for stashing two people who weren't going to be doing much moving or talking. But I'd been here often enough that I knew the terrain. Three buildings down from Chessie was an older structure that looked ripe for renovation and currently was only half occupied. There was an empty suite on the bottom story; the lock on its door was easy to pick. I stayed long enough to make sure the echoes ate a quick meal, and then I stepped through the door, pulling it shut tight. Slipped inside Scar's body to lock the door from the inside so no other squatters looking for shelter could break in as easily as I had. Slipped back into Chessie's head and made my way to Brianna's place.

She lived on the third story of a narrow building in an apartment with slanted rooflines, minimal furniture, and piles of fabric reaching almost to the ceiling. Wherever there wasn't a bolt of cloth, there was a basket of dried flowers. Brianna did keep small spaces cleared out for the normal human functions of eating and sleeping, but it was easy to see that crafting her fine headpieces consumed most of her time and attention.

"You need a bigger space," I remarked as I handed over the bread. I wedged myself behind a round wooden table so I could stay out of her way as she carried out plates and glasses.

She laughed. "That's what Nico says. But I want to wait until I'm making real money before I start *spending* money on the business." She handed me a glass of water and sat across from me. "Anyway, I keep thinking that Nico and I will get a place together soon, and then I'll make sure I have a room set aside just for sewing."

"When *are* you getting a place together?" I demanded. "Shouldn't you be getting married pretty soon?"

"My mother thinks we should wait a few months to make sure we really know each other. Nico's mother—I don't think she wants us to get married at all," she said, pouring some water for herself. "She hasn't said it in so many words, but I know she's disappointed that Nico's with me. His father was a low noble, and Nadine has spent her whole life grooming Nico to be in that class. She doesn't want him marrying a former lady's maid like me. She wants him to marry a noble."

"But Nadine was a merchant's daughter herself," I said.

"She never forgets that she dragged her husband down socially. And I'm even lower than she was." Brianna sipped her water. "Sometimes I think she's right, and I should step out of Nico's life. And other times I think—I love him and he loves me and none of the rest of it matters."

"I think you'd find it pretty hard to convince Nico that you aren't good enough for him," I said. "I think you might find it difficult to push him out of your life."

She broke into a smile that transformed her whole face. She was a fairly ordinary girl, with light brown hair and wide cheeks and a rather brisk practicality that made her take most events, good and bad, in stride. But when she was happy, she had moments you'd almost call her beautiful. "I think so, too. I tried that once and it didn't go so well."

"So you should plan the wedding," I said. "Let his mother sigh."

"You don't think it would break her heart if Nico married me?"

"I don't know. I've never met her. I've only known Nico for the past two years."

She leaned back in her chair and studied me. That was one of the many things I liked about Brianna; she always appeared to be listening to what you said and what you didn't say. She always appeared to be paying attention to the details you let fall—and putting them together to form a more complete picture in her head. Of course, it was also one of the things that made me nervous about Brianna, but I didn't think we'd spent enough time together for her to figure out my entire story.

It would certainly be interesting if she ever did, though.

"I know you're cousins," she said at last. "But I always thought you were related through Nadine's side of the family. That's not the case?"

I laughed. "Well, Nico isn't entirely convinced we're cousins. But he likes me, so he humors me and pretends he believes."

"He hasn't told me that much about you. So how are you cousins? And how did you get to know each other?"

I hesitated a long moment. Until I'd met Nico, I'd told no one, *no one*, the story of my parentage. I had learned in the hardest way possible that information is the wickedest weapon there is; I knew that trust was a luxury I simply could not afford. To this day, I couldn't explain why I had chosen to tell Nico the truth. I couldn't say why I had believed he wouldn't betray me. But I had and he hadn't, and I had never been sorry. A couple of months ago he had asked me if he could tell Brianna I was his cousin, and I had agreed, but as far as I knew, he had given her no other details.

I was quiet long enough that she lifted her hands in a gesture of release. "It's fine. I don't need to know."

"No, I'll tell you. You just have to promise you won't repeat anything I say."

"Not that I know anyone I *could* repeat it to, but of course I promise."

"We're cousins through his father's side," I began.

She frowned, clearly trying to remember. "I think his father had a brother and a sister. I've never met the sister, but the brother is Malachi Burken—the king's inquisitor and one of the people I dislike most in the world."

"Malachi is my father," I said quietly.

She stared. "He *is*? Then I'm sorry, I shouldn't have said that—"

"You couldn't possibly dislike Malachi more than I do."

"I didn't know Malachi had any children."

"I don't think anybody knows."

"So what happened?"

I stuck to the tale the way I had told it to Nico, which was, of course, incomplete. "Before Malachi became the king's inquisitor, he had a small estate in Empara. My mother was one of the housemaids, and she caught his eye." I shrugged. "When she ended up pregnant, he threw her out of the house. She went to stay with a woman named Angela, who used to be a governess at a noble's house. I can't remember how they knew each other. My mother was living with Angela when I was born."

"Where is she now?"

"My mother? She died of a fever when I was two years old. I don't have any memories of her at all."

"That's so sad! This whole tale is sad!"

I shrugged again. "It is, I suppose. It all seems so long ago and there are so many parts of it I never experienced for myself. I just know what Angela told me."

"So how did you learn that Malachi was your father?"

I laughed. "Because Angela never stopped cursing his name! 'Your father, Malachi—I hope the triple goddess shows him only justice, no mercy!' That sort of thing. He had left for Camarria by this time, but sometimes she would drive us by the estate he'd owned, so I could see where I would have lived if I'd been legitimate. She took me by Nico's house, too, at least a dozen times. She wanted me to know that I was related to nobility, even if nobody acknowledged me."

"But you never went up to the door and introduced yourself?"

"Even Angela didn't have that kind of nerve, and she was pretty brave."

"Where is Angela now?"

I was sure Brianna was going to get tired of this litany. "She died."

"Chessie! How awful! What happened to her?"

I had never told anyone that story and, much as I liked Brianna, I was not about to relate it to her now. "She fell and broke her arm and never had it set properly. It got infected and the infection spread. It all happened faster than you would have thought."

"Maybe she was already sick with something else and just wasn't strong enough to heal."

"I've often thought the same thing."

"How did you end up in Camarria?"

"I was young and restless and I thought I might have a chance at making a living here." *I was young and terrified, but I knew there was no future for me in Empara.*

"How old were you?

Thirteen. "Seventeen."

She gestured in the general direction of the palace. "You must have realized Malachi was here. Did it ever occur to you to introduce yourself to him? To tell him who you are?"

Not once. Not ever. "I was curious about him," I said. "I've gotten glimpses of him, from time to time, when he's on public parades. But I've never tried to meet him. I don't want to know him. I don't want him to know me. By the way he treated my mother, I know everything I need to know about him."

"He wouldn't be the only lord to take advantage of a serving girl and treat her cruelly," Brianna said. "He might regret that, now that he's older. He might be overjoyed to learn he has a daughter."

I put my elbows on the table and leaned forward to look her in the eyes. "*You* have had some dealings with the inquisitor," I said quietly. "Do *you* think he's the kind of man who secretly conceals a soft heart?"

She was quiet a moment, briefly showing an expression of deep sadness. Brianna had been lady's maid to Marguerite, the noblewoman who had been executed for killing the king's bastard son. She must be well aware that Malachi was the one who had ordered the execution—had ordered it, had hired the archers, and had given them the order to fire on the lady and her echoes. "No," she said on a sigh. "If he was my father, I don't think I would ever tell him, either."

I sat back in my chair. "And so I won't."

"You said that Nico didn't believe your story at first," she said. "Why not?"

"Well, I can't entirely blame him," I said candidly. "When someone just approaches you in Amanda Plaza one day and says, 'Hey, you're my cousin,' you might wonder what her angle is."

"He could ask Nadine, I suppose."

I nodded. "And he has. I believe her answer was something like, 'I never heard that particular story, but it sounds exactly like something Malachi would do.'"

"So how did you convince Nico?"

I fished under the collar of my shirt and pulled out a delicate gold chain hung with a single charm. It featured three long lozenge-shaped emeralds forming a triangle, with three small round emeralds placed at each joint, as if acting as hinges. Three diamond-shaped emeralds were set in the middle, their points touching at the very center. All of them were held together in a heavy setting of the finest gold. Emeralds were the traditional stones of Empara, and these were of exceedingly high quality. I could probably get a fortune for the necklace if I was ever desperate enough to sell it, but I was determined to never be that down on my luck.

"I showed him this," I said. "Angela said my mother stole it from the house the day he turned her out. Angela believed it belonged to Malachi's mother. Malachi owns an emerald ring with the exact same pattern."

Brianna frowned. I could tell she was sifting through her memories. "Not that I've ever seen him wear," she said.

"Oh, he doesn't wear it," I answered. "That's why Nico believed me—because no one's ever seen the ring on Malachi's hand. But Malachi showed it to him shortly after Nico started working for him. Said he didn't have any sons of his own, and it was his only valuable piece of property—and that it would be Nico's when he was gone. When I showed Nico my necklace, he recognized the pattern, so at the very least he knew someone in my life at some point had been in Malachi's house, stealing things from his wardrobe! But I think it made him more inclined to believe the entire story."

"Has he ever asked Malachi about you?"

"I begged him not to, and he swore he wouldn't."

"Then he didn't," said Brianna. "Because Nico always keeps his word."

At that precise moment, we heard the doorknob rattle and Nico stepped into the apartment. He was a handsome man—strongly built, with dark curly hair and blue-green eyes—but what made him really attractive was his smile. There was a general air of happiness about him that I always thought sat oddly on an inquisitor's apprentice. I often wondered if that personality trait might one day lead him to give up the inquisitor's trade. I thought Nico was too good for the job he'd chosen.

"Hello, love," he said to Brianna, walking over to drop a kiss on the top of her head. "And, Chessie! What brings you here tonight?"

I rose to my feet so I could give him a brief hug. Even though Nico wasn't positive I was who I claimed to be, he liked me; we had quickly developed an easy rapport and a genuine affection. Of course, there was much he didn't know about me—and perhaps much I didn't know about him—but none of that seemed to matter. He always felt like an ally to me in a world that had very few reliable resources.

I laughed as I pulled away from him and dropped back onto my chair. "Looking for information, of course. I would never come just to *visit*."

"That's what I like about you," he said in an admiring voice. "You use people, but you're honest about it." He turned to Brianna, who had also stood up and was now rummaging around in the tiny area that passed for a kitchen. "What can I do to help?"

"Sit. I just need to bring the food to the table."

In a few minutes, we were sharing a meal and trading anecdotes about our days. Only Brianna spoke without carefully choosing her words, as Nico and I had friends and employers we didn't want to betray with offhand comments, but we all contributed something to the conversation.

"I do have something I want to ask you, if you're willing to share," Nico said as Brianna cleared away the plates. "Who would I talk to if I wanted to find out about Biddelton's?"

"The new tavern by the Montacorci Bridge? Halloran invested in it, but I think he has partners. I could ask Jackal." I drank more water. "I thought it was legitimate."

Nico smiled. "Mostly. Just want to check up on something."

"So then *I* have a question. Is there a new inquisitor on your team? Tall, skinny fellow who's almost bald, even though he can't be much older than you."

Now Nico grinned. "You know I can't start identifying Malachi's men. How would they do their jobs?"

That meant I was right. He would have said no if I was wrong. "Oh, I'm *so* sorry. I'm so embarrassed that I've put you in an awkward position."

Brianna sat down again and handed around small plates of some kind of lemony confection. "It's very entertaining to listen to the two of you talk," she remarked.

"Ask me something else," Nico invited. "Ask me whatever it is you came here to talk about."

"What do you know about someone named Lord Dezmen?"

Now Nico looked surprised. "The Pandrean noble? How did he come your way?"

"He was asking questions down in Sweetwater. You know, about that lord who got murdered?" I lifted my eyebrows, and Nico just nodded. I went on, "Jackal heard a whisper that someone didn't like the questions, and you know Jackal. He gets curious. He sent me out to offer a helping hand if someone tried to hurt Lord Dezmen."

"Jackal as a benevolent guardian. I do like that image," Nico said.

I grinned. "I think he had reasons he wasn't sharing with me."

"I take it nothing happened to Dezmen while he was out?"

I stared at him. Was it possible this information hadn't filtered back to the palace through Malachi's vast network of spies? "Well, now, that's interesting," I said at last.

Now Nico was frowning. "So something *did* happen?"

I nodded. "Two men attacked him. I had Scar and Red with me, so we were able to chase them off, and the lord escaped with hardly a scratch. But why don't you know that?"

"I'm sure Malachi knows, it's just that nobody bothered to mention it to me. Did that make Lord Dezmen reluctant to keep asking questions?"

"Not from what I was able to determine."

"So what did you want to ask me about him?"

I spread my hands. "Why bring him in to investigate this murder? I never heard of that before. Doesn't Malachi have enough men to solve every crime committed in Camarria—or in the whole province of Sammerly, when it comes to that?"

Nico nodded a few times as if confirming something that hadn't been said out loud. Brianna dropped her gaze to the table, maybe hiding an emotion she didn't want me to see. "It all stems from Jamison's death," Nico said quietly, "and the way it was handled. A bastard royal was murdered, and a high noble was executed for the crime. Every aristocratic family in the western provinces has expressed shock and outrage at Marguerite's death. Even nobles from Banchura and Thelleron spoke out against the harsh sentence. There are people who think Malachi manufactured the evidence against Marguerite, just so he could say he had solved the crime. They think she was innocent."

I glanced at Brianna. "I thought she confessed."

"She did," Brianna said, addressing the table.

I didn't ask the next obvious question. *Did she do it?* I was willing to bet Brianna knew the answer, one way or the other, but right at the moment it didn't matter.

Nico continued, "So when another lord turned up dead, it seemed best if someone else led the investigation—someone that all the nobles, high and low, could agree was both qualified and impartial. That way, whatever he discovered, no one could accuse Malachi of manipulating the evidence."

"So it was Malachi's idea to bring in Dezmen."

Nico was silent.

I couldn't keep the astonishment from my voice. "It was the *king's* idea?"

"I wasn't in the room when they made the decision."

I turned that thought over in my head. "The king doesn't trust Malachi?"

Now Brianna glanced at Nico. "Tell her what you've told me before. The king thinks Malachi is more loyal to the queen than to him."

"Malachi and Queen Tabitha are both from Empara, so that makes sense, I suppose," I said. But I was still thinking, *The king doesn't trust Malachi?*

"Right," Nico answered, "but it doesn't have much bearing on this particular case, since it doesn't appear as though the murdered man was from Empara. No, it's like I said. Because the dead man was a lord, nobles throughout the kingdom want the investigation to be handled by someone who is himself of noble birth."

"Malachi's noble—low noble, at least," I pointed out.

"Right," Nico said again. "But in the eyes of many, his profession has, let us say, rubbed all of that nobility off of him."

"I agree with them," I said. "I think it's a despicable profession."

Nico made an ironic half-bow from across the table. "Thanks so much for your high opinion of me."

I grinned. "I think you're too good to be an inquisitor."

"So do I," said Brianna, picking up her fork to start on the lemon tart.

I did the same. "Although I must say, I do like being able to ask you questions and find out things nobody else knows," I said. "So you should keep the job as long as it's handy for *me*."

"It's the only reason I stay with Malachi," Nico said, taking a bite of his own dessert. "To be of use to you."

We seemed to have drifted right off the topic of Dezmen, and I couldn't think of a casual way to get back to it. I wasn't even sure what else I wanted to know. *Do you think he's an honorable man? Is he kind? Would you trust him? Is there some lovely Pandrean noblewoman that his parents have arranged for him to marry? How long do you think it will take him to solve this crime? How long might he be in the city of Camarria, where I might see him again at any time?*

Stupid questions, really. "This is awfully good," I said to Brianna as I finished up my tart. "I think it's the best thing that's happened to me all day."

CHAPTER SIX

The next day was sunny and fine, warm enough to make you think summer might have decided to come back. In the morning, I had errands to run for my landlady—depositing rent fees and picking up cleaning supplies—work I did to get a discount on my own charges. The errands only took a couple of hours, so I was able to get to Amanda Plaza before either of the men I was meeting there.

It was, as always, a busy, constantly changing scene: clerks dashing across the patterned brickwork, children investigating the statues and fountains, couples sauntering across the bridge and pausing at the midpoint to kiss. There were two wedding parties clustered near the statues of the triple goddess, led by priestesses in the red robes of joy; the brides and grooms took turns tossing coins into the grate, wishing for boundless love and unbreakable fidelity, I supposed. I liked that one group of revelers was made up of nobles in lace and embroidered satin, while the other group looked to be working-class men and women in cotton and leather. All equal in the goddess's eyes.

I threaded my way through the crowds to the shadow of the bridge. A popular meeting spot, it was already sheltering a half dozen men and women of dubious character. I nodded to the two I knew, but offered no conversation. The base of the bridge at Amanda Plaza wasn't a place you went for socializing. Everyone was there with a goal in mind.

My current goal was to find a place to leave Scar and Red while I met with Jackal and Lord Dezmen. There were no convenient benches in this part of the plaza, so, in the end, I just settled them on the ground as close as they could get to the northern footing of the bridge. As long as they appeared wide-eyed and alert, posed as if they were patiently awaiting someone, no one would bother them, not even people who knew them.

I then made a circuit of the plaza just to scout the terrain. I strode right on by the statues of Queen Amanda and her echoes—the wife of Edwin, and the first queen of the Seven Jewels—but I paused for a moment to study the least interesting feature of the whole square. It was a blank stone wall behind a slightly raised dais. A stage of sorts, though a gruesome one. It was the place where criminals were publicly executed by a team of archers. I wondered if Brianna was able to walk through the plaza without breaking down in tears. Or maybe she paused to toss flowers against the wall and whisper a prayer to the goddess. Maybe she just avoided the place altogether.

By the time I made my second promenade around the square, Lord Dezmen was already standing in front of the statues of the triple goddess. He had paused before the one for justice and took the pose that I had already come to associate with him—feet slightly apart, hands behind his back, contemplative expression on his face. Behind him, his echoes had fallen into the same stance.

I sidled over from behind him, so I was practically at his shoulder before he realized I was there. I felt him jerk in surprise when I started speaking. "If you're going to stand and stare at something, face outward," I recommended. "If you're going to fall into a fit of thinking, put your back against a wall. At least make it *appear* that you're paying attention to your surroundings."

"Excellent advice," he said, smiling over at me. "I depend on you for such insights."

We both repositioned ourselves so our backs were to the statues and we each had a good view of the plaza. Dezmen's echoes arranged themselves in a similar fashion. Of course, any determined assailant could just vault over the arms of the goddesses and attack us from behind, but that didn't seem too likely on this bright day.

"Have you had any more adventures since I left you here a couple of days ago?" I asked.

"No, life has been singularly dull."

"Dull isn't so bad when it means no one is trying to kill you."

"How about you? Any excitement?" he asked.

"My life is *always* exciting," I said, casting my eyes down demurely. "But, of course, I can't tell you any of the details."

"So where do we need to go to find your friend Jackal?"

"He's meeting us here. And he's usually very prompt, which means—yes, there he is. Coming our way."

Dezmen followed my gaze and tried to pick Jackal out of the crowd. It wasn't hard. If you were looking for someone named "Jackal," you would probably identify the tall man with the slight swagger and the intense expression, especially if he appeared to be heading straight for you. His hands were empty and his face was arranged in a smile, but he still exuded an air of coiled menace. I saw more than one nursemaid pull a small child out of his path, noticed how a banker's clerk completely changed course to avoid stepping in his way.

"Hey there, Chessie," Jackal said as he joined us, but he kept his eyes on the noble's face. "Why don't you introduce me to your friend?"

I gestured at each man in turn. "Lord Dezmen. And Jackal."

Jackal's gaze went past Dezmen to rest briefly on each of his echoes, who were watching him with a muted version of Dezmen's own deep curiosity. "I understand you've been having an interesting time of it," Jackal said.

"Much more than I expected," Dezmen admitted.

Jackal brought his attention back to the lord. "Really? You're looking into a murder, and you didn't think people might be upset with you?"

Dezmen considered for a moment, as if weighing his words. "I didn't think I had gotten close enough to the truth to make anyone react so violently," he said at last.

That caused Jackal to raise his eyebrows. "Well, that makes me curious," he said softly. "Where were you asking questions, then— and where do you expect to find the truth?"

Dezmen glanced around the plaza, as if my earlier lesson had started to sink in. "Is there someplace we could talk where we're unlikely to be overheard?"

Jackal jerked his head toward the southern edge of the square. "I saw a fine carriage parked a few streets over. Looked like it might belong to a noble lord. If it's yours, we could take a ride."

Dezmen nodded and glanced at me. "Want to come?"

I did, but it was hard to know how to bring Scar and Red along. "Is there room for all of us?" I said, gesturing at his echoes.

"Should be. Come on."

I roused my own echoes, who followed us at a discreet distance as the five of us wove through the crowd to the side street where the carriage was waiting. It was a long, open vehicle with four benches, two in the middle that faced each other, with an additional bench behind each one. A middle-aged coachman sat on a high perch, idly keeping the team of horses in check. He tipped his hat to Dezmen and straightened in his seat as we approached.

I was almost shocked when Dezmen turned to offer me a hand up. I couldn't remember the last time anybody had thought I was frail enough to need assistance to do anything, and I was pretty sure Dezmen didn't count *helplessness* among my attributes. Merely, he was showing the ingrained courtesy of the nobility. I couldn't help smiling as I grasped his fingers and stepped up with as much grace as I could muster. He urged me to the forward-facing bench in the middle. Jackal climbed in beside me, giving me a droll look. Dezmen took a seat on the bench directly opposite from ours, while the echoes settled on the row behind him.

The streets around Amanda Plaza were narrow and crowded; this was the oldest part of town, and it had never been built to accommodate heavy traffic. I was optimistic that we would move slowly enough that Red and Scar could keep up if they jogged along behind us. If not—well, I would make an excuse and disembark if they fell too far behind.

The coachman clucked to the horses and we set off at a sedate pace, bouncing over the uneven cobblestones on the street. "You were saying," Jackal prompted in a low voice.

We all leaned forward so we could talk. I realized Jackal had been right; this was the perfect place to have an undisturbed conversation. No one from the street would be able to hear us, and the clatter of horse hooves and wagon wheels would prevent the coachman from catching a word.

"I didn't think I'd asked enough questions to arouse suspicion," Dezmen said. "I'd inquired about a horse that Leffert had stabled. And—"

"'Leffert'?" Jackal interrupted. "That's the dead man's name?"

"It's the name he used at the inn where he spent a few nights. I don't know if that's his real identity. So as I say, I'd asked about his horse, and I'd found the inn where he stayed. He left behind some clothing in the rented room, but nothing of any value. His horse is still in the stables where he left it. It's a fine beast and I assume the stable owner will sell it soon to cover the cost of its care and feeding. I took charge of Leffert's saddle and tack, and I've been looking them over, but they don't appear to be marked with any useful secret initials that will lead me to more information."

"So you've learned nothing," Jackal said.

"Exactly. So why would anyone be so alarmed by my investigation that they'd send someone after me? I'm at a loss."

"What's the name of the stables where the horse was left? What's the name of the inn?" Jackal asked.

"The inn is called Market House. It's near the big flower market. The stables—I didn't see a name. It's run by someone called Geordie."

"I know them both," Jackal said. He was frowning. "But that doesn't make sense."

"What doesn't?" I asked.

"Neither of them are places Halloran has a stake in. So *he* wouldn't care that the lord here was poking around."

"Who's Halloran?" Dezmen asked.

When Jackal didn't answer, I said, "Somebody Jackal hates, mostly for no reason. He's the one we thought didn't like your questions."

"I have plenty of reasons," Jackal said.

"Who does own them, then?" I wanted to know. "The stables and the inn?"

Jackal shook his head. "Market House is a little place. A man and his wife have run it for years, and as far as I know, no one else is involved. Geordie had backers when he started his business, but they're all paid up now. I should know, I was one of them." He focused on Dezmen. "You're right. If those were the only questions you were asking, no one should have been rattled."

"I have to think that there's someone who knows why I've been brought here, and he's not going to wait until I find something out," Dezmen said. "He's just going to try to stop me before I make any headway at all."

Jackal settled back in his seat and studied the lord for a minute. "So who knows why you've been brought here?" he asked.

Dezmen shrugged. "Who doesn't? *You* know. I have to think your Halloran rival knows. And—"

"I'd hardly call him a *rival*."

"And anyone else who keeps track of what happens in Camarria probably knows," Dezmen went on.

"Everyone at the palace knows, and every noble in the city knows," Jackal added.

Dezmen narrowed his amber eyes. "Why would you think a noble might be involved?" he asked.

"Leffert's a lord, or so we all believe," Jackal answered. "He could have been caught cheating at dice. He could have been caught bedding another man's wife. I can think up plenty of reasons another lord would have wanted to kill him."

"And then dump his body on the east side?"

"It's what I'd have done if I'd killed him. Better than leaving him in my own house to be found by the servants," Jackal said.

"Very well. We'll add the entire nobility of Camarria to our list of suspects," Dezmen said.

Something about his tone made me suspicious. I stared at him. "You know who killed him, don't you?"

His smile was faint. "I don't. But I know why he was killed."

"And?" Jackal said.

"He failed at the job he was hired to do. And whoever hired him was either angry—or wanted to make sure Leffert never talked about his employer."

All the half-answers were making me irritable. On the excuse of trying to scratch over my left shoulder, I looked behind me to check on Scar and Red. They were barely ten yards behind the carriage, walking on opposite sides of the street as if out for an idle stroll. The horses were clopping along so slowly the echoes were having no trouble keeping up.

When I faced forward, Jackal was staring at Dezmen and Dezmen was staring back. What had I missed? I asked, "What job was Leffert hired to do?"

Jackal was the one to reply, in a hard, disbelieving voice. "Kill Prince Cormac."

"*What?*" I looked between them again, but they were still staring each other down. Dezmen didn't nod or in any other way confirm Jackal's guess, but it was clear that he was right. "Wait a minute," I said. "It's been two months since the assassination attempt. Why kill Leffert *now?*"

"Because there was a second attack on Cormac's life," Jackal said slowly. "One that nobody knew about."

"*What?*" I said again. Now I was staring at Dezmen, too. "Is that true?"

He gave me a half-smile. "You were right. Jackal does know everything that happens in this city."

"There were rumors at the time," Jackal said. "They didn't seem credible, so I dismissed them. But I see they were right."

I was still trying to make sense of it. "So you're saying that someone tried to kill Cormac, and failed. So then someone else—a nobleman this time—tried again. And when he wasn't successful at the job, the noble was killed."

"That's exactly what he's saying," Jackal responded.

"And you were brought in to work on the case because—"

"Because of all the reasons I've already given you," Dezmen said. "Because if nobles are leading assassination attempts, it could mean that the western provinces are truly gearing up for war."

Jackal hitched forward on the seat. "You keep saying Leffert is noble," he said. "But you also keep saying you don't know who he is. I thought all the lords throughout the kingdom were related in some fashion. So why can't you identify him? And if you can't identify him, how can you be sure he's noble?"

Dezmen nodded. "If he was a high noble, you're right, someone would know him. There are probably fewer than five hundred high nobles throughout the Seven Jewels. But there are hundreds of low nobles in every province, and they're not as easy to keep track of. Well, that's not true. Within each province, the governors have a registry of all their nobles, high and low. But the high nobles of Thelleron, for instance, have no interest in the low nobles of Alberta. To figure out who Leffert really is, I would have to discover what province he was from and then ask that governor to verify his identity. And if he was from Orenza or Alberta or Empara... Well, you see the problem."

"You might have just as much trouble with the governors of Thelleron or Banchura, who *seem* like they have no reason to hate the crown, but who might be planning a rebellion that you don't know about," I said with a certain zest. This not only was a problem without a solution, it was a problem that seemed to add layers of complexity by the hour. I was starting to enjoy piling on more.

Dezmen nodded at me. "As you say."

"The one thing the king knows is that this Leffert fellow is not from Pandrea," Jackal said. "Which must be the real reason you were brought in to investigate."

Dezmen nodded again. "Correct. He was a pale-skinned man with fair hair. So even though the list of potential suspects is almost limitless, the king knows *I*, at least, am not among them."

"I don't see that at all," I objected. "You could have *hired* a pale fellow to attack the prince. That's what I would have done if I were you."

Both Dezmen and Jackal burst out laughing. "She looks like a sweet scrap of a thing, but her mind is devious," Jackal said.

"That's because I've been around *you* too long," I flashed at him.

"But the question remains," Jackal said. "How can you be sure Leffert is noble?"

Dezmen glanced at me. We had had this same exchange the day I met him at the gardens. "Because of his clothing, his jewelry, and his presence at an event where only nobles were allowed. It's certainly possible that someone from the merchant or working classes was dressed up to play a part—but it's highly improbable. This appears to be a blow against the monarchy struck by a member of the ruling class. And the king is very anxious that we discover who tried to strike that blow."

"Is he afraid?" I asked.

"Who, the king?"

"Cormac, I meant. If there have already been two attempts on his life, doesn't he think there might be a third one?"

"I think they're all a little nervous," Dezmen admitted. "But the members of a royal house are always at risk because there are always malcontents who dislike the regime. People have been trying to kill members of the ruling class since before the days of Edwin. That's why there are echoes."

"What?" I said. "I don't follow."

"Back before the Seven Jewels were united, the provinces were always at war. The legend is that the triple goddess endowed the high nobles with echoes as a way to keep them safe—so that potential assassins wouldn't know which of three or four bodies was really the lord, and which one was just a shadow."

"I never knew that," I said.

"Did it work?" Jackal asked.

Dezmen laughed. "Well, there was still a great deal of dissension in the provinces even after Edwin united them all, but I don't know how often rebels tried to kill off the high lords. Some people say that in times of peace, fewer echoes appear to the nobility, and in times of unrest, their numbers grow again."

"So are we living in a time of few or many echoes?" Jackal wanted to know.

"Many," Dezmen said with something like a sigh. "For the past ten or fifteen years, more and more babies are being born to the high noble houses with echoes appearing in their beds a day or two later. It's been making a lot of people very uneasy."

I was sure that must be a sign that the triple goddess was preparing us for war, or something, but I was more interested in something else he'd just said. I hoped my voice sounded like I had only a casual interest. "Do only high nobles get echoes?"

Dezmen made an equivocal motion with his head. "That's what everyone always says. That echoes are only bestowed on high nobles, and *legitimate* high nobles at that. But I know a couple of low nobles in Pandrea who each have one echo. And, human nature being what it is, I have to assume that there are a few bastards out there trailing their own shadows."

"Makes me glad I'm not noble," Jackal said. I could tell his gaze was shifting, and he was watching Dezmen's echoes instead of Dezmen. "I'd find it highly inconvenient to be followed by witnesses everywhere I went."

I saw Dezmen open his mouth as if to correct him—*That's not what it feels like at all*—and then decide it wasn't worth trying to explain. "We've strayed from the point," he said. "Which is my investigation into Leffert's death."

He hadn't said, *Don't tell anyone anything I've told you today.* But, of course, I had to assume that every bit of information he'd given us had been deliberate. He knew Jackal traded in knowledge, and he expected to get a return on the goods he'd offered, even if he didn't know when that payoff might appear.

He expected Jackal to share what he'd learned—whenever it suited Jackal to do so.

"I'll keep my ears open," Jackal said, "and let you know if I discover anything interesting."

"How will I get in touch with you if I have something I want to ask?"

Jackal grinned and rearranged himself more comfortably on the bench. "I'm supplying you a bodyguard, don't you remember? He knows how to find me."

Dezmen swiveled his head to look around. His echoes mimicked him. "I don't see him."

"Back at the plaza. He's waiting for us. You can make your own arrangements with him, but it might be easiest to meet there every morning at a certain time of day."

Dezmen looked at me. "What about you?"

"What about me?"

"What if I want to get in touch with *you?*"

I tried to ignore Jackal's spreading smile. *So you've made a conquest of the Pandrean lord, have you?* My tone was belligerent. "Why would you?"

"You carry messages, don't you? Maybe I'll have work for you."

I glanced at Jackal. "Who'd you pick for his bodyguard?"

"Bertie."

I nodded. A strong choice. Bertie loved a good brawl, and he would just as happily watch one as initiate one. But he wasn't stupid, as some of the big men were. I sometimes wondered if he was missing some of the basic human components, like empathy, but I'd never seen him be cruel just for the fun of it. And he was intensely loyal to Jackal. I glanced back at Dezmen. "Bertie can get a message to me, too. But if you want, I'll come by Amanda Plaza every couple of days and see if there's something you need."

"Good enough," he said.

The carriage had come to a standstill as the driver waited for a couple of vendors to get their toppled carts out of the narrow street. I figured I had played my part by now and didn't need to ride back to the square to oversee Dezmen's introduction to Bertie. I placed a hand on the side of the carriage and came to my feet.

"I think I'll just head on home from here," I said. "Good luck in your investigation! Try not to make anyone else mad enough to kill you."

"Wait, let me get the door for you," Dezmen said, but I had swung over the side of the vehicle and dropped lightly to the cobblestones before he'd even finished speaking. Dezmen looked a little put out, but Jackal was grinning. Jackal always favored people who didn't need to be taken care of.

I waved to them both. "See you in a few days, probably!" I called, then turned on my heel and headed back in the direction from which we'd come. Just in case either man was watching, I sent the echoes on ahead of me so no one saw them fall in step beside me. I wanted both Dezmen and Jackal to think that *some* of the time I could operate on my own. I had survived this long by keeping my secrets, and I never wanted anyone to start wondering about me.

I had enough of my own questions. I didn't want anyone else to start asking new ones.

CHAPTER SEVEN

It was Scar's turn to work the following day. If I was going to maintain the fiction that the echoes and I were three distinct people, I figured we all had to appear to have separate lives at least some of the time. We would be going to a rougher part of town, so I dressed both Red and Chessie in more masculine trousers and jackets and covered their hair with soft caps. I didn't bother to make up Red's face, but once I was in Scar's body, I put special care in highlighting the gash across one eyebrow and darkening my chin, as if a beard might just be coming in. I added a cap and Scar's slight scowl, then set off for the warehouse district.

It lay at the southwest corner of the city, where the Charamon Road brought hundreds of travelers into Camarria every day. Dozens of these were merchant wagons, carrying goods from all the other provinces and off-loading them here. The district was busiest during the harvest months, but an astonishing array of products arrived every day through all seasons—fruits and grains, flowers and bulbs, leather and wool, raw lumber and finished furniture, jewelry, clothing, livestock, and art.

The district encompassed maybe ten square blocks of gloomy brick buildings and mazelike streets, all packed with carts and horses and people. If you ever wanted to learn colorful new curse words, that was the place to go. There were a couple of warehouses where I was most likely to find work, where I liked the owners and the overseers, and where no one asked me too many questions. So I headed to one of those as soon as I arrived. I stashed the echoes in an alley that ran between the warehouse and the neighboring building; it was too narrow to accommodate carts, so it was likely that they could sit there undisturbed for hours. A lot of drifter types tended to hang around the warehouse district—sometimes looking for work, sometimes looking for handouts—so nobody who noticed the echoes would give them a second thought.

The foreman looked moderately pleased to see me. He was a powerfully muscled man whose ruddy skin was oiled in a perpetual sheen of sweat. "Yeah, plenty of work today, just got a whole shipment of hothouse bulbs from Alberta. All in crates. Not too heavy, not too fragile, but there's a lot of 'em. Dickie'll show you where to put 'em."

I spent the next few hours unloading raw wood crates and stacking them against a sooty wall. Dickie and two other taciturn men worked alongside me; we didn't exchange a word once we received the initial instructions. It was one of the things I loved about being in Scar's body. There was this sense of physical and emotional freedom, as if I was just a little bit unmoored from the world. Red was a smiler and a flirt; she chatted with customers and laughed at their jokes and let them take a physical liberty if she liked them. Chessie wasn't as warm, but she talked a lot. She displayed a certain jaunty attitude and was quick with a comeback if someone gave her an opening.

But Scar just existed. Just got to the job at hand and didn't waste breath or energy caring about what anyone else was doing. If the other laborers started arguing, Scar hung back; if they started boasting about their recent nights carousing through Sweetwater, Scar remained silent. By now, everyone knew that Scar was unsociable, if reliable. Most everyone left Scar in peace.

I spent so much time trying to make Scar look male that sometimes even I thought of that incarnation as *him*. So it was always a slight shock to slip into Scar's body and remember just how feminine it was really was. But then I developed even more zeal for the deception. I loved the loose, easy way I could swing my arms when I was working and spread my legs when I was sitting. I loved the fact that a grunt counted as a conversational contribution and no one would ask me if I was having an off day when I didn't smile. I loved the fact that no one offered to help me unless I asked for assistance with some particularly awkward load and that everyone expected me to do my share. I loved the feel of my body bulking up.

From what I knew about echoes, they were all supposed to be identical, but mine had subtle differences, and one of them was in the tone and definition of their muscles. Scar had slightly more mass; Red had greater manual dexterity and faster reflexes. Chessie could outrun them both. Impossible, I know, but it was *true*.

The day was long and wearisome, broken by a short pause for lunch, which I shared with Red and Chessie. The pay was good, though, and I was pleased with myself when I pocketed the coins at the end of the day. On the way home, I detoured through a small vendor's market and picked up special treats for dinner—baked fish, fresh fruit, some sweet cakelike offering that made me hungry just to look at it. I bought an extra portion and dropped it off at my landlady's on my way to my own apartment, slipping into Chessie's head before I knocked on her door. She was so pleased that I figured she wouldn't raise my rent for at least six months.

Not a bad day, all in all. Calmer than some of the recent ones. Calmer than some of the upcoming ones, too, I would bet, though it was hard to say why. Even though I had no set plans to interact with the Pandrean lord again, I had a premonition that he was not out of my life quite yet, and it seemed pretty obvious *his* life was going to be eventful.

I tried to ignore the feeling, but I couldn't help but be just a little pleased at the thought that I would see him again.

The following day I settled into Red's body and took another shift at Packrat. The crowd was small enough that Dallie had a lot of time to lean against the counter and complain loudly about the men who had treated her badly.

"Steer clear of drunkards, that's my advice to you, Red," she told me.

"I always do."

"And sweet-talkers! Always *making* promises. Never *keeping* promises. A man starts telling you all the things he's going to do for you, you just run the other way."

"Yep. I prefer a quiet man."

She turned so that her back was to the corner booth where Scar and Chessie appeared to be enjoying a pitcher of beer and an idle game of dice, and she jerked her thumb over her shoulder. "You and Scar, now. *He's* a quiet one. But I'm never sure if you're actually together."

I picked up a tray of drinks and smiled at her. "Sometimes we are and sometimes we aren't. But we take care of each other even when we're on the outs. I guess we'll just always be friends, no matter what."

Dallie snorted. "Oh, you think that now. But you wait. Men are no good. *All* men."

I delivered the drinks to the table where Jackal was sitting with Pippa and a couple of his other friends. "Even though Dallie tells me all men are no good, I brought you some beer," I said. I nodded at Pippa. "Maybe you should find yourself some better company."

Pippa gave a slinky shrug. "It's not like you can trust women, either."

"Well, Dallie has a point," Jackal said fair-mindedly. "Most men are bastards." He waited until I'd set down the last glass, then he pulled me onto his lap. "But women can't get enough of us."

"Eh, I can take them or leave them," I said. Then I cleaned my hands on my apron and reached up to toy with his thick hair. "But *you*, Jackal, you're so handsome and strong and clever. I'd never get sick of *you*."

They all laughed, and Jackal swiped at my butt when I jumped to my feet. "None of your sassy talk, Reddy-girl," he said. "Not unless you mean it."

From five steps away, I paused to blow him a kiss. "You'll know it when I mean it," I said, and sashayed back to the bar as the table burst into laughter again.

The crowd picked up around dinner time, so there was no time for either commiserating or flirting, but that was fine with me. When things slowed down again, I made up a platter and took a quick break with Chessie and Scar so we could all eat. I was still at the table, finishing up my meal, when a group of men walked in, all talking together. They headed to a booth over by Jackal, but one of them caught sight of me and broke off from the others to head my way.

I was already on my feet because I knew he'd be wanting to talk to Chessie. It was Morrissey, whom I hadn't seen since our little adventure under the bridge. He murmured a hello to Red before dropping into her seat across from Chessie and next to Scar. I didn't have time to slip out of the bar, pretending to be on an errand, so I let Red lean against the wall as if listening to the conversation while I flung my consciousness back into Chessie's body.

"How's it going, Morrissey?" I asked. "Did you ever take care of that business that had men hunting you down all over the city?"

"I did," he said. "But it wasn't easy."

"Well, when was anything ever easy?"

"Never, if you go by my life," he said. He tapped his fingers on the table. "So have you thought it over?"

"Thought what over?"

"That job I asked you to do. Fetching my nephew from Empara."

There had been so much additional excitement in the past few days that I had not spared a minute to consider his request. I shook my head. "I just don't see that trip being in my future."

"I'm not going to stop asking."

"Isn't there someone else who can go? When it comes to that, why can't *you* go get him?"

"I can't be away from the city that long," he said evasively. "And there aren't many others I would trust with my money *and* to take care of the boy."

"Why don't you send JoJo? You'd trust him, wouldn't you?"

Morrissey snorted. "He's too dumb to find his way there, let alone back."

That tallied with my experience of JoJo, but it still seemed a little harsh. I'd never been entirely sure of the relationship between the two men, who could almost always be found together. If they were lovers, as I suspected, they were careful not to show any affection in public; people in Sweetwater tried to keep all personal details to themselves, since information was always power in someone else's hands. I never asked questions because I never wanted anyone to pose similar questions to me.

I glanced over at the table of men who had walked in with Morrissey and realized JoJo wasn't among them. "Was he too dumb to find his way to Packrat tonight?"

Morrissey shook his head. "He's out looking for his brother."

"What happened to his brother?"

"Well, that's the thing. No one knows. He's been missing for the past three days."

It was always cause for alarm when someone from Sweetwater just dropped out of view. While people frequently had perfectly good reasons for disappearing for brief periods, it was more likely that some unsavory past had caught up with them. It was easy to inject sympathy into my voice. "Sorry to hear that. Does JoJo think his brother was picked up by Malachi's men?"

"Maybe, but Malachi tends to make arrests in public so the rest of us think twice about carrying out any unlawful activities."

This was true. I had witnessed any number of dramatic scenes where Malachi's men had come swarming into some quiet spot in the middle of the day, scooping up men who were just sitting at a table downing a glass of ale or women who were just having an idle conversation. "Does JoJo think his brother had an accident? Is lying in a ditch somewhere?"

Morrissey shook his head. "That crossed his mind, of course, but it's strange, because Covak is missing, too."

For a moment, I couldn't place the name. "'Covak,'" I repeated.

"Fellow that Trout works with some of the time."

"Oh, that's right! JoJo's brother is Trout..."

My voice trailed off, and it was all I could do not to gape at Morrissey across the table. *JoJo's brother was Trout. Trout and someone else—probably this Covak fellow—had attacked Lord Dezmen at the botanical gardens. Now Covak and Trout were missing.* My blood ran so hot that I could feel it burn through the veins in Chessie's body, in Scar's, in Red's. Red shifted on her feet and almost dropped her tray. Scar gazed down at the scarred wood and played idly with the dice.

I tried to think of something to say so that Morrissey wouldn't be put off by my silence, but he didn't even seem to notice. "Yes, and they had a couple of jobs this past week that they thought were going to bring in a lot of money. JoJo says Trout wasn't too generous with details, but he was already planning how to spend it."

"Maybe that's where they are. On one of those jobs," I said, hoping my voice didn't show my strain.

"Maybe, but JoJo doesn't seem to think so. So he's off trying to find them." He shrugged. "Most of the time it's best not to interfere in someone else's business, but you know, when it's family... He's got to go looking."

"He does," I said. "Well, I wish him luck."

Morrissey muttered a word of thanks and heaved himself to his feet. "Let me know if you change your mind," he said. He nodded at Scar, glanced over his shoulder to nod at Red, and then made his way across the bar to join his friends.

I sat there a moment, trying to still the clamoring of my heart long enough to think this through. Leffert had tried to assassinate Prince Cormac and had failed; then Leffert had been murdered. Dezmen had been brought in to investigate Leffert's death; then Covak and Trout had tried to kill—or at least harm—Dezmen. When they failed, they themselves were killed, or at least neutralized in some fashion.

Whoever wanted Cormac dead was very, very keen on making sure no one knew he was behind the attempt.

And was very, very ruthless.

Which made me wonder how long it would be before someone tried to kill Dezmen again.

I didn't have a chance to talk to Jackal until nearly midnight, since he was doing business all night long and there were never fewer than three other people sitting with him. When the last of his confederates finally left, I abandoned the table I was cleaning to cross the tavern and drop myself in his lap. As he smiled and drew me closer, I leaned in to murmur in his ear.

"The men who tried to kill Dezmen are missing. Maybe dead." I kissed his cheek and nuzzled his neck.

His whole body went rigid for a moment, then I felt him force himself to relax. "How'd you find out?" he asked, nibbling on my lip.

"Morrissey told Chessie and I was listening. One of the missing men was JoJo's brother."

"Morrissey know why?"

"Doesn't seem to."

"This is bad news for the Pandrean lord."

"You'd better tell Bertie to be especially careful."

He pulled back just enough to look me in the eyes. "Bad news for you, too."

I blinked at him. "Why?"

"You were there with Chessie, weren't you, when she scared off his attackers? Someone could have seen her. Seen all of you."

"The only ones who saw us were Trout and Covak," I retorted, "and I doubt they were describing the three of us when someone was slitting their throats." The minute I said it, I was sorry. I shivered at the image my words conjured up, and I clung a little more tightly to Jackal.

He stroked my back. "They might not be dead," he said. "They might be very much alive, and telling someone everything they know. If you recognized them, they probably recognized you. Everyone knows you and Chessie and Scar work as a team."

"Maybe, but none of us *know* anything. I mean, Chessie has no idea who hired Trout and Covak. That seems to be what someone is trying to conceal. I think we're safe enough."

I didn't actually feel safe. Truth be told, I never felt safe—had not for a minute felt safe—not since Angela died when I was eleven and I had learned exactly how brutal the world can be.

Jackal looked concerned. "I'm not so sure," he said.

"Well, I'll be careful. I don't know what else I can do."

He lifted a hand to play with a heavy fall of my hair. "You could come home with me like you used to. Always plenty of security around my place." He tipped his head in the direction of the echoes. "Plenty of room for Scar and Chessie, too. I know you'd be worried about them."

I kissed him. "You're sweet," I said. "And devious. You know I don't want to start things up with you again."

"I promise. This time no other women."

I laughed. "Jackal, every temple in the kingdom will fall into dust before you're able to keep that promise."

"Well, no other women for a few months. At least till all this craziness with Lord Dezmen is past."

I patted his cheek and slipped to my feet. "I don't think so. But I appreciate the offer."

He stayed in his chair and watched me with somber eyes. "Let me know if you change your mind."

People had been saying that to me all night. "I will."

I spent another half hour working alongside Dallie to finish cleanup, then headed on home. The conversations with Morrissey and Jackal had seriously unnerved me, so I kept the echoes bunched tightly together and proceeded down the dark streets in a state of high alertness. I kept myself in Scar's head because Scar was the best fighter, but I made sure both Chessie and Red had daggers in their hands. If Scar went down, I could instantly slip inside one of their bodies and do a little damage.

But we made it to my lodgings without incident. I checked three times to make sure the door and the windows were locked, then I hung a string of decorative bells over the doorknob. Anyone who tried to enter by stealth in the middle of the night would make enough noise to wake me up.

It was still difficult to relax enough to fall asleep. Usually I slept on the outer edge of the bed in case I wanted to leap up quickly for some reason, but this night I slept in the center with an echo on either side of me. I didn't expect them to act independently enough to protect me, oh no. My reasoning was that if someone broke in to kill me, he might take out one of the echoes instead, giving me enough time to fend off his attack and escape from the room altogether. I hated myself for thinking that way. It would be a terrible thing, a heartbreaking thing, to sacrifice one of the echoes to save myself.

But I could think of worse things. I could remember them.

CHAPTER EIGHT

Morning sunlight chased away most of the terrors of the night, though my muscles felt sore from the cramped, protective posture I had held while I slept. Today was Chessie's day to earn the family income, so I dressed in practical clothes and hustled to the financial district to check in with some of my regular clients.

"Yes," one of the bankers told me. "I have a packet that needs to be delivered to the palace." He handed over two heavy leather bags connected by a strap I could wear over my shoulders to distribute the weight.

I didn't ask what was in them, though I knew it was money; the housekeeper withdrew funds almost weekly to pay salaries and cover sundry expenses. I wasn't always the one to make the delivery, but this client, in particular, always sent the money by me if he could. He trusted me not to steal and I relied on him for steady work, so we both did our best for each other.

"Deliver it directly to Lourdes?" I asked, naming the terrifying woman who ran the royal household. She was large, intense, and overbearing; I had frequently had the thought that if I *had* been foolish enough to try to keep a few coins for myself, she would only have to look at me to know the truth.

"As always. She's expecting it within the hour, so don't waste time." He handed me a few coins in payment and I was out the door.

I didn't often have a reason to go to the palace, but I always appreciated the chance when I did. The building was purely beautiful, all warm red brick with a copper roof and accents in white and black stone. The huge courtyard was almost completely enclosed by the curving walls of the east and west wings, and it was always bustling with endless streams of people coming and going. I found an open spot on a stone bench and left Scar and Red sitting there, apparently entranced by the pageant, then I headed in through the great front door.

The first few times I'd acted as a courier for the banker, I'd carried the money around back to the entrance that servants and tradespeople always used. But Lourdes herself had instructed me to come to the main entrance, which opened into a marbled foyer that was big enough to stage a theatrical production. I could never stop myself from gazing around like a country girl come to the city for the first time, entranced by the polished floors, the high painted ceiling, the artwork and statuettes and busts of forgotten heroes. This was Lourdes's territory; you could usually find her prowling around between the pillars and the decorative suits of armor, or stepping forward to welcome some high-ranking visitor who had just come through the door.

Today she wasn't immediately in view, so I caught the attention of a passing servant girl and showed her the bags of money. She nodded and scurried off, and I stepped behind a column to wait. There was, as always, a great deal of activity in the palace foyer, and I wanted to keep out of the way of the rushing servants and the visiting nobility.

I hadn't been in place more than five minutes when a certain commotion began issuing from one of the doors that led back into the recesses of the palace. I shrank even closer to the column to make myself invisible. First, three royal guards strode out, crossing the gleaming floor in strict formation, and then they were followed by the entire royal family. I pressed myself against the cool stone of the pillar and stared. Never before had I seen any of them from such a close vantage point.

At the head of the procession was King Harold, a solidly built man with black hair, stern features, and a regal carriage; his face was pulled into a frown and he didn't bother looking at his surroundings. His three echoes looked so much like him that, if they hadn't been a step behind him, it would have been hard to say which was the original, although usually echoes had a certain *dimness* to them that made it clear they were shadows. I supposed it was important for a king's echoes to be just as solid as the king so that any potential assassin would not know which body to target.

Directly behind him came Queen Tabitha. Her face was as clear-cut as a cameo, with strong bones and smooth skin. Her hair was so styled with braids and ribbon that it was hard to tell the color, though I thought it was a chestnut brown. Her three echoes also seemed almost as alert and sentient as she was, and all four of them looked around with much more interest than Harold had showed.

The two princes were next, walking side by side and talking in low voices. Cormac was handsome and dashing, with hair as black as his father's, slashing cheekbones, and a decided chin. Jordan looked much less dramatic but somewhat more likable, with softer coloring and a generally more pleasant expression. Like their father, they had three echoes apiece.

The last one to appear was a girl about twelve years old, whose two echoes trailed behind her. Because she was the only child Tabitha and Harold had produced together, and because she had two older half brothers, and because no one in the kingdom expected her to inherit the throne, nobody in Camarria paid her much attention. Indeed, I had to think for a moment to remember that her name was Annery. Most people, if they talked about her at all, simply referred to her as "the young princess."

Studying her as she slouched past, I had to say I wasn't much impressed. She was small-boned and scowling, with an expression that said she had been forced to wear the pretty green dress and the gauzy headpiece. She was making no effort to hold her head high, as I was sure a princess should; she didn't thank the maid who ran along behind her to give her something she'd dropped. It was too bad, because I thought she could have been lovely if she actually smiled. She had her mother's green eyes and an attractive wash of red through her brown hair. But she didn't look like someone who would grow up to inspire the love of an entire kingdom if she ever happened to wear the crown.

The whole royal party had almost disappeared out the yawning front doors before I realized there was one last person in the group. He followed behind them in a soundless glide, moving with such stealth that it was possible to overlook him entirely. But once he caught my attention, I could not look away.

He was bald and black-eyed, a sturdy man of medium height and no particularly distinguishing features. Yet there was an intensity about him that radiated power and menace. All the onlookers who happened to be in the foyer as the king and his family strode through had already drawn back to the margins of the room to allow them unfettered passage. But as this fellow stalked noiselessly behind them, everyone pulled back another pace or two, pressing against each other in their desire to get out of his way. When he turned his head to glance at a group of young men clustered near a pillar, they all hastily looked down at their feet as if hoping they could simply make themselves disappear. As his head swiveled around in my direction, I heard a young woman nearby make a noise of strangled fear.

Malachi Burken. The king's inquisitor.

My father.

I was almost completely behind my own pillar by now; I certainly didn't want to attract his notice, either. I had turned my head so that I was in profile to him, but I could track him out of the corner of my eye. Nothing on my side of the room seemed to snag his interest, and he looked away. He lifted his gaze toward the ceiling as if checking the integrity of the braces on the roof, and then he returned his attention to the royal family. Five more paces and he, too, was out the door.

Every single person remaining in the foyer released a sigh of relief. I could almost feel the stone walls bow outward from the collective exhalations. Even for blameless citizens who had no reason to fear the inquisitor, Malachi was the most frightening man in Camarria.

I had caught similar glimpses of him in the decade that I had lived in the royal city. Those first few years, I was terrified of accidentally encountering him on the street, convinced he would take a single look at me and recognize me as his daughter. I realized just how foolish I had been to come to Camarria, when almost any other place in the Seven Jewels would have been safer if I did not want to run into my father. And yet, that had been part of the draw of the royal city—knowing that Malachi was here—knowing that he had no idea that *I* even existed. I began to loiter in the palace courtyard, hoping to catch a glimpse. I was always one of the first ones to line up on any parade route on the days I thought he would be part of a royal procession. I *wanted* to see him; I wanted to keep track of him. I wanted to fix my gaze on him while I hated him with all my heart.

But I never wanted him to turn his head and see my face.

"Chessie," said a voice behind me, and I spun around to discover that Lourdes had made her way over to me. "They told me you were here, but I couldn't find you."

I lifted the money bags from my shoulders and passed them over. She held the center strap easily with one hand, as if the coins weighed nothing. I supposed she handled deliveries twice that large on a regular basis because it must take a small fortune to run the affairs of the palace. "The king and the rest of them were leaving just as I got here," I said. "I wanted to stay out of the way."

"Of course." She studied me for a moment, as she always did, trying to determine if I had lifted even a copper from one of the bags. I maintained my expression of pure innocence. "Thank you," she said at last, turning away without another word.

Sulky, terrifying, or rude—that seemed to sum up the inhabitants of the palace. Not for the first time, I was glad I didn't live there.

Before making my way to the door, I took one more quick look around the foyer, just in case anyone else I recognized might be crossing the polished floor. Well, I would only recognize one other person currently residing in the palace, and surely he was already out tending to his own affairs. And I didn't even care if I saw him again or not. At any rate, he was nowhere in sight. I gave my head a slight shake and made my way to the door. I had more errands to run. Time to stop gawking.

Nothing in the rest of the day was nearly as unsettling as the visit to the palace, though I completed a half dozen errands for other clients and eventually earned a tidy sum. At day's end, I returned to the banking establishment where I'd made my first stop to deposit most of the coins I'd collected.

I couldn't have said what I was saving up for. I never expected to purchase a house or a horse or a fine wardrobe. I never expected to leave the royal city, buy farmland in Alberta or Thelleron, start raising crops, and begin shipping my surplus to a warehouse on the outskirts of Camarria. But it made me feel more secure to have that money steadily piling up in my account. Something I could rely on if a disaster befell me and I couldn't rely on myself.

I did keep enough of the day's coins to treat myself to another fine meal, which I split with the echoes as soon as we got back to the apartment. I triple-checked the locks before I went to bed, tying the string of bells to the doorknob again. But I took my usual place on the outer edge of the mattress. I slept more peacefully and woke feeling much more rested than I had the day before.

You have to be careful, but you can't let yourself be consumed by fear, or there's no point to even being alive. That was the lesson I had taken away from Angela's death. As long as I stayed away from the Pandrean lord, whatever trouble was creeping along behind him would stay away from me.

I believed that, and yet the minute I was out the door, I found my feet taking me in the direction of Amanda Plaza.

I knew that Dezmen and Bertie had made plans to meet there every morning, I just didn't know what hour they had set for their rendezvous. In case it was an early one, I arrived shortly after dawn and took up a spot close to the bridge where I could see everyone coming and going. I'd dressed for the cold because the morning was frosty, and I didn't know long I'd have to wait. On my way, I'd picked up some fruit and fried bread from a vendor, so the echoes and I ate in companionable silence while we watched the endless flow of activity across the plaza.

I'd been there somewhat more than an hour before I saw the Pandrean lord make his way through a tangle of passing schoolchildren and pause before the statues of the triple goddess. For a moment, he stood so quietly he might have been praying, then he made the traditional obeisance to the goddess, touching his forehead for justice, his heart for mercy, and his lips for joy. His echoes copied him exactly.

I left the echoes behind as I crossed the plaza to greet him. I was only a few feet away when he turned his back to the statues and caught sight of me. He smiled like he'd seen his best friend for the first time in a year.

"Are you here by chance, or are you looking for me?" he asked.

"Not really *looking* for you, but curious to see how your investigation is going," I replied. "I see you've managed to stay alive so far."

"Yes, though I understand Jackal thinks I might be in more danger than I realize because of—" I shook my head to indicate he shouldn't voice any suspicions out loud. "Because people might be missing," he ended lamely.

"Right. Although until we know *why* they're missing, it's all speculation. Have you learned anything in the past three days?"

He shook his head. "Nothing. And I'm sure today's errand will be equally fruitless since I'm headed to the main temple to ask the priestesses a few questions. Seems like Leffert spent some time there in the days before he died. Maybe he met with the man who hired him. Or maybe he was merely praying." Dezmen shrugged.

"You ought to be safe at the temple," I observed. "You probably don't even need Bertie's protection."

"Come with me, if you're not doing anything else," he invited. "I could use the company. Bertie's not much of a talker."

"Well, I've heard him talk a *lot*, but probably not about things that would interest *you*."

"Exactly. So will you come along? Now that you're here?"

I knew what I *should* say: *I have to earn my own living, you know. Every day that I saunter around the city with you is a day I can't add a coin to my bank account. I don't have a rich father or a wealthy estate, no one to care for me if I can't care for myself. I live by my wits and my willingness to work.* What I *did* say was, "Sure. For a couple of hours anyway."

He waved at someone in the crowd. "There's Bertie."

A moment later we were joined by the big man, whose face showed its usual goofy grin. "Hey, Chessie," he said, then he looked around for Scar and Red. They were already jogging over to join us, and they returned Bertie's friendly wave.

"Looks like we're all here," Dezmen said. "Let's go."

We made up a procession almost as large as the royal family's as we exited the plaza. We were hardly unobtrusive, which worried me, but I had to think an attacker might be daunted by our sheer numbers, which comforted me. The streets were crowded enough to make it necessary to walk single file much of the way, so there weren't many opportunities for conversation. But I enjoyed the stroll anyway.

It wasn't long before we arrived at the most famous temple in the city, a gray stone building sitting on a small island of green. It was surrounded by a stream narrow enough to jump across if you were feeling energetic, but most people took one of the three wooden bridges instead. We clattered over the one that was painted red for joy.

The temple itself was constructed of three large round sections connected by a central core. Each section had its own door, painted red or black or white to reflect the goddess's moods, and outside each door was a statue of the goddess in one of her traditional poses. Most visitors chose their entrance depending on whether they had arrived looking for joy, justice, or mercy.

Dezmen, not at all to my surprise, circled the building until he found the door for justice. I hung back as he reached for the handle.

"There are too many of us," I said. "Scar and Red and I will wait out here."

"So will I," Bertie said. "I'll just walk around the perimeter, easy-like, so people know I'm here."

There were three uncomfortable-looking metal benches arranged in a triangle and located on the lawn just outside the door. I settled onto the one that overlooked the black bridge and, beyond it, the variegated horizon of the city. Scar and Red took the one on my left, which basically had a view of the temple.

"All right," Dezmen said, pushing the door open. "I don't anticipate this will take very long."

I got bored within five minutes, so I had Chessie take a contemplative pose and let my mind slip into Scar's body. I got to my feet and joined up with Bertie as he walked past us on his second circuit.

"You bring any weapons?" I asked. It seemed like the sort of thing Bertie and Scar would talk about.

Bertie nodded and showed me some of the gear he'd stashed in various pockets. A couple of knives, of course, both of them razor sharp, as well as a short, weighted metal stick clearly designed for bashing in a man's head. Looped through his belt was a length of heavy twine wrapped around a core of wire. "Tie someone up with that, and he won't find it easy to cut his way free," he said with satisfaction.

"Might have to get me some of that," I said, impressed. I'd never had a reason to tie someone up, but who knew when the occasion might arise?

"I'll bring some to Packrat someday and leave it with Red," he said.

"That would be great."

I didn't have much to offer after that, but Bertie launched into a gruesomely detailed account of a fight he'd seen a couple of days ago—between two professionals, from what I could tell, so no one I needed to feel sorry for—and that took up the next fifteen minutes of our promenade. Just as he was describing the way it looked when a man had had his eye gouged out, I saw Dezmen and his echoes exit the temple and head over to the benches.

"Hey," I said, "looks like we'd better get back."

I flowed into Chessie's body and glanced over at Dezmen as he dropped down next to Red. His echoes took their places on the third bench. "You don't look like you learned anything exciting," I said, but I was slightly distracted. I had to concentrate, because I was trying to position everyone just so. I had Red turn a little toward Dezmen, rest her elbow on the back of the bench, and arrange her features into an expression of great interest. I let Scar amble back with Bertie and then lean against the temple wall as if only half listening. Bertie dropped to a crouch at Scar's feet and continued to scan our surroundings, watching for trouble.

Dezmen shook his head. "I spoke to the abbess—a rather formidable woman—who told me the only interaction any of the priestesses had had with Leffert was to collect his body and prepare it for burial. If he came to the temple in the days before his death to meet with some criminal contact, none of her priestesses witnessed the encounter."

"That's disappointing," I commented.

His face showed resignation. "I didn't really expect to learn anything here. But I felt I couldn't overlook the possibility that someone might know something."

We fell silent momentarily as a group of seven people tramped solemnly over the black bridge and headed toward the door for justice. They were all dressed in dark clothing and wore expressions of grief or rage. Clearly they had suffered some kind of devastating loss; clearly they wanted to demand that the goddess deliver retribution.

Once the door had closed behind the last one, Dezmen released an infinitesimal sigh. "You know, I've been to this particular temple maybe a dozen times in my life. And I'm not sure I've ever seen anyone enter the door for joy."

"I've noticed that myself," I said. "There are always crowds of people looking for mercy or justice—*those* two sections are always full—but only a handful of people ever sit in the pews set aside for joy, looking delighted with the world."

I thought it might be time for Red to enter the conversation, so I slipped into her head and stirred a little on the bench. "Why do you think that is?" I asked. "Do people just not have any happiness in their lives?"

Dezmen glanced at me. "Or do they not credit the goddess when happiness comes their way?"

"Oh!" I let my eyes get big and my ready smile come to my face. "You're right! People like to blame the goddess when something goes wrong, but when things are going *well*, it doesn't occur to them that she's behind their good fortune."

Dezmen kept his eyes on Red's face, so I stayed in her head. "Exactly. I'm guilty of that myself. Although I *try* to remember to thank her whenever she has granted me her special favor. In fact, while I was in the temple, I lit a candle on the altar for joy."

I skipped back to Chessie and spoke in a slightly sardonic tone. "Really? What's made you so happy in the past few days?"

He glanced back at me with a grin on his face. "I'm glad to be alive," he said. "So I thanked her for bringing you into my life." He lifted a hand to gesture at Red and Scar. "All of you." He turned back to Red. "Let me express my deepest gratitude."

I was right there behind her eyes, smiling at him. "I didn't do anything," I said. "It was Chessie and Scar who kept you alive in the botanical gardens. Mostly Scar."

Dezmen nodded and turned his attention over to the third echo, so I scrambled into Scar's head. I found it pretty easy to bounce between two of my incarnations, but it was tricky to skip among all three, especially when conversation was required. "I can't thank you enough," Dezmen said, raising his voice so it would carry the extra distance. "I think my echoes and I would all have been floating facedown in that reflecting pool if it hadn't been for you."

I raised a hand in acknowledgment and deprecation. "I never mind a little fighting," I said in Scar's slightly rough voice. "'Specially since our odds were pretty good that day."

I brought myself back into Chessie's body so I could control the conversation a little more. "Don't let Red fool you, though," I said. "She's pretty fast with a blade. She works in an east side tavern, and she can take care of herself when someone gets rowdy."

That nudged Dezmen's attention back to Red, but I was waiting for him, and I gave him a sideways smile. "I don't like to be taken advantage of," I said.

"Well, it's good that you have each other's backs," Dezmen said. "How did all of you meet, anyway?"

I stayed in Red's body and rearranged myself a little on the bench. "My mother and I lived in a tiny apartment over a tiny bakery in a working-class section of town. Not far from Amanda Plaza. One day Chessie showed up, sort of worn and bedraggled. She'd just arrived in Camarria, didn't know anyone, didn't have much money, was looking for work. My mother could be—" I paused, as if thinking over the sins and virtues of this imaginary woman. "She could be hard as iron. Just unyielding. But every once in a while something would touch her heart, and she would turn into this soft, warm, loving creature. She took one look at Chessie and just fell in love. Offered her a job, offered to let her stay in our apartment. Gave her a life, basically."

I spun over into Chessie and offered up a laugh. "She was always warm and loving to *me*," I said. "Not one harsh word from her *ever*."

Back to Red, and a tone of indignation. "That's because *you* weren't her daughter. *You* weren't the one she'd always had such hopes for, but instead you only wanted to consort with some hopeless boy with no prospects and no name."

Dezmen had been glancing between us with some amusement. Now he jerked his head in Scar's direction but kept his eyes on Red. "So he was already in the picture?"

I nodded. "He'd always been around. Kind of a street urchin. His mom left when he was a baby, his dad was…unreliable. He'd take odd jobs with anyone who'd hire him. Sometimes he'd be staying with an uncle, sometimes with a friend. He lived pretty rough."

"And your mother didn't like him."

I shrugged. "Oh, she didn't *dislike* him. She fed him anytime he showed up, and she'd cut his hair or buy him a new shirt when he got too shabby. She just wanted better for me. You know." I shrugged again. "But he's always been my best friend."

The story wasn't true, of course, but a few of the elements were. There *had* been a bakery, and a woman who ran it, and she'd been kind to me in a brusque, offhand way. I'd told her that Red and Scar were my siblings, both damaged from a childhood illness. *He doesn't do much except sit quietly in a corner, but he's no danger. She barely talks, but she'll work all day long if I'm nearby and she can see me. We can both mix dough and roll out bread and tend the oven. I can deal with customers and make change. I'm strong. I'm honest. I'm desperate.* Red and I worked for her for nearly five years. It was the first lucky break I'd had.

The tale seemed to satisfy Dezmen. "It's a good thing to have people who've been in your life so long," he said, nodding seriously. "They know everything about you, good and bad, and love you anyway."

I skipped back to Chessie and made a derisive sound. "Good *and* bad," I said with great emphasis. Then back to Red to burst out laughing.

Grinning, Dezmen glanced between us again. "You argue like sisters," he said.

I stayed in Red's mind and studied his face. "You say that as if you have personal experience."

He nodded. "I do. Three sisters. I'm the oldest."

"Are you close to them?"

"Somewhat close to Darrily. She's only a year younger than I am. But the other two—" He spread his hands. "They're ten and eleven years younger, and mostly I just think they're brats. Darrily at least has some thoughts in her head, although sometimes I find her a little shallow." He laughed. "I've said that to her face, though, so don't be shocked at the things I'm saying behind her back. She's very focused on who's getting married, and who's in the middle of a scandal, and all this society stuff, and I find it a little tedious."

I darted back into Chessie's brain. "Says the man who is friends with Prince Cormac."

He glanced over at me and laughed. "Well, yes, it is hard to avoid *society stuff* when Cormac's in the room. But lately we have much more sober things to talk about—such as who wants to kill him and why."

I nodded. "So tell me what you're planning to do next to solve that puzzle."

Dezmen frowned. "There's a low noble named Wimble who lives here in Camarria. Not very respectable. Every few weeks he throws parties that draw a certain element of noble society—the kind of people who are looking for danger, but in a controlled environment. There might be illegal substances available there, and a certain kind of woman—" He looked a little embarrassed as he glanced between Red and me.

We both nodded, but I spoke. "I know the type," I said dryly. "I've even heard of this Wimble. A few folks I know have been suppliers for him."

"Seems that a few days before he assaulted Cormac, Leffert was at one of these parties. I thought I might go to the next one and ask around. See if I can find anyone who remembers anything he said."

"Sounds reasonable enough. When's the next one?"

"The day after tomorrow."

I put my hands on my knees and pushed myself to my feet like a woman who was clearly done with this conversation. "Then I hope you learn something."

Red didn't stand, and neither did Dezmen. In fact, he gazed up at me with a serious expression. "I thought maybe you'd come with me."

I dropped back down onto the bench. "*What?* Why?"

"Sometimes people will talk to a pretty girl when they won't talk to a high noble."

I glanced over at my echo. "In that case, you should take Red."

He glanced at her, too, but brought his attention back to me. "I would, if she was willing and you weren't. But you've been on this case with me from the beginning. You might overhear something that would make sense to you when she wouldn't even notice."

I spoke as Red. "That's true," I said in a judicious voice. "Chessie pays a lot more attention to things than I do." I smiled at Chessie. "I'll help you with your makeup, though. I'll pick out your dress."

In a voice of irritation, I spoke as Chessie. "I haven't even agreed to go!"

"You will, though, won't you?" Dezmen asked in a wheedling voice. "I think people will find me a lot more approachable if I come to the party with a woman on my arm. And I think maybe you'll learn something."

"Oh, all right," I said as ungraciously as possible, though secretly I was delighted. To attend a party at a noble's house! True, it was a dissolute noble and the party was likely to be no more high-minded than a typical night at Packrat, but it would still expand my experience wonderfully.

I tried not to think about how much I would enjoy looking pretty for Lord Dezmen's sake. *That* was simply ridiculous. Instead, I should be worrying about how I was going to bring Red and Scar along on the expedition. It might take a little creativity.

"Do you want me to meet you there? What's the address?" I asked.

"No, of course I don't want you to meet me there! Cormac will put a carriage at my disposal, and I'll pick you up at your place, as courtesy demands."

The last thing I wanted was Lord Dezmen knowing where I lived. I never invited anyone to my small apartment; not even Jackal had been there. It offered too many clues about who I really was.

"Well, you won't," I said. "I'll meet you somewhere and we can arrive together in style, if that matters to you."

He eyed me—for a moment I thought he might argue—but he seemed to quickly realize that I wouldn't budge on this point. "Very well. How about the front entrance of the botanical gardens? That's somewhat along the route."

"Tell me a time and I'll be there."

We finalized details and then we all rose to go. Scar and Red ranged themselves around me, while Bertie and the echoes clustered behind Dezmen, and we all clattered over the black bridge. "Day after tomorrow," he said as our groups prepared to split off.

"At the gardens," I answered. "I'll be there."

103

❧ ❧ ❧

I spent half of the next day earning a living and the other half shopping for clothes. Nothing in Red's flashy wardrobe was suitable for an event at a noble's house. Besides, most of the dresses she owned had had beer spilled on them at one time or another. I wanted something that looked daring but sophisticated, something that showed off my figure and my coloring. Something I could afford that didn't look cheap.

I browsed the secondhand stores in the district that sat squarely on the divide between the noble side of town and the merchant neighborhood. I got lucky in the third shop I tried, where I found an emerald-green silk gown with a deep scoop neck, a cinched-in waist, and three-quarter sleeves that dripped with lace. It was a little too big for me, and I wasn't much of a needlewoman, so once the clerk wrapped it up for me, I headed straight to Brianna's. By this time it was the dinner hour, and she was already back from the flower markets.

"Oh, this is lovely," she said as she held it up by the shoulders. "And you need it by tomorrow? Lucky for you I don't have anything *really important* that I need to be working on tonight."

I laughed at her. "You're helping the king investigate a terrible crime!" I pointed out. "What could be more important than that?"

She gave me a wry look. "I am not entirely enamored of our king."

Of course not; he had had her mistress put to death. I nodded soberly. Then she added in a more cheerful voice, "But I do not favor anarchy, either, so I will do what I can to help! Come on, you'll have to strip down so I can get this properly fitted."

Once I was standing barefoot in my flimsy underthings, she slid the cool silk over my head. For a moment I was blinded by green darkness, then my face emerged through the neckline. Brianna started tugging the fabric into place, then moved behind me to fasten buttons.

"Red will have to help you get dressed tomorrow night—you can't do these up yourself."

"She'll be happy to."

I felt her fingers at my waist and under my arms as she estimated how much fabric she would need to take in. "This should go pretty quickly," she murmured. She circled around me so she could check the fit of the neckline. "Oh, but see how beautiful your emerald necklace looks with this dress!" she exclaimed. "It's like you bought them together!"

She steered me to a corner of the room, where a tall cheval mirror was half hidden behind a pile of boxes. I peered around the obstacles to try to get a good look at myself. She was right; the triangular pendant seemed to blaze above the scooped neckline of the dress. Both the gems and the fabric were a fierce and triumphant green.

"It might look perfect, but I'm not going to wear it tomorrow night," I said. "If it's the only thing that ties me to Malachi, I don't want anyone seeing it and starting to wonder."

"But no one's ever seen Malachi wear that ring. And the necklace is so beautiful."

"I'm not taking any chances." I ran my fingers through my hair, which was flat and a little grimy after several days of neglect and too many hours crammed under a cap. "Too bad my hair is so short. I won't be able to do much with it."

"Wait right here," Brianna said, disappearing into a small room off the main one. I continued to primp and pose before the mirror, craning my neck to try to see myself from all sides. It was amazing how much my appearance changed simply with the addition of a piece of high-quality clothing. My face looked more sculpted, my bearing almost regal. Maybe that was because I was standing on my tiptoes, trying not to trip over the hem.

Brianna was back in a moment with various items fluttering from her hand. "Hold still," she said, reaching up to set a hairpiece on my head. "If I wrap that with green ribbon and a little lace—and then sew on a few dried flowers—that would look lovely, don't you think? And no one would notice your short hair."

"That would be so pretty! But do you have time to make something like that? *And* alter the gown? I've already asked you to do so much."

She smiled at me in the mirror. "I miss helping Marguerite dress," she said. "This will be fun."

"Well, at least let me go buy dinner for us and bring it back while you're working."

"Sounds like a deal."

I took the echoes with me to buy food and brought them upstairs when I returned—it had been a chilly day and I didn't want to leave them shivering in an abandoned building. Brianna just greeted them absently and kept on working. I served us all and cleaned up the mess afterward, then sat talking idly with Brianna while she sewed. It was three hours before she was done, and I was starting to feel guilty about how much effort she was putting into the project, but she seemed to be happily absorbed in fixing the dress and crafting the headpiece. It was surprisingly restful to pass that much time with her, just existing companionably. I didn't have many female friends in my life—Dallie was probably the one I spent the most time with, and while I liked her, she complained so much that she soon became annoying. But I'd never heard Brianna complain about anything. Not for the first time, I thought how lucky Nico was to have found her. Which had made me lucky, too.

"There," she said, when she had put on the finishing touches. "Let me show you how to pin this in place, and then I think you're ready to go."

We returned to the mirror and she arranged the headpiece on my hair while I watched. Its effect on my face was even more dramatic than the dress. My cheekbones seemed higher, my skin fairer, my eyes bigger. "I'm not one to brag about myself, but I don't think I'm going to need to be embarrassed about my looks when I'm at that party tomorrow night," I said.

"Well, you're half noble yourself, and I've always thought that you had an air of refinement," Brianna said.

I laughed at her. "Refinement? Me?"

"You don't talk like the street girls I know. Your accent is better. You just have a certain way."

"That's all Angela's doing," I said. "She was a governess in some high noble's house before she retired. She schooled me like I was going to be a lady someday, even though we both knew I wasn't."

Brianna unclipped the headpiece and carefully wrapped it in soft paper. "Well, you can certainly act like it tomorrow night," she said. "I can't wait to hear all the details. Come over later in the week and tell me how it goes. That's how you can pay me back."

We wrapped the gown, too, and folded it just enough to fit it into a large carrying bag. Then I rousted the echoes, who were drowsing on the sofa, thanked Brianna again, and headed out into the dark. I was a little disconcerted to realize how much I was looking forward to the following night. I honestly couldn't remember the last time I had been so eager to see the next day arrive.

CHAPTER NINE

It took me two hours to get ready the following afternoon, but I was inordinately pleased with the results. I'd spent most of the time inside Red's body, dressing Chessie like she was some kind of oversized doll. Applying makeup with a practiced hand, buttoning up the back of the green dress—which fit perfectly, all thanks to Brianna—pinning the hairpiece in place. Not until I stepped into a pair of simple heeled boots did I slip back into Chessie's mind, and then only so I could grin at myself like an idiot in the sliver of mirror I had tacked up near the front door.

"Don't be so full of yourself," I warned my reflection. "Bad things happen when you let down your guard."

The last thing I did was rummage around for the right jewelry. Except for the emerald pendant, most of the pieces I owned were cheap and flimsy, but I had a friend who bought and sold quality goods, and over the years I'd bought a few items from him. So I was able to add a gold necklace hung with a charm stamped with the letter C, and a slim gold ring set with a band of tiny emeralds. Fancy but understated.

I couldn't bear to leave my emerald pendant behind, though; I was a little superstitious about keeping it with me at all times. As if my identity might disappear if it no longer hung around my neck— as if *I* might disappear. So I fastened it around Red's throat instead, and tucked it under the collar of her shirt.

Then we were all ready to go.

I arrived at the botanical gardens nearly an hour before our proposed rendezvous time, and not because of my usual determination to check out a meeting site long before anyone else arrived. No, the minute I started walking down the street, I realized that the hem of my dress would be horribly soiled if I continued on foot for even another few blocks, so I paid a carriage-for-hire to take me the rest of the way. A criminal waste of money for an able-bodied woman, but I was not going to let a small expense ruin my carefully created appearance. Anyway, I never minded waiting. I sat on a bench outside the main entrance, Scar and Red on either side of me to lend some warmth, and watched the world go by until Dezmen arrived.

He pulled up in a royal carriage blazoned with the king's heraldry and boasting two guards riding on the bench with the driver. Scar and Red and I were on our feet as he and his echoes disembarked. I saw him look past me once as he scanned the area, searching for me.

Then his gaze came back, and he simply stared.

I hadn't practiced my curtseys since Angela died, but I thought I wasn't too shaky as I dipped in his direction and straightened up again. "Lord Dezmen," I said in a cool voice. "I'm pleased to see you."

"I suppose it sounds rude to say I wouldn't have recognized you without Scar and Red standing beside you," he said. "But I don't think I would have. You look magnificent."

He didn't look too bad himself. He was always fashionably dressed, but tonight he wore dark velvet, antique lace, and a chain of opals that glittered across his chest like so much captured firelight. He was a study in shadow and sand—his skin and his suit so dark, his eyes and his shirt and his jewels so fair. Side by side, our colors would make us a striking pair.

"Red picked everything out for me," I said.

He nodded in her direction. "Then you did an excellent job."

I skipped into her head briefly to grin at him. "Thanks. I thought so, too."

Dezmen returned his attention to Chessie so I returned my consciousness to her body. "But do you plan to bring them along? I don't think it's necessary." He gestured at the carriage. "I've got a couple of royal guards with us. I think we'll be safe enough."

I glanced around. "Did you leave Bertie behind, then?"

"Like I said. Royal guards. Didn't seem like we would need more protection."

Leaving the echoes behind wasn't an option, of course, so I just had to brazen this out. "Well, *I* will feel more comfortable with my friends at my back, and I think you should have brought Bertie, too," I retorted. "Scar and Red can wait in the carriage. I just want them with me."

I slipped into Scar's mind. "We won't be any trouble. But we want to be there."

"Fine. It'll be a tight fit but—fine. Everyone into the carriage."

It took a little jostling before we all were settled inside, since the carriage was a conventional one with only two facing benches. Dezmen wasn't a bruiser like Bertie, but his shoulders were broad enough to make it impossible for him to share one seat with both of his echoes. So I sat between his and he sat between mine, though I went to some trouble to make sure he didn't realize that. I stayed in Red's head for much of the short trip, quizzing him about palace gossip. I was pretty sure he was glad when we finally arrived and he could stop trying to answer the questions.

"One last thing," he said as the carriage came to a halt. "How do you want me to introduce you? While I very much like the name Chessie—"

"Call me Chezelle," I said. "It sounds so much more pretentious."

He cocked his head to one side. "I like that. Elegant."

It also happened to be my real name, but I didn't want him to know that since it might make him start wondering. "I've used it before when I needed to be fancy. But I'm guessing this party will be the fanciest place I've ever been."

He grinned. "Or the most debauched. I guess we'll see."

One of the guards opened the carriage door, and Dezmen was the first one out. Even before his echoes disembarked, he turned to offer me his hand. His fingers were much warmer than mine on this chilly night, and I almost didn't want to let go once I was on the ground, but of course I did.

"Ready?" he asked with a smile.

"I hope so," I said.

He crooked his arm and I rested my hand at the bend of his elbow, and we promenaded up a short flagstone path, trailed by his echoes. We had arrived at an ornate residence in a neighborhood filled with similar buildings—all three and four stories high, over-decorated with small turrets and architectural features and painted accents. It was obviously a much finer district than the one where I lived, but it was the sort of neighborhood that made me sniff with disdain. It was filled with people who wanted to appear better than they were, who wasted time and money trying to prove they were as good as the high nobles they envied. I had never seen any point in trying to be like someone else. I was always too busy trying to make sure the person I was remained alive and fed.

While most of the other houses in the area were quiet and showed only a few lights at their windows, this one was illuminated from top to bottom. A muted roar spilled out from the closed doors, a combination of music, voices, laughter, and the constant clatter of feet shifting along a hard floor. There were a lot of people inside.

"Shall we go in?" Dezmen murmured as we reached the front step.

I nodded because I was too distracted to speak. Part of my attention was focused on the echoes as the carriage edged away from the house. I didn't see any other vehicles waiting in the street, so I was suddenly worried that the coachman would have to travel several blocks before he found a place he could pull over and wait for us to leave the party. How far away could the echoes get before I started to feel faint and panicky? What excuse could I give if I suddenly turned away from Dezmen and went racing after the carriage?

I was inexpressibly relieved when the driver pulled over again almost immediately, having left just enough room for other coaches to stop in front of the house. I supposed he didn't feel the need to lumber down to whatever alley the other drivers were using—the royal insignia on the carriage would prevent any neighbors from complaining about his presence.

I smiled up at Dezmen just as a servant opened the door to admit us. "Yes, let's," I replied, and we stepped inside.

We immediately were in a large open room that was just as over-decorated as the exterior, with polished marble for the walls and floors, and gold leaf on dozens of surfaces from the crown molding to the excessive number of statuettes. It was difficult to get a good look at the furnishings, however, as so many people were crammed into the space. Close to a hundred, was my initial guess, and that didn't include the servants slipping through the crowd carrying trays of food and wine.

Everyone was dressed in what I imagined to be the highest kick of fashion—silk and satin for the women, velvet and wool for the men, lace at every throat and wrist, jewels on every finger. What took me most by surprise were the scents, which were a combination of face powder, perfume, cologne, and distilled spirits. Usually when I was in the middle of a crowd, the odors tended more toward sweat, piss, and beer.

"Gorsey," I whispered to Dezmen. "Everyone looks and smells so nice."

He grinned. He appeared to be much less impressed with the pageant than I was. "If only they were so nice in their hearts."

"So what do we do now?"

"We walk around and see if anyone looks interesting enough to talk to."

To me, that seemed like a daunting proposition in a sea of strangers, but Dezmen was perfectly at ease. From a passing foot-man, he snagged two glasses of wine and handed one to me; his echoes lifted their own glasses from the server's tray. Then we began strolling slowly forward, nodding to anyone who noticed us, and catching snatches of conversation.

"The sweetest filly I ever put my money on..."

"But I told him I wasn't that big a fool..."

"He believed it, can you imagine?..."

"Everyone knew the marriage would be a disaster."

We'd been there maybe twenty minutes when we were hailed by a young man standing in a knot of people who looked remarkably similar to him. Same age, same style of clothing, same somewhat giddy expression that I assumed came from drinking too much wine in too short a time. "Dezmen! Didn't expect to see you here tonight."

"Hello, Randall," Dezmen replied, giving him a warm smile. "I hear such things about Wimble's parties that I thought I'd come see one for myself."

"Oh, they're great fun," Randall said. "Anything you want, you can find here. Card games in the rooms over there." He waved toward a closed door on the far side of the room. "The stakes are steep, but that shouldn't matter to *you*. Upstairs you can find—" He glanced at me and blushed. "Well, nothing that would interest you, probably."

I took a tighter grip on Dezmen's elbow and bestowed a dazzling smile on young Randall. "I'll make sure his attention doesn't go wandering," I said, to make it clear I knew just what kinds of diversions were lounging in the upper-level rooms.

Randall smiled back at me. Apparently, he appreciated a woman who wasn't easily offended. "And if you like smokes or berries, there's a woman in the courtyard out back. She can set you up with anything you want."

"Most excellent," said Dezmen. "You must come to most of Wimble's parties."

"I do," Randall said, "but I missed the last two. Traveling for my father, you know. Can't tell you how glad I am to be back from Banchura."

"I can imagine," said Dezmen. "Well, we're going to prowl around a little and see what catches our attention. Good to talk to you."

I realized, though Randall probably didn't, that Dezmen had no interest in him if he couldn't describe anything he might have seen during the last party at Wimble's house. When the young man nodded and turned back to his friends, I spoke to Dezmen in a low voice. "So we're looking for people who were here when? About four weeks ago?"

"Yes. That's when Leffert was here last."

"Seems like an odd sort of thing to keep asking people. 'So do you come to all of Wimble's parties? Really? Even the last one? Oh good, then I have a question for you.' People might start wondering."

"Most of them are probably too drunk to remember what we ask about."

"Then they might be too drunk to remember what happened four weeks ago."

"I know. But we might get lucky."

I gave him an arch look. "Did Leffert consider himself a lover? You might get your best information from the women upstairs. Or the men, depending on his tastes."

He made a face. "That occurred to me. But I think I'd prefer seeing if I can discover anything on this level instead."

We continued our slow circuit through the crowd, greeted by a few more nobles who recognized Dezmen and seemed surprised but pleased to see him. Two of the people who were *most* delighted with his presence were a pair of young women I estimated to be about twenty years old. At a guess, they'd come here on a dare or in a fit of defiance, and their parents would probably disown them if they were discovered at such a disreputable location. They were quite a contrast: One had the pale skin, blond hair, and blue eyes of the Banchura native; the other had the dark coloring that was classically Pandrean. But they both had two echoes lined up behind them, and they both giggled and fawned over Dezmen, stroking his velvet sleeves and wondering if he thought he might dance later in the evening?

"Oh, will there be dancing?" he asked. "I confess, this doesn't seem like the venue."

"Well, it's not *proper* dancing," said the Banchuran woman. "It's more—intimate."

"My father would say it is wanton," said the one from Pandrea, and they both went off into gales of laughter.

Dezmen met my gaze, laughter on his own face. "Chezelle? Do you think we might stay for the dancing?"

"Oh, I hope we *do*!" was my enthusiastic response. "But you'll have to pair up with one of these girls, since I'd feel ever so awkward having your echoes follow us around." I glanced about the room as if searching for a friend. "I'd have to find someone else who wanted to be my partner."

"That settles it. You have to stay," said the Pandrean lady. "We'll look for you later!"

They tripped off arm in arm and I grinned at Dezmen. "I can hardly wait."

His expression had turned severe. "I don't think you have any idea what their idea of dancing entails."

"I think I have a better idea than you do," I retorted. "I'm pretty sure I've been in a few rooms where it was done, and I'm guessing you haven't."

He smiled again, not saying yes or no, and regarded me for a moment. "I think we both still have a lot to learn about each other," he finally replied.

I laughed. "What next? We haven't found out anything useful so far."

"I think I might need to visit the card rooms and play a few hands. I don't know if you want to come with me and watch or—"

I glanced around. I was feeling more comfortable about being here and talking to random strangers. None of them had been very intimidating—or even very impressive—in our brief conversations so far, and I was starting to think I could hold my own. "I'll circulate for a while out here. I think once you're not standing next to me I might find myself a lot more popular."

Unexpectedly, that made him frown. "I don't want to expose you to the overeager attentions of a bunch of drunken louts."

I laughed at him. "I think I can take care of myself. Now go."

He protested once more, but gave in when I pointed out that we were here to gather information, and it made more sense to split up while we tried to do it. He and his echoes headed for the card room, looking back at me twice before disappearing through the door, and I made another pass around the room.

I did, in fact, draw much more attention now that Dezmen wasn't beside me, and I quickly developed a useful conversational gambit. *My father would be so mad if he knew I was here, but I'm having so much fun! Do you come to all of Wimble's parties?* If the lords I was talking to were not regular visitors, I moved on. If they had been here four weeks ago, I asked if they'd ever met my friend Leffert. *He's the one who told me to come, but I haven't seen him tonight. Do you know him? Do you know where he is?* No one seemed unduly suspicious when I brought up his name—but no one confessed to having talked to him last month, either.

By the time I had made my way toward the back of the room, I was a little overwhelmed by the heat, the perfume, and the glare of candlelight glinting off of gold statuary. The back door was standing open, and the wash of cold air felt so welcome that I decided to go outside for a few minutes. The courtyard was much less crowded and much more pleasant, softly lit by a few lanterns and decorated only with a few benches and widely spaced planters filled with leafy greenery.

Its scents were entirely different, too, a blend of sweet and acrid smoke fumes from a couple of different kinds of burning herbs. These were far more familiar odors to me, and I relaxed even more. I glided through the sparse groups of people, mostly men, all of them more interested in drugs than women at the moment. I glanced from face to face, wondering if there was anyone I should approach.

"Chessie."

It was such a shock to hear a woman speak my name that I froze in place and wondered how quickly I could dig my concealed knife from its sheath on my left ankle. This wasn't someone who had just met me tonight; this was someone who knew me. "Chessie," she said again, and I turned in her direction.

I spotted her right away, leaning against an ornamental tree, her arms crossed, her fair hair and bony face barely visible in the shadows. But I recognized her, too, and I relaxed again. She was a slim, smart, older woman who trafficked in every kind of illegal substance that could be found in the Seven Jewels, both those that could be inhaled and those that could be swallowed—"smokes and berries," as young Randall had said. More important, she was one of Jackal's friends.

I crossed the patio to talk to her, my skirts making whispering noises against the stone. "Hello, Gina," I said in a low voice. "Call me Chezelle here."

She looked me over, taking in the green gown and the exquisite hairpiece. "You taking up a new line of work?"

"In a manner of speaking, but not what you're implying," I replied. "Helping someone who's looking for information. He thought some people would be more likely to talk to me than to him."

"Probably right about that," Gina agreed. "What kind of information?"

I glanced at the men drifting around the courtyard. "About someone who was here the last time Wimble had a party. I don't think he was a regular visitor, but maybe someone who comes here pretty often would remember him."

"What's his name?"

"Leffert."

Gina shook her head. "I don't know him. But I can tell you who was here at the last party. And the party before that." She nodded at a group of young men who had just burst into laughter. They had appeared dazed and a little sleepy when I first walked out, but they were reviving a little as whatever they'd ingested started to wear off. "Those three. They're always here." She jerked her head toward a solitary, morose man who hovered over a stone planter and stared at the shrub inside as if attempting to puzzle out a divine script. "That one." Then she moved her hand to indicate a foursome—two men and two women—who clustered together in the shadows on the far side of the courtyard and passed a lighted object from hand to hand. "And that group. But I wouldn't waste your time with them. I never see them talk to anyone but each other. And me, of course."

The three cheerful young men looked to be my best bet. "Thanks," I said. "I'll tell Jackal you were helpful."

She grinned. "Now that's what I like to hear."

I studied the young men a moment, strategizing. Two were dark, one was fair; the fair man and one of the dark-haired lords were tall, while the other was short. Other than those superficial differences, they didn't have many distinguishing characteristics. They were all young, rich, and irresponsible enough to be wasting their family's money at a place like this. It was not hard to think I could outsmart them. I reached up to unclasp my necklace and coiled it in the palm of my right hand.

With a nod of farewell to Gina, I turned toward the open door of the house and picked my way daintily across the courtyard. I didn't glance at the knot of laughing men, but I stealthily opened my hand just as I was passing them. Two steps later, I gasped with dismay and laid my hand against my bare throat. "Oh no! My necklace!"

I turned back to hunt for it, bending low to peer at the flagstones. It was hardly a coincidence that I was facing in the direction of the young lords, who had a mighty fine glimpse down the front of my dress.

The shorter lord broke off his conversation with his fellows to say, "Did you lose something, my lady?"

Still bent over, I looked up at him woefully. "Yes, my gold necklace! Oh, I have to find it!"

The other two stepped back and scuffed at the flagstones with their feet. "Gold, you say?" asked one of the tall ones. "You'd think that would be easy enough to see even in this light."

The blond one reached down to scoop something up. "I found it!" he said triumphantly. "At least—I found *a* necklace. I don't know if it's yours."

"It's just a little charm with the letter *C*," I said hopefully.

"Ha! Then it *is* yours," he said, handing it over.

"Oh, thank you, thank you, thank you!" I exclaimed, clutching my hand to my heart. "My mother gave it to me, and if I ever lost it—and then had to explain *where* I lost it—" I indulged in a little shudder.

"It's my belief that it's always better if your mother doesn't know where you spend your time," said one of the tall ones, and the three lords laughed.

The short one seemed to be the friendliest. "So your name begins with a *C*?" he asked. "Would you be willing to tell us what that name is?"

I hesitated, as a lady should, and then smiled, as a conspirator must. "Chezelle."

"I'm Trev," he said, then waved at his fellows. "Jordie. Barton." I thought the blond was Jordie and the dark-haired fellow was Barton, but the introduction had been so casual I couldn't be sure.

"So are you enjoying the party, Chezelle?" asked the one I thought was Jordie.

"I *am*. I've never been before. But it's ever so much fun." I don't know when I had gotten it into my head that "ever so" was a phrase silly young noblewomen used, but it had spilled out of my mouth at least ten times tonight. Each time, I felt some of my own intelligence spilling out along with it and evaporating in the scented air.

"We're here all the time," Trev boasted. "Never miss one."

I glanced around as if making sure no one was listening, and then I leaned forward to talk in a lower voice. "I heard that *he* was here at the last party. That man they found dead a few weeks ago."

Jordie and Trev looked momentarily confused, but Barton was nodding. "That's right. Leffert. You remember, Trev, we talked to him for half an hour. I was shocked when I learned whose body had turned up over on the east side."

"Leffert— Oh, you mean the fellow who kept going on about his horse? *That's* who got killed? I didn't realize that."

"I didn't put it together, either," said Jordie. "Well, that's a damn shame. He seemed like a nice enough fellow."

"What was he like?" I asked with the slightly gruesome eagerness of someone fascinated by the horrible things that happen to other people.

Barton shrugged. "Oh, you know. Seemed like the type who would fling himself headlong into anything. Kept talking about his horse, and how he'd be willing to take on any comer in a race. I saw him go into the card room and bet a roll of coins on a bad hand. That sort of thing. I'd guess he was reckless in everything else he did, too."

"Well, if he was hanging around in Sweetwater at night, you could hardly get any more reckless than that," said Jordie.

"What else did he talk about?" I wanted to know. "I mean—here he is, he doesn't know he's going to *die* in a few days. I keep wondering what his last words were."

Trev looked like he was cudgeling his brain, trying to come up with some detail that would please me. "I remember wondering if he was a little deeper in debt than he should have been, and if that was why he kept making those high wagers."

"Why'd you think that?" Jordie asked.

"Because he was asking for the names of secondhand jewelers, don't you remember? He said he wanted to buy, but I thought he was really looking to sell."

"That's right!" Barton exclaimed. "He wasn't from Camarria, so he didn't know the best places to go."

I could think of a dozen, but I wasn't sure which shops these lords were more likely to patronize. "I know where *I* would have told him to try," I said. "Someplace off of Cheater's Row, down by Amanda Plaza."

"That's what I said!" Trevor replied, pleased. "I've sold three rings there in the past six months."

"Yes, but there's got to be four jewelers on that one street," Jordie complained. "Which one would you recommend?"

"Candleback's," Barton said without hesitation. "Always the best prices."

Trev was nodding. "That's what I told him. Don't know if he went there, but he asked for directions."

I sighed. "So he went in and sold his mama's bracelet, maybe, and then just a few days later he was *dead*. It just seems so monstrous. And so *sad*!"

"We don't want you thinking about sad things," Trev said in a firm voice. "What can we talk about to cheer you up?"

I gave him a saucy smile, though I was really calculating how quickly I could exit the conversation now that I had discovered what I wanted to learn. "I don't know! What would you *like* to talk about?"

Trev sidled a little closer and put his hand on my arm. My skin was bare and cool; despite the fact that he'd been out in the chilly dark for some time, Trev's palm was feverishly warm. The effect of the "berry" Gina had sold him, no doubt. Some drugs could make you so hot you'd strip off all your clothes and run into a snowbank for relief. And die, of course, if there was no one nearby to rescue you from your stupidity.

"I'd like to talk about *you*," he said. "What made you come here tonight? Are you having a good time? Do you think you'll be back? Did you come with some friends or by yourself?"

As Trev spoke to me, Jordie and Barton drifted away, engaged in their own low-voiced conversation. Clearly, once Trev had signaled his intent to pursue me, they were leaving him a clear field.

"Oh, I wouldn't dare come *alone* to such a place!" I answered, edging away. He followed, giving my arm a squeeze. "Of course I'm with friends!"

Now Trev slipped his arm around my waist. He was so close that my shoulder pressed into his chest, and I could feel the heat radiating from his whole body. "Will they miss you if you stay out here for a while and talk to me?" he asked in a low voice, squeezing my arm again. "I'd like to learn more about you. Chezelle. I'd like to learn *everything* about you."

For a moment, I contemplated my next move. I wasn't afraid—not yet. Trev might be feeling amorous, but he didn't look too steady on his feet, whereas I was sober, I was armed, and I was a lot stronger than he had any reason to expect. I was pretty sure I could fight him off without much trouble. The wild cards were Jordie and Barton. If there was a struggle, would they haul Trev away from me or help him hold me down? I didn't think I could count on Gina to come to my defense. She had a reputation for refusing to interfere, and I wasn't sure even her friendship with Jackal would move her to step in.

Better to extricate myself as quietly as possible. I smiled again and turned my head so I could lean my forehead right up against Trev's own. "I've got a knife, and I know how to use it," I murmured, my mouth so close to his I might have been planning to kiss him. "I'll cut off your balls or slit your throat—your choice. So take your hands off me and let me walk away, or you'll be leaving this party in a lot different shape than when you arrived."

His eyes, mere inches from mine, widened first in confusion and then in unease. He dropped his hands and stepped back so quickly that he almost stumbled. I saw Jordie glance our way, though he didn't break off his conversation with Barton, but I kept most of my attention on Trev.

"I didn't mean anything," he whined. "I just thought—you seemed to like me."

I tugged on my gown as if pulling the fabric back in place, though his gentle pawing hadn't done much to dishevel me. "I do like you," I said. "But I don't like to be touched by men I've just met."

He stared at me a moment by the playful lantern light, looking so woebegone that I almost felt sorry for him. "Well, then, would you like to—like to sit down somewhere and talk?"

"No," I said. "I'm going to go inside now. You stay out here for a while."

"Will you come to Wimble's next party?"

I couldn't help laughing. I hoped not, but I supposed Dezmen might still be investigating poor Leffert's death. "We'll see," I said. I picked up my skirts with both hands—a little tricky, since I was still clutching the locket—and gave him another stern look. "You stay out here," I repeated. "Goodnight." I headed back inside without another glance. To my relief, he didn't follow.

The heat inside was oppressive after the cool air outside, and the mingled scents of bodies and alcohol had intensified. I wasn't sure how much longer I could stand to be there; fortunately Dezmen must have come to the same conclusion. I had been back in the house only about five minutes when I saw him pushing his way through the crowd, clearly looking for me. The press of people was so thick that his echoes followed him in single file.

"There you are," he said, when he had made his way to my side. "I was a little alarmed when I came out of the card room and couldn't find you."

"I was out in the courtyard, making new friends."

"Where's your necklace?"

I was surprised that he realized it was missing—surprised he had even noticed I was wearing one. In my experience, men don't pay too much attention to women's jewelry. I held up my hand to dangle the chain in front of him. "I...mmm...dropped it, and some nice young men helped me look for it."

"Your new friends, I take it. Did they have anything useful to offer you? Besides their skills in locating lost items."

I couldn't hold back my laughter. "They did, but maybe we should discuss that once we're out of here. How about you? Did you make any friends, and did they tell you anything helpful?"

"I'm not sure," he said. "But I agree. It's time to go."

He nodded toward the door and fell in step behind me as I eased my way through the crowd. I felt his hand on the small of my back—the lightest touch—as if to guide or protect me, I couldn't be sure. Either reason should have annoyed me, and yet I was pleased at his thoughtfulness; he was treating me with the same care he would have given to any high noblewoman who might have been rash enough to attend such an event with him. I didn't feel the slightest inclination to pull out my blade and threaten to cut him open.

No one but the servants seemed to notice we were leaving, and they didn't even bother to see us through the front door. I reflected that we had spent more than two hours in Wimble's house and I had never once laid eyes on our host. It seemed like a strange way to run a party.

The royal coachman must have been watching the front door because the moment we stepped outside, he set the equipage in motion. A few minutes later, we were all climbing in and squeezing together on the two benches.

As we got settled, Scar and Red made a big show of yawning and stretching, to prove they had been sleeping while they waited. I skipped over to Red's body to ask drowsily, "So did you learn anything?" Scar just blinked at us all and said nothing.

I slipped back into Chessie's head. "Maybe," I said. Dezmen and I had once again situated ourselves on opposite benches, next to the other's echoes, and we both perched on the edges of our seats as the carriage lurched into motion.

Dezmen nodded at me. "You first. What did you find out?"

"Our friend Leffert was a young hothead who would fling himself into any pursuit. Liked to gamble. But maybe he wasn't very good at cards because, last time he was at one of these parties, he was asking for a good pawnshop."

I could only catch glimpses of Dezmen's face as the carriage passed under occasional streetlamps, but I could tell he was frowning by the tone of his voice. "That doesn't exactly tally with what I learned," he said. "He was a gambler, yes, but he seemed to have plenty of money to throw around. Somebody said that he bet a stack of gold coins on one turn of the cards and lost it all. And he laughed."

"He wouldn't have laughed if he was worried about funds," I agreed. "But then, why go to a dealer in secondhand jewels?"

"Only one way to find out," said Dezmen. "Did you get the name of the shop he did business with?"

"The one that was recommended to him was Candleback's. No idea if that's the one he picked. Seems like a good place to start, though."

Dezmen nodded. "Do you know where it is?"

"I do. Not far from the flower markets."

"Would you have time to go with me tomorrow?"

I bent a stern gaze on him, which he couldn't see in the dark, of course. "I have my own responsibilities to attend to, you know."

"I'll pay you. You run errands and deliver parcels for a living, right? This isn't much different. Acting as my guide."

As it happened, I didn't have anything urgent lined up on the following day, so it would be easy to accept his offer. But I made sure my tone was begrudging. "Well. I'll have to rearrange my schedule a little. But I suppose I could meet you by noon tomorrow in Amanda Plaza."

"Excellent! And then we'll go see what the folks at Candlewax have to say."

I flitted over to Red's body so she could burst out laughing, then jumped back to Chessie to say, "Candleback's—with a *B*."

"See, this is why I need you. You know the city so well."

"I should," I said. "I've lived here ten years."

I felt the carriage slow, then the coachman called down from his perch, "Where shall we drop off the young lady and her friends, my lord?"

I raised my voice to call back an answer. "The botanical gardens!"

The carriage picked up its pace again, but a passing streetlight showed me Dezmen's face, creased in protest. "We're not dropping you off anywhere," he said in a voice of finality. "We're taking you home."

"You're not," I said, my own voice pleasant but firm. "I don't bring anyone to my lodgings."

"I won't come in. I just want to make sure you're safely home."

"I'll be safe."

"It's nearly midnight! You can't walk home at this hour—the goddess only knows how many miles!"

I laughed at him. "I walk home at midnight *all the time*. Anyway, Scar and Red are with me, and all of us have weapons. And we know how to use them."

He crossed his arms stubbornly. Beside me, his echoes did the same. Suddenly I was much less charmed by his protectiveness than I had been at the Wimble house.

"You're a remarkably capable woman and I'm sure you can take care of yourself," he said quietly. "But I have never in my life taken a lady on a carriage ride then pushed her out in the middle of the street to make her own way home in the dark, and this is not going to be the first time I do it. You have your pride, I suppose, but I have my principles."

An impasse, to be sure. He obviously was not going to yield, and there was absolutely no chance that I was going to take him to the street where I lived. I sighed, then I laughed and leaned back against the cushions as if capitulating. "I suppose you'll insist on driving around until daybreak if I don't give in," I said.

"That is exactly what I was just about to say."

I sighed again in great irritation. "All right, then. But you can't come upstairs."

"I already said I wouldn't."

"Have him head toward the flower markets and then follow the street that runs south."

We were silent for the rest of the ride except whenever Dezmen relayed my instructions to the coachman. Soon enough, we had turned onto the narrow street where Brianna had her apartment, and I directed him to stop in front of her building.

"And don't just go in the front door to wait until we've driven away, *pretending* this is where you live," Dezmen said suddenly. "I want to see your hand waving out of the window of your own rooms."

That was exactly the reason I had picked Brianna's apartment instead of some other building on some other street. It was a little unnerving how well I understood him—or how well he understood me—when we were still essentially strangers to each other.

"You *are* the suspicious one," I said.

"Only because you're so devious," he retorted.

By then we had come to a complete halt and one of the guards jumped down to open the door. I didn't wait for Dezmen to disembark and hand me out of the vehicle; I just gathered my skirts and hopped down on my own, followed by Red and Scar.

"See you tomorrow. Noon, Amanda Plaza," I said as I turned to go.

"See you in two minutes as you wave from the window," he retorted.

I made a noise of exasperation, then flounced up the short walk, into the building, and up the stairs. I tried to gauge my knock so that it was loud enough to wake Brianna but not so loud that Dezmen could hear it from the street. I was already formulating my apologies when the door was wrenched open and my cousin Nico stood there, holding a candle and looking rumpled and irascible.

"What in the name of— Chessie! Is something wrong?"

Over his shoulder, I caught a glimpse of Brianna hovering back by the bedroom door. "It's Chessie? Did something happen at the party?"

I gestured at the echoes to stay in the hallway and stomped over the threshold. "No. I'm fine. Stupid Lord Dezmen thinks I'm too fragile to walk home in the dark. I have to wave from the window to prove I'm actually inside my apartment. Blow out the candle."

I saw the unholy amusement on Nico's face before he complied. In the dark, I felt my way over to the window, pulled back the curtain, raised the sash, and stuck my upper body out through the frame, waving madly. I saw Dezmen's hand poke out through the carriage window and he waved in return. The carriage began moving slowly down the street.

I closed up the window again and turned back to my hosts. "Sorry. I didn't want to take him to my place."

"Can I light the candle again?" Nico asked.

"Yes. Or you can go back to bed. I really am sorry."

By the light of the renewed flame, I could see Brianna come deeper into the room. "Well, I'm not! I want to hear all about the party! Was it fun? Did everyone admire your dress? Did you learn anything exciting?"

I edged toward the door. "It *was* fun," I admitted. "We learned a couple of things, but I think I'm not supposed to talk about them. No one came right out and said they admired my dress—*or* my lovely hairpiece!—but there was a young lord who was *most* attentive, so I think he liked the way I looked. Oh, and Dezmen didn't even recognize me when he first saw me, so that was very satisfying."

Nico yawned. "If you're going to stay up and talk fashion, I'm going back to bed."

"We're not," I said. "I'm going home."

He tilted his head. "I might be of Lord Dezmen's opinion," he said. "It might not be a good idea for you to walk home alone."

I shook my head. "I'll be fine."

"Are Scar and Red with you?"

"Yes. And all of us are carrying weapons."

He looked uncertain, but did me the favor of letting me make my own decision. "All right. Come back sometime when you feel like you can tell us all the details."

"I will. Thanks. And sorry again."

I was pretty sure that one or both of them watched from the windows as Scar and Red and I exited the building and headed down the street toward my place. It had occurred to me that my lovely green skirts could be a serious hindrance if we really did have to fight, so I slipped my dagger from my ankle sheath and carried it openly; Red also showed her blade. But the precautions were unnecessary, since the only people we encountered on the street were drunks and lovers and night watchmen. No one who was interested in us.

Home safe. Oddly reluctant to take off my fancy gown and beribboned hat. Oddly reluctant to return to my ordinary self.

Already looking forward to the morning.

Chapter Ten

I couldn't just sit in my apartment killing time while I waited for noon to make its laggard appearance, so I checked in with a couple of my regular clients and couriered a number of packages across town. Always satisfying to receive a few coins. I put some in Chessie's pockets, some in Red's, some in Scar's, to minimize the loss if a pickpocket happened to catch one of us off guard. I was usually pretty alert, no matter which body I was inhabiting, and able to outwit even the nimblest thief; but the echoes weren't nearly as sensitive, and I'd lost a little money over the years. Still, I liked to split up the money when I could, and I didn't mind skipping between incarnations as the situation dictated.

I was in Amanda Plaza ahead of the designated hour, so I bought pasties from a vendor, and the three of us munched on an impromptu meal while we waited. I'd only been there ten minutes when Bertie wandered over, wearing nondescript gray clothing and his usual daft grin.

"I take it his lordship survived the evening without me?" he asked.

I nodded. "He was alive at midnight, at any rate, unless someone intercepted him on his way back to the palace."

Bertie's grin intensified. "Well, I think I could take down a couple of royal guards all on my own. Wearing their fancy livery and carrying their dress swords. *Pfft.*" He made slashing motion that I assumed represented him slitting someone's throat. "But I *wouldn't*. Because then Malachi would surely get involved. So his lordship was probably safe enough."

Just then—as if to prove him right—Dezmen and his echoes arrived, dropped off by a coach-for-hire. Clearly, his lordship didn't want the palace servants knowing where his investigations were taking him so he hadn't requested a royal conveyance today. Bertie and I strolled over to meet him as he was paying the driver. Scar and Red trailed behind.

"Can we walk there, or should I retain this fellow?" Dezmen asked me.

"We can walk," I said.

"Anyway, I don't think we'd all fit," Bertie added.

Dezmen nodded, offered a brief word of thanks to the driver, and turned back to me. "Then let's go."

We only crossed two bridges to get to the street commonly known as Cheater's Row. Not because the shop owners were untrustworthy; on the whole, they were considered among the most honest in the city. No, the place got its name because most everything you could buy there was secondhand but of extremely high quality. You could don those jackets and boots and shawls, and cheat the world into thinking you were something you were not. In fact, it was in one of these discreet boutiques that I had purchased my green gown just the other day.

Candleback's was dead center in the middle of the street, an imposing two-level storefront graced with bow windows and stone pillars. It wouldn't have looked out of place in the banker's district. I didn't see any security guards posted nearby, but I assumed they were there. Eva Candleback was not the kind of woman who took chances.

"I'll wait right out here," Bertie said, leaning against one of the pillars where he would have a good view of the whole street.

I followed Dezmen and his echoes inside, but I was concentrating on deploying Scar and Red. It was in times like these that having echoes was the most advantageous, since I could practically be three places at once. I positioned Red almost directly across the street from Candleback's, but one shop over, having her sit on a shaded bench and focus on her hands as if she was reading a prayer book. A spindly potted shrub partially hid her from sight, but when I slipped behind her eyes, I had an excellent view of Bertie and the front of the jewelry store.

I sent Scar a little farther down the street in the other direction to hunker down in the narrow space between two buildings. Completely out of sight, but able to watch whatever traffic drifted past, either on foot or on horseback. Perhaps catching a glimpse of trouble before trouble had a chance to do any damage.

Once they were in place, I refocused on my immediate surroundings inside the shop. It was a quiet, dignified place with plush furniture and sober, well-dressed clerks whose serious expressions convinced you that you could trust them to treat you fairly.

One of them approached as soon as we entered and shut the door behind us. He didn't give me a second glance, but he murmured a greeting as he bowed low to Dezmen. Anyone who walked through that door accompanied by two echoes was bound to get the most solicitous attention. At the moment, we appeared to be the only customers on the premises, which also worked in our favor.

"Good afternoon, my lord. I'm Curtis. How may I be of service to you this afternoon?" the clerk asked.

Dezmen glanced at me, but I hung back. I was well acquainted with the place, but not with the people; there would be no benefit to me participating in the conversation. Dezmen looked back at the clerk and said, "I understand you buy and sell jewelry."

"The very finest pieces at the very best prices," Curtis replied. "Are you interested in purchasing? Or selling?"

"I'm interested in learning about someone who might have sold something to you."

I watched as the clerk's friendly face became more guarded. "Ah. That is unfortunate. One of the promises we make to our distinguished clientele is that we will not share the details of their transactions with anyone else. You understand."

"Most admirable," Dezmen said. "However, this particular client will not mind if you discuss his private business, since he is dead."

Curtis tried not to look shocked. "My condolences."

"I have reason to believe," Dezmen went on, "that he visited your shop a day or two before his demise. I thought that if I could discover what transactions he concluded here, it might give me some clues as to how—and why—he ended up dead."

Curtis appeared undecided. "What was his name, if I may ask?"

"Leffert. That's all I know."

Curtis seemed to search his memory but didn't find a match. "He was here when?"

"About four weeks ago."

"Do you have any idea what kind of property he brought in for us to evaluate?"

"None at all."

The clerk shook his head. "Then—"

Dezmen leaned closer. "Let me describe him. He had fair skin and dark hair, and eyes that were very blue, so I am given to understand. He was high-spirited and impetuous. A little argumentative. If, say, he tried to sell you a brooch and you offered him a price, he might have loudly declared that you were trying to cheat him. If you offered him a second, slightly higher price, he would have accepted the offer without thinking it over. Then he would have laughed."

I had drifted over to one of the bow windows, but I could hear the conversation clearly enough, and that detailed description made me glance at Dezmen in surprise. As far as I knew, Dezmen had never met poor Leffert. My guess was that someone at Wimble's last night had described Leffert's style of card play and Dezmen had adapted that information to conjecture about the man's behavior in a pawnshop.

Curtis's expression smoothed out. "Ah. I believe I know the gentleman you are referring to. I did not assist him that day. Let me fetch the proprietor."

"Of course."

Curtis disappeared through a heavy door that I presumed led to a room lined with safes that held an extraordinary bounty of jewels. Dezmen and his echoes merely waited. I leaned my head against the window glass, as if I was looking out at the street, but in reality I was checking in with the echoes. I slipped first into Red's mind, then glanced slowly up and down the street. There was a steady stream of traffic in both directions, all of it purposeful and none of it alarming—women pointing and sighing as they peered through tall windows, men striding past with brisk urgency, people stepping in through shop doors or stepping out again. Two carts went by, the horses managing a light trot even through the knots of shoppers. The bright sunshine made it easy to forget that the day held an unwelcome chill.

I skipped up to Scar's body and uncoiled myself from my easy crouch. Poking my head out from between the two buildings, I took in the scene from a different vantage point, but nothing seemed amiss from this angle, either. Bertie saw me, grinned, and waved. I waved back before ducking back into the shadowed alley.

I was back in Chessie's head in time to hear a woman introduce herself to Dezmen. "Hello, I'm Eva Candleback. I understand you have some questions about one of my clients."

I casually turned from the window so I could get a glimpse of her, because Eva Candleback was famous among my class of society. She was tall and white-haired, with a straight posture and beautiful hands. She had the air and manner of a noble, all elegance and refinement; there were many who supposed her to be some lord's bastard who had succeeded so well at her profession because her family had backed her venture when she launched it forty years ago. I'd often wondered if she had an echo or two stashed in the back room or on the upper level. It would certainly give credence to the story.

"Thank you for meeting with me," Dezmen said, his voice as courteous as hers. "Yes. There was a young nobleman named Leffert who was here a few weeks ago—and who died shortly after his visit here. I am endeavoring to discover what he might have sold and whether or not it played some role in his death."

"I remember the man very well, but he sold nothing at my shop."

I saw Dezmen frown. "He didn't like the price you offered?"

"No, what I mean to say is that he wanted to buy an item, not sell one."

Dezmen glanced at me briefly before returning his attention to Eva Candleback. Buying, not selling? That hardly fit with our picture of a desperate rogue who had gambled too often or too deeply and needed to restore his finances. "And did he buy anything?"

"He did. A large amethyst ring set in a heavy band of gold. He was quite particular about the size of the gem—he said he wanted it to be so large it could be glimpsed from across the room. I had showed him several pieces of much higher quality, but he found them unsatisfactory. This particular item caught his fancy immediately and he purchased it without a moment's hesitation."

"Amethyst," Dezmen repeated. "Perhaps he was a noble from Alberta who wanted to flaunt his heritage."

"He certainly wanted to give that impression." Eva Candleback's voice was very dry. It was easy to deduce that she had not been impressed by the volatile young man.

"You found him very free with his money? He didn't haggle over price or seem worried about funds?"

"Not at all. He had all the coins he needed and he instantly counted them out."

"I believe you, of course, but this is not entirely what I expected," Dezmen said. "Let me ask you a few more questions."

I figured this could take a while and not yield much more information. So before he set out to try to murder the prince, young Lord Leffert had purchased some secondhand jewels to make it appear as if he were a noble from Alberta. That raised all sorts of interesting questions. Was he *really* from Alberta and determined to wear its colors so that everyone would know that the residents of that province despised the crown? Or was he from some other region of the Seven Jewels, bent on stirring up trouble that would then be credited to one of the western provinces? Was he a messenger or an anarchist? And who had funded him to take on either role?

As Dezmen and Eva Candleback continued to talk in low voices, I flung myself back into the bodies of my echoes. Not much happening down where Scar was skulking, so I bounced back over to Red. From her eyes, I peered toward the other end of the street, where a huge carriage was just lumbering out of view, and then glanced over at Candleback's to see how Bertie was faring.

He was having a conversation with a couple of young men who appeared to have asked for directions because I saw Bertie point in the general direction of Amanda Plaza. Then his arm dropped down as if his hand had suddenly become too heavy to hold, and his mouth opened and shut three times before his head slumped forward. I saw the red stain spread over the front of his gray shirt before I saw the tip of the blade poking through from behind. Together, his two assailants lowered his limp body carefully to the ground. Bertie had never made a sound.

I leapt back into Chessie's body and slammed down the bar that would seal the door. "Outside," I said in a harsh voice. "Bertie's been attacked. Two men are trying to break in."

Dezmen and his echoes whirled to stare at me. "How—?"

"Red saw it all. She signaled."

On my words, there was the sound of shattering glass as someone began smashing through the windows. The many small panes were held together with an iron framework, however, and it would take a little time for anyone to pry these apart far enough to squeeze inside.

Eva didn't pause to ask questions, she simply pivoted on one heel, stalked to a bell pull hanging on the wall, and gave it several hard yanks. I heard the clamor of heavy bells pealing out from overhead and footsteps pounding down from all over the building. Three men burst through the connecting door, all of them brandishing short swords and knives as if they knew how to handle weapons. One was Curtis, the clerk who had greeted us when we arrived.

"What's wrong?" Curtis demanded.

Eva waved toward the front of the store, where one assailant was breaking through the second window and another seemed to be tugging madly on the door, which rattled against the bar I had thrown in place. Two of the clerks ran forward with fearsome yells, and I saw one of them hack at the dirty fingers that poked through the broken glass. Someone yowled in pain but I couldn't tell if he was inside or outside. Over the crashing and the shouting, another sound rolled our way—a cacophony of bells in all sorts of timbres.

"What's that?" Dezmen demanded. He and his echoes had drawn back against the wall—not out of fear, I thought, but out of a prudent desire to stay out of the way of the people who were clearly more skilled in combat. I noticed that he had a deadly little dagger in his hand, and he held it like he'd used it before.

"All the merchants on the street have a pact to come to each other's aid," Eva replied. "When one of us sounds an alarm, the others ring their own bells to send the message up and down the row. In a moment, the street will be flooded with defenders."

"That'll chase them off," Dezmen said grimly. "I'd like to catch one and interrogate him."

I sank to the floor in my own out-of-the-way corner, hoping everyone thought I was too timid to take part in the battle that still raged at the front of the store. Curtis was wrestling with the heavy bar, while one of the other clerks panted behind him, waiting to leap out when the door was wrenched open. "Maybe Scar will stop one of them," I said.

"That would be good," Dezmen agreed.

I barely waited to hear his words before I flung myself into Scar's body and came running out of the alley. I spent one quick moment taking in the scene outside the shop. The two assailants were still scrabbling at the windows, trying to find a way in, but suddenly one of them looked over his shoulder and started shouting. About ten men were pouring out of nearby storefronts, waving clubs and daggers and barreling down the street toward Candleback's. The two thugs abandoned their attempt to break in and raced away, splitting up to draw off their pursuers. I saw one of them slip between two buildings close to where Red was stationed, but I didn't have time to jump into her head and give chase, because the other one was headed straight toward me.

I charged directly at him with a yell of bravado. This close, I could see that he outweighed me by at least a hundred pounds and was wild with desperation besides. We collided with sickening force, our bodies hitting so hard that for a second I was sure we were both off the ground, chest to chest, breathlessly staring straight into each other's eyes. He wasn't somebody I knew, but in that moment I memorized his face so minutely that I would recognize him if I ever saw him again.

Then I felt a blade cut through my back like a sliver of fire. I gasped with the pain, too astonished to cry out or even try to jerk away. My feet hit the ground, then my knees, then my face, as I was suddenly too weak to keep myself from falling. My attacker, instead of lingering long enough to finish me off, sprinted away.

Terrified of losing consciousness, I flung myself into Chessie's body and shot up from the floor with an inarticulate cry. Everyone in the shop whirled to stare at me—Dezmen, his echoes, Eva, and Curtis, who stood in a pose that suggested he was guarding the open door. The other two clerks must have rushed into the street to follow the marauders.

"What's wrong?" Dezmen demanded.

I shook my head, trying to orient myself. My back was sore from where the blade had gone in, but I didn't feel any wetness on my back, so I didn't appear to have picked up a corollary wound.

"Scar and Red—are they all right? What's happening?" I asked, shoving myself away from the wall and toward the door. Dezmen and his echoes followed as I pushed through the knot of people and stepped outside, looking around as if trying to piece together the last few moments of action.

Curtis gave us a quick update. "They've run off now—both men."

"And no one followed?" Dezmen asked, his voice almost angry.

Curtis shrugged. "There's always thieves and swindlers. We don't try to catch them, we just chase them away."

Eva had come out behind us and gestured at the prone figure of Bertie, motionless and covered with blood. "Who's this? Someone who attacked or someone who defended?"

"Oh, no— Bertie!" I exclaimed. I was desperate to go to Scar but I couldn't just step over the body of a man who'd been my friend for five years. I dropped to a crouch next to him and gingerly put my fingers to his neck. It wasn't necessary. He was clearly dead. I gazed up at Dezmen, tears coming to my eyes. "My lord, he—he doesn't have a heartbeat."

Dezmen's face set into a hard frown. "It appears these men are even more ruthless than we thought."

Eva's attention went from the body to Dezmen. "You know the people who were breaking in? Who killed this man?"

"No—but I know they were trying to find *me*," Dezmen replied.

I couldn't wait another second. I transferred myself to Red's body and jumped to my feet with a faint shriek, pointing at the crumpled body that lay on the street. "Scar!" I cried, and began to run.

As soon as Red was launched toward Scar, I arrowed back to Chessie and let out another cry of dismay. In a second, we were both racing toward the fallen echo.

Red was only a few paces behind me as I reached Scar's side and dropped to my knees to check the extent of the damage. I'd been able to feel the pull of the echo's existence, so I knew the wound hadn't been fatal, but I hadn't been able to gauge how bad it was. But Scar gazed up at me, blinking and breathing. Blood had seeped out onto the street and stained the cobblestones, but there was no hint of red on the front of the shirt so the blade hadn't gone all the way through. In fact, the wound was lower than I'd thought, and more superficial. It appeared to have entered near the bottom of the ribs and sliced sideways, with any luck missing the lung and any internal organs.

Please let me have this kind of luck.

"Let me have your scarf," I said to Red, holding out an imperious hand. She gave it to me just as Dezmen and his echoes came skidding up and dropped to their knees beside us. Just what I didn't want—witnesses to my battlefield ministrations. I didn't want to pull off enough of Scar's clothes to reveal a woman's body.

"Is he all right? How badly is he hurt?" Dezmen demanded.

"Not sure. I want to bind him up and get him home. Then I can assess."

"We need to clean that wound. Should we take him to Candleback's? I'm sure they'd give us a room."

"No," I said sharply. "He doesn't—he doesn't do well with strangers gawping at him. I need to get him home and take care of him there."

As I spoke, I was attempting to roll Scar to one side so I could wrap Red's scarf around the wound. But with Dezmen watching so closely, I didn't want to move from Chessie's body to Scar's so the hurt echo could sit up and make the maneuver easier.

"He's too weak," Dezmen exclaimed. "Here, I'll help you." He scooted around so he could lift Scar's head and upper body from the ground.

By this time, we'd attracted quite a crowd, which made me even more nervous. Scar lolled bonelessly in Dezmen's arms while I wrapped the scarf twice around the gash. Curtis was leaning over us. "Do you want to bring him to the shop? We've got water and clean cloths. And brandy, too."

"Thank you, no, I want to get him home," I said again. "But he can't walk like this. Can someone hire a cart?"

"There's a stand one street over," Curtis said. "Shall I go fetch one?"

"Thank you, that would be most helpful."

Dezmen carefully laid the echo back on the cobblestones, and Red leaned over to place her cheek against Scar's. Her long hair fell forward in an auburn curtain, obscuring both their faces.

"I think a journey across the city, bouncing over road hazards, might well aggravate his wound," Dezmen said in a low voice. "I think you'd be better off staying here for an hour or two."

"Perhaps," I replied, in an equally quiet tone. "But I know Scar, and I know how much he hates public attention. Trust me. He will be happier at home."

Dezmen shrugged in silent acquiescence. "What do we do about Bertie? How do we get word to his family—to Jackal? Where do we take his body?"

At that, someone pushed through the crowd and dropped to a crouch beside us. I recognized Pherson, a slim, ageless man who'd been running errands for Jackal as long as I'd known him. It hardly surprised me that he was here; I'd have placed good money on the bet that *someone* with ties to Jackal had been loitering here on Cheater's Row half the afternoon. It was a good place to pick up odd jobs and odder information.

"If you don't mind, Chessie, we can take care of Bertie for you," Pherson said diffidently. "You've got Scar to worry about, but I've got a couple of the boys here with me, and we've got nothing else to do."

I nodded my thanks. "And tell Jackal...tell him I'm so sorry. Tell him I'll be there in a day or two to fill him in on everything I know."

"I'll do that," Pherson said, rising to his feet and edging back through the crowd. He was barely out of sight before I heard the jingle and clop of horses heading in our direction, and the rattle of wheels against the cobblestones.

The onlookers pulled back to make room for the vehicle, and most of them started drifting away. I glanced over to find that Curtis had requisitioned a roomy wagon big enough to haul a few head of cattle, though it didn't look like it came with any amenities such as benches. I supposed we could let Scar lie on the floor of the vehicle while Red and I knelt beside him for the journey across town.

"Good, there's room for all of us," Dezmen said, coming to his feet.

I stared up at him. "All of who? *You're* not coming with us. Not you, not your echoes."

"I most certainly am."

If I hadn't been hunched over a bloody body in the middle of the street, I'd have stamped my foot in sheer frustration. "Didn't you just hear what I said? Scar wants to be at home. Alone. With Red and me and no outsiders."

"I'm hardly a stranger. Anyway, this is my mess. I brought you along with me, I put you in danger, I'm going to see this through."

140

"We don't need you. We don't want you."

"Well, you've got me," he replied. "You can let him bleed to death while we argue about it, or you can let me help you into the wagon."

Goddess do away with arrogant nobles who think they can make the world bend to their will, I fumed silently, but I didn't have much choice. Looked like I'd be bringing the Pandrean lord back to my apartment after all.

CHAPTER ELEVEN

It was a slow and awkward process to load the hurt echo into the wagon. Before we started, I risked one quick dip into Scar's body to try to gauge the extent of the damage. Painful, but not critical, I thought. I slipped back to Chessie's mind as Red and I looped Scar's arms over our shoulders and pulled the echo to a seated position, then a standing one.

In fact, it would have been difficult to get Scar into the cart without Dezmen's assistance. Even though the wound didn't seem that bad, Scar was a deadweight, and Dezmen and I had to work together to lift the echo into the wagon with some degree of gentleness. Red climbed in of her own accord and curled herself around Scar's body; Dezmen, his echoes, and I all arranged ourselves as best we could on the hard wooden floor of the wagon.

"Amanda Plaza and then south on Menneton Street," I called to the driver. I winced as the cart jerked into motion, feeling the pain that jolted through Scar. It was hard to tell through the bright colors of Red's scarf, but I thought the wound might be bleeding again.

"How bad do you think it is?" Dezmen asked over the clatter of wheel and hoof.

I shook my head. "Didn't look too deep. But painful. I think he'll be fine once I get him home."

"And Bertie," he added. "I haven't even had a moment to let that sink in. He died for me. He *died*."

I nodded numbly. "He was a strange guy. A little goofy. Never so happy as when someone was fighting and he got to watch—or take part. But he wasn't a mean man. Mostly he thought the world was funny."

"Does he have family?"

"I don't think so. Maybe a brother or cousin somewhere. No wife. No kids. Jackal was his family, basically."

Dezmen resettled himself in a futile effort to get more comfortable in the jouncing cart; his echoes copied him. "What will Jackal do?"

I looked over at him. "Well, if he can figure out who killed Bertie, I imagine he'll do something pretty terrible."

"What about those other two men? The ones who attacked me in the gardens? You said they disappeared. Did they ever show up again?"

I shook my head.

"So they're probably dead," Dezmen concluded.

I was so tired I leaned against the side of the cart. "That's what everyone assumes."

"So. Leffert. Those two men. Bertie. All dead. All because someone wants to cover up who hired Leffert to assassinate the prince."

I had closed my eyes, but now I opened them again and stared at Dezmen. "What about the men who killed Bertie today? They ran off, but where did they go? Will *they* be killed because they failed to do what they were hired to do?"

"Maybe not," Dezmen said. "I didn't get a look at their faces."

I did, I almost said. "Scar might have," I answered instead. "He was close enough."

"That might be useful," Dezmen said, "but I don't see how."

I closed my eyes again. Between the fear and the adrenaline and the swaying of the cart, it was too hard to concentrate on the conversation. I only opened my eyes and spoke again as we passed landmarks and I had to give the driver additional directions.

We were almost at my apartment when I realized that Dezmen was staring at me fixedly. "What?" I snapped.

"This isn't where you directed the coach last night."

"No, it's not," I said. "I told you I didn't want you to take me home."

"What exactly are you so afraid of?" he asked in exasperation.

More things than I could possibly name, I thought. Aloud, I said, "I like my privacy."

"So who lives at the place we went to last night? Since somebody must have let you in at midnight."

"The woman who's in love with my cousin."

"I suppose you didn't stay there safely once I drove off."

"I suppose not."

"You're almost more trouble than you're worth."

I eyed him with a level of exasperation to equal his own. "I could say the same thing about you, Lord Everybody Wants to Kill Me."

"At least I'm *trying* to proceed with caution. But you—"

I shrugged. "No one ever tried to harm me until you came along."

That might have been the biggest lie I'd ever told, but I didn't have time to feel a twinge of guilt, since we'd reached my street and I had to tell the driver where to pull up. It took some time and effort to ease Scar out of the cart, and Dezmen had paid off the driver before I'd had time to think about digging out my own money. Then he came over to where Red and I stood in the street, bracing Scar between us, and gently moved me aside to take my place. "You get the door," he said. "I'll help him inside."

"But—"

"And don't even try to tell me to go away before he's settled."

I wanted to kill him, but I didn't want Scar to suffer, so I huffed with irritation and hurried ahead of them. It was late afternoon—much earlier than I was usually home—and naturally the landlady and several of the neighbors were hovering about in time to watch our little procession trying to navigate the stairs.

"Chessie! Gorsey, what happened to you? And to poor Scar?" the landlady cried.

"A careless coachman almost ran him over," I called over my shoulder as I dashed up the stairs to unlock the door. "He's pretty bruised, but I think he'll be all right once I patch him up."

"Let me know if you need anything. And let me know—*gorsey!*" she exclaimed again. I supposed she had just realized that the three Pandreans with me were a lord and his echoes. Although they were all soberly dressed for today's excursion, it was a certain bet they were still the finest creatures to ever step over her threshold. She'd probably never been this close to an echo in her life.

Well, she had. She just hadn't realized it.

I didn't bother with explanations, though I heard Dezmen murmur a polite greeting to her as he passed. I just flung open the door and hurried straight to the bedroom to lay a towel over the top quilt to protect it from Scar's blood. Then back to the door to usher the others through and close and lock it behind them.

"We'll take it from here," I said to Dezmen, reclaiming my spot at Scar's side and guiding the three of us into the second room. We placed the echo on the bed and I took a moment to order my thoughts.

"Water," I muttered, making a list out loud. "Salve. Bandages. Clean clothes."

Back out in the main room I found that Dezmen had settled onto the couch while his echoes sat on nearby chairs. He was looking around with interest, though honestly there wasn't that much to see. Maybe that's what had caught his attention, the fact that my lodgings were so sparse and spare.

"I'm going to clean him up—it might take a little while," I said as I rummaged around for supplies. "I suppose you can make yourself some tea, or something, while you wait. Unless you'd like to just go home, which is what I think you should do."

"I'll stay, thank you," he said. "I think we have a lot to discuss."

Pretty much what I had expected. I was too distracted to argue, so I just nodded and continued gathering what I needed.

Back in the bedroom, I closed the door behind me. It took me some time to strip off the bloody clothes, to clean and bandage the wound, and get Scar comfortable. Once I finished, I briefly slipped back into the echo's head to gauge the extent of pain. The salve had helped, but the gash ached with a pulsing fire that would probably keep me awake all night if I was actually confined to this body. It was something of a relief to return my consciousness to Chessie.

"I'll just leave you two here and see how quickly I can get rid of the obnoxious high noble," I murmured, well aware that I was talking to myself. Red climbed onto the bed next to Scar while I bundled up the soiled clothes and towel. Laundry day might have to come sooner than usual this week. I left the bundle in a corner, took a deep breath, and crossed into the main room again, once more closing the door between the two rooms.

Dezmen was still sitting on the couch, but in a position so relaxed it could have been called sprawling. His echoes likewise were lounging in their chairs, but their eyes were closed while his were open. They didn't stir and sit up when he did, which was the first time I had ever noticed them moving independently from their original. Or, well, *not* moving.

"How is he?" Dezmen asked, scooting over to make room for me on the couch. There was really nowhere else to sit. I never entertained company, so I never needed more than three seats.

"All right, I think. Red's going to stay with him. I hope they both fall asleep."

"That would probably be best," he agreed.

I hadn't invited him up and didn't want him here, but I felt a begrudging sense of duty as a hostess. "Do you want something? Water or anything?"

"Water would be great, thanks."

I stood up and gestured at his echoes. "What about them? I've never seen them so still."

He nodded. "Every once in a while—usually after a time of great stress or a great expenditure of energy—when we get to a quiet place, they'll grow still like that. I know people who can release their echoes completely, which I've never been able to do, but I can—shut them down, I suppose. It's a very odd feeling. It's like walking around on a sunny day without your shadow behind you. But sometimes it's a little freeing. Like taking off all my clothes and running around naked."

"Huh," I said, glancing again at the motionless echoes. "Well, don't do that."

He laughed. "Wasn't planning on it."

I fetched water for both of us then rejoined him on the couch. I was thirstier than I'd realized; I gulped the whole glass down in a few swallows before setting the goblet on the floor. Dezmen did the same.

"Scary day," he commented.

"Terrifying," I retorted. "And Bertie—" I shook my head. I still couldn't take it in.

"Let me know if there's something I should do. Pay for a memorial service, maybe. And if you find out he *does* have a family—"

"I'll ask Jackal."

"What I want to know," he said, "is why? Why today?"

"What do you mean?"

"I've been looking into Leffert's death for a couple of weeks now. Asking a lot of people a lot of questions. Most of the time, I've been left in peace, but two of those days, someone tried to kill me. Why? Why today, when I was at Candleback's, and why nine days ago at the gardens?"

I shook my head, almost too weary to try to think it through. "Maybe those were the only times that good opportunities presented themselves."

"I doubt it. If someone was following me, there were a lot of places along my various routes when I would have been vulnerable."

"Then— What do they have in common? Eva Candleback and the man you were meeting in the garden? Who was he, anyway?"

"Nobody. A stranger. Someone Leffert had hired while he was here."

"Hired to do what?"

"Act as his valet while he stayed at the Market House Inn."

"So—clean his clothes and help him dress."

"Exactly. He said he didn't run any errands, didn't meet with any mysterious strangers, didn't even learn if Leffert was the man's real name."

"Well, whoever attacked you must have thought there was *something* he could tell you."

Dezmen nodded. "And thought there was something Eva Candleback could tell me."

"Leffert bought an amethyst ring. Big enough to see across the room. So he wanted everyone to think he was from Alberta."

"But I already knew he had the ring. It was on his body when he was found dead. So I already knew he was from—or pretending to be from—Alberta."

"Maybe that's it, though," I said slowly, intrigued despite my weariness. "Maybe there was a *different* piece of jewelry that Leffert acquired while he was here. The valet would have known about it if he was helping Leffert dress. Eva Candleback would have known about it if she'd sold it to Leffert. Was there some other piece that you found in Leffert's belongings?"

There was a long, long silence. Sensing a mystery, I felt a renewed surge of energy and straightened up where I sat to bend a searching gaze on Dezmen's face. His expression was neutral, but for someone who was generally as open as Dezmen, that meant he was trying to conceal something.

"What?" I said flatly. "You know something that you're not telling."

He narrowed his amber eyes but didn't answer.

"Oh, this is rich," I said. "You complain that I'm keeping information from *you* when all this time you've been hiding something from *me*."

"It's part of the investigation," Dezmen said. "Only three people know about it. Cormac, Harold, and me."

I was baffled. "Why?"

"It seemed like it might be a clue to Leffert's identify, but we didn't want anyone to know we had the clue."

Still gazing at him, I settled back against the couch. "What is it? Tell me. I'm in so deep already that you *have* to trust me."

He hesitated, then capitulated. "A pin. Very old, heavy, and ornate. Leffert was wearing it when he attacked the prince, and in the struggle, Cormac ripped it from Leffert's jacket. He said Leffert almost went berserk when he saw the pin in Cormac's hand and he showed more interest in getting the pin back than in trying to strangle Cormac."

"Leffert was trying to kill Cormac with his bare hands?" I asked. "I don't think I realized that before. I thought—a knife, or even poison—"

Dezmen nodded soberly. "A knife can be traced to its maker. A poison can be traced to the apothecary who sold it. But if you throttle a man, the only weapon is you."

"What happened? How did Cormac get away from him?"

"He grabbed the pin—Leffert loosened his hold on Cormac's throat. Cormac was able to cry for help, and a couple of footmen rushed in. They were good enough to scare Leffert off, but not good enough to tackle him and keep him in place. By the time the guards arrived, Leffert had run. No one saw him leave the palace, and no one laid eyes on him again until his body showed up on the east side."

"But Cormac still had the pin. Which no one else knew he had."

"Well," Dezmen said. "The working theory is that whoever hired Leffert knows Cormac has the pin. Since whoever hired Leffert probably killed him. And looked desperately through all his things trying to find something."

I raised my eyebrows. "You know this for certain?"

He nodded. "That was one piece of information that the valet *could* give me. The day after Leffert disappeared, the valet returned to his room at the Market House and found the place a shambles. Someone had clearly sorted through every single one of Leffert's possessions—even slit open the pillows and mattress for good measure—searching for something. The pin's as likely as anything else."

I shrugged. "Could have been looking for money. If Leffert had been paid a tidy sum in advance—"

"Maybe," Dezmen said. "But money's anonymous and jewelry isn't."

"So. Whoever hired Leffert knows you're investigating his death. He knows that *you* know Leffert tried to kill Cormac. He's covered his tracks really well, so he's not concerned when you talk to the proprietor of the Market House or the low nobles at Wimble's party. But when it seems you might be about to discover something about this mysterious pin, he wants you dead."

"Which is why I think the pin is the key to his identity."

"And what have you learned about the pin?"

Dezmen shrugged. "Nothing yet. I figure I'll have to travel to Alberta and start showing it around to see if I can find someone who recognizes it."

"Alberta?"

"It features an intricate pattern set in amethysts. Intricate and distinct. Someone will have seen it before." He sighed and stretched his legs out. His echoes stayed motionless in the chairs. "But I thought I would discover everything I could in Camarria before I set out for Alberta. Where no one will want to talk to me because everyone in Alberta hates the king."

I tapped my finger against my knee. "You might be able to learn something here. If you talk to the right people." Dezmen gave me an inquiring look and I went on. "Whoever killed Bertie today obviously thought you were showing Eva Candleback the pin and that she might recognize it. That means some other jeweler could recognize it as well. I know someone who trades in really high-quality stuff. Name is Ronin. He'll know the pattern on that pin, I can almost guarantee it. You can have your answer tomorrow."

"Excellent," Dezmen said. "I'll come pick you up in the morning."

I laughed and instantly started remembering all the reasons I wouldn't be free tomorrow—or the day after that, now that I thought about it. "Not so fast," I said. "I'm going to stick around here for a day or two to make sure Scar's recovering. Anyway, I think we'll have to plan our visit to Ronin's really carefully. We don't want to be followed. We don't want to lead some cold-blooded assassin to Ronin's shop to kill him *and* us."

"What do you propose?"

"I'll get Jackal to help us. He'll figure something out."

Dezmen grimaced. "See, this is what I don't like. The more people who get involved, the more people who know about the pin."

"I won't tell Jackal *why* we need to get to Ronin's in secret. Just that we do."

Dezmen looked unconvinced. "I still don't like it."

I flopped back against the couch cushions. "Fine. Continue on with your own investigation, which has turned up exactly nothing to date. See how far you get."

"I wouldn't say I've learned *nothing*. It's just—"

I spread my hands in a gesture that meant *I don't care.* "You think about it. You let me know when you want me to introduce you to Ronin."

Now he was the one to gesture, as if to say, *Fine. I don't really have a choice.* "You might be right," he said aloud. "As long as Ronin doesn't know *why* I'm interested in the pin, it shouldn't matter if he sees it."

"All right, then. Should I meet you at Amanda Plaza in—three days? That will give me time to talk to Jackal and see if he has any ideas about how to keep us safe."

He nodded. "Sounds good. I have a couple of other things I need to take care of, too, so—in the morning, three days from now. I'll meet you at the plaza."

Since we seemed to have settled everything, I figured he'd finally leave, but he made no move to get up. The afternoon was pretty far advanced by now, with the low gold of the setting sun making bars of brightness across my floor. Surely there must be commitments awaiting him back at the palace. Surely the prince would like to hear a report of the day's activities. Or, considering that the day's activities had included chaos and murder, maybe not. I shuddered.

I shoved myself to a more upright pose, braced my hands on my knees as if about to push myself to a standing position, and said pointedly, "Do we have anything else to discuss?"

Dezmen still sat relatively relaxed on the couch, but now he was letting his gaze wander around the room. "So you and Scar and Red all live here?" he asked.

I tensed a little. "Yes."

He brought his attention back to me. "Where do you all *sleep?* I just got a glimpse of the bedroom, but I only saw one bed."

"If we all slept together all the time and took turns making love to each other, I don't suppose that would really be any of your business," I said.

He didn't look offended or even salaciously intrigued. He just tilted his head to one side and said, "I was under the impression that Red and Scar were a couple and you were their friend."

Because that was the impression I wanted to give you, you idiot. "Well, that's the truth of it," I said.

"But there's only one bed," he repeated.

"Red and Scar usually sleep on the bed. I sleep on the couch. Unless they're fighting, and then Scar sleeps on the couch and Red and I share the bed. Sometimes they'll start fighting in the middle of the night, so I'm sleeping on the couch and I wake up and find Scar on the floor."

"But Red always gets to be in the bedroom?"

I laughed. "She's the beautiful one. That's generally how life works."

"She's not the only beautiful one," Dezmen said.

It took me a moment to catch his meaning, and then I laughed again, half embarrassed and half pleased. "Thanks for the compliment," I said. "But it doesn't change anything."

"Well. It still seems like a small place for three people."

I was pretty sure that we'd never had a previous conversation where I'd mentioned how long we'd been living together, so I figured it was safe to prevaricate now. "They used to have their own place, but we decided about a year ago we could save a lot of money by sharing expenses, so they moved in."

He was looking around again. "So all the furnishings—such as they are—are ones that you picked out?"

"Pretty much everything, yeah."

"But the place is so *impersonal.* It could be a guest room at an inn. Where are the mementos, the drawings you bought from some painter in the plaza, the vases full of flowers—the *anything* that makes it feel like it belongs to you?"

I stared at him, full of hot resentment. "First, I'm not a wealthy lord, who can go about buying *paintings* and *wall hangings* and *decorations* whenever I feel like it. I save every coin that I don't need to spend on food and clothes, and I'm happy to do it."

"I didn't say—"

"And second," I said, raising my voice to speak over his, "I learned a long time ago that *things* won't keep you safe. I learned a long time ago not to have an attachment to anything I couldn't carry with me everywhere I went. I like the idea that I can walk out the door tomorrow morning and if the place catches fire and burns to the ground, I won't have lost anything I care about. Every day when I leave, I ask myself, 'Will it matter if I can't come back tonight?' and the answer is always no. I like that. That's freedom."

"That's abandonment," he shot back.

That was so much more accurate than he knew. "Just as well I don't care what you think of me," I said tightly.

"I worry about you," he said. "And I can't figure you out."

"Here's an idea," I said. "Don't bother doing either of those things—worrying about me or trying to figure me out."

He studied me a moment. "I didn't mean to make you mad."

"I'm not mad!"

"You *sound* like you're mad."

"I'm flustered. All this attention from a high noble—it makes my head spin."

"I have never seen anyone less impressed with my bloodline than you," he scoffed.

"Hang around Sweetwater a little more," I invited. I was pleased to note that my voice sounded calmer; we seemed to have gotten past the dangerous personal talk and back to an easy banter. "You'll find a lot of folks who aren't impressed with a noble heritage."

"What a marvelous idea!" he said. "I don't think I've quite met my quota of people who'd like to rob me or see me dead."

"Most of the people in Sweetwater would be happy to let you live," I said. "It's true they'd be happy to lift your purse and steal your opals, but murder's a serious offense and most people don't indulge. Camarria is one of the safest cities in the kingdom."

"Until I showed up and started asking questions, apparently," Dezmen answered.

I nodded. "That's how you know you're getting close to the truth. Because someone is desperate enough to kill to keep a secret."

Dezmen sighed. "And now we're talking about the case again."

I looked at him a moment in silence. What else did he think we were likely to talk about? It wasn't like we had hobbies in common. "Pick another topic, then," I said at last.

He leaned forward. "So how'd you meet up with Jackal? He seems like a useful friend to have—but a dangerous one."

"He's both of those," I agreed. "Red met him first, when she started working in a tavern down near Sweetwater. She introduced me, and I started running errands for him. He likes me, I trust him. The relationship has been good for both of us."

"I could tell he likes you."

I smiled. "He likes Red better. She's more of a flirt."

"I can see that. Did it ever go further than flirting between them?"

I gave him a *mind your manners* look. "You'd have to ask her— though I'd advise you not to! What a question!"

He grinned. "So I can't ask you the same thing? Whether you've ever been romantically involved with Jackal?"

"Well, I haven't, but no, you can't ask! Why would it even occur to you?"

"Like I said. Trying to figure you out. Trying to figure out what kind of men you like."

"Why would you want to?"

"Why do you think?" he replied, then he leaned even closer and kissed me.

His mouth was warm, his lips full and supple, and beneath them my own lips felt thin and uncertain. I couldn't remember the last time someone had kissed me when I was in Chessie's body, and it felt different, somehow, than it did when someone kissed Red. Or maybe it was that Dezmen's kiss was so different than Jackal's. Gentler, lazier, the kiss of a man with all the time in the world at his disposal and a willingness to spend it. Jackal's kisses tended to be brisk with purpose, but Dezmen's kiss was full of curiosity and a desire to go exploring. He lifted a hand to touch my cheek with one fingertip, then cupped his palm under my chin. His skin held a faint, sweet, indefinable scent.

A moment more the kiss held, and then I jerked away from him and stared. "What did you do that for?" I demanded.

He was laughing. "Why do you think?" he repeated.

I put the back of my hand against my mouth but didn't go quite so far as to try to scrub the kiss away. "I have no idea! Since even you must have figured out that I'm not the kind of girl who tumbles into bed with every man she meets, even if he *is* a high noble."

"Didn't even cross my mind," he said amiably. "It was a kiss, not a seduction." He glanced around the apartment again, as if he hadn't been studying it for the past half hour. "Anyway, I can't even imagine where I *would* seduce you, since there doesn't seem to be anything remotely passing for privacy here."

I scowled. Of course, I didn't *want* to sleep with the Pandrean lord, but he was right; the logistics would have been impossible. "Well, you shouldn't go around kissing people just because you feel like it" was all I could think to say.

He reached for my hands, keeping them even when I would have pulled away, and laced his fingers with mine. I stared down at the striped interplay of our skin tones, dark and light, dark and light. "All right, I won't," he said. "Just you."

Now I looked up at him. "No, *not* me. I'm not getting involved with you in any capacity other than—well—what I've been doing," I said lamely. It was hard to think clearly when he was still holding my hands.

"Don't you like me?"

This time I succeeded in wrenching myself free. "I like you well enough, I suppose, but goddess have mercy on my soul! You're a high noble and I'm a street urchin, and I'm not *interested* in the only kind of relationship that would be possible between us."

He was watching me, but he didn't seem either surprised or discouraged by my reaction. Actually, if I'd had to put a name to the expression on his face, I'd say he was pleased with himself. "It was just a kiss. It doesn't have to mean anything else."

"And it doesn't have to happen again," I said firmly.

He shrugged, which I took to mean *we'll see*, not *all right, you win*. "I'm hungry," he said. "Should we go get food and bring some back for the other two?"

"No," I said. "You should go and get food, if that's what you want, but at any rate you should *go*. I'll stay here and take care of my friends. And I'll see Jackal tomorrow and find out what he thinks about setting up a visit with Ronin. And two days after that, I'll meet you back in Amanda Plaza."

"All right," he said, but he didn't stand up like a man who was planning to leave right away.

"In the meantime, try not to do anything that might you killed," I added. "Don't visit any jewelers. Stay away from the Market House. Maybe just stay inside the palace altogether."

"Cormac was inside the palace when Leffert tried to kill him," Dezmen reminded me. "So that doesn't seem so safe, either."

"Then I'm out of ideas," I said. I came to my feet and gazed down at him with a clear message on my face, so he slowly rose off the couch. Behind him, I saw his echoes shake themselves awake and stand up as well; they were instantly synchronized with him again. I couldn't help wondering if he'd sent them into that state of stillness on purpose because he thought it would be less awkward if they weren't hovering over us when he kissed me. But that would mean he had planned on kissing me almost from the moment we stepped into the apartment. "Just try to stay safe," I added.

"I will. You, too. No forays out into the street at midnight."

I laughed. "Of course not."

He stood there a moment longer, as if he had other things to say and was just trying to formulate them, but I made impatient shooing motions to urge him toward the exit. "All right, then," he said, heading for the door, the echoes right behind him. "I'll see you in a few days."

I locked the door as soon as all three of them were through it, and I tried with all my will to avoid going to the window to watch them walking down the street. I lasted about ten seconds before flinging myself across the room and pulling the curtain back. Dezmen and his echoes were standing in the street, gazing up, either waiting for me to wave goodbye or memorizing the facade of the building so it could be located again. Or both, more likely. I did wave; they all waved back. I watched till they were out of sight.

Chapter Twelve

I had never seen Jackal so furious. He didn't pace and shout and threaten, as so many men did when they were angry, but he simmered with a slow, building rage that showed in his severe expression and tightly controlled movements. I knew for certain that if the men who had killed Bertie were somehow brought before Jackal right now, Jackal would rip their throats open with his bare hands. And he wouldn't need anyone's help to do it.

I was glad I hadn't been the one to deliver the news about Bertie's death, though apparently Jackal hadn't bellowed and howled then, either. But Pherson told me privately he had almost thought Jackal was going to pick him up and throw him through the tavern window just to work off some of his fury.

I waited till Red's shift was almost over and she could take her break sitting at the table with Scar, who was sore and weak but passably mobile. Then I slipped into Chessie's body and nerved myself to approach Jackal. Three men and a woman were at his table as I walked up, but he made a wordless gesture and they all moved to a nearby booth so he could talk to me alone.

"I'm sorry," I said simply.

He nodded curtly; condolences weren't of much use. "Did you see anything?" he asked.

"I was inside Candleback's. Scar got a good look at the face of one of the men, though."

"Describe him."

I shared every detail I could remember, but I could tell nothing sounded familiar. "Imported, maybe," Jackal said. "Brought in for just this job."

"Lord Dezmen asked if there was anything he could do," I said. "Pay for a memorial service, maybe. Give money to a wife or daughter, if he had one."

"It's a kind gesture, but I'll take care of it," Jackal said. "I'm the one who gave him the job, so it's on me."

That explained some of his rage, I thought. It wasn't just that a friend was dead, but that Jackal had in a real sense put that friend in harm's way. "I'm sorry," I said again. "We'll understand if you don't want to be involved in this investigation anymore."

Jackal's dark eyes bored into mine. "More than ever," he said in a hard voice. "Now I actually care that the murder is solved."

I swallowed. The king's inquisitor might not need to see that justice was meted out to Leffert's killer. Jackal wanted to take care of that all on his own. "Then maybe you can help us with something else," I said. "There's a reason the Pandrean lord wants to speak to Ronin. I'm not supposed to tell you why."

"I don't care why."

"It seems logical that Dezmen is going to be followed no matter where he goes, and I don't want to lead anyone to Ronin's place and put *him* in danger. Can you think of a way to get Dezmen across town so that no one sees him?"

Jackal thought it over for less than a minute. "We'll bring Ronin to him," he decided. "Not here—there are too many eyes and ears. My house in Crescent Lane, probably."

I nodded. Jackal owned at least a dozen properties—some of them businesses, some of them residences—and he moved around between them often so that no one knew where he might be next. But insofar as he had a place he would refer to as home, it was the house in Crescent Lane. The neighborhood was shabby genteel, full of merchants who wished they were nobles or nobles who had fallen on hard times—not much different from the district where we had attended the party at Wimble's house, though it was quieter, wealthier, and haunted by its former elegance. It was where Jackal had brought me most often when he and Red were lovers.

More to the point, it was a street where tradesmen came and went on a regular basis, so even if someone spotted Ronin entering Jackal's house, it shouldn't rouse any suspicion.

"That works," I said.

"Give me a few days to set it up."

"Sounds good."

I thought about saying *Ronin might need to be compensated for the loss of a day's earnings.* But I was pretty sure Jackal had already thought of that—and would take care of it. Jackal was a man on a mission now, and there weren't many details he would overlook.

I stood up, hesitated just a moment longer. "I'll miss him," I said. "I keep looking over here and expecting to see him sitting at your table. With that silly smile on his face."

"He was a happy guy," Jackal said. "He liked his life. There are days I wish I liked my own half as much."

There were days I wished I liked mine at all. "Yeah," was all I could think to say in response. I nodded and headed back to my own table.

It was a relief when Red's shift was over and we could all go home. After the chaos of the past few days, we needed a good night's rest, so I planned to sleep in the next morning. Besides, we needed to look our best tomorrow because it was Counting Day.

In the morning, I took turns slipping from one body to the next so I could bathe thoroughly and scrub every last trace of grime from my face and hands. As a rule, I kept myself relatively clean, but I tended to be lax about filing down the broken edges of my fingernails and rubbing cream into my face to keep my complexion smooth. But today I needed to look even better than I had when I attended Wimble's party. Today I needed to pass as a lady. With two echoes.

Once a year, everyone in the Seven Jewels who claimed even a single echo was required to make an appearance at one of the temples in the kingdom. Didn't matter which one. Didn't matter what time of day. You didn't have to sign a register, light a votive candle, or even speak to a priestess. You just had to show up. The goddess would know if you were there.

And she would know if you weren't. Angela had impressed this knowledge on me from a very early age. *If you don't go to temple on Counting Day, Chezelle, the goddess will know you do not honor her. She will know you do not deserve echoes. She will take them away from you—they will disappear overnight from your bed, the way they appeared when you were a tiny baby. The goddess gave you the gift of echoes and she can take that gift away. Is that what you want? No? Then never, ever miss a Counting Day.*

When I was little, Angela had taken me to the temple in the small town half a day's drive from the back road where we had our modest house. The temple was tiny, the size of a cottage, and the priestess who served it must have been a hundred years old and blind on top of it. We lived in a rural part of Empara then, nothing but farm and forest and the occasional market town crossroads for miles in any direction. Certainly no high nobles owned property anywhere in our vicinity. I was always the only person who showed up at the temple with echoes at my back. The priestess would tilt her head when we walked in, as if judging by our footfalls how many had entered the building—and how many of them were echoes. We would sit dutifully in one of the three pews, Angela praying, me trying not to squirm with impatience, the echoes copying my every movement. When we stood up to leave, the priestess would step over and offer us the ritual benediction, which Angela always accepted on behalf of all of us. As the priestess touched my forehead, my heart, my lips, her eyes always looked just beyond me. At my echoes, maybe. At a ghostly manifestation of the triple goddess, invisible to me. At her own memories. Who could tell? I just knew I was always happy to step back outside into sunshine and fresh air. Angela always took us past a market stand on the way home and let us buy treats, but first we had to cast off the matching bonnets and pull on different shoes and jackets so we didn't draw attention because of our identical looks. And then we would be home and I wouldn't give another thought to Counting Day until it rolled around again.

My first year in Camarria, I almost missed Counting Day. I had just turned fourteen, I was still working at the bakery, I had barely clawed out a place of safety for Scar and Red and myself, and I had forgotten what day it was. The baker had sent me to the warehouse district to pick up a delivery of honey that she had ordered specially from Thelleron, and on the way back I happened to walk past a temple on the southwest edge of town. I saw people exiting the building in groups of two and three—more people than you usually see leaving a temple in the middle of an ordinary day—and so I idly watched them, wondering if they were members of a wedding party. In another moment, I realized that the two- and three-person groups were all originals and echoes. *Must be the wedding of a noble,* I thought.

The next moment, I remembered what day it was.

My heart started pounding. I was flooded with terror. *Counting Day, Counting Day, I missed Counting Day. I'll wake up tomorrow and Scar and Red will be gone.* But no. No. It was still daylight. In fact, it was still afternoon. The goddess had not despaired of me yet.

I didn't have time to go home and change into respectable clothing—anyway, at that point in my life, I didn't *own* any respectable clothing—but I thought it was likely the goddess would be able to recognize that my echoes belonged to me even if we weren't dressed alike. Still carrying the jars of honey that I had distributed among us, the three of us slipped inside the temple and sat in the back pew. I didn't synchronize the echoes' motions with mine. I thought it might be best if anyone who saw us thought we were three friends who had decided to stop at a temple when it happened to be Counting Day. The other originals wouldn't know I was a woman with echoes; the priestesses might not know, either. But the goddess would, or so I hoped, and she was the only one who mattered.

We stayed about twenty minutes and I silently recited a few of the standard prayers. None of the visiting nobles noticed me, none of the priestesses approached me, and when we left, no one offered us a benediction. I was anxious and edgy the rest of the day, constantly looking over my shoulder to make sure Scar and Red were still there, so fretful that the baker finally sent me home early because my fidgeting was giving her a headache. That night, I slept between the two echoes, my hands clasped around their wrists, and I probably woke up a dozen times to check that they hadn't vanished. But when the morning came, they were still beside me, solid and reassuring as ever, and I finally started to relax.

I never forgot another Counting Day.

Once I acquired a little money and could improve my wardrobe, I decided that it would do the goddess the most honor if I showed up at her temple well dressed and in tune with my echoes. I now had three sets of what I considered "Counting Day clothing," and I rotated these every year. Each set consisted of a simple dress made of fine fabric and two matching dresses in a slightly paler shade; from my observation, that was how most high nobles arrayed themselves and their echoes. All of our accessories were identical, down to our high-heeled leather shoes. Well—the echoes didn't have emerald necklaces, but as I hid mine under my high neckline, it didn't matter.

This year, I laid out silk lavender dresses trimmed with velvet bands in royal purple. While I waited for our hair to dry, I inspected the wound on Scar's body. It was healing nicely, though it would be another week or more before I could stop tending it. I fashioned a pad and wrapped gauze around Scar's torso to keep it in place, making the bandage as flat as I could so it wouldn't be visible under the close-fitting bodice.

Hair was the real challenge, since we all wore it at different lengths and the color varied besides. My solution was to coil Red's hair on top of her head and cover it with a simple headpiece so you couldn't really tell how long it was. Scar and I had matching headpieces, all of them graced with a few floating ribbons that would draw more attention than the color of the hair itself. Or so I hoped. I wasn't a particularly deft needlewoman, and I'd spent about a week putting these confections together. Brianna probably could have done the job in a couple of hours—but then I would have had to explain why I wanted the items. It was easier to do the work myself.

Dresses, hairpieces, matching bracelets, and little net reticules. We crowded together in front of the sliver of the mirror and eyed our reflections. We looked as identical as three manifestations of the same person could look.

Leaving the apartment was the next challenge, since obviously I didn't want anyone to spy us all together and start wondering madly. But I had practiced this part before, too. Staying in Chessie's body, I walked out the door, down the steps, and out into the street, encountering no one. Once I got half a block away, I ducked between a couple of buildings, waited a few moments, then flung myself into Scar's head. Another exit, similarly unobserved, and now two of us lurked between buildings.

I projected myself into Red's body and left the apartment for a third time, locking the door behind me. This time I wasn't so lucky because the landlady was coming out of her door at the same time.

"Well, don't you look fancy, Miss Red!" she exclaimed, looking me up and down.

I tossed my head and struck a pose. "Interviewing with a noble-woman who might want a companion. I thought I'd try to dress the part," I said. "Do you like it?"

"Very much so! That's a good color on you! I thought I saw a flash of purple go by just a moment ago, but maybe it was someone else."

I laughed. "Oh, that was me! I forgot the old woman's address and I had to go back and get it."

"Good luck," she said. "I hope you get the job."

Once we made it outside, the landlady fortunately turned in one direction and I was able to hurry the other way to join up with Chessie and Scar. Even so, we loitered in the shadows a few moments until I was pretty sure the landlady was out of sight. Then I shifted back into Chessie's head and we set out in the direction of the temple, the movements of the echoes perfectly timed with mine.

I'd never believed that fine clothes make a fine lady, but I had to say, some small, shallow, frivolous part of me loved the way I felt when I was all dressed up. I always felt prettier, sassier, more confident, more audacious. Shopkeepers nodded at me with respect, hoping I'd stop in and spend money on their wares. Coachmen driving by took care to slow their vehicles so they wouldn't spatter mud in my direction. Maybe it wasn't the clothes—maybe it was the fact that the echoes trailing behind me, matching me step for step, signaled that I was a wealthy woman, a high noble, one of the most envied members of society.

I knew the truth, of course, but for this one day, it always felt so good to pretend.

I headed to the city's main temple, the one I had visited with Dezmen nearly a week ago, and we clattered over the bridge painted red for joy. In a spirit of defiance, I chose to enter by the door for joy as well. Maybe the world was harsh and terrifying; maybe I had just lost a friend to a shocking act of casual violence. But I had to hope there was still beauty and grace and happiness in the world. I had to believe that one day I would find those things.

It was barely noon—too early for most nobles, in my experience—and the circular tower dedicated to joy was almost empty. Normally I was the kind of person who would slink toward the back so I could observe everyone else in the room without being seen, but on Counting Day I wanted to make sure the goddess couldn't miss me. So I headed to the very first pew and sat right in the middle, an echo on either side. I folded my hands piously and stared at the statue of the goddess on a dais just a few feet in front of me. She had her hands lifted toward the ceiling in exultation and wore a radiant smile on her bronze face. *Someday I want to be that joyful,* I thought.

I was never sure how long I had to stay on Counting Day before the goddess would record my presence, but I typically lingered about an hour. I always found that hour oddly restful. It was the one time in my life I didn't feel like I should be rushing off somewhere, doing something productive to earn my living or ensure my safety. The goddess had commanded me to come and sit; so I sat, and let her reassurance wash over me. I was not especially devout, but on Counting Days I felt a particular closeness to the deity. I felt her hand on my head. I heard her voice say, *I remember you. Your name has been recorded.*

Maybe that was the real reason I observed Counting Day so faithfully. I wasn't afraid of losing the echoes; I just wanted to believe that someone somewhere still knew my name.

As the hour passed, I heard the door open and close a few times, saw the light strengthen and fade as the door admitted and then blocked out the sunshine. I could hear the shuffling of feet, the rustle of clothing, an occasional murmur of voices as priestesses bestowed benedictions. I wasn't paying close attention, but I guessed that twenty or more people had come and gone while I maintained my vigil. Impossible to know without looking how many were originals, how many were echoes, how many were just ordinary people who had dropped by to speak a prayer.

I found myself reluctant to leave as the hour came to a close, but I could think of a dozen things I should probably do before the day got much older. As soon as I stood up, a red-robed priestess was by my side, offering a benediction. I nodded, and she touched her cool fingertips to my forehead, my heart, my lips. *May you know justice, mercy, and joy.* She repeated the ritual with Scar and Red before stepping back to let us pass. The echoes and I turned as one to head toward the exit.

And as one, we froze in place and stared.

Lord Dezmen and his echoes stood in the aisle, watching us, and their faces wore matching looks of bewilderment and shock. It was clear the goddess wasn't the only one who knew my name.

CHAPTER THIRTEEN

For a moment I was tempted to sit back down, since I didn't think Dezmen would cause a scene in the temple, but obviously that would only be a temporary solution. I could tell by Dezmen's dawning expression of determination that he wouldn't let me simply walk away without an explanation, and I'd already learned how persistent he could be. I squared my shoulders, an action that the echoes copied, and I strolled forward to meet him in the aisle.

"Lord Dezmen," I whispered. "I see you have come to the temple for Counting Day."

"As have you," he replied in a low voice. "Let me escort you home."

Maybe a few of the other people in the pews noticed us, maybe they didn't, but I saw one of the priestesses frown in our direction. *Please take your conversation outside.* I didn't answer Dezmen, just brushed past him and stepped through the door, squinting in the bright light.

He was beside me in an instant. The second the door closed behind us, he caught my hand in his, lacing his fingers tightly with mine, and I felt his echoes clasp hands with Red and Scar. I couldn't help glancing down just once to see our intertwined fingers again, light and dark. I wondered how often we would have to hold hands before I stopped being fascinated by that sight.

I had been caught in a flagrant deception, but I didn't have to be meekly apologetic. I tugged against his hold and said, "I don't want you to take me home."

He tightened his grip. "Fine, we'll go somewhere else. There's a public house not far from here. We can ask for luncheon in a private room."

I just couldn't keep the contrary words from spilling out of my mouth. "I'm not hungry." It wasn't even true. I was starving.

"Fine," he said again. "We'll just drink. I know that I myself could down an entire bottle of wine."

I don't want any wine. I didn't say it. I didn't say anything.

He pulled me toward the bridge that was painted white—the color of mercy—though I really think he chose it because it led more directly toward his destination, and not because it matched his mood. The six of us crossed like a trio of handfast lovers, our shoes and boots making a racket against the wood. Neither Dezmen nor I spoke for the next ten minutes, as he towed me through the streets with a single-minded purpose. Soon we were in a high-end shopping district, much more crowded than the temple had been, and each storefront was more elegant than the last.

It wasn't long before Dezmen stopped before a quiet establishment with a hand-painted sign offering luncheons, dinners, and spirits. Not releasing my hand, he opened the door and ushered me inside, our shadows following close behind.

The proprietor, who was dressed nearly as finely as Dezmen, hurried over and pronounced himself most willing to serve us a meal in a private room. Within a few moments, Dezmen had put in an order—not even asking me what I'd like to eat—and the six of us had settled around the small rectangular table. Dezmen and I sat in the middle, our echoes on either side of us, and stared at each other. I had never seen his dark face so serious, his amber eyes so watchful.

"Who are you?" he finally asked.

I wondered if he thought I'd been carrying out an elaborate masquerade—thought I was a low noble from Alberta or Empara who'd been hired by Jackal to bollix up his investigation. The fact that Jackal would have *loved* to partake in such a complex charade didn't make the idea any less ridiculous. "I'm nobody," I said. "I'm Chessie."

"You're a woman with two echoes. Who don't act like echoes. So not only are you of noble blood—you're able to do something no one in the kingdom can do. You're not nobody. I just can't figure out who you are."

"I'm a noble's bastard," I said. "He didn't want me. I grew up on the streets just like any other abandoned child, except I had three bodies to take care of. Everything else you know about me is exactly the same."

"Three bodies," he repeated. "That you can—*somehow*—pass between, is that right?"

I jumped to Red. "Yes. Anytime I want." I jumped to Scar. "I just have to *think* it, and I'm in the other echo's head." I returned to Chessie. "It's proved very useful in making people believe there are three separate people."

His eyes followed me as I skipped from body to body, and now he focused tightly on Chessie again. "You don't even know, do you? How rare that is. How impossible." He swept his hand out to indicate all three of us, and his echoes did the same. "First off, most nobles can't even release their echoes to the point that they can stand or sit or turn or eat or do *anything* except exactly what their originals are doing. And yet you—you can let yours stray some distance away, have completely independent motions, walk on the other side of the street—how do you *do* that?"

I made a tangled gesture with my hands; Scar and Red remained still. "It's hard to explain. It's like—it's like—maybe it's like when someone is playing a musical instrument. One hand plays one note, one hand plays another note. They're coordinated, but they're not identical. Or like when you're dancing. Your feet make a tapping motion and your hands move from side to side. It's like the echoes are different parts of my body, and they can do different things. But they're all part of one body. I still control all their movements."

He shook his head. "Maybe. I can see that. Sort of. But then— moving from one echo to the other. I can't even fathom—" He shook his head again.

"No one else can do that?" I asked. "Truly?"

He managed a slight laugh. "Well, there are stories that King Edwin could! On the battlefield, when his original was killed, he flowed into the body of an echo. And that *is* one of the original purposes of the echoes, you know—to be a repository for the spirit of an original who is murdered. But I never heard of anyone, even Edwin, hopping around from body to body just because he felt like it."

I had often wondered, and now I knew. "Oh" was all I could think to say.

There was a knock and then two servants entered, bearing trays. I was glad to see that, despite my contrariness, Dezmen had ordered a hearty meal for the six of us—bread, cheese, roasted chicken, some fruit, and three bottles of wine. That last seemed excessive, since I didn't plan on having more than one glass. Though perhaps he felt he and his echoes each needed a whole bottle of their own.

Except for Dezmen's murmured thanks, we were all silent until the servants left again, carefully closing the door behind them.

"Food first," he said, "and then the rest of the conversation."

"There's not much else to tell."

This time his laugh was incredulous. "Oh, I think there is. But come on. Eat up."

We all fell to eating as if we hadn't had a proper meal in weeks—though I, at least, had not had one this good in an appreciable amount of time. Dezmen continued to watch me closely, perhaps wondering if I could possibly be real, so I deliberately synchronized the echoes' movements with every one of mine. It was the easiest way to eat a meal, anyway.

When we were done, he leaned back in his chair and crossed his arms, still studying me. His echoes repeated the motions and stared at Scar and Red.

"So," he said. "Start at the beginning. Tell me about the noble who fathered and abandoned you. And how you ended up here. And what you've had to do to maintain this unbelievable masquerade."

"I don't think my tale is as fantastic as you seem to think it is."

"Well, I want to hear it anyway. We're not leaving until I've heard the whole story."

I eyed him across the table. It was a stupid thing to say. He was taller than I was, and bulkier, but if I made a run for the door I didn't think he could stop me. I could probably take him in a fight, since I was pretty sure my combat skills were better than his and I could mobilize the echoes as well. So I would only stay and tell him the whole story if I wanted to tell him the whole story.

And, goddess have mercy on my soul, suddenly I did want to tell him. Tell *somebody*. Shift some of my terrible burden onto somebody else's soul.

But not now. Not yet. I would tell him the part that a few others knew, and keep the rest of it to myself. As always.

"It's an ordinary tale," I began. "My father was a noble who seduced a housemaid. When it turned out she was pregnant, he sent her away. She took refuge with a woman named Angela, who used to be a governess for another noble. My mother died when I was a baby, so Angela raised me. We lived in a small house in rural Empara until I was seventeen."

"A girl and two echoes," he said in a marveling voice. "Living in a cottage in the middle of the countryside. And nobody started asking questions?"

"From the time I was little, I could release the echoes," I said. "And Angela always made sure we were dressed differently. Nobody realized they were my echoes. We just looked like a group of children playing together."

"But if two of them barely spoke—"

"If anyone asked, Angela would say, 'Those others just aren't right in the head. It's so sad.' People seemed to accept that."

"Could you always skip between bodies?"

I shook my head and gave a vague answer. "That came later. When I was fourteen or fifteen. When I started realizing how odd it was that I had echoes and I started exploring what I could do."

"What did Angela think about *that* little trick?"

"She was gone by then. Caught a fever and died."

He frowned. "By the time you were fifteen? That's hard."

By the time I was eleven. I just nodded, not bothering to correct him. I'd given him so many half-lies already. "I spent a couple of years scraping up jobs at the nearby farms. All three of us could work, so we'd usually earn enough to feed ourselves. But those were lean times."

"What made you decide to come to Camarria?"

"One of the farmers' wives had a sister who lived here—the baker woman I told you about before. She said her sister would give me a job if I wanted to go to the royal city. I thought maybe life would be easier in a big place where there were more opportunities. And it was, after a while, but the first couple of years were pretty rough."

"I can imagine!" he exclaimed. "Or rather—no, I *can't* imagine trying to do what you did. Become completely responsible for yourself—*and two echoes*—at the age of fifteen. *I* wouldn't have survived such an ordeal. I don't know many people who would have."

I shrugged. "You'd be surprised to find out what you can do when your only goal is survival. Life got easier as I got older and I could get better work. These days I'd almost call it easy. At least in comparison."

"But it should be easier still," he said. "You're of noble blood— the existence of your echoes proves that without a doubt. You should be able to petition the crown to make your father provide for you financially. There was just such a case a couple of years ago, though it was an estranged wife suing on behalf of her infant daughter. Her husband had accused her of dallying with the gardener and turned her out of the house, but when her newborn daughter suddenly sprouted a couple of echoes, the lord had to admit that he was the father. He was forced to put a portion of his fortune in trust for her."

"Yes, but that was a girl who was born in wedlock to a woman who could prove she had been the man's wife! I doubt the law would be so interested in a bastard child like me."

"Maybe not, but King Harold would be," Dezmen argued. "He had a bastard son himself and loved him very much! That son is dead now, of course, which makes Harold even more tender on the subject. I think he would be moved by your story—and find some way to make your father acknowledge you."

"I don't want anything from my father, thank you very much."

Dezmen leaned back in his chair and studied me a moment. "But you do know who he is?" he said at last.

That had been a bit of a slip; if he thought I knew my father's identity, he would pester me until I revealed it. I had survived so long by keeping that fact a secret from almost everybody, so I was surprised at how much I wanted to tell Dezmen the truth. But I needed to think it over another moment. "I know who he is," I said. "Angela made sure of that."

"Well?" he prodded. "I'm acquainted with most of the high nobles in the country, even those in Empara. I might even be able to guess at his identity."

"Oh, I think you'd be surprised."

"Tell me, then. Don't make me keep asking."

I gave him a long and level look, still assessing. Every time you share information, it becomes a weapon in someone else's hands. Why was I so convinced Dezmen would never use that weapon against me? He watched me steadily, willing to wait for as long as it took for me to decide to trust him. I offered a tiny shrug and said in a flat voice, "Malachi Burken. The king's inquisitor."

Dezmen's amber eyes widened and he looked almost as shocked as he had when he'd seen me at the temple. "Malachi *Burken*? Sweet holy goddess, I don't blame you for not wanting to claim him as a father! There aren't that many people I dislike, but Malachi gives me the shivers every time I see him."

"I have the same reaction," I said dryly. "And I've only ever seen him from a distance."

Now Dezmen was frowning. "But hold on a moment. Malachi's your father? That doesn't make sense."

"Angela was very, very certain." I wasn't going to offer the proof of the emerald necklace. There was virtually no chance Dezmen had ever seen Malachi's matching ring, so the pattern of the jewelry would not convince him.

"I believe you, but it's still almost incredible," Dezmen said. "Malachi doesn't have any echoes of his own."

"So?"

"As far as I'm aware, no child ever acquires echoes unless one of his parents also has them."

"Maybe his father or mother had echoes. Maybe the trait somehow skipped a generation."

Dezmen was watching me with those light-colored eyes. "Or maybe the goddess gifted you with echoes because she had a special purpose in mind for you."

I laughed tiredly. "What purpose might that be?"

"I don't know, but it will be interesting to find out."

I shrugged. "So far my only purpose has been survival."

"Well, that will be easier now."

"I can't imagine why."

He looked puzzled by my response. "Because you're going to take your rightful place in society, of course."

"No, I'm not. Why would you think that?"

"Why wouldn't you?"

"I just told you! I'm not going to march up to King Harold and claim Malachi as my father!"

"You don't have to do that. All you have to say is that you were orphaned at an early age. There's no question that your blood is noble—the echoes are proof of that. The king will make some provision for you. At the very least, you'll be able to afford a decent place to live, good clothes, and good food—"

I placed my hands flat on the table and leaned forward, my face intense. "I *have* a decent place to live," I said. "And good clothes and plenty of food. I'm not looking to change my situation."

He stared at me a long time, his blank bafflement slowly changing to narrowed speculation. "What are you afraid of?" he asked quietly.

Afraid wasn't a strong enough word; *brainlessly terrified* might cover it. But to tell him that would be to tell him everything, and I wasn't ready for that. "I'm a rural bastard who became a city urchin," I said flatly. "If I try to take my 'rightful place' among the nobles, I will become the greatest oddity in the Seven Jewels. People will either mock me or pretend to fawn over me, laughing behind my back at my terrible manners, speculating about my parentage. The life I lead now is peculiar enough, and precarious at times, but it is *my life*. I have no interest in exchanging it for a stranger's."

I could see by his continued close regard that he didn't quite believe me, that he realized I was leaving something unsaid, but that he thought it best not to press me for a more complete answer. At least not right now.

"I realize this is all very new for you," he said. "You must have had limited contact with other high nobles until now. It might never have occurred to you that you could change your circumstances." He waited for me to confirm this. I just shrugged. "I would urge you to think about it for a few days. Consider what your life might be like. You don't have to go into society. You don't have to be acknowledged by your family. But you ought to seek an audience with the king. If you let me tell him of your existence—"

"No," I said so quickly that the word almost caught in my throat. "No. Promise me. Not a word to him. Not a word to anybody. I don't— You're right. I need time to think it over. Promise me you won't say anything."

He kept that calm gaze on my face, and I could almost see the words trembling on his lips. *What are you afraid of?* But this time he didn't speak them. "Of course not," he said at last. "It is, as you say, your life to do with what you will. I only wish you would let me smooth the way for you."

I tried to summon a smile, but I could tell it was strained. "So far, nothing you've done has simplified my life," I told him. "If anything, you've made it more complicated."

"I do apologize. But that was never my intention." He picked up a bottle of wine, silently offering to pour me a glass. His echoes made similar offers to Scar and Red. The three of us nodded, and the three of them poured. I took a few swallows and found the alcohol oddly steadying. After he sipped his own wine, Dezmen said, "I am still astounded that you have managed to pull off such a deception. How many others know the truth about you?"

I shook my head. "Since Angela died, no one."

"Not even your cousin?"

"He knows that Malachi is my father, but not that Scar and Red are my echoes. No one knows about the echoes."

"Not even Jackal? Not even your lovers?"

I was pretty sure he suspected that *Jackal* and *your lovers* might be one and the same. There had been a couple of other boys, but they had always been so young and urgent and self-absorbed that it had been easy to mislead them during our short relationships. Jackal had been the one who required the most subterfuge. I arched my eyebrows and spoke in a supercilious tone. "That's an indelicate question, Lord Dezmen. Would you ask the noblewomen of your acquaintance how they entertain *their* lovers?"

He laughed as if he couldn't help himself. "I suppose not, but I am consumed with curiosity about how you could have managed it! There is—for the rest of us—well, I suppose it *is* indelicate, but my echoes do everything that I do. So if I am to take a lover, I really need to take three. You understand."

"Yes, thank you, I am able to perfectly construct the image in my mind." He laughed again, and I went on, "But since I can, as you have observed, allow my echoes to operate independently, I do not need to worry about that particular … function."

He grinned. "Very interesting. And so—Jackal. He really doesn't know? He's the kind of man who seems to ferret out others' secrets, so I would have thought he would have stumbled upon this one."

"He's the one I always thought was most likely to discover the truth," I said. "But if he has, he has kept the knowledge to himself."

Dezmen tilted his head. "Would it be a problem? If he knew? Would he use it against you in some fashion? Or can you trust him?"

"I don't know," I admitted. "Jackal trades in information. That's his currency. That's his fuel. That's his *life*. He might keep my secret. Or he might sell it to someone else for information he wanted more. I don't think Jackal would ever deliberately harm me—unless I crossed him, which I make sure I never do. But if he thought the information might do him some good and wouldn't hurt me in any substantial way—he might reveal it to someone, so I've never told him."

"So no one knows."

"Except you."

"Except me."

"And, of course, it raises the same question," I said.

"What question is that?"

Once again, I leaned across the table, and stared at him with all the intensity I could muster. "Can I trust you?"

Now his dark brows drew down over his pale eyes. "I'm offended that you think you have to ask me that."

"You don't know me well enough to be offended by anything I might think of you," I said. "And I don't know you well enough to be able to tell if anything you say is true."

Now he stared back, his face setting in uncompromising lines. "Then I suppose I will just have to prove myself to you. And I will begin by assuring you that, yes, you can trust me—with your name, with your life, with the very fact of your existence. I won't mention you to the king."

"Or anyone else."

"Or anyone else," he repeated.

"Then I suppose I feel safe enough," I said. "For now."

He settled back against his chair and continued to regard me. "So nothing changes? You go back to your grubby little apartment—"

"It's not grubby!"

"And continue on with your odd jobs, and your odd life?"

"And *you* go back to the palace and do whatever it is you do, and why would you think anything would change?"

"Because it *feels* different," he said. "Like the world has been upended. Like I am standing on the ceiling or breathing underwater. Like my eyes are someone else's." He touched one finger to the corner of his eye. His echoes did the same.

I laughed. "Because some girl you barely know has a couple of shadows? You haven't experienced much in the way of cataclysms if *that* has rocked you off-balance."

He watched me a moment. "Because some girl turns out to be something I didn't expect," he said softly. "Yes. That's why the world is made new."

His steady gaze made me want to gulp down the rest of the wine, or throw my head back and laugh, or smooth down my skirts and give him a sideways glance, all the while pretending I wasn't blushing. Instead, I sat up straighter, placed my hands on the table, and spoke briskly, "Well. I think we've covered everything. I'll check with Jackal to see what he's set up with Ronin, and then I'll let you know when our next meeting should be. I assume a note sent to the palace will find you?"

"You can assume a note to the palace will be read by one of Malachi's spies."

I smiled. "I'll be very discreet. I'll just say, 'Tomorrow morning,' and you'll know to meet me at Amanda Plaza."

He frowned. "But it might take days for Jackal to set up the appointment with Ronin. We were always planning to meet at the plaza tomorrow. I think we should do that anyway. There might be some other lead I want to chase down."

"I've got my own work to do, but I can tell Jackal that you plan to be there in the morning and he can send someone—"

I stopped abruptly. *He can send someone else to guard you, now that Bertie is dead.* I had gone several whole hours without remembering that terrible fact.

"Did you ask Jackal?" Dezmen asked gently. "If there was anything I could do for Bertie's family?"

"He said he would take care of it. His responsibility. But I know he was impressed that you offered."

"Of course. Let me know if he thinks of something."

I glanced toward the doorway because it had just now occurred to me that there hadn't been any soldiers crowding up behind

Dezmen when we left the temple. "So you just went out on your own today? Didn't bring any royal guards to keep you safe?"

"So far I've only been attacked when I seem poised to learn something that someone wants to keep secret. I figured I couldn't be in much danger just going to the temple."

I shook my head. "I'm surprised you're still alive."

"I could say the same thing about you. Which reminds me." He glanced between Scar and Red, and I was amused by the thought that he couldn't tell them apart. "One of your echoes was badly injured a couple of days ago. How is he—*she?*"

Just to be difficult, I didn't indicate which one was Scar. "Healing pretty well, though I'm trying to keep activities limited. The wound wasn't as bad as I thought at first."

"That was lucky."

"It was," I agreed. I pushed myself to my feet as if I was impatient to go, and the echoes scrambled up alongside me. The truth was that I would have preferred to sit there all day, arguing with the Pandrean lord. *You're an idiot,* I told myself. "So," I said, resuming my brisk voice. "Jackal will let us know when he sets something up, and when he does, I'll meet you at Amanda Plaza."

He and his echoes were also on their feet, coming quickly around the table. "Chessie—"

"I have to go," I said, turning toward the door.

He caught my arm and pulled me back around to face him. "I just want to ask—"

I skipped over to Red's body, a safe distance away. "You've already asked plenty of questions," I said. I was gratified to see him drop Chessie's arm and look over at me in frustration. He needed to know that he could *not* force me to have a conversation I didn't want. I had only stayed so long because I was willing.

"But everything feels so unfinished," he said.

"Not from my point of view. I'm done." I opened the door and this time he didn't try to stop me. "I'll see you in a few days."

"All right."

His voice was so low and troubled that, for the life of me, I couldn't refrain from turning back one last time to look at him. Chessie and Scar filed out ahead of me while Dezmen and I exchanged a final glance. I felt the faintest smile at the corners of my mouth. "Maybe by then," I said, "you'll have learned to breathe underwater."

CHAPTER FOURTEEN

The next two days went by like normal days, the kinds I'd been living for the past couple of years, when my life had finally, *finally*, slipped into a routine of some predictability. Scar's wound was in excellent shape, but the rib cage was still tender, and it didn't seem like a good idea to seek out heavy labor. So I stayed away from the warehouse district and took more jobs running errands and carrying money, information, and light packages from one edge of the city to another.

I tried to tell myself that I wasn't bored half out of my mind. I tried to tell myself that I didn't miss seeing the Pandrean lord, laughing at him, sparring with him, fighting for our lives. But, honestly, all I wanted to do was prowl around the outskirts of the palace, hoping to catch a glimpse of him as he set off on some adventure without me. It was all I could do to stay away from the royal neighborhood altogether for those two days. Well, I only went by once, and even then I only crossed the palace courtyard a couple of times, pretending to be looking for someone. Dezmen never made an appearance. I wondered where he was.

Finally, just for the distraction, I picked up an extra half-shift at Packrat that second night. When Red took her break, Chessie sidled over to meet with Jackal. He told me that he'd sent Pippa to be Dezmen's new bodyguard.

"Didn't know she did that kind of work," I commented. Pippa was lithe and smart, and I'd never doubted she knew how to garrote a man in a back alley, but she didn't have the physique of a typical fighter.

"What she lacks in size, she makes up for in brain," Jackal answered. "She's a hard woman to catch by surprise, and that makes her good in a fight. Also, she wanted the job. Bertie was her best friend." Jackal shrugged. *And she'd love the chance to strangle the man who killed him.*

I shivered. I had told Dezmen that Camarria was one of the safest cities in the kingdom, but these days it seemed that everyone I knew was willing to commit murder. It was unsettling.

"So have you set up a meeting with Ronin?" I asked.

"Tomorrow. Noon. I'll bring him to my house a couple hours beforehand so anyone who might be following Lord Dezmen won't see Ronin arrive. And he'll stay until long after the lord is gone."

"That works," I said. "Does Dezmen know?"

"Pippa was supposed to tell him this morning." He gave me a brief inspection. "Do you plan to be there?"

I nodded. "I figure it might make things smoother if I'm in the room, since I know them both. Also—" I couldn't help a slight laugh. "I'm in pretty deep now. I'm curious about the answers."

Jackal's face set. "I don't care about answers anymore," he said. "I just want justice."

Much to my annoyance, I dressed with a certain amount of extra care the next morning, putting one of Red's clingy tops on Chessie's body and making sure my hair didn't look quite so hopeless. Once I'd made up Red's face, I made up Chessie's—then I scrubbed off all the cosmetics in a fit of embarrassment. Then I reapplied them.

"Idiot," I said with a sigh, regarding myself in the mirror. I still didn't look much better than usual, and Dezmen probably wouldn't even notice the improvements. "You deserve to fall off the highest bridge in the city and break your stupid neck."

But I made it to Amanda Plaza without suffering that fate. Dezmen and his echoes were there before me, standing before the statues and contemplating the goddess of mercy. He didn't seem to notice my approach, but when I said his name, he spun around, his face instantly breaking into a wide smile.

"You *are* here!" he exclaimed, looking so delighted at my presence you'd have thought he hadn't seen me for months. "I wasn't sure Jackal had told you the arrangements had been made. I wasn't sure you'd come."

"I said I would."

He surveyed me a moment. "And don't you look nice!"

I was simultaneously pleased and embarrassed that I had taken extra care with my appearance. "As do you, I'm sure."

"The minute you left the public house the other day, I thought of all these things I hadn't asked you," he went on, speaking in a rush as if afraid we would run out of time to talk. "When Scar got stabbed right in front of Candleback's—did the wound appear on your body, too? I didn't notice you bleeding, but you were wearing a jacket, and the blood might not have seeped through."

I glanced around to make sure no one else was close enough to hear. I could see that Pippa had arrived, but she was hanging back under the bridge, waiting for us to finish our conversation and summon her over. "No," I replied. "Only Scar was wounded. But I've often wondered—"

"Yes?"

"How does it work for everyone else? If someone slices open a vein on *your* body, will your echoes bleed as well?"

He nodded. "Yes. If it happens to me, it happens to them. If I have a fever, they do. If I break a bone, both of them do, too."

"But if one of *them* gets hurt—do you?"

"No. But that happens very rarely. Echoes mimic the actions of their originals so closely they don't have much chance to suffer accidents on their own. But I thought it might be different for you."

"Why?"

"Because Scar has that mark on his face—*her* face—and the rest of you don't."

I was grinning. "We do, though. We've had it since I tripped and fell when I was about five years old. The echoes fell down right next to me. All of us screaming, all of us bleeding—you can imagine how frantic Angela was."

"I've never noticed that scar on anyone else!" he exclaimed.

"That's because I cover it up on Red and me. But it's there." I brushed back my hair to show him. "See?"

He leaned so close I could catch the faint sweet scent of his skin. I found myself holding my breath. "You're right—I see it," he said, and straightened up. "But you've done an excellent job of hiding it."

"Part of the masquerade."

"I still thought it might be different for you than the rest of us with echoes," he went on. "Because you can move from body to body, maybe whatever body you're in becomes the original for that moment. In which case, if you were in Scar's head when that fellow drove the knife home—"

"Which I was."

"Then all three of you would have suffered the wound." He looked down at me. "But you didn't? Then it seems safe to say that Chessie—that *Chezelle*—is the original and at least some of the rules apply."

"That's how it's always felt," I agreed. "Good to know that's right."

"I was also wondering something else. You let the echoes wander some distance from you. How much are they able to see and feel that *isn't* coming through your senses? Can they feed you information from wherever they're standing?"

I shook my head. "Not really. They can navigate forward and manage not to trip over anything, but they operate in a gray haze—it's almost like I'm feeling my way in a deep fog. If I really want to see what's going on in front of them, I just throw myself back into one of their bodies."

"How far away from you can they get and still be connected?"

"I don't know. I've never pushed it too far. I was never willing to risk that something might happen to one of them."

"We could try it someday—you and I. I'd be there to protect them so you could go as far as you liked."

The idea of relying on anyone for that much security was both appealing and appalling. "Maybe," I said, a little flustered. "I think we have a lot more important things to worry about first."

On those words, I glanced over my shoulder again and motioned to Pippa. She just jerked her head in a generally southern direction, indicating that we should set out toward Crescent Lane ahead of her. Apparently she preferred to follow at a distance so she could notice if anyone else seemed particularly interested in Lord Dezmen and his route.

"We should get going," I said. "We want to be at Jackal's by noon."

We set off in our usual parade-like fashion, Dezmen and I side by side, his echoes behind us in strict formation, my echoes trailing along like tourists, the bodyguard falling in step as we passed. Good thing we weren't aiming for stealth; we never could have managed it.

The walk to Jackal's house was a pleasant one through well-kept neighborhoods, though the houses got smaller and correspondingly less impressive as we went. Most of the foot traffic was made up of people in the middle strata of society—the merchant class and the working folk—bustling about on business affairs or important chores. I saw a few thieves and beggars, but they didn't tend to do much business in these districts during the daylight. At this hour, the streets belonged to the more respectable members of society.

Jackal's house was a solid structure of veined gray marble, accented with a black roof, black shutters, a black door, and a black wrought-iron fence to hold the whole place together. It looked both elegant and worn, as if it had done its best for as long as it could and was now just going to coast along, hoping not to draw too much attention. The shrubbery out front was well maintained but stringy, sporting leaves of a faded green. Even the birds pecking at the soil looked thin and exhausted.

By contrast, the man who answered the door was young and muscular, full of energy and ready to battle all comers. I knew from experience that there were never fewer than five employees on the property, all of them armed and primed for trouble. The things Jackal valued most tended to be kept in this house, and he didn't want to take chances.

"Jackal here?" I asked the doorman as six of us crossed the threshold. Pippa hung back, knowing she wouldn't have to keep Dezmen safe as long as we were inside the house.

The man shook his head. "He said he wasn't interested in your business. But the person you're supposed to meet arrived about an hour ago. He's in the upstairs study."

"Thanks."

The lower level of the house was filled with oblique sunshine filtering through half-closed draperies. The whole place was sparsely furnished—some rooms, I knew, were entirely empty—because Jackal was more interested in creating the impression of affluence than living the requisite lifestyle. One of the big downstairs rooms was crammed with wide couches and soft chairs, and that was where he entertained groups of friends in disrespectable pursuits. A couple of the upstairs bedrooms were outfitted with every comfort to accommodate Jackal and any overnight guests he might have. A few of the rooms were locked, and I imagined they held all sorts of treasures, but I had never bothered to try to find out what was inside.

The upstairs study was the place where Jackal conducted his serious business. It was located in the dead center of the house, had no windows and only one door. There was a large table in the middle of the room, eight chairs around it, and a patterned blue carpet beneath it. If you didn't count the lamps and wall sconces, the room held nothing else.

I was familiar with the house, so no one had to show us where to go. I left Scar and Red in one of the half-empty downstairs rooms and led Dezmen and his echoes up the polished staircase. We encountered another one of Jackal's men upstairs, but he only gave us a quick inspection before turning away.

The door to the study was closed. I knocked and opened it without waiting for a reply. Ronin was sitting at the big table, reading a book and sipping from a glass of water; a large tray of refreshments sat in the middle of the table, enough to keep him satisfied if he had to wait for hours.

He looked up when we came in, and nodded at me in recognition. Ronin was a ghost of a man, small and bald and unremarkable in every way. You wouldn't notice him if he passed you on the street, and I always thought he liked it that way. He had done very well for himself by presenting an unassuming appearance and focusing only on business. He was smart, though, with a phenomenal memory and an unerring sense of value. My guess was that, over the years, he'd traded in more goods and made more money than Eva Candleback.

"Chessie," Ronin said. "Jackal didn't tell me who was coming, just that he wanted me to be here."

I glanced over at Dezmen with an inquiring expression, and he just made a gesture of indifference. My interpretation was that he didn't care if I introduced him or not. There weren't that many Pandrean lords circulating around Camarria trailed by their two echoes, however; a few questions in the right circles and Ronin would learn his name instantly. But I appreciated Jackal's bow toward secrecy.

"This is Lord Dezmen," I introduced him. "And Ronin."

Ronin nodded again, not unduly impressed. Bankrupt lords and ladies came to his shop all the time, desperate to swap their heirlooms for income, and plenty of them had echoes at their backs. "I understand you want my opinion on a piece of jewelry," he said.

Dezmen slipped into a chair across from Ronin, his echoes sitting beside him. I remained on my feet, unaccountably restless. "I do. I suppose Jackal has made it clear that discretion is essential—"

"You don't have to worry about Ronin," I interrupted. "He never tells anyone anything." It was true. I'd known Ronin for almost as long as I'd lived in Camarria and he'd never passed on a single piece of gossip about who was buying, who was selling, or how much they were worth. Along with Jackal, he was one of the few people in the city I mostly trusted.

Dezmen reached into a jacket pocket and pulled out a piece of cloth bundled around a small object. He unwrapped it carefully and set it in the middle of the table. Ronin leaned in to examine it without touching it; I came close enough to peer down.

It was a round gold pin maybe two inches in diameter, made of a worn and heavily fluted gold. The top was encrusted with amethysts—long narrow ones and small round ones—laid into the design of a many-petaled rose. In the soft interior lighting, the gold looked smooth and worn from much handling, but the amethysts were crisp as icicles.

I saw Ronin hitch his chair nearer to the table as he took out a loupe and studied the brooch for a moment. "Interesting," he said at last.

"Do you recognize the pattern of the jewels?" Dezmen asked. "Would you be able to name a family or a region that claimed this heraldry?"

"I don't think so," Ronin said, "but I don't think the pattern is what makes this piece so distinctive."

Dezmen glanced at me, but I just shrugged. I didn't have any idea what that meant.

Ronin looked at Dezmen. "May I handle it?"

"Please."

Ronin carefully lifted the piece off the table, holding it so that he could examine it from the sides and the bottom. Then he pulled out a thin metal tool and probed gently at the central jewel in the purple flower. I almost gasped when the stone came loose and tinkled onto the table, but Ronin didn't look concerned. He just reinserted the gem with the same sharp tool, then laid the pin back on the table.

"The amethysts aren't original to the piece," he said. "The gold is very old, very pure, but the stones are cheap and recent. They were set into the pin to make you think that it belonged to someone from Alberta. Which is, I suspect, what you believed."

"Yes," Dezmen replied.

Ronin nodded. "This is what is known as an envoy pin. Very popular, oh, two hundred years ago, when there was a great deal of feuding between the high nobles. The lords would communicate with each other by sending messengers bearing one of these pins. The visible jewels would be inserted in the fittings to mislead anyone who might intercept the courier. So, for instance, Lord Dezmen, if you had commissioned a messenger and had given him an envoy pin, you would not set it with opals, because then anyone would know it came from a Pandrean noble. You would, perhaps, fit it with sapphires so that someone would believe it originated in Banchura instead."

"Ah," said Dezmen. "But then, how would anyone know the message was really from me?"

Ronin picked up the pin again and turned it over to reveal the heavy clasp. He tried twisting the clasp to one side, but it wouldn't budge; he held the pin between his two hands and made as if to unscrew two halves, but nothing happened.

Dezmen and I leaned closer, both of us fascinated. "There's a secret compartment," Dezmen breathed. "That's why the pin is so thick and heavy."

"Yes," said Ronin. "The trick is finding it."

He turned it faceup again and tried pressing on various combinations of the amethyst stones, but got no results. Finally he held it close to his face and ran a thumbnail around the exterior, clearly searching for a break in the metal. "There," he said, a second before I heard a faint *click*, and the lid of the pin came off.

Ronin gazed into the inner workings of the brooch for a moment, his face showing no expression, then turned the item so Dezmen could see inside. I caught nothing but a flash of green.

"Emeralds," Dezmen said. "So then this envoy pin was sent by someone from Empara?"

"That would be my interpretation," Ronin replied.

"Do you recognize the pattern? Does it belong to any particular family?"

Ronin shook his head. "I'm familiar with most of the symbols used by high nobles throughout the Seven Jewels, and this isn't a herald I recognize. Certainly it could be from a minor branch that I just have not encountered before, but I tend to doubt it."

"You've never seen this pattern before?"

"Once—but I couldn't identify it then, either."

"Then how will I trace who the pin belongs to?"

"My guess is that it's the symbol for some small regional temple. The arrangement of gems in groupings of three would seem to indicate a religious affiliation, and the obscurity of the design would argue that it was adopted by some local branch that had only one or two locations."

Dezmen sat back in his chair and regarded Ronin for a moment. "I find it hard to believe that a priestess of *any* temple, no matter how obscure, could be involved in the particular activity that I'm investigating."

Ronin permitted himself a faint smile. "Perhaps not. But I have found that people with no heraldry of their own sometimes adopt the symbols of organizations that are important to them. I once knew a man who had been abandoned on the steps of a temple when he was a baby. The priestesses took him in and cared for him until they could find him a foster home. Once he was a man, he always wore a ring with the fleur-de-lis pattern of that temple." He tapped the side of the pin. "Whoever sent this envoy pin might feel a similar strong tie to a local temple for some emotional reason."

"That makes sense," Dezmen allowed. "Is there any register that lists the designs of all the temples in the kingdom?"

"Not that I'm aware of," Ronin said. "If you want to find this particular outpost, you'll probably have to travel to Empara."

Dezmen groaned. "And search the whole province for one specific building out of what must be thousands! That could take—months. Years."

"It does seem to be a difficult quest," Ronin agreed. "But I'm afraid I can be of no more help to you." He set the pin down on the table between them, and I finally had a chance to get an unobstructed look at the pattern inside.

Three long emeralds forming a triangle. Three small round emeralds at each joint. Three diamond-shaped stones in the middle.

Identical to the necklace I wore around my neck at that very moment.

Identical to Malachi's ring.

Malachi.

I tried to rein back my stampeding terror, but it was all I could do not to wail aloud. As it was, I must have made some kind of sound as I jerked upright and took a few clumsy steps backward until I blundered against the wall. Dezmen looked over at me in concern.

"Chessie? What's wrong?"

I shook my head and tried to produce a normal voice. "Just—I thought of something. I'll tell you later."

He frowned at me a moment longer before returning his attention to the calamitous object sitting so innocently in the middle of the table. I tried to still my breathing, but there was no way to slow my racing pulse. It was an effort to keep my hands hanging loosely at my sides instead of drawing them up protectively over my face, my heart.

"So I'm assuming that something like this would be very rare," Dezmen said. "A man might own only one or two—and if he lost it, he would be very eager to get it back."

"Particularly if it was found in the hands of someone who had committed some sort of crime," Ronin said. "Yes. Although in this case—" He spread his hands. "It hardly seems to matter, since no one is able to identify the design and therefore identify the sender."

"*Someone* will recognize it."

Ronin didn't even glance at me. "No doubt."

I had showed him my necklace three years ago, after I had come to trust him. It was a reckless move because if he ever realized that Malachi possessed a piece of jewelry with a matching pattern, he would be able to put at least some of the puzzle pieces together. But he had told me much of what he had said to Dezmen today. *It looks like a design from a rural temple, but it's not one I've seen before. It's beautiful, though, and very expensive. You could almost set your price and I'd be willing to buy it.*

I'd never been that desperate for money. But I was starting to think that the price of owning the necklace could be more than I was willing to pay.

Now Dezmen sighed. "You might be right. I might have to set off for Empara."

"It's what I would advise," Ronin answered. He snapped the lid back on, showed Dezmen how to open it again, and then folded his hands on the table while Dezmen rewrapped the envoy pin and stored it in his pocket. "Is there anything else I can do for you?"

"Nothing, thank you. You've been most helpful. May I offer some remuneration for your professional advice?"

Ronin's thin smile reappeared. "Thank you, I've been generously compensated."

Dezmen slid a fat gold coin across the table anyway. I hardly saw Ronin's hands move, but the coin vanished instantly. "Nonetheless. I'm grateful for your time and expertise. If I have future questions of a delicate nature, I'll be sure to consult you."

Ronin inclined his head. "Thank you, my lord."

Dezmen and his echoes were on their feet. "All right, then, let's go."

I thought it might be more than I could do to push myself away from the support of the wall. My breathing had gone back to normal, but my heart was still racing, and my hands were the temperature of snow. The look I gave Dezmen was so stark that it stopped him in his tracks.

"Chessie?" he said uncertainly.

My voice was hoarse. "Let's go."

Frowning, he offered me his arm, something he never did—and I took it, something I never would have expected to do. I wondered if he could feel the ice in my fingers through the layers of his jacket and his linen shirt. "Maybe we should get some food and talk about what to do next," he said.

"Maybe," I croaked.

Jackal's servants—or bodyguards or brawlers or whatever they were—watched us out the door to make sure we didn't steal anything. Scar and Red were behind us as we stepped back out into the chilly sunshine, passed through the wrought-iron gate, and set out in the general direction of Amanda Plaza. Pippa followed after the whole entourage.

"Where would you like to have lunch?" Dezmen asked.

I shook my head. "I can't eat. I'd throw up."

He looked down at me, his face furrowing. "What's wrong? What happened back there? What did Ronin say, or what did you see—" His voice trailed off. "You recognized the pattern," he said quietly. "In the envoy pin. You know who it belongs to."

I nodded.

His free hand came up to cover mine, and I could hear the excitement in his voice. "Who is it?" Then the worry. "Chessie, your hands are so cold!"

"We have to go somewhere we can talk."

"Your apartment?"

"Not if someone's following us."

"A public house, then. We'll get a private room."

"Not if someone might be listening at the door."

"Then—"

"Just come with me."

CHAPTER FIFTEEN

I led Dezmen through a warren of streets, through neighborhoods that quickly became less respectable. I wouldn't have called them dangerous, though I noticed that Dezmen looked around a little uneasily and glanced over his shoulder once to make sure Pippa was still behind us. In about fifteen minutes, we'd come to an area that held a few abandoned buildings, a couple of meager establishments that were still operating, and a long, narrow metal bridge that arched over a drainage canal. It used to connect two halves of a fairly prosperous business district, but these days it just stood watch over its domain like the skeleton of minor king.

When you stood in the middle of that bridge, you could see around you for a good fifty yards in all directions, and nobody could overhear you unless you knew they were there.

"You keep watch down here. Don't let anyone get close," I directed Pippa as I climbed onto the bottom steps, my feet ringing loudly against the metal. The six of us thundered across the span until we reached the center point, where I came to an abrupt stop. Scar and one of Dezmen's echoes took two steps beyond us; Red and his second echo were on our other side. Somewhere along the journey I had gathered up my echoes and bound them to me, so that every move I made they copied exactly. I could not think clearly enough to allow them to act on their own. I couldn't think clearly at all.

Therefore, when Dezmen made an exclamation of concern, grabbed my shoulders, and turned me toward him, his echoes caught Scar and Red in their arms and gazed down with similar expressions of worry. Scar and Red stared back up at his echoes, as I stared up at Dezmen. I shivered in the insistent breeze and realized I would never be warm again.

"Chessie, what is it? What do you know?" he asked urgently.

I freed one hand enough to dip it beneath the collar of my shirt. Scar and Red repeated the motion, though they had nothing to show for it. But I pulled out my necklace. Hung with the emerald charm.

Dezmen glanced from the pendant to my face and back to the pendant. "But that's—that's the same pattern. Isn't it? The one in the pin?"

"Yes."

"Why are you wearing the same design? I don't understand. How are you connected to all this?"

"It belonged—" My throat closed up. I shook my head and tried again. "The necklace. Angela said my mother stole it when she was kicked out of the house. It belonged to my father. He owns a ring with the same design."

"Your father..." He repeated, puzzled, as if he had forgotten who my father was, or never believed me when I told him.

Even though Pippa was the only person visible for half a mile, and she was facing away from us as she slouched against a pile of old rubble, I leaned forward and whispered in Dezmen's ear. *"Malachi."*

His hands clenched on my arms and I felt his whole body stiffen. "The inquisitor?" he breathed. "Gave this pin to Leffert? *Wanted Leffert to murder the prince?* It makes no sense."

"I know."

"Chessie, are you sure?"

I shrugged against his hold, but he didn't drop his hands. "I have the necklace, which I was told belonged to my father. My cousin Nico has seen a ring of the same design in Malachi's belongings. The pin was in the possession of someone who was hired to murder the prince. I don't know any other way to add the pieces up. Malachi wants Cormac dead."

"But why?"

"I don't have the faintest idea."

Dezmen was frowning, but he no longer looked incredulous; he looked as if he was trying to reorder his thoughts. "Certainly Malachi would have the resources to have me followed—or to have me killed," he said slowly. "And the resources to eliminate anyone he thought had botched the job. There is no question he is a ruthless man. But a murderous one? He does not have that reputation. He'll have a man interrogated, and he'll happily see a woman executed in Amanda Plaza—but to order someone's assassination? Worse, to kill someone himself, in stealth? I have never heard anyone even whisper such an accusation about Malachi."

I started trembling so violently that I could not conceal my shivers. Dezmen exclaimed aloud and drew me against his chest, cradling me so close I could feel the heat of his body for my entire length. It was a comfort, but it was not enough to keep me warm.

"He has done it before," I whispered. "And I saw him."

I felt his arms tighten around me as he kissed the top of my head. "Tell me," he said.

"When I was a girl. Living with Angela. He came—he came to the house. I was in another room with the echoes. Angela was in the kitchen, and I heard her shriek. I left the echoes behind and I came running."

I drew a deep, ragged breath. Sweet goddess, I had not let myself think about this for so long. That terrible, terrible day.

"I stopped in the doorway and they didn't see me at first," I went on. "I saw a man holding—holding Angela by the throat and pressing her against a wall. I don't think her feet were on the floor. She was struggling and choking and—and I just stood there. Staring. I didn't know what to do. He said, 'I understand you have my daughter.' That's when I knew who it was. My father."

Dezmen drew a sharp breath. "Had he been looking for you all that time?"

"I don't know. Why would he have been? Then he said, 'Is she here?' He set her down and let go of her throat, and she gasped and coughed and almost fell over. And he said it again, 'Is she here?'

And she stood up and she *spit* at him and she said, 'May the goddess never have mercy on your evil soul, Malachi Burken.' I think she knew he was going to kill her."

"He *killed* her? You said she died of a fever—"

"He killed her," I said into his jacket. "He asked her three more times if I was there, and when she didn't answer, he pulled out a knife and he cut her throat. In an instant. She was covered in blood and lying on the floor so fast I hadn't even had time to move."

"Dear holy goddess," Dezmen breathed. "Sweet mother of us all."

"All that time, I'd just been standing there. Watching. And when he killed her I—I made a sound. He saw me. And he came— he came for *me.*"

His arms tightened so much I briefly couldn't breathe. "Chessie!"

"I ran," I said. "Through the house. Up the stairs and into one of the bedrooms. I don't know what I was thinking. That I could climb out the window, maybe, and go running through the yard."

"Where were the echoes?"

"Hiding in the downstairs room where I had left them. I don't think he knew they were there. I don't think that whoever told him about me had told him that I had echoes. So he didn't know."

"What happened then? How did you get away?"

"He followed me. I could hear him climbing the steps and crashing through the hallway. I had crawled into the closet and was curled up on the floor, under a blanket, as small as I could go. I heard him open one door, and then another door, and then he came into the room I was in and he yanked open the closet. And I didn't breathe and I didn't breathe—and then he grabbed the blanket and pulled it off and dragged me out into the room."

"Chessie," Dezmen breathed. "Dear goddess. *Chessie.*"

"For a minute, he just stared at me. Like he couldn't believe I was real. He was holding my arm so tight I thought he might break the bone. He said, 'All this time I believed you were dead.' And I had this thought—this strange, wild, unbelievable thought—that he had *come for me.* That he *wanted* me. That maybe he hadn't kicked my mother out of the house, but she had run away, and he had searched for me all that time."

"How did he find out you were alive?"

"I don't know."

"What happened then?"

"He said, 'What do they call you?' And I said my name was Chezelle. And he laughed. I'll never forget that. Holding my arm in one hand and a bloody knife in the other hand, and he *laughed*. He said, 'I should have guessed. She loved that name.' I just looked at him and said, 'Have you come here to kill me?'"

Dezmen gasped. I could feel his hands pressing against my back as if, all these years later, he was trying to be a shield for me, trying to place himself between me and my deadly father.

"And he said, 'Yes,'" I whispered.

Dezmen's lips were against my ear. "But he didn't kill you, he didn't," he murmured.

I gave my head the faintest shake. "He just kept staring at me. He said, 'I expected you to look more like her.' I thought—I thought if he kept talking to me, maybe he wouldn't kill me, so I said, 'Did you love her once?' and he said, 'No one ever loved anyone as much as I loved her.'"

I felt Dezmen lift his head as if he had to think that over. "He said that about his housemaid?"

"I don't know, maybe he was obsessed with her. Maybe he was in love with her and she was cruel to him. Maybe that changed him."

"Maybe."

"He just kept staring at me. I said, 'She wouldn't want you to kill me.' And he laughed again. And he lifted up the knife."

Dezmen gathered me closer, bending his head over mine again, murmuring my name in my ear. I had been blank with terror. What would it be like to die? The whole world pressing against me—the heat, the color, the music of a summer afternoon—suddenly lost, completely invisible, no longer perceptible against my skin. Pain first, no doubt, tremendous pain, but surely it couldn't last long? Then oblivion. An obscure life lost to its final obscurity.

"But he couldn't do it," I whispered against Dezmen's throat. "He had come there to murder me, but he couldn't do it. He dropped the knife and he let go of me and he put his hand over his eyes. I thought he might have been crying. He left the room and he left the house and he never came back."

"Chessie, Chessie, Chessie," Dezmen chanted, running his hands over my back, over my shoulders, then wrapping his arms around me and drawing me against his body. "Sweet goddess, and there you were! Alone in a house with a dead body! What did you *do*? How did you survive?"

"I told you some of this part before," I reminded him. "I packed up clothes for the echoes and me, and we left the house, walking as far away as we could get. Like I said, we worked on a few different farms in Empara for a couple of years, and then eventually made it to Camarria."

Dezmen lifted his head again, pulling back enough to look at me. I had had my face buried against his jacket for so long that the sunlight hurt my eyes, and I squinted up at him. "Even though you knew Malachi was in Camarria. That was a little risky, don't you think? What if he changed his mind?"

"It was risky," I acknowledged. "But—I wanted to know where he was. I didn't want to be living in some quiet town in Empara, thinking I was safe from him, only to have him show up suddenly at my door. I thought at least if I was in the same city, I could keep track of him a little better."

"Have you ever seen him again?"

"A few times. From a distance. When I've delivered a package to the palace or watched a parade go by. I always pull back into the shadows. I don't think he's ever seen me. I don't think he realizes I'm here."

Dezmen took a great, gusty breath. "No wonder you didn't want me to tell the king about you! If Malachi learns you're in the city—"

"I'm afraid of him," I said. "So afraid. And that's why I said it."

"Said what?"

"That I can believe he tried to kill Cormac. That I can believe he killed Leffert, probably with his own hands, and probably killed the men he sent after you at the botanical gardens. I think there's nothing he wouldn't do. I don't know *why* he wants Cormac dead, but if he does—" I shivered.

Dezmen moved his hands up to either side of my face and peered down at me. "I'm not ready to talk about Cormac yet. I still want to talk about you," he said. "Now I'm going to be worried about you every single minute. If Malachi realizes you're here—if he goes after you again—"

"I don't think he will."

"Chessie, it's not safe for you here!"

Now I pulled back from the comfort and shelter of his arms. That quickly he had gone from being a haven to being a problem. Scar and Red similarly disentangled themselves from his echoes. "I'm as safe here as I am anywhere," I said coldly. "I've managed to take care of myself for the past several years without any help from anyone else."

"But I want to help you," he said urgently. "I *can* help you."

"Oh, really? The first time I met you, someone was trying to murder you, and *I'm* the one who kept *you* alive."

I thought this was a very good point, but he brushed it aside. "Let me take you to Pandrea," he said. "Malachi will hardly come after you if you're living on a country estate, surrounded by guards and servants."

I stared at him. "Pandrea! I don't know a soul there. What would I do? What would— *Pandrea!*"

"Well, you'd know me. And my family, of course, and all of my friends."

"They'd think you'd lost your mind," I said. "What would you tell them? 'Oh yes, here's this urchin I met in Camarria—someone's trying to kill her, so I thought it would be a good idea to drag her here so all of you could stare at her and whisper behind her back.'"

"That's not what would happen. They'd welcome you."

"High nobles don't *welcome* girls like me."

"Girls with two echoes?" he said softly. "I think they would."

I jerked back as if he'd slapped me. "Ah. So this is just your way of forcing me to change my life the way *you* think I should change it. You're determined to see me join noble society—"

"I'm determined to see you live," he retorted. "And if *joining noble society* helps you stay alive, then yes! I'll do everything I can to make sure that's what you do."

"Well, I'm not doing it," I said. "I'm not going to hide in Pandrea just because *you* think it's a good idea."

"But you—"

I held up a hand and he fell silent. "But I *will* go to Empara with you, since that's obviously what you have to do next to follow this bloody trail. I'll go to Empara with you and help you find the temple that claims this particular design. And then ... we'll see what we learn."

He stared down at me a moment, his face creased in worry and frustration. "But, Chessie, if it's not safe for you in Camarria—"

"Maybe it will be," I interrupted, "once we figure out what Malachi's up to. Maybe we can learn something that will help us destroy him."

He watched me a while longer, obviously thinking that over. "I'm starting to wonder," he said, "if the king suspects something like this."

"Suspects that his inquisitor tried to murder his son?" I said, astonished. "That seems pretty unlikely."

"I know. But it was always just a little odd that he didn't want Malachi looking into Leffert's murder."

I remembered the conversation I'd had a few days ago with Nico and Brianna, when Nico suggested, but wouldn't come right out and say, that the king didn't entirely trust Malachi. But all I said to Dezmen was, "Why not?"

"I think Harold is just a little—uncertain—about Malachi. And this was his way of putting Malachi on notice."

"But if he doesn't trust Malachi, why would Harold name him inquisitor?"

"Malachi came to Camarria when Tabitha married Harold. I don't know how many of the details you know, but from what I've been told, the marriage negotiations took almost a year. There was so much animosity between Camarria and the western provinces that Harold could hardly find a family from the west that was willing to marry off their daughter to the king. Tabitha's parents insisted that Malachi be part of the deal—that he be appointed to the staff of royal inquisitors so he could protect Tabitha if there was ever any trouble. He was good enough at the job that he rose pretty quickly through the ranks—but—maybe Harold thinks his loyalty is more to Empara than the crown. So if the crown is under attack—if people are trying to kill the prince—maybe Harold doesn't trust Malachi to discover the truth."

"That makes your job easier, then," I said. "If you find any evidence against Malachi, Harold will be ready to believe it."

"*If* we do," Dezmen said. "I'm not feeling entirely optimistic about our chances."

"Maybe Nico can give me some advice about where to start."

"So you *will* come with me? Because I think I'll need your help."

I was starting to recover, so I gave him a saucy smile. "I'll come. Because I *know* you'll need my help."

"When do you want to leave?"

"I need a day to organize myself and let Jackal know I won't be around for a while. I could leave the day after tomorrow."

He was watching me again. "But if Malachi is having someone follow me, it might be dangerous for us to go straight to Empara. That could send him into a fit of murderous rage, don't you think?"

I narrowed my eyes at him. "Maybe."

"But if we stop in Pandrea first—"

I threw my hands in the air. "I am *not* going to hide away in Pandrea for the rest of my life! I told you!"

He was laughing. "No, no. I am not planning to kidnap you and bury you on my estate! I swear! But you have to admit Malachi will be much less suspicious if we go there instead of to Empara.

Particularly if I say I've received an urgent message from my father, asking me to come home."

"I suppose that makes sense."

"And then I could introduce you to my family."

"Why would you want to do that?" I said in exasperation.

He was still laughing. "Why do you think?"

He put his arms around me; his echoes put their arms around Scar and Red. All three of us looked up in surprise; all three of them kissed us. It was as if I had never properly been kissed before—as if, every other time it had happened, I had been wrapped in silk, my mouth and my hands and my skin sheathed in fine fabric, blunting sensation, dulling desire. But now every barrier was stripped away, now every part of my extended body thrilled to the heady contact. I could have been naked, I could have been dipped in fire, and I could not have felt this kiss any more keenly. I leaned into that long embrace and I felt my body dazzle into dissolution.

When Dezmen finally lifted his mouth, I just blinked up at him. "Oh," was all I could say.

He grinned. "Is that a good reaction? A bad reaction?"

"That's what it's supposed to feel like."

"Ah. With echoes, you mean."

I could just nod.

"Yes, it's entirely different, isn't it? Would you like to try it again?"

He took my silence as an affirmative. The second kiss was just as intense, just as magical as the first. I wondered if my skin was glowing; I was certain my face was flushed with delight. I put my arms around his back and strained against him, and I felt that kiss shock through me from my mouth to my tingling toes.

Then I placed my palms against his chest and pushed myself away, panting a little. He made a strangled sound of protest. "Just when it was starting to get interesting," he said. He was breathless himself.

"We are *not* traveling halfway across the Seven Jewels misbehaving in the coach," I said sternly. "So don't think once you've got me trapped in the carriage with you that I'm going to be—be—hugging and kissing you for the whole journey."

"No, indeed, a coach is a most awkward place for lovemaking," he said, trying to sound serious but unable to subdue his laughter. "Even in a well-sprung vehicle, it's nothing but hard bumps and sudden stones in the road and swerving to avoid a herd of goats. Much better to wait until we've taken rooms for the night."

Now I frowned at him. "Two rooms. One for each of us. And our echoes. We will *not* be sharing quarters."

He lifted a hand to touch my cheek. If I'd had to find a word for it, I would have described his expression as tender. "We will do whatever you like," he said. "This is all very new and unexpected for me, too, you know. I have no particular plans or designs. I just— wanted to kiss you. I might want to kiss you again. In fact, I'm pretty sure of it. But I'm certainly not going to do it if you don't want me to."

I don't want you to was the retort I wanted to make. But it wasn't true and I doubted I could make the lie convincing. I just wanted to create the space that allowed me to say no. "Well, good," I said, a little huffily. "I'm glad we've got that settled."

He smiled. "So am I," he said. "So then—the day after tomorrow? Shall I pick you up at your lodgings?"

I shook my head. "I don't want anyone following you to my place. I'll meet you at the plaza."

"With all your luggage? That seems inconvenient."

I laughed. "I don't think I'll be packing that much."

"Then I'll see you there in a couple of days."

The six of us clattered down off the bridge, the noise of our passage giving Pippa plenty of warning that we were on the move. It belatedly occurred to me that, even if she'd been too far away to overhear our conversation, she'd been close enough to see us kissing if she'd been facing in our direction. And while I wouldn't care that she saw Dezmen and Chessie in an embrace, she would certainly think it odd that Scar and Red had been swept up in the arms of the echoes. Could I explain it away? *The echoes do everything their originals do, but I didn't realize they would take hold of Scar and Red like that. I was afraid Scar would be mortified, but he said he'd always wondered what it would be like to kiss a man.* Maybe—or maybe it was better just to let her wonder. I doubted she would ask anyway, though if she carried the tale to Jackal, Jackal might.

Or maybe she hadn't seen. Or maybe she didn't care.

At any rate, she didn't speak as we approached, she just fell in step behind us. I had released my echoes again and they were walking along hand in hand, as they so often did. I wasn't capable of giving them much more independence than that, since my head was still in something of a whirl.

It had not been the day I anticipated.

I could hardly remember the last time I had had one of those.

Chapter Sixteen

Jackal, when I finally tracked him down the following day, didn't ask any inconvenient questions—about Ronin, about Dezmen, about echoes, about the trip I planned to take. "You think it will help the lord discover something about the murder?" he said. "That's all I need to know."

"I don't know how long we'll be gone," I said. "A couple of weeks at least."

"Then I'll see you when you get back."

It took me a little longer to find Morrissey, who was helping a friend tear down a building on the east side. I didn't ask what they were intending to build in its place. JoJo was one of the other men on demolition duty; he waved when he recognized me, but didn't offer his usual smile. I figured he was still mourning for his brother. I didn't ask him any questions, either.

"So it turns out I have to go to Empara," I told Morrissey. "If you still want me to fetch your nephew for you—"

His crumpled face smoothed out as if he'd heard good news for the first time in a year. "I do! Chessie, this is great! When are you leaving? When can you get there?"

"Details are sketchy," I said. "And there are stops to make on the way. But if you tell me where to find your sister, I'll pick him up on my way back."

He begged a piece of paper from the building owner and scrawled down an address in a town on the northeastern border of the province. I could imagine few things more tedious than traveling four or five days with an unknown kid who couldn't be happy about his own situation, but I thought it might be a good idea to have a cover story in case Malachi's men really did follow us to Empara.

Besides. It couldn't hurt me to do a favor for Morrissey. You never knew when he might be in a position to do me a favor in return.

That evening, I paid my landlady a month's rent in advance, just in case, and promised to send more if my trip was unexpectedly extended. Then I headed over to Brianna's to see if my cousin might have any useful information to offer.

I had to be careful, though. Nico wasn't just related to Malachi; he worked for the man. I couldn't be entirely honest about the reasons for my journey.

Not that I had ever been entirely honest with anyone about anything.

Brianna was pleased to see me, especially since I showed up with pastries I had purchased at a specialty shop, and she promised that Nico would arrive before the night was over, perhaps in time for dinner. In fact, he walked in when we were halfway through our meal, and he pulled up a chair to join us.

"So I suppose you've come to see if you can worm some information out of me again, while pretending you're just here out of cousinly affection," he said.

I laughed. "But, Nico, I do feel great affection for you," I said soulfully. "I've missed you so much! Ever since—well, when *was* the last time I saw you?"

He took a big bite of a boiled potato. "A week ago," he said around his food. "When you came to Brianna's door in the middle of the night."

"See? I wasn't looking for information *that* time."

He swallowed and grinned. "You were still using me. As you always do. So I suppose you want another favor."

"I do, but it's a small one."

"Tell me, then."

I tapped my fingers on the table, as if trying to determine how much to say. In truth, I'd plotted out almost every sentence of my conversation. "It turns out that Lord Dezmen's investigation will lead to Empara, although that's not information he wants widely known." I gave him a serious look. "By the king. By Malachi. By anyone."

Nico wiped his mouth. "All right."

"He asked me to go with him. At first I said no, but then I thought… it's been years since I was there. Maybe it's time I looked for some answers about my own past."

He nodded. "Not a bad idea."

"But I'm not sure where to begin. I remember what the house looked like—the one I lived in when I was growing up—but not exactly where it was. I thought maybe, if you're willing, you could ask your mother to help me. She might be able to tell me where to go or who I can look up when I want to start asking questions."

He nodded. "I'm willing, and I'm sure she'd be glad to help, but—I told you before, Chessie—she didn't know any gossip about Malachi and a servant girl. I did ask."

"I know. But maybe if I talk to her—if I can remember more details—something I say will spark a memory. Or she might know where the house is, if I describe it. Or she might know someone else who knows."

Brianna spoke up. "What will Lord Dezmen be doing while you're trying to trace your own history?"

I affected indignation. "You can't ask me that! I can't reveal the secrets of his investigation!"

Nico grinned. "Not even who he's going to be asking questions about?"

"*Especially* not that!"

He leaned back in his chair. "Empara. That's interesting, though. It's always been the least fractious of the western provinces. Well, ever since Harold married Tabitha. Wonder if something's happened to stir up trouble."

I spread my hands. "I wouldn't know. Anyway, I think the trail only winds through Empara—I don't think that's where Dezmen expects to find the answers."

Nico eyed me. "Uh-huh. I believe that."

"Well, he doesn't seem to have found any answers yet," Brianna said, pushing herself to her feet. "Now, who'd like some of the sweets that Chessie brought? They look *very* good."

I stayed another half hour, but I was impatient to get home and start packing. As I'd told Dezmen, I wouldn't be bringing much— but I *did* have to organize luggage for three people. It would take a little time.

Once Nico promised to send a note to his mother, telling her to expect my visit, Brianna walked me to the door. Before she opened it, she slipped a small metal pot into my hand. "What's this?" I said.

She smiled. "A little paint for your cheeks and your lips. In case you have an occasion where you want to look pretty."

"I don't think it's going to be that kind of trip."

She glanced over her shoulder at Nico, who was gathering up the dinner dishes. "You're traveling with the Pandrean lord, aren't you?" she murmured. "And you like him, don't you?"

"I never said that!"

She patted my face. "Take it with you anyway. Just in case."

"Just to make you happy," I said, and hugged her goodbye.

"I want to hear everything as soon as you get back."

I laughed and headed out the door. "I doubt there will be much to tell."

"I hope you're surprised."

Scar, Red, and I were at Amanda Plaza shortly after dawn the following morning, which was overcast and cold. I was quickly regretting my tendency to show up early for every rendezvous because I was chilled straight through within ten minutes. Fortunately, on this day Dezmen had chosen to arrive ahead of our scheduled meeting time. He was on foot, followed by his echoes, but not by anyone who might be considered a bodyguard.

"I thought you'd be here already," he said. "We couldn't get the carriage down the street, so we're a few blocks over. Come on. Do you need help carrying anything?" He glanced at the echoes. "*Any* of you need help?"

I shook my head, settled the strap of my bag over my shoulder, and fell in step beside him, all the echoes behind us. "Where's Pippa?" I asked.

"Not bringing her along on this trip."

"So if we're attacked on the road, I hope we can defend ourselves."

"I've hired a couple of guards. Just like I hired the carriage. I'll send them back to Camarria once we're in Pandrea, and we'll go on to Empara in my own coach. It seemed like the fewer people making the whole trip with us, the better."

That sounded logical enough. "All right, then," I said. "As long as you've put a *little* thought into our safety."

He looked down at me soberly. "You must be joking," he said quietly. "*Your* safety has become my topmost concern."

I glanced away, a little embarrassed. And a little pleased. I had been trying hard not to think about those kisses on the bridge two days ago. Naturally, I had thought about almost nothing else. "Well, then," I said, not sure how to answer. "As long as you haven't been careless."

In a few minutes, we arrived at a wide city street where the carriage was waiting, out of the way of traffic. It was bigger than most of the vehicles that trundled around Camarria on an ordinary day, but not as massive as some of the coaches I'd seen bowling along the Charamon Road, carrying large groups of paying passengers—or noble families and their assorted echoes.

Inside there were only two benches, facing each other across a small space, but both benches were long enough and wide enough to comfortably seat three people. I insisted on taking the backward-facing row, and I settled in with my echoes beside me. I was pleasantly surprised to find the interior outfitted with amenities like heavy blankets, jugs of water, a bag of dried fruit, and a couple of loaves of bread.

"We'll stop as often as you like, but I've found that it makes the trip easier if there are some comforts for the road," Dezmen explained. I heard a few noises as our bags were lashed to the back of the coach, and in a few moments we were under way.

We passed the first hour or so of the trip with desultory conversation, looking out the windows and commenting on city landmarks as we passed them. *Have you ever been to the southern market? It's a lively place... So that's the silver bridge everyone talks about? It just looks gray and ugly to me... Cormac took us to a theater production there one night. The play was marvelous, but the whole building smelled like mold.*

We fell silent as we finally made it to the city limits, passed the warehouse district where Scar so often worked, and headed out at a pretty good clip in a southwesterly direction. I calculated it would take us four days to reach the border of Pandrea, and another half-day or more to make our way to Dezmen's property, assuming he lived anywhere near the center of the province. It was hard to imagine being able to come up with enough conversation to fill so many hours. I thought my best hedge against both awkwardness and boredom would be to sleep as much as I could.

I had just wriggled on my seat a little, trying to get comfortable enough to start napping, when Dezmen reached into a pocket of his greatcoat and pulled out a book. "Do you like Narmier?" he asked.

"Do I like what?"

"Fenton Narmier," he said. "He's my sister Darrily's favorite writer."

"Oh," I said. "I've never had much time for reading, though Brianna is always giving me books."

"When we were children, every time we were on a long journey, my father would read out loud to us in the carriage," Dezmen said. "It was a way to keep us reasonably quiet and well behaved."

I was trying to remember. "Don't you have a bunch of sisters? All with echoes? That must have been a big carriage."

"My father and Darrily and I would be in one coach, and my mother and younger sisters would follow us in a second one," he explained. "My other sisters weren't interested in books, but Darrily and I loved them, and we've both developed the habit of reading because of my father. Even now, I sometimes look forward to travel just because it's the only time I get a few days to sit and read for hours at a time."

"Oh," I said again.

My lack of enthusiasm made him smile. "I think you'll like this one," he said. "It's about a girl who dresses up as a boy and gets mistaken for the prince."

"She gets mistaken for Cormac? Or Jordan?"

"No, no, it takes place in a made-up country. Haven't you ever read any fiction?"

"I told you. I never had much time."

He opened the book and smoothed down the first pages. "Let me read for a while. If you don't like it, I'll stop. But let me get through a chapter at least before you decide."

"I'm sure it will be fine," I said. It would be better than trying to talk for four days, at any rate. Besides, he probably wouldn't even notice if I fell asleep while he was reading.

I squirmed into a more comfortable position, eventually resting my shoulder against Scar's shoulder and my leg against Red's. Now that we were free of the city, the road had leveled out and the ride was smoother, though I expected that to change as we crossed some of the emptier miles between major provinces. Still, the rocking motion of the coach and the sheer tedium of travel were already combining to make me drowsy. My eyes were half closed as I nodded to Dezmen across the narrow space that separated us. "Let's hear it," I said.

He cleared his throat. "'Chapter One. I didn't really think about it when I saw the footman's clothes drying on the line. I just thought, "If I was wearing his uniform, no one would even notice me. I'd be invisible. Aren't servants always invisible?" I was tired of being noticed everywhere I went, so anonymity seemed like a welcome change.'"

Dezmen was right; I enjoyed the book from the very beginning. I forgot to be sleepy, I forgot to fret about what I might find in Empara, I forgot to feel embarrassed and weird and hopeful as I was cooped up for half a week in a confined space with a man who had made it clear how much he liked me. I wouldn't have said that the hours flew by, but they certainly passed in an agreeable fashion, and I was almost reluctant to stop for lunch because we were in the middle of an exciting chapter. But hunger and a keen desire to get out and walk off some of the stiffness of travel persuaded me that lunch was a very good idea.

When we were back inside the coach to resume our trip, Dezmen offered me the book. "You can read the next few chapters if you like," he said.

I eyed it warily. "I don't think I'd be very good at it." When I noticed his expression, I added, "Don't you dare ask me if I know how to read!"

He grinned. "I wasn't going to! Though there would be no shame in it if you couldn't."

I snatched the book from his hand. "Angela made sure I had all the skills and knowledge any lady required, even a low noble," I said. "I can read and do sums and sew a straight seam. I used to be able to play a few songs on the harp, too, but I haven't touched one in so long that I'm sure I couldn't produce a note."

He leaned back against the cushions. "Good," he said. "I just finished chapter seven. So start with the first page of eight."

I flipped to the proper place, took a deep breath, and started reading. I was a little self-conscious about my voice and my pronunciation, and there were a couple of phrases I stumbled over because they were the sorts of words that people never used in ordinary conversation, but I found that, once I got into the rhythm of it, I didn't mind reading out loud. Twice the story became so intense that my voice dried up and my eyes skimmed ahead just so I could see what happened next. Once I even turned the page so I could finish the whole scene.

"Hey. Not fair. I want to hear the story, too," Dezmen complained.

I shushed him with a wave, still scanning the words. "You already know the story. You've read the book before."

"But I can't remember."

I ignored him until I finished the chapter, then I sat back in satisfaction. "Well! That was even better than I hoped."

He nudged me with his foot. "Come on. Back to the book."

By the time we reached the inn where Dezmen wanted to stop for the night, my throat was a little sore and my tongue felt strangely thick. He took the book from my hands as we pulled up in the stable yard. "I don't trust you not to stay up all night reading it without me," he said.

I gave him a straight look. "When I'm in my own room. By myself."

"That's what I meant."

So he wasn't going to try to seduce me. It was both a relief and a disappointment. I gnawed on that thought as the servants carried in our bags and Dezmen finalized the transaction with the innkeeper. What did I want from the Pandrean lord? We came from such different places in the world that I didn't entertain the thought we could have any kind of permanent connection, but even a temporary one could be full of delights. He was handsome and charming and funny and kind. Even if he didn't make me a part of his life forever, I couldn't imagine that he would repudiate me with disdain once he grew bored.

He wouldn't become the kind of man who shoved a pregnant housemaid out the door. He wouldn't turn out like my father. I wouldn't end up like my mother.

If I wanted him, I could have him, for a while at least, and no doubt enjoy myself very much. Then I would be sad for a while once he moved on, but sadness was a given. You expected pain when you let someone into your life; it was an inescapable part of the bargain. I tended not to be afraid of pain. I'd had enough of it in my life already, I knew how to endure it till it faded.

So why was I resisting the idea of falling into bed with Lord Dezmen?

Partly, I thought, because I wanted to prove—to him and to myself—that I didn't have to be interested in him just because he was interested in me. He might be a noble lord and I might be a working-class woman, but I didn't have to swoon over his face and his money and his manners. This would be an unequal relationship in so many ways that I needed to have that one single advantage—the ability to say I didn't want it—if I was to have any power at all.

And partly it was because I liked having him flirt with me and show he wanted me; I didn't know how long I could expect those attentions once he was sure of me.

And partly it was because I wasn't good enough for him. In three or four days we would be surrounded by his family, on property his ancestors had owned for generations, and I didn't want him to suddenly be mortified by my very existence.

For all these reasons, it seemed best for me to keep my distance as much as I was able.

The innkeeper snapped his fingers at a servant and motioned for us to follow him. "Upstairs," he said, leading the way. "Our two very best rooms."

In a few moments, we were settled in. Judging by the chamber I was given, the "best rooms" were designed for travelers with echoes: There was one luxurious bed in the center of the room and three narrow ones lined up beside it. The landlord turned to me with a grimace.

"I hope this is all right," he said. "The smaller beds are comfortable enough, and we don't have any other rooms that sleep three."

I skipped over to Red's body and gave him a bright smile. "After spending all day in the coach, I could sleep on *rocks* and feel grateful," I said.

I moved over to Scar's head and spoke in my deepest voice. "I'll let my sisters share the big bed while I take one of the small ones. I never care where I'm sleeping."

"That's all right, then," the landlord said. "There's a private parlor down the hall. We'll lay out a dinner there in—half an hour?"

Back to Red. "That sounds good. I *have* to wash my face!"

As soon as he was gone, I got all of us cleaned up, though I couldn't do much about our wrinkled clothing. I knew some people thought travel was glamorous, but I had never found it anything except wearisome, inconvenient, and numbing.

Still. One day done. And it had not gone so badly.

When Dezmen knocked a little while later, the three of us stepped out into the hall to meet him and his echoes. "Food's ready if you're hungry," he said.

"Starving. Let's go."

During the meal we talked idly about the trip, the book, and how far we might get on the journey tomorrow. I found myself yawning long before my usual bedtime. You wouldn't think that hours of just sitting in a moving vehicle could make you so tired, but I almost couldn't keep my eyes open.

"Do you think anyone has followed us this far?" I asked, shaking my head to clear it.

"I was wondering the same thing. I thought I might go down to the taproom to drink a beer and see who else might have checked in for the night. If I spy anyone with a villainous face who's watching me too closely, I'll assume that he was set on our trail by Malachi."

Alarm woke me right up. "Gorsey. Do you think someone might try to murder us in our beds? You'd be much easier to kill *here* than in the royal palace."

"My impression is that we're only at risk when we come too close to discovering some key piece of information. I don't *think* Malachi wants to start piling up corpses if he doesn't have to. But make sure your door is tightly locked." There was a short pause. "Or you could sleep in my room if you want. The six of us should be able to fend off one or two attackers."

I felt myself flush, whether from embarrassment or gratification it was hard to say. But I tossed my head and gave him a minatory look and said, "I prefer to take my chances, thank you very much."

He grinned and stood up. "Well, you can consider it a standing offer for the duration of the trip," he said. "Anytime you feel afraid—or lonely—or bored—or, you know, anything—just come find me. I'll do what I can to put you in a better frame of mind."

I couldn't help it. I started giggling and I couldn't stop. The invitation was so offhand and casual that I wasn't flustered and I couldn't be offended. "That's so generous!" I exclaimed, also coming to my feet. "I'll let you know if I suddenly need—cheering up."

"I hope you do."

The six of us walked the short distance to my bedroom door, then Dezmen and his echoes nodded and continued on down the stairs. I looked after them a moment before entering my room. As soon as Scar and Red were through the door, I carefully locked it behind us. Then I glanced around at the space, which suddenly seemed big and empty, and I couldn't keep myself from sighing.

CHAPTER SEVENTEEN

In the morning, we were on our way again directly after break-fast. The day was slightly warmer than the one before, perhaps because the skies weren't so overcast, or perhaps because we were farther south. However, in virtually every other respect, the second and third days were repeats of the first. We read, we talked, we took two rooms for the night, and we flirted warily over dinner, though we slept alone with our echoes. And the next morning, we were again on our way shortly after dawn.

The only difference was that at the end of the third day, we veered off the Charamon Road and took a southerly highway that was a little rougher and narrower than the main route that tied the whole kingdom together. Early in the evening of the fourth day, that road delivered us directly into Pandrea.

There was no river or mountain range or geographical fea-ture to mark the border, though Dezmen pointed out a signpost on the road. I hitched forward to peer out the window and get a better look at the landscape. For some time now, we'd been traveling through progressively flatter countryside, but here in Pandrea it seemed like the acres rolled out for miles without any hills or rock formations to interrupt them. Most of the land clos-est to the road was a tangle of overgrown green, but not far in the distance I could spot field after field of cultivated farms. Some of them were full of dry stalks from crops that had already been scythed down; others looked like they held winter wheat or other plantings almost ready for a second harvest. Pandrea was legend-ary for its rich soil and fertile fields. They said there had never been a drought or flood season so severe that Pandrea had truly suffered.

I watched the land roll by for a mile or two, but the scenery didn't change much, so after a while I settled back against my seat. "It seems very serene," I said politely.

Dezmen grinned. "A peaceful land for a peaceful people," he said. "It's not as dramatic as Orenza or Empara—or even eastern Banchura, which is right on the ocean—but there's a calm, productive, methodical happiness to the province. At least, that's how it's always seemed to me."

"Do you miss it when you're gone?"

He nodded, then he shrugged. "There's always an underlying air of excitement in Camarria. Even when there aren't murder attempts and betrayals! There's the sense of much important activity occurring, and there are always people coming and going at the palace, and you could walk the streets and find something to entertain you at any hour of the night or day. Pandrea's not like that. None of our cities are even half as big as Camarria, and the smaller towns are fairly sleepy unless it's market day. When I'm at my estate, I could go for a couple of weeks and not see anyone except the servants—unless I make an effort to socialize. It's a very different life."

"So you have your own property? I don't know how the high nobles divide up their assets."

"My parents and my sisters live at the manor house in the middle of the land my father owns. I have a smaller property about five miles away."

"You'll inherit the manor house eventually?"

"I will, or one of my sisters. My father hasn't decided yet. I imagine it will depend a good deal on who takes a husband or a wife that my father approves of—and produces heirs quickly enough to suit him."

He was laughing as he said it, as if his father's eccentricities amused him, but I gave him a sharp look. "And if your father *doesn't* like your bride? You could be left penniless?"

"No, the house I live in now is mine outright, and each of the girls will be endowed with some of the land my parents own jointly." He looked me straight in the eye and said, "So you needn't fear that the minute my father meets you, I'll be disinherited and left on the streets to scramble for a living."

I felt a hot blush prickle across my skin. "I wasn't thinking anything of the sort!" I lied. "I hardly think I'm any kind of factor in your future! I was just trying to understand how it works."

"Ah."

"But are you worried that the manor house won't go to you? Will you be disappointed if it doesn't?"

"I don't know," he admitted. "I enjoy the peace of the countryside—but after a month or two, I get restless. I've traveled the length and breadth of Pandrea, and I've visited all the other provinces at least once. I wouldn't mind spending half my time on my estate and half my time in Camarria. I couldn't do that if I owned my father's property. It takes someone who's willing to commit most of his time and energy to it every day."

His answer made me happier. If my very existence destroyed his credit with his parents, at least he wouldn't be entirely miserable. "Maybe your sister Darrily would be a better choice, then."

He laughed. "Darrily is even more restless than I am. If she had her way, she would live in Camarria or Banch Harbor the whole year round. No, if it's not me, it's most likely to be one of the younger girls. But there's time yet. My father's still keen for the life, and I don't see that changing soon."

I glanced out the window again. The sky was beginning to bruise with night; I didn't think we could travel much longer and still see the road. "When will we reach your property?"

"In about half a day. We can't make it tonight. In fact— Yes, here it is! The inn where we'll be spending the night."

We pulled into the courtyard and Dezmen handed me out of the carriage. I noticed right away that the ostlers were all Pandreans; so was the servant who came out to fetch our luggage. We passed through the taproom on our way to find the proprietor, and everyone seated at the tables or waiting on the tables was Pandrean. So were the landlord and his wife, who greeted Dezmen with the familiarity of longtime acquaintances.

Red and Scar and I were the only light-skinned people I could see in the whole place.

It was an odd feeling, disorienting. I drew closer to my echoes and slipped into Red's body because that was the incarnation in which I always felt most prepared to deal with the looks and comments of strangers. Keeping my expression impassive, I glanced around. Were the servants and the patrons eying me sideways, trying to get a glimpse of my face without staring outright? Did they wonder what had brought me here, did my presence make them uncomfortable, did they think they'd have to keep an eye on me because I might be a source of trouble? I had never paid too much attention to the Pandreans I saw on the streets of Camarria—because you could see all kinds of people in the royal city, people from every province and even from some foreign nations, and all of them had their own distinctive looks—but still I had always noticed when one of them walked by. I wondered if they usually felt the way I was feeling now—as if all eyes were upon them, as if they didn't belong. It was a strange and unsettling thought.

The landlady, at least, didn't seem to find me troublesome. She smiled as she led the way to a staircase and up to the second floor. "Lord Dezmen stops here often, but I don't recall that he's ever brought company with him," she said. "Especially a pretty girl!"

Still in Red's body, I returned an easy smile of my own. "Don't be imagining a romance! My friends and I have been doing some work for him in the city, and he thought we could get more done if we came to Pandrea. Where it is *much* quieter than I anticipated."

She laughed. "I'm sure it is! There's always some bustle here at the inn, but even so it hardly compares to Camarria. But then, nothing can."

"You've been to the city?"

"A few times. I have a brother who lives there. He loves it. But after a week or so, I have a headache that won't stop until I'm back in the countryside."

"I wonder if it will be the opposite for me. I'll have a headache from all the silence!"

She laughed and unlocked a door to usher me into a room. It was small enough that the two medium-sized beds took up most of the space, but the curtains were a merry yellow and the rug was a warm riot of color, so it had a cheerful aspect. "Lord Dezmen's room only has the two beds also," she said. "But we can bring in cots for the echoes, so this nice young man can share his room. I'm afraid we don't have any other open rooms tonight."

"I'm sure Lord Dezmen would be happy to have my friend sleep over," I said, managing not to laugh. "We'll sort it out! Thank you so much."

As soon as we'd all cleaned off the grime of travel, we headed back downstairs, where the landlord had cleared off a table for six. This was a small place with no private parlors, so we sat in the middle of the public space and ordered our meal. I thought the girl who waited on our table was trying hard not to stare at me and the echoes, though she was very polite. She even flirted slightly with Scar, who winked at her in response.

As soon as she'd walked away from our table, I slipped back into Chessie's head and said to Dezmen, "So is this what it feels like for you?"

"Is this what *what* feels like?"

"Being the only person who looks like you in the entire building. Or, I don't know, in the entire *province.*"

"Ah." He glanced around, as if he hadn't noticed that my echoes and I were the only ones with pale skin tones. "It's a shock the first time it happens," he admitted. "My father always had dealings with merchants from Alberta and Thelleron, so I'd seen plenty of people who *weren't* Pandrean from the time I was a boy. But the first time we traveled to Empara City—I do remember staring. Everyone looked so *odd*. I was pretty young, so it was a while before I realized they thought *I* was the odd one."

"Did it make you feel uneasy?"

"Not fearful, no. Pandreans tend to be respected across the Seven Jewels because they've always had such good relations with the crown. But it did make me feel like a—a curiosity, I suppose. I remember a little girl came up to me once and just wanted to touch my face. Her mother jerked her away, telling her not to be rude. But a lot of other people couldn't stop staring, which was just as rude. And I've had women approach me simply because I'm Pandrean, simply because there's some status in being seen with a Pandrean man. *That* made me feel uneasy."

I grinned. "It sounds horrid."

"Darrily revels in it," he said. "She wears dresses in shades of yellow and gold—colors that really show off her skin—and she carries herself like she's the queen of the whole realm. She loves it when people practically trip over themselves to be introduced to her. She's a flirt, as you might have guessed, but she's really in her element when she's outside of Pandrea."

"She has a lot more self-confidence than I do, then."

"Darrily has a lot more self-confidence than most people."

The meal was good, the waitress continued to smile at Scar, and I became a bit less self-conscious as the evening progressed. Maybe if I stayed in Pandrea for a week or a month or a year, I would stop noticing how different I looked from everyone else.

Of course, I had no plans to extend my stay in Pandrea for any length of time.

After the meal we returned to our rooms, which were across the hall from each other. Dezmen laughed as he unlocked his door. "The efficient proprietor has already brought up some cots," he said, opening the door wider so I could glance in. "So send Scar on over anytime you like and he can have the second bed."

"I think we'll be able to work out an arrangement of our own," I said.

"Let me know if you change your mind."

I couldn't think of an answer to that, so we stood there for a moment outside our separate doors, each waiting for the other to come up with something to say.

"I guess I'll see you in the morning," was the best I could manage.

He and his echoes filed into his room. "I guess you will."

Shortly after noon the next day, we arrived at Dezmen's estate. We'd spent most of the hours in the coach arguing. Well, that word was too strong. Disagreeing.

He thought I should introduce myself as a woman with two echoes. I refused categorically. "Why would I even *think* of doing that?"

"Let's see—because that's what you actually are?"

"But I don't want anyone to *know* that."

"You don't want anyone in Camarria to know. Fine. But here in Pandrea, why not practice what it feels like to be a noblewoman with echoes? You're not acquainted with a soul here, so you can resume your old life the minute we leave. Unless you find you like the new one."

"See, this is the way secrets get unraveled," I said to him. "You pretend to be one kind of person under one set of circumstances, and another kind of person under other circumstances. But when you least expect it, suddenly those circumstances intersect. Someone who met me in Pandrea will show up at the Packrat in Camarria and ask where my echoes are. You *know* that's the way it would happen."

"Since the only people you're likely to meet are members of my family, and none of them, I assure you, would frequent the kinds of establishments that Jackal runs—"

I shook my head. "I'm not doing it. I've managed to survive this long because I'm careful and I'm consistent. I'm not going to risk all that just to make you happy."

"This isn't about making *me* happy," he said, sounding nettled. "I just thought it might be an interesting experiment for *you*."

"In fact, I'm going to remove *all* of the risk," I said. "I'm not even going to meet your family. You say your house is about five miles away from theirs? Good. I'll stay there while you ride over and visit with them."

He looked disappointed. "You don't want to meet them? But they'd like you. And you'd like them, my father and Darrily in particular."

Why? Why would they like me? Why wouldn't they be wondering why one of the heirs to the estate was consorting with an urchin girl who could never quite scrub the dirt of the city off her face? "I think I will be more comfortable remaining in the background as some professional acquaintance you're traveling with—someone you don't have to explain," I said. "Would you have introduced Pippa, if she'd come with us? Jackal?"

"Pippa—maybe not," Dezmen admitted reluctantly. His face lightened. "But Jackal? Absolutely. My father's always liked a rogue. And I have no doubt that when it suits him, Jackal can be as entertaining as sin. He'd have the whole dinner table listening to him, spellbound."

"He would," I agreed. "But I wouldn't. I don't want to try."

He pressed the point a little longer, and came back to it later after we'd sat in silence for about an hour, but I was adamant. I felt strange enough here in Pandrea, with my pale skin and my undefined relationship with a high noble. I didn't want to become an object of intense curiosity—or hostility—as that noble tried to explain exactly how I had become enmeshed in his life.

As we pulled up in front of his property, I was even more glad I had made this decision. I had envisioned his estate as something along the lines of Jackal's Crescent Lane house, but in better repair and situated on an extensive, well-kept lawn. But I had lacked imagination. It was at least two times the size of Jackal's house, a rambling, four-story manor covered with climbing yellow roses and surrounded by an intricate garden. Very little was in bloom this late in the season, though a few of the roses still glowed like opals against the silver-gray of the stone, but it was easy to picture how glorious the place would look at the height of spring.

"It's *beautiful*," I exclaimed, staring out the window. "How do you ever bring yourself to leave?"

"It *is* beautiful," he agreed. "Which is why I'm always happy to come home. But—" He shrugged and didn't finish the sentence. Mentally, I completed it for him. *It's not enough.*

Clearly he had never been running for his life, fighting for his food, praying for some kind of sanctuary, any kind of safety, if even for a night. Or this *would* be enough for him. He'd never want to leave.

I saw the front door open as our coach swept up, and a footman or a butler or a steward stepped outside, waiting for us. He was, of course, Pandrean. I was gripped by a moment of doubt.

"Do your servants know I'm coming?" I demanded. "What did you tell them?"

"They know I'm bringing company to the house. I didn't specify what kind of company," he said. "Since you don't want to be a noble with echoes, I think it will be best to explain you as a professional acquaintance. That way no one will know what to expect of you. You can be as rude and unfriendly as you like."

That made me grin slightly. "And Scar and Red? I could say she's my maid, I suppose, though she's actually dressed better than I am—"

"A maid would be expected to dine in the servants' hall and conform to patterns of behavior that are even more strict than those laid down for nobles! No, you will all be professional acquaintances. And perhaps Scar and Red will be too unwell to want to leave their rooms."

He had scarcely finished speaking before the carriage came to a full stop and the door was opened a second later. "My lord," said the footman/butler/steward. "It is very good to see you again."

"You, too, Jankins," Dezmen said, climbing out of the carriage. As soon as his echoes were on the ground, he turned to offer me a hand. "I've brought some guests with me, as I mentioned I might."

"Yes, my lord."

"This is Chessie Bur—Burkelow. Chessie Burburkelow," he said, stumbling over the name he had manufactured on the spot. I felt my blood run chilly through my veins as I realized he had been thinking of me as Chessie Burken. Chezelle Burken, even.

My true name. Which *no one* had ever said aloud in my presence.

I glared at him, both for the near mishap and the ridiculous appellation that I was now stuck with. Then I tried to gather my dignity as I turned to nod at Jankins. How was one supposed to address servants? "Good afternoon," was all I said.

"Welcome to the house, Miss Burburkelow," he said.

Scar and Red had managed to climb down from the coach without any assistance. I hurried to introduce them so that I could determine what they were called, but I discovered it was not so easy to produce reasonable names on the spur of the moment. "These are friends of mine," I said. "S-Scarborough and—and Rita. Uh, Morrissey."

"One room for Miss Burburkelow and another for her friends, preferably near each other," Dezmen said. "The Morrisseys are unfortunately suffering from travel sickness, so I think they might be glad to retire to their rooms and stay there."

I skipped over to Red's body and leaned against Scar's arm. "It's just that my head hurts so much," I murmured. "I think if I could just lie down and sleep, I'd be better."

I switched to Scar, patted Red on the back and kissed her forehead. "It's been a long few days for both of us," I said in my raspiest voice.

"Of course," said Jankins. "We have rooms ready. Let me summon some footmen to help with the luggage."

Dezmen gestured for me to precede him through the door into the wide hallway, so I did, and the rest followed. I looked around as quickly as I could, trying not to appear like a country yokel who'd never even seen the palace. From what I could tell, the interior matched the exterior, being full of warmth and whimsy and touches of homey color. There were cobalt blue tiles on the floor in the hallway, intricate paintings on the walls, baskets of flowers just inside the door, and a burnished wooden stairwell leading up the four stories. It seemed like the sort of place you would expect to hear laughter drifting over from rooms just out of view.

A neat, middle-aged woman bustled over. "Don't all of you look exhausted!" she exclaimed. "Who'd like a late lunch and who would just like to lie down?"

There was another round of introductions—the woman was known simply as Grillis—and she instantly took charge of my echoes and me while Dezmen went off with Jankins. She showed us to adjoining chambers on the second floor, each of them the size of my entire apartment in Camarria and holding twice as much furniture. Red instantly stretched out on the bed and looked ready to fall asleep, and Scar sat beside her, yawning. Grillis and I hastily retreated to my room.

"I think they'll take luncheon in their room, if it isn't too much trouble," I said.

"No trouble at all! And you? Lunch in your room or downstairs?"

I hesitated. "If Lord Dezmen is eating downstairs, I'll join him. If he's not, in my room, please."

"He'll eat in the smaller dining hall. He always does. Everything will be ready in half an hour. Shall I have hot water brought up for all of you first?"

"That would be most appreciated."

As soon as the water and my luggage arrived, I cleaned myself up and dug through my bag to try to find clean clothes. This was another reason I didn't want to meet Dezmen's family. I only had one outfit with me that might be almost barely acceptable to wear in a polite drawing room, and even then the housekeeper's dress was probably just as fine as mine. And I hadn't brought matching outfits for Scar and Red, because it hadn't occurred to me that I should. There was no possible way I could attire us like an original and her echoes. Even if I wanted to, I couldn't play the part Dezmen had hoped I would play.

And, of course, I didn't want to.

He was already in the dining hall when I went downstairs and Jankins kindly led the way through a short maze of hallways and parlors. The "small" dining room was bigger than my bedroom but otherwise not particularly imposing. There were only two place settings at the long table, directly across from each other and right before a large window that overlooked the grounds out back. This view showed more gardens, complete with walking paths and a few ornamental stands of trees. There might have been a water feature on the far edge of the lawn before it gave way to the wilder acres of meadow and woodland.

"What a lovely home you have, Lord Dezmen," I said as I took my place across from him. "For some reason, I hadn't pictured you as much of a gardener. But this rivals the botanical gardens where we met in Camarria."

"I can't take much of the credit. My mother oversaw the laying out of most of the flower beds when she and my father lived here before I was born. I've managed to maintain the plan she created, but I haven't added to it. My skills don't lie in that direction."

A noiseless footman offered us platters of cheese, bread, cooked meats, and fruit, and I helped myself to liberal amounts. I was starving. When he withdrew, I spoke around a mouthful of food. "Angela and I had a garden. No flowers—just a few rows of vegetables. I used to like to dig in the dirt, but I don't think I've touched a seed or a trowel in ten years."

"Do you ever miss country living?"

I shrugged. "It was so long ago. A different life."

"Well, feel free to stroll through the gardens here while I'm gone. Pluck as many flowers as you can find. Though it's not the time of year for flowers."

"Are you going over to your parents' house this afternoon?"

He nodded. "And possibly tomorrow morning. They'll want me to stay for dinner, but I—"

"Don't worry about me," I interrupted. "I've just spent *days* with you in the carriage. I won't miss you at all while you're gone."

He grinned. "Just when I think you couldn't extend me another courtesy, you surprise me with the depth of your generosity," he marveled. "Then make yourself free of the entire house while I'm gone."

"So how long do you think we need to stay here?"

"My father will have accounts he wants to go over with me, and land business to discuss, but that shouldn't take more than a few hours. I don't see any reason we can't leave tomorrow by around noon."

"And how long from here to Empara?"

"Maybe three days to the border of the province. And then—it depends on where exactly we're headed. You said your cousin has given you directions to his mother's house. Do you know where the closest town is?"

"Yes, she lives by Amilloch."

"Oh, I've been there. It's near where Queen Tabitha's family has its estates."

I nodded. "Tabitha was already married to Harold by the time I was born, but Angela took me by the Devenetta property once show me where the *queen* used to live. She seemed to think I would be very excited about seeing it, but I wasn't."

Dezmen grinned. "Children. They never realize what's important in life." He sipped his water. "Interesting, though, that all these people—Malachi, Tabitha, your cousin—all lived in the same vicinity."

"Well, you said Tabitha's parents insisted that the king hire Malachi, so they had to know the Burkens for a long time," I answered. "And Malachi is Nico's uncle—his father's brother. Nico says his mother wanted to stay near the Burken family so Nico could have all the advantages that might come from knowing them."

"Seemed to work out for him," Dezmen said. "If he's the inquisitor's assistant."

"He's too kind to have such a job for long," I said.

Dezmen looked unconvinced. "Maybe. Most people have a side that isn't as kind as you'd like to think."

That was an opening hardly to be overlooked. "Do you?"

He thought about it. "Under the right circumstances, could I be cruel? Oh, I think so. I've just never been pushed to a drastic limit." He gestured at the walls around us. "I live in luxury. I have a loving family. I'm not persecuted. I haven't been betrayed. I've had no *reason* to develop malevolence."

"You still could have," I pointed out. "Just because there's something twisted inside of you."

"I could have," he answered, "but I don't think I did."

I leaned my chin on my hand and regarded him. "So you're just the dull, respectable person you appear to be, with no grim secrets and no hidden desires?"

He made an ironic half-bow across the table. "Yes, exactly. I'm pleased that you see me so clearly."

I laughed. "You must admit it makes you sound somewhat boring."

He seemed to be struggling to put a thought into words. "I don't look at it that way," he said. "I think all the advantages I've been given—the wealth, the ease, the sense of honor—I think I have to put them to good use. Or else *I'm* the one doing the betraying. If I just live a life of idleness, I have wasted the gifts that were lavished on me. That's why I am happy to be doing this investigation for the king. I am glad I can be of some use."

Now I tilted my head. "And have you been of *some use* to the king before now?"

He tried to hide a smile. "Perhaps. And my father before me, perhaps."

"That *does* make you more interesting," I said. "Can you tell me any of those stories?"

"One or two, maybe." He touched a napkin to his lips. "But not now. Now I need to head to my parents' house and meet with my father. Perhaps when we're back in the coach tomorrow."

"This could be better than the Narmier book."

He laughed. "Not quite." He came to his feet. "Like I said, wander as you like throughout the house and grounds. I'll be back late and gone again in the morning. Plan to be under way again by noon."

"I will."

After he left, I headed upstairs to check on the echoes. Servants had brought them a tray of food, but I had left them in a slumberous state, so they were still lying on the bed, curled up together, until I nudged them awake. I sat with them while they polished off the meal, but I kept glancing at the bed and thinking how comfortable it looked. I was sure the one in my own room was just as inviting.

As soon as they were done eating, I had them lie down again, headed to my own room, and stretched out on the bed. It was even softer and more luxurious than I had expected. I hadn't slept well during our travels, since the mattresses at the inns had sometimes been hard or lumpy.

"Time for a nap," I said, rousing just enough to strip off my outer clothes before settling back in under the covers. In moments, I was asleep.

Hadn't locked the door. Hadn't left a weapon within reach. It was the first time since I was a child that I could remember falling asleep in an utter, unquestioned belief of my absolute safety.

CHAPTER EIGHTEEN

It was morning before any of us stirred again. When I went to get dressed, I found that Dezmen's servants had busied themselves on my behalf, cleaning, repairing, and pressing every item of clothing except the ones that were actually on my body. I had to assume they had done the same for Scar and Red as well. Now I was even more regretful that the quality of my wardrobe wasn't higher.

And more relieved that I hadn't tried to pass myself off as a noblewoman and her echoes.

Scar and Red accompanied me downstairs for breakfast and then outside to the back gardens, where bright morning sunshine made a valiant effort to chase away the persistent chill. We promenaded down the pathways, walking slowly, looking for the last lingering blossoms of the season. Because Dezmen had said I could, I plucked a scarlet rose and tucked it behind Red's ear, and picked a yellow flower that I couldn't identify and merely held it to my nose to enjoy its sweetly delicate fragrance.

Not until we turned back toward the house did I realize that someone had joined us in the gardens and was standing on the main graveled path, waiting for us to see her.

I came to a sudden stop but allowed Scar and Red to continue on a few more paces before stumbling to a halt. I had just enough presence of mind to make sure Red reached for Scar's hand, but most of my attention was focused on the woman before us.

She was Pandrean, clearly a noble, and probably about my age. Her black hair was combed back in a style that showed off the angles of her face; her silk dress was a figured gold, accented

233

with an embroidered blue shawl wrapped around her shoulders for warmth. Opals glittered on her earlobes, around her wrist, on her fingers, at her throat. Her eyes were the same amber shade as Dezmen's. Behind her stood two echoes, dressed exactly as she was, watching me with exactly the same expressions on their faces.

At a guess, this was Dezmen's sister Darrily.

"Hello," I said cautiously. I resisted the urge to blurt out, *I'm not a thief! Your brother told me I could pick as many flowers as I wanted!* I was betting she wasn't there because she was worried about the garden.

Her eyes flicked from me to my echoes, and I had a moment of cold terror wondering if she was comparing our faces and realizing how similar they were. But then her gaze settled fixedly on me for a moment before she said, "You must be Chessie."

I nodded and gestured at my echoes. "And those are friends of mine. Scarborough and Rita."

"My brother mentioned them," she said, still studying me, "but you're the one whose name came up most often."

I flung my consciousness into Red and, still hand in hand with Scar, strolled closer to the newcomer. "Are you Lady Darrily?" I asked, peering at her curiously, then taking a moment to glance at her echoes. "You're *much* prettier than Dezmen said."

That made her laugh, which made her even prettier. "I don't think I want to know how he described me!" she exclaimed. "Brothers can be so completely—unappreciative."

I smiled. "I don't have a brother, so I don't know, but I think you might amend that to 'men can be so unappreciative' and still be right."

I bounced quickly to Scar and gave Red an indignant look. "Hey. I compliment you all the time."

Returning to Red's body, I lifted a hand to pat Scar's cheek. "When I *ask* for compliments."

"You can train lovers to say all the right things," Darrily agreed. "But there's no training a brother."

Back to Scar. "That makes us sound like dogs or horses."

Darrily laughed again. "No, no, no. Much more complex."

Back to Red. "Can I train you to sit and talk with me some-where?" I said, tugging on Scar's hand. "I think the lady would like to visit with Chessie."

Darrily didn't even bother with a polite protest. "It was lovely to meet you," she said, watching my echoes head to a bench close to the house.

I was back in Chessie's head before she turned that smile on me. "Have you seen all the gardens?" she asked. "Or would you like to walk some more?"

"I'd be happy to keep walking," I said. She and I fell in step down the gravel path, her echoes trailing behind. When we had gone a few paces, I said, "But I wonder. What did Lord Dezmen say about me? Since it's clearly made you curious."

"I think it was the fact that he was trying *not* to talk about you that caught my attention," she said. "He was being cagey about everything, in fact. Though he admitted he was doing some work for the king, and, of course, my father knows better than to press him on *that* topic! But he told us about some of his adventures, and he would say something like 'Chessie thought—' and then he would stop a moment and then go on with, 'Well, *I* thought it didn't feel right, either.' After someone does that three or four times in one conversation, you start to notice."

"He probably just couldn't figure out exactly how to explain the work I've been doing for him."

"No, he explained it just fine when I asked him outright, 'Who's Chessie?' He said, 'She runs errands for one of the better-known criminals in Camarria, who has also been roped into my investiga-tion.' And then he talked excessively about Jackal, and why Jackal's been so helpful, and how much my father would like Jackal. Instead of giving more details about Chessie, which I think he would have been perfectly happy to do if Chessie was just some business acquaintance with a colorful background."

"I'm not so colorful," I demurred.

"That's not the point."

"The point is you're horrified at the notion that your brother might have developed an affection for me," I said in a flat voice.

I was staring down at the path, but I felt her quick glance in my direction. "Not horrified. Not even surprised," she said. "Dezmen has never cared for society ladies. All my friends would swoon over his graceful manners and his beautiful eyes, but he never displayed the slightest interest in any of them. He thought they were shallow and ridiculous. But the governess my mother hired for my sisters and me? Dezmen could talk to her for hours. And she was one of the plainest women I have ever seen."

"I think he likes smart people. I assume she was highly educated."

"Yes, and not remotely frivolous. He was very depressed when she took a job with one of my mother's friends instead. All the other girls he's ever liked have been much the same. Different in some fashion. Funny or intelligent or creative. He tried to learn to paint once when my father hired a woman to do portraits of the whole family. He was never any good at it, but he obviously loved spending time with the artist."

"Your parents must worry about his marriage prospects if he shows such lamentable taste in women," I said. I looked briefly her way, then down at my feet again. "Of course, he didn't marry any of those unsuitable girls, so maybe not."

"I do think they worry somewhat," she agreed. "Though they're both a little unconventional themselves. I doubt they'd disinherit him if he brought home a barmaid he'd met in Camarria." I could hear the sudden smile in her voice. "In fact, they probably expect it."

I wanted to say, *Well, I'm not a barmaid*—but sometimes I was, and anyway, that wasn't the point, either. "So why are you telling me all this?" I said. "Does Dezmen even know you're here looking for me?"

She laughed again. It was a sound like silver and honeysuckle on a moonlit night—dreamy and beautiful. It was hard not to at least smile in response, but I managed to refrain. "He doesn't, and he'll be very annoyed when he finds I've been here. I was just curious. I wanted to see what kind of person you were."

"You can't tell that in five minutes."

"You can tell a lot," she argued. "For instance, you can tell that I seem silly and self-absorbed, but that I'm much more observant than some people think, and I love my brother and I want him to be happy."

I wheeled around to face her, and we came to a halt between a pair of tall green shrubs. She didn't look at all discomposed by my stormy expression. "I can't tell that at all," I said rapidly. "Maybe you came over here to tell me it's just fine if your brother falls in love with me. Maybe you hope he does, and you hope he runs off with me because then your parents will leave *you* all their money and all their property."

"If you knew my parents, you would realize how funny that is," she replied calmly.

"Or maybe you came over here to warn me away, but once you saw me, you realized I wasn't the right type to attract your brother, so you knew you didn't have to worry. Or you—"

"Well, *that's* not true, at any rate," she interrupted. "You're exactly the type I expect him to fall in love with, except so much prettier than the other girls."

"I don't know why you're telling me all this," I said stiffly.

She tilted her head to one side, studying me with an expression so similar to Dezmen's that it was eerie. "Because I love my brother and I want him to be happy," she repeated. "I don't know if you're the one who *can* make him happy. I can't tell *that* in five minutes. But if you are—I want you to know that it will be all right. Because Dezmen said something that made me think you're pushing him away."

I couldn't imagine how a fact like *that* had been dropped into a conversation that wasn't entirely, minutely about what kind of relationship I had with Dezmen. Even *Chessie insisted that we get two rooms at every inn* suggested that we had been thinking about other arrangements. "My life is complicated enough already," I said. "Dezmen just makes it more complicated."

"Other people tend to do that," she said. "Life is much simpler when it's just you." After a moment she added, "But it's worse."

You have no idea what you're talking about, I wanted to say. Simple was better. Simple had always worked for me. Know your role, know your risks, know your terrain. Limit your circle of acquaintances to those you think you can trust, but never trust them entirely. Never relax and never reveal.

Dezmen had already caused to me to bend and splinter all of my own rules. Falling in love with him would shatter them.

"Well, it's been interesting to talk to you," I said, pivoting on one heel to head back toward the house.

She followed my lead but gave me another quick sideways glance. "And now I've made you angry. That wasn't my intention."

"Not angry. Just puzzled. I'm not used to people interfering in my life."

"Oh, people are *always* interfering in mine!" she said. "You mean that's not acceptable behavior? I didn't know!"

She laughed again, the sound so infectious that this time I couldn't hold back a grin. "People tend to leave me alone," I said.

"I apologize for upsetting you. But I *am* glad I had a chance to talk to you. And I hope you have a very good trip back to Camarria." She gave me another one of those sideways looks. "Or wherever you're going next."

"If Dezmen didn't tell you, I certainly won't."

She sighed. "No. Even though I've just met you, I can tell you're not the kind of person who gives secrets away."

Now I was the one to laugh. "You're right! You *are* observant!"

"Anyone could tell that," she assured me.

By this time, we had reached the bench where Red and Scar sat, apparently deep in conversation. Once we were a few feet past them, I slowed down as if I wanted to rejoin my friends, and we both came to a halt. "It *was* interesting to meet you," I said, this time with a little more sincerity.

She held out a hand impulsively; her echoes did the same. I reluctantly took hers and ignored the echoes. "And *so* interesting to meet you," she replied. "I hope you'll come back for a visit some-day—when you can tell us some of the details of your adventure."

I wondered if she meant the adventure of this particular trip or the adventure of my life. Either one would probably shock her to silence. But what where the chances that I would ever return to Pandrea? "I'll look forward to that," I said, because I had to say something.

She smiled, squeezed my hand and dropped it. "Travel safely! Goodbye!"

I took a seat next to Red and watched as this surprising young woman and her echoes disappeared through the back door into the manor. Darrily hadn't asked me not to tell Dezmen that she'd come by, but I didn't think I would mention it anyway. I didn't want to repeat the conversation to him, I didn't want to detail my own reactions—and I didn't want to hear him talk about governesses and artists and the other unusual women who had caught his attention in the past.

I couldn't tell if I was miffed or reassured to learn that I fit neatly into his romantic pattern. I couldn't help but wonder what made me different. Or maybe I *wasn't* different. He hadn't married any of those other girls, after all, and there was no reason to think…

I shook my head. A dangerous direction for my thoughts to be tending. I needed to finish my packing and be ready to set out the minute Dezmen returned from his father's. I waited a few more minutes, to be sure Darrily was gone from the house, then I pushed myself to my feet and led Scar and Red back inside. It was time to set out, finally, for Empara.

Four days later, right around noon, we pulled into the town of Amilloch. I was kneeling on the floor of the carriage so I could get a better view out of the window, as I had been doing almost since the minute we had crossed into Empara a day ago. My emotions were in such turmoil that it was hard to sort them out; I couldn't tell if the pressure in my chest was pain or longing. *Empara.* I had never thought to come back. I had never expected to find that scared little girl waiting for me behind every bend of the road.

Much of our travel had been down narrow passages winding through the heavily forested tracts of land that furnished most of Empara's wealth. It was late enough in the season that at least half of the trees were either bare or flaming with autumn colors, but plenty of them still flaunted their cloaks of vibrant and variegated green.

It was impossible to describe to anyone who hadn't been to Empara on a summer day how dense, how impenetrable, how all-encompassing that green could be. Even when sunlight could work its way through the interwoven susurration of leaf and branch, it merely spattered the treetops with bright shocks of beauty, as if shaking emeralds down from an overstocked sky. If you stood too long beneath one of those spreading canopies of relentless color, you would have a hard time distinguishing other shades; you would imagine the air itself was green, and it was infiltrating your lungs, and tinting your skin and your blood. Sometimes you would swear you could taste it.

That had not been our experience today, but I still knelt at the window and remembered the flavor of summer.

It had almost been a relief to break through the woodland and come to more cultivated parts of the province, though even the farms were separated by patches of forest, and every village was sheltered by a windbreak of trees. We passed fewer lumberyards and more stockyards as we moved deeper into the territory, but there was never a moment where, at least in the distance, you couldn't see a stand of pines or a mass of hardwoods.

Amilloch was the largest town we'd come to since we crossed the border. It was an easy blend of the provincial and the sophisticated, since it was not only a market town, but also the seat of local government; both farmers and nobles came here to do their business, replenish their supplies, and socialize with their friends. It was a busy place with a welcoming air.

We used to come here, Angela and I. Not often, because she was always cautious about where and how often she showed me in public. But two or three times a year, when she needed something she couldn't barter for with the neighbors or buy from the traveling peddlers—or when, I suspected now, the solitude and the secrecy and the isolation grew too much for her to bear.

"Do you recognize the place?" I heard Dezmen ask from behind me.

I nodded, and then I shook my head. "Some of it. The big plaza with the clock tower up front—that was always here. And all of the buildings on the main street look familiar. But a lot of it looks new."

"Well, the whole province has prospered since Tabitha married Harold," Dezmen observed. "And while Amilloch isn't as big as Empara City, I'm sure that a lot of the new money has flowed down its streets. So I'm not surprised the place has been built up somewhat."

I glanced at him over my shoulder. He had been remarkably understanding about my fascination with the unfolding countryside. He hadn't bombarded me with questions, hadn't wondered aloud how strange this all might feel to me. He'd merely tossed me a pillow to place under my knees so I could stare out the window in comfort.

"When I was a little girl, even the shortest journey seemed to take forever, so I can't judge distances," I said. "How close is Amilloch to the Devenetta estates?"

"Twenty or twenty-five miles—a day-trip there and back," he said.

"And they still live there?"

"Tabitha's parents? Yes. And two brothers and a sister, I believe, though some of them may have established their own households by now."

I pushed myself up into a crouch and then back onto the bench to sit beside Scar like a normal passenger. "Nico's mother only lives about thirty minutes outside of Amilloch, he said. He was going to send her a note to tell her we were on the way."

Dezmen was watching me. "Do you want to go straight there? Or find our inn first and take a break from traveling?"

I grimaced at my rumpled clothing. "Let's get cleaned up so that we can look halfway presentable when we meet her."

The establishment where Dezmen had booked us rooms was small and discreet, not like the fancy inn we passed as we clopped down the main street. "I didn't think it would do us any good to run into other nobles I might know, since we're on a rather delicate mission," he explained.

"I'm much more comfortable in a smaller place," I assured him.

He smiled. "I admit, that was another consideration."

It was both irksome and endearing to realize that he knew me so well.

Our rooms were small, overstuffed with beds, and side by side along a narrow hallway. Neither of us spent much time getting ourselves and our echoes freshened up, but I at least felt better once my face was washed and I'd put on slightly less wrinkled clothing.

I was downstairs a few minutes before Dezmen, and I conferred with his coachman, studying a map of Empara along with the directions Nico had scrawled to his mother's house. "Should be simple enough to find," the coachman said as Dezmen and his echoes emerged from the inn.

Dezmen helped me into the vehicle and said, "Then let's go talk to the widow Burken."

CHAPTER NINETEEN

Nadine Burken lived in a large cottage just one turn off the main road. Angela had taken me there a few times when I was a child, so I could gawk at the house where some of my relations lived, but now I assessed it with an adult's more knowledgeable eye. It was a well-maintained and charming property, the home of someone who didn't have to worry overmuch about money. The grounds around it, while not extensive, had all been put to good use with vegetable gardens, a chicken coop, and a small barn that probably held a milk cow and maybe a horse. My guess was that even though her husband's family had been horrified that he had married a merchant's daughter so far beneath his station, they'd made sure she had had enough to live on while she was raising his son. That, or Nico's father had amassed a certain amount of wealth before he died and he'd left it all in her hands. It still couldn't have been easy for Nico, straddling the line between low noble and a more inferior class. Clearly, being taken up by Malachi had been the best thing that could have happened to the fatherless boy.

Or the worst thing, depending on what you thought of Malachi.

There was no formal drive, so the coachman pulled up along the side of the road and waited for us to disembark. "I'm leaving Scar and Red in the carriage," I told Dezmen when my echoes made no move to get out. "I don't want her to be distracted by wondering about them."

"What does she know about you?"

"What Nico's told her. And anything else she might have found out, if she started asking questions."

"We might solve two mysteries on this trip," he said.

I gave him a sharp look. That had been in the back of my head this whole time, but I hadn't expected his mind to be running along the same lines. "We're here to investigate Leffert's death," I said.

His only reply was, "Ah."

I couldn't ask him what that meant because the front door had opened, and a woman stood there waiting for us to come up the walk. She was on the shorter side, a little plump, with dark blond hair pulled back into such a large bun that I was sure her hair had to fall to her waist when it was unbound. She looked to be about fifty years old, and a lot of the worry of those fifty years could be clearly read in the lines of her face—but there was still a fair bit of merriment around the lips and eyes.

"I never thought I'd see a Pandrean lord come calling at my house!" she exclaimed. Her voice had a soft country burr I instantly recognized—and it instantly made my gut twist with homesickness. Angela had always insisted that I speak with *proper* elocution, as she did herself, but all our neighbors and everyone we encountered in the nearby towns had had an accent just like Nadine's. I had completely forgotten the sound. "And with two echoes! Gorsey!"

Dezmen bowed to her as if she were Tabitha herself, the echoes perfectly imitating his movements. "I hope we haven't called at an inconvenient time," he said. "We can come back if you tell us when."

"No—no—not inconvenient at all! It's just more amazing than I was expecting."

"My name is Dezmen, and as you've guessed, I'm from Pandrea," he said. "I was led to believe that you might be expecting my visit. My companion is originally from Empara."

Nadine was finally able to drag her attention from her exalted guest and focus it on me. For a moment I could tell that she forgot Dezmen entirely because she stared at me so intently. I let her get her fill, though I wondered what she was looking for and what she saw.

"So you're Chessie," she said, coming partway down the walk to get a closer look, practically brushing past Dezmen and his echoes to do so. "Nico told me he met you. Told me the story you told him."

"I don't think you quite believed me."

She was still staring, but not in a rude way; merely, she was trying to take in as much information as she could. "I didn't *disbelieve* you, but I'd never heard anything you could take as proof one way or the other. Malachi was a cold man—even his own brother would have told you that. There were almost no stories about him at all."

"I can't say I'm surprised," I said.

But she couldn't take her gaze off my face. "You have her look, though—it's uncanny. Your eyes could be her eyes."

I felt my heart try to clamber out of my chest. "My—my mother's eyes?"

"No. I'm sorry. Mirrabet. My husband's sister. You look like your aunt. If she *is* your aunt, if you *are* Malachi's daughter."

"I truly believe I am."

I felt Dezmen take a step closer. "Maybe Mirrabet would like to meet Chessie," he suggested.

I threw him a look of horror. If Mirrabet learned of my existence, Malachi would discover it, and then my life was as good as forfeit. Though perhaps Malachi would be less likely to murder me once he realized his sister knew about me; my death would be harder to explain away.

But Nadine was shaking her head. "Mirrabet never wanted anything to do with Nico, and he was legitimate," she said. "She allowed me into her house while my husband was alive, but once Brandon died, she cut the connection. I don't see her welcoming any baseborn children into her life. I'm sorry if that sounds cruel."

"It sounds like what I've come to expect of the Burkens," I said. "Nico's father must have been much different from everyone else in his family."

For a moment, a sweet smile came to her mouth, and I saw the laughing girl she must have been when she snared a noble's heart. "Brandon was the youngest, and everyone loved him, and that made him a loving man," she explained. "I knew it would be catastrophe for him to marry me, but he insisted that his family would welcome me, and I allowed myself to believe him. It turned out that

I was right and he was wrong, but he never stopped believing that they would change their minds." She shrugged. "He died before they could. And once Brandon was gone, it was like I was dead to them, too. Some of them accepted Nico, and some of them didn't. Malachi was good to him—which went a long way toward making me like Malachi. Or *almost* like him."

"He is not a man who inspires easy affection," Dezmen murmured.

She laughed. "No, he is not! But maybe he has a softer side after all. If he fell in love with his housemaid—"

"Or forced himself on her," Dezmen said gently. "Which might fit the circumstances better."

Nadine nodded soberly. "Yes. Well, that doesn't redeem him at all." She studied me again. "I can't get over how much you look like Mirrabet."

I didn't know exactly how to answer that, so I just said, "I'm glad I do, if that means you believe me."

"I think I have to." She gazed at me another moment, then gave her head a quick shake. "But we needn't stand out here in the cold garden and talk about it! Come inside, and I'll make you some tea."

In a few moments we were clustered around a small table in a gleaming kitchen, sipping tea and trying out an assortment of sweets. The interior of the house was just as charming as the outside. The rough stone walls were covered with quilts and bits of framed lace, the crooked mantel held an assortment of vases and flowerpots, and the smells of lemon and sugar and yeast drifted down every hallway. I had never seen the inside of Malachi's house, though Angela had driven me past the outside often enough, but I was already sure I would have much preferred to grow up in this cottage than that manor.

"I mean, you *could* go introduce yourself to Mirrabet—she might have grown more tolerant with age," Nadine said, as if our conversation hadn't been interrupted by ten minutes of handing out plates and distributing food. "It's been years since I've seen her. She might have changed."

I blew on my tea to cool it. "If I expected her to listen to me, I'd have to present some proof," I said, not bothering to mention the "proof" hanging around my neck at this very moment. "My mother's been dead more than twenty years, but maybe some of the other servants would remember her. Is anyone still at Malachi's house?"

Nadine shook her head. "It's been closed up for a long time. Malachi used to come back a couple of times a year when Brandon was still alive, but he hasn't been here for at least a decade. You'd think he'd sell the place or at least rent it out, but as far as I know, there's not a soul on the property."

"What about the servants who used to live there?" Dezmen asked. "A butler or valet? They might remember Chessie's mother."

'They might, but—there was some story—" Nadine sat there a moment, a slight frown on her face, trying to conjure a memory. "Right before Malachi took the job in Camarria—oh, I remember! The steward and the housekeeper were both found dead in the kitchen. The steward stabbed her, so the story went, then cut his own throat. The whole floor was covered in blood. My husband was still alive then, so I got all the details. Apparently, they had become lovers, then they had a quarrel, and then one day he grabbed a butcher's knife and did them both in. It was quite shocking."

My whole body chilled so drastically that I cupped my hands around my mug just to try to absorb some warmth. I didn't risk a look at Dezmen, but I was sure he was thinking the same thing I was: *The steward didn't kill the housekeeper; Malachi murdered them both.* The servants knew something he didn't want them to repeat. I couldn't imagine that that secret was the fact of my existence, but the timing was certainly about right.

Maybe my mother had told the servants she was pregnant before she revealed the truth to Malachi. They were shocked at how poorly he treated her and unwisely showed their disapproval. In a rage, he killed them both. Or maybe it was even worse. They hadn't expressed any opinions at all—what servant would have the nerve to condemn Malachi?—but his anger and his shame were so great that he murdered them anyway.

Or maybe he had another secret that he didn't want shared with the world. Something more important than my small life.

"That does sound horrible," Dezmen said, realizing that I was temporarily unable to summon words.

"Maybe that's why Malachi doesn't like to return to the manor. He's the one who found them," Nadine said.

I'm sure he was, I thought. "Well, it doesn't sound like there's anyone who might remember my mother," I said.

Nadine briefly touched my wrist. "I'm sorry. And you came all this way to find out."

I shook my head. "That's not the only reason I made the journey. I'm also here to help Lord Dezmen with his investigation."

Now Nadine returned her attention to Dezmen's handsome face. Her gaze flicked briefly to his echoes, crowded together at an even smaller table in the corner of the kitchen. I thought it must usually serve as a chopping block. "What are you investigating?" she asked.

"A matter for the crown," he said. "I'm sorry I can't give details."

Nadine looked impressed anyway. "I understand."

"I have a piece of jewelry that includes a pattern picked out in emeralds. I've been led to believe it's the pattern adopted by some small temple in central Empara. I would like to find that temple. Even if you don't recognize it, we thought you might know someone who could point us in the right direction. Maybe the priestesses at some *other* temple nearby."

She laughed. "Now I'm intrigued! I suppose you can't tell me *why* you want to track down the design."

He smiled and shook his head. "I can't." Reaching into his pocket, he pulled out the envoy pin and unwrapped the thin cloth that covered it. Sliding a fingernail under the top half, he pulled off the heavy lid and placed the pin before Nadine on the table.

She studied it a moment. "May I touch it?"

"Certainly."

She carefully picked it up and tilted it back and forth so that the hidden emeralds glittered like a cat's eyes. "I *have* seen this design before," she murmured. "But where? It was a long time ago. I was with Brandon, and Nico hadn't been born yet. We were at—we were at—oh, I know." She sat back in triumph, laying the pin back on the table.

I could read the astonishment on Dezmen's face. Could it really be this easy? "Truly? You know this heraldry?" he demanded.

She nodded. "Yes! It belongs to a tiny little temple probably a half-day's ride from here. We were there when Brandon's cousin got married. *She* was only a low noble, like all the Burkens, but she was marrying a high noble, so his family insisted that they have a small wedding in the most out-of-the-way place imaginable. This was the design embroidered on the altar cloths."

"How can you remember that?" Dezmen made no attempt to hide his amazement.

She laughed. "I'll tell you how! I was pregnant with Nico and very sick to my stomach. When I told the priestess I was going to vomit, she showed me into a little room off the main sanctuary. I spent the whole wedding ceremony kneeling on the floor, throwing up into a bucket." She tapped the envoy pin. "I was kneeling on a rug with this pattern woven into it. I felt like I was staring at it for hours."

Dezmen moved restlessly; I could feel his excitement. "Do you remember where the temple is?"

"Not precisely, but it shouldn't be hard to find. It's right on the edge of the Devenetta family estates."

I felt myself jerk upright, and I could see Dezmen stiffen. "'Devenetta'? Queen Tabitha's family?"

"Right. Brandon's cousin married one of Tabitha's cousins. Apparently this little temple had served the Devenettas for generations, although they always went to a larger temple in Amilloch for Counting Day and other big events." She smiled again. "But they went to the *little* temple to celebrate any weddings to low nobles."

Dezmen drew a deep breath. "Well. It ought to be easy enough to find, then. Thank you so much for your help. I had envisioned spending weeks trying to track down this particular detail. How can I thank you for solving my mystery?"

She laughed. "You don't have to thank me! Although I would very much enjoy it if you stayed for dinner. I don't often have the opportunity to cook for others."

"We couldn't impose," I demurred. In truth, I surmised that, like me, Dezmen was itching to leap up, run for the coach, and set the horses galloping toward Devenetta land.

I saw Dezmen glance at the window, gauging time of day by the angle of the sun. I realized that we probably only had a couple of hours of daylight left—and that we couldn't know how long it would take us to find the temple—and that we couldn't know how long we might need to poke around before we stumbled upon something, *anything*, that looked like a clue. "We'd be happy to stay for a meal, but only if you let us help," he said.

I managed to summon a look of derision. "*You* can cook?" I demanded.

"No, but I can cut things up if someone gives me directions, and I can carry heavy pots, and generally make myself useful," he replied.

Nadine made shooing motions designed to send us from the kitchen to the adjoining front room. "Nonsense, you and your echoes will just trip me up," she said. "Go sit down while I put a few things together. This won't take long."

The four of us slipped into the other room and found seats on a worn sofa, a rocking chair, and a somewhat rickety three-legged stool. We hitched them close together so Dezmen and I could hold a whispered colloquy.

"*The Devenettas!*" I breathed. "What can that mean?"

"I don't know," he answered just as quietly. "But if there really is some plan to assassinate the prince, and Malachi is involved, could the Devenettas be involved as well?"

"You said Tabitha's parents wouldn't agree to the marriage unless Malachi was brought onto the inquisitor's staff. Could they have been plotting all this time?"

"I suppose—but Harold and Tabitha have been married more than twenty years! And while they seem to hate each other, in all other respects, the marriage has been a success. It enriched Empara. It calmed down the rebellion among the western provinces. It produced an heir ..." His voice trailed off.

"What? What are you thinking?"

"Harold has been in correspondence with the king of Ferrenlea, discussing a visit from one of the foreign princes. Maybe they've been talking about arranging a marriage between Princess Annery and an heir from Ferrenlea."

"But the princess is still a child! Is she even twelve years old yet? Twelve?"

"Something like that. But just because they're discussing marriage doesn't mean they'd have a ceremony until she's of age."

"I don't see why Annery's marriage would make anyone want to kill Cormac."

Dezmen shrugged. "Maybe someone started thinking Annery might make a good queen in her own right. Here in the Seven Jewels, not across the ocean in Ferrenlea."

"If Cormac was dead, Jordan would be next in line for the throne."

Dezmen shrugged again. "If you're going to murder one prince, you may as well murder two."

I took a deep breath. "That would require you to have a terrifyingly cold and ruthless heart."

"I think a man who would murder his servants probably could summon just the right amount of ruthlessness."

I tried not to shiver. "I have no proof but—as soon as she said it—"

"I thought the same thing," he interrupted. "Malachi killed them. I don't know what he was trying to conceal, but he obviously will go to any extreme when it comes to keeping his secrets."

"Then I think it's even more important," I said in a low voice, "that he never finds me again."

"I agree."

It wasn't long before Nadine called us back into the kitchen, where—in addition to making us a meal—she had expanded the main table so that the echoes could sit with us. She'd laid out five place settings of cracked and mismatched china, lit four candles, and placed two platters and one tureen on the table.

"We'll just eat family style and pass the food from hand to hand, if that works for you," she said shyly as she took her seat. "I know it's not very grand, but—"

"It's perfect," Dezmen said, pulling out his chair as his echoes did the same. "I'm famished."

The food was delicious, and I liked Nadine Burken more and more the longer we sat and talked with her. It was hardly a surprise that the conversation quickly turned to Nico.

"Do you seen him often?" she asked wistfully.

"I usually make a point of dropping by every couple of weeks." I smiled. "We're both in the business of gathering information— except we gather it for different people—so sometimes we help each other out. Other times we just make fun of each other. I like him a great deal."

"He's the most wonderful boy." She sighed. "I had such high hopes for him when Malachi took him up. What *couldn't* Nico do once he was in Camarria? But I've started to think that—well—even though Malachi is working for the king, his profession is violent and vulgar. I don't know if Nico will ever have a chance to take his place in society. And now that he's involved with this serving girl—"

"Brianna," I said gently. "You'd like her. She really loves him."

"I'm sure she does, but so often love isn't enough," Nadine replied. "I should know. I thought it would be, and it wasn't. When I think how much better Brandon's life would have been if he'd married someone his parents approved of—"

"Did *he* think his life would have been better?" Dezmen asked.

"He never said so. He never seemed to have regrets. But I had regrets for him."

Her words made my heart shrink into a tight little ball. I mean, it wasn't like I had planned to pursue this romance—or whatever it was—with Lord Dezmen. I hadn't imagined myself sitting at his table, presiding over his household, hanging on to his arm as we attended events at the palace. But it was distressing to think that if he *did* invite me into his life, if I *did* accept, he would spend the rest of his life wishing he hadn't.

Dezmen lounged back in his chair, completely at ease. "Oh, I don't know," he said. "I think I'd rather marry for love and risk the consequences than marry for my family's sake and end up despising the woman I was stuck with."

Nadine laughed and, in spite of myself, so did I. "Some arranged marriages work out quite well, if both of the parties are agreeable," she pointed out.

"Certainly. And some of them are complete disasters! The most obvious one that comes to mind is Harold and Tabitha."

Nadine sighed. "That *is* a sad case, isn't it? There was no end to the gossip around these parts while he was courting her. Well, you can imagine! Nothing that exciting had happened in central Empara since—since *ever*!"

I tried to assume the girlish tone of someone flighty enough to care about court politics. "Oooh, tell us some of the gossip," I said. "It all happened before I was born."

"Well, Harold's advisors had determined he should marry a girl from the western provinces, but apparently there weren't very many candidates. She had to have three echoes, just like Harold, and she had to be somewhere between twenty and thirty years old, and she had to not be married to someone else. There weren't too many single girls of the right age—because, as you know, nobles tend to marry off their children the first chance they get!—and only a handful had three echoes. I believe there was a girl in Banchura, and two in Thelleron, but Tabitha was the only one in the western provinces who met all the conditions. It was Tabitha or nobody."

"That put her parents in an excellent negotiating position, I would think," said Dezmen.

"The Devenettas couldn't *wait* to make the deal. They've always been arrogant, since they're the richest family in this part of Empara, but the opportunity to be connected to the royal house made them insufferable. They were practically *throwing* Tabitha into Harold's arms."

I looked up at that, to find Dezmen and his echoes frowning. "Really?" he said. "The way I always heard the story, the Devenettas drew out the negotiations for almost a year."

Nadine nodded emphatically. "They did. Because *Tabitha* wouldn't agree. Now, you'd think any girl would be excited about the prospect of becoming a queen, but not Tabitha. She flatly refused to marry Harold. The Devenettas had to lock her up for six months—in a stone tower in a castle, just like the heroine in a children's fable—before she finally agreed. Her parents pretended that they were the ones who resisted the alliance until the deal was sweet enough, but they were just covering for a most disobedient daughter."

"That's some story," Dezmen said. "I wonder why Tabitha was so adamant against the match?"

I glanced over at him. "Maybe because she was young and fanciful and he was old and ugly?"

"He wouldn't have been that old when they got married," Dezmen argued. "Forty, I would guess, or thereabouts. And he's not an unattractive man."

"No, but she was only twenty-five at the time, and beautiful," Nadine said, siding with me. "There were always men flocking around her, and she could have had her pick of any young lord in the western provinces. In fact, it's something of a mystery as to why she was still unmarried at that age, since she'd had numerous offers."

"She was enjoying all the attention," I said cynically. "Who wants to give that up just to become someone's wife? Even if that someone is the king?"

"Well, she did eventually give in—obviously," said Nadine. She turned to Dezmen. "I thought that once she was married and settled in, she might come to appreciate Harold. I never met him, of course, but Brandon always thought he was a good man."

"He is, I believe, and a good king," Dezmen answered. "It seems to me that Tabitha enjoys being queen, but there's never been any affection between her and Harold. Cormac says they despise each other and that it's nothing short of miraculous that they managed to produce even one child together."

"Does the prince dislike her as well?"

"Cormac tends to speak diplomatically of such things, but I believe both he and Jordan avoid her as much as possible."

Nadine sighed. "So then. All the turmoil and heartache and screaming and scheming that went on as Tabitha's parents forced her to accept the king. All that for nothing. No good came of it at all."

"Well, except for peace in the realm," Dezmen said with some astringency. "Which I would count as a greater good than the happiness of one stubborn girl."

Nadine smiled at him. "But then, you are not a romantic."

He put his hand to his heart and made her a half-bow. "I can be, when circumstances require," he said. "But it's true that I rarely find politics a romantic business."

By this time it was nearly sunset, I was sure my echoes were half starved, and I had so much to mull over that I really just wanted to get back to the inn so I could sit and think. Dezmen's thoughts seemed to have been running on the same track because a moment later, he pushed his chair back and stood up. "You have been the most gracious hostess imaginable, but we have taken too much of your time," he said. "Thank you for your insights—and your food—and your delightful charm of manner."

She blushed and stammered and waved off his thanks, and within a few minutes we were on our way again. She had insisted that we take a sandwich for the coachman and a loaf of bread for ourselves, though I was pretty sure Scar and Red would devour the bread before we were out of sight of the cottage. I paused to hug Nadine before stepping out the door; Dezmen gave her an elegant bow.

"Come back if you have more questions!" she called, waving to us as we climbed into the coach. "Give Nico my love!"

"I will!" I responded, waving out the window as, with a few lurching turns, the coachman got us facing the right way on the road again.

"Come back anytime!" she added. "I'd love to see you again!"

I laughed and repeated, "I will!" Then I pulled my head back in the window, and we were on our way to Amilloch.

Dezmen and I sat there in the gathering dark, staring at each other. I was the first to speak. "So the Devenettas *wanted* Tabitha to marry Harold."

"That's what it sounds like."

"They didn't put a whole bunch of conditions in place. They didn't, for instance, say that Harold had to hire Malachi or they wouldn't agree to the marriage."

"It seems doubtful."

"Then how did he end up on the inquisitor's staff?"

"My very question," Dezmen said. "Though I suppose they *could* have made it a requirement of the marriage just because they had so much negotiating power."

"But why would they want to? How did they know him? I couldn't figure out a casual way to ask Nadine."

"I was having the same problem," he said. "But Malachi's cousin was married to a Devenetta. Perhaps that's the only connection there is."

"At any rate, we know there is *some* connection," I said. "Because of the emerald design on the pin."

"I feel certain we'll discover more when we find the temple," Dezmen said.

"Let's hope we learn all the answers tomorrow."

CHAPTER TWENTY

We arrived back at our inn in Amilloch about half an hour later. After our first flurry of speculation, Dezmen and I had fallen mostly silent, each of us lost in our own thoughts. I had finally remembered to hand out the bread to Scar and Red, but I knew they were both still hungry. As we made our way down the hallway to our rooms, I was already planning to go back to the taproom and ask that meals be sent up for the echoes. But then Dezmen smiled at me as we paused outside our doors, and I found myself smiling back.

"I know it's been a long day," he said in a coaxing voice. "But *my* evening, at least, would be much improved if you would agree to sit with me for a while. Your echoes must be starving, and I confess I could stand to eat a few bites. There's a table in my room—not very big, but I think all of us could fit around it if we didn't mind crowding."

I opened my mouth to say no, but the words that came out were, "All right. Give me a few moments to freshen up."

His whole face lit up; his echoes were smiling. "Excellent! I'll go order a light dinner."

Twenty minutes later the six of us were crammed around a table designed to seat four. We'd dragged in a couple of chairs from my room and waved away the proprietor's offer to bring in another table. "It's just for one meal," Dezmen told her. "But thank you."

I'd had a meal at Nadine's barely an hour ago, so I was surprised at how hungry I was; maybe it was just that I could tell Scar and Red were ravenous, and I matched them bite for bite. Dezmen and his echoes ate with similar gusto. Once the meal was over, we redistributed ourselves around the room more comfortably, and I found myself seated on a sofa next to Dezmen, half turned to look at him.

"I don't know why it is," he said, "but food tastes better whenever you share it with someone."

"Really? I've never noticed. Now I'll have to start paying attention."

He smiled. "Or maybe it's just that I particularly enjoy sharing my meals with you," he said. "It will seem very strange to be back in Camarria and not expect to see you every day at every meal."

A not-very-subtle attempt at flirtation. My heart did a hard slam against my chest, but I managed to reply coolly. "If we solve this puzzle tomorrow at the temple, you might not have cause to see me again for *any* meal, ever."

"I hope that's not true," he said seriously. "I hope I'll be able to convince you to keep me in your life in some fashion—no matter what we learn tomorrow."

My voice was still steady. "That seems unwise. Weren't you listening to Nadine? It's foolhardy for two people to—to get involved—if they don't come from the same class and background."

"Well, your background is different, I'll admit, but I maintain you're in my class. Your echoes are proof of that. Though I wouldn't care if you weren't, you know. You think I'm very proper and stuffy, but—"

"But you've always been drawn to the odd girls, the ones who didn't fit in or didn't behave the way a noblewoman should."

"I knew it!" he exclaimed. "Darrily rode over to the manor house, didn't she, and found you? She was gone for a couple of hours and wouldn't say where she'd been, but there's this expression she has when she's done something reprehensible—"

I laughed, which made me relax a little. "I liked her," I said. "I think. She's very blunt."

"She can be. Or she can be completely devious and close-mouthed when it suits her purpose. What did she *say* about me? None of it was true."

"Even the part about you falling in love with unsuitable women?"

"I never saw them as unsuitable," he responded.

"So it is true."

He shrugged. "It's true that I've never been drawn to the women I met through polite society. They always seem to be carefully constructed versions of who their parents want them to be. I'm sure a few of them are genuine and thoughtful and much more interesting than they appear, but I've never been moved to try to find out." I couldn't think of an immediate reply, and after a beat of silence, he said, "What about you? What kinds of men have you fallen in love with?"

Normally I would have returned a guarded answer, but I was too tired to prevaricate. "I don't know that there have been any I've actually fallen in love with," I admitted. "The ones I've permitted myself to be with have been…" I paused, trying to find the common characteristics. "Incurious," I said at last. "They've all been, oh, passionate about life, full of energy and enthusiasm, and happy to share their days with me. But they tended to be more focused on themselves than the people around them. They didn't care that I didn't tell them my secrets. They didn't want to know."

"Even Jackal?" he asked.

I had never confirmed his suspicions about Jackal, so I just laughed. "Don't you think Jackal would be one of the most selfish lovers imaginable? Very brash and full of himself."

"Well, I don't spend much time imagining other men in bed, so I haven't given it any thought," he retorted. "But *incurious* is not a word I would apply to him in most circumstances."

"Perhaps not," I acknowledged. "But Jackal thinks he knows me. So he doesn't need to ask questions."

"Nobody ever knows anybody," he answered. "You always need to ask questions."

"You're right," I said sardonically. "You are a romantic."

He smiled. "You should give me a chance to prove it."

It's better if I don't. The words were whispers at the back of my throat, they lay like candy on my tongue, but I couldn't speak them.

Dezmen would be unlike any lover I had ever taken, I was certain of that. From everything I knew about him, he would be generous, he would be playful, he would take his time. Already he made me feel intriguing and unusual—I could only imagine that he would go to some trouble to make me feel even more precious if we were in bed together.

He would break my heart, of course. Was that a good enough reason to refuse him now?

"I can't see a future for us," I said at last.

He shifted closer, taking one of my hands in his and cradling it against his chest. "Can't you? I can see several. They're all tumultuous—but they're all interesting."

I became aware that my echoes were both turned toward his echoes, that they were all handfast as we were. I had released them after the meal and I had not consciously gathered them up to me again, and yet here they were, synchronized to my motions. As they always were during any time of great stress. Or great excitement.

"All those futures end badly," I said.

He lifted his other hand to stroke my hair. I tried not to lean into that touch as a cat leans into a caress. "None of them do," he replied softly. "In one or two versions, we may decide we don't suit each other for the rest of our lives, but we don't part in pain and anger. I don't have any plans to hurt you. I don't think you plan to hurt me."

"Sometimes it happens anyway."

"Sometimes," he acknowledged. Now he placed his hand behind my head, pulling me slowly forward. I could feel Scar and Red leaning in toward his echoes. "Does that mean you should never take a chance to be with another person?"

"It means you should be careful about who you let get close to you."

His mouth was now an inch from mine. "How careful do you want to be?" he whispered.

Maybe it was the fact that he asked. Maybe it was the fact that the day had been so long—the trip had been so long—I was tired and slightly melancholy and a little lost. Maybe it was because his face was so close and I thought his face was so beautiful. Maybe I was curious or rebellious or lonely or rash. Maybe I was a little bit in love with him.

All of those things. "I don't want to be careful at all," I said, leaning in to kiss him.

Desire kicked through me like a physical blow. His arms closed around me, and it was like being wrapped in heat. I strained against him, wanting to get closer, wanting to feel more. I hooked one leg over his thigh and pressed my hips against his, and felt his whole body react. I felt his echoes react against my echoes, heightening my own sensations, making my body feel even more alive.

"This might be going faster than I planned," he whispered.

"It's not going fast enough," I replied and kissed him again.

His hands were against my back, slightly cupped, as if his fingertips were poised to count each of my separate ribs. There were too many layers in the way; I wanted to feel his flesh against mine. Impatiently, I pulled free of the embrace, earning a wordless protest from him, and pulled my shirt off over my head with one quick motion.

"Oh, now," he breathed. "This is a different kind of beautiful."

I laughed. I felt reckless and daring and, unexpectedly, wildly sure of myself. "Come on. You, too," I said, making an impatient motion.

"Gladly," he said, tearing off his own shirt and throwing it carelessly on the floor. Across the room, our echoes were disrobing with equal abandon. Pretty soon it was going to start looking like laundry day in here.

"Mmmmm," I said, flattening my palms against his chest. His skin was a fine-grained brown, silky and smooth, lightly bunched with muscle and sleek to the touch. I curled my hands around the arched cages of his ribs and felt them expand when he took in a sharp breath. "I have to agree. Beautiful."

He laughed and drew me closer, kissing me again. It was different this time, hotter, more sensuous, bare skin to bare skin. I writhed against him on the little sofa, which was suddenly much too small, before I broke apart with a gusty breath and tugged at his hand.

"Come on. Stand up. All of it off. Everything," I commanded.

I was already on my feet, but he resisted for a moment, grinning up at me. "I never pictured you as being the impatient one," he said.

With one hand, I continued urging him to stand; with the other, I was undoing my own clothes, pulling them down, kicking them aside. "I don't want to think too much," I said. "I don't want to have time to change my mind."

"Well, in that case—" he said, and jumped to his feet. He dropped my hand so he could undo buckles and buttons with alacrity. All around the room, more clothes dropped into piles on the floor.

Completely naked now, he turned and faced me. When I would have stepped back into his embrace, he put his hands on my shoulders to hold me an inch or two away. I could feel the warmth of his body heat the air between us and tickle against my skin. He loosened his hands and ran them slowly from the tops of my shoulders to the bottommost tip of my longest fingers, then slowly reversed the journey. I felt my whole body shiver in response.

When he reached the tops of my shoulders again, he repositioned his hands just slightly, and followed a new line down the front of my chest, detouring slightly outward at the fullest portion of my breasts. He flattened his palms as he traversed the inward curve of my waist and the outward flare of my hips, so I could feel the whole surface of his hands leaving behind streaks of fire. Again, he retraced his path, this time pausing as his hands came to rest on my breasts, covering them completely. He bent down to kiss a spot just above his steepled fingers. I made a sound that I couldn't even describe.

I felt his echoes kiss the exact same spot on my echoes. But it was not like three actions, three reactions, three choked cries. It was one body, more alive than it had ever been, saturated with sensation, sparking with desire. With another of those wordless sounds, I fell forward, twining my arms around Dezmen's back, shifting my weight to one foot so I could wrap the other leg around one of his. I could feel the shock of excitement as the length of my body pressed against the length of his.

"Stop playing. Now. The bed," I breathed, not even trying for coherence.

"But I want to go exploring," he whispered at my ear.

"Explore some other time," I retorted, and lifted my mouth to press it against his like a woman starved for sustenance.

I felt him laugh as he swept me from my feet and tumbled me onto the bed—as his echoes laughed, as my echoes laughed, as we were all one tangle of hands and arms and hair and kisses. We clung to each other and rolled so I was under him and his weight was pressing upon me from above.

"Stay with me," he murmured. "Don't go skipping to Scar and Red. Be Chessie the whole time."

"We're all Chessie," I answered, and then gasped as his body entered mine.

It was like nothing I had experienced before, as if every inch of my skin was being touched at once, as if every part of my body moved with a delirious synchronicity. I had been sleepwalking through every other lovemaking session, pantomiming, pretending. I had felt something, but it had been partial, insufficient, disappointing. This was all of me being loved and all of me responding. I threw off any notion of restraint and moved with Dezmen with a sense of wild abandon. My cry of satisfaction came from three mouths, but it was the cry of a single soul.

Afterward, we lay silent for a few minutes, still closely entwined, me burrowing into Dezmen's dark skin as if into the safest shadow. I felt his hand run rhythmically up and down my back; I felt him drop a kiss onto the top of my head.

"So that's what it's supposed to be like," I said at last.

He kissed my head again. "When you make love to someone who has the same number of echoes? I believe it is. It makes all my other experiences in bed seem—pedestrian in comparison."

I chuckled, then I tilted my head up to look at him. "Wait, so—you've never made love to someone with two echoes before?"

He shook his head. "No."

I freed myself just enough to push up on one elbow. He rolled back to gaze up at me lazily. "I find that hard to believe," I said.

"Young noblewomen with multiple echoes are encouraged to maintain some decorum, so it's not like it's easy to find bed partners," he said with a wicked smile. "I admit I've had liaisons with older women who didn't have reputations to worry about—but none of them had two echoes. A couple of them had one."

"So then—what did—if your echoes always do exactly what you do—"

He was still grinning. "Often there's a maid who is willing to provide the missing body. Eager to, in some cases. Some people—men *and* women—are infatuated with the idea of bedding an echo. There's a whole class of prostitutes that specializes in that service."

"Well, then, you should have had ample opportunities to satisfy your curiosity."

He grimaced. "I find myself uninterested in sexual encounters that are only about the body. If I don't know the woman—if I'm not interested in the woman—I can't muster any enthusiasm for the act."

"So it was different? This time? With me?"

He stretched up to kiss my mouth and then settled back against the pillow. "Different because it *was* you, first and foremost," he said. "Your face, your hands, your laugh, all of you. But because of the echoes…" His voice trailed off. "Different in a way I can't explain. Like, I suddenly understand why people could care so much about such a simple act." He watched me a moment. "What about you?"

I dropped back down to nestle against him, turning so my back was against his chest. "My first time ever in bed with the echoes at the same time," I said. "And it feels like I never actually made love before. Or did it fully clothed. Or did it while I was half asleep. And now I know what it's supposed to feel like."

264

He wrapped his arms around my ribs, drew me tighter, and kissed my cheek. "Now I've ruined you for other lovers," he whispered in my ear.

I laughed, but I felt a stab of despair. It was true. Nothing could compare to this experience; it would be pointless to try to re-create this moment of completeness. Once Dezmen left my life, I would be doomed to a dull and passionless existence.

Of course, he was still in my life at the moment, his rough cheek pressed against my smooth one. I tilted my head and sought his mouth with my own, kissing him as if I had just discovered kissing. "Then let's go for complete ruination," I whispered back.

He did not bother to reply, but his actions made it clear that he considered it an entirely satisfactory plan.

I woke in three distinct stages, each following the previous one after a slow beat of comprehension.

It's morning.

I'm awake.

I'm in Dezmen's bed.

I opened my eyes and sat up in one single spasm of alarm to find Dezmen already wide awake and watching me. On his face was both humor and comprehension. He didn't make a move to catch my arm or try to hold me in place.

His echoes all lay there, too, watching my echoes as they sat up in their own beds and stared down in panic.

"Good morning," Dezmen said. "You seemed to sleep well."

"I—" Like a virginal idiot, I clutched the bedsheet to my chest, as if that might make him forget what the curves of my body looked like. "I suppose I did."

He didn't answer, didn't move toward me, just waited for me to decide how I felt about the situation. Against the white bed linens, his face was a dense and delicious brown, the skin of his body a saturated creamy darkness. I was filled with a sudden, urgent desire to run my palms along the rippled topography of his chest.

I took a deep breath. The words were hard to say aloud. "I feel like I want to go running from the room," I confessed. "But I don't know why. I feel like I'm scared. But I don't know why."

Now he lifted a hand, very slowly, so I could flinch away if I wanted to, and he just touched his fingertips to my cheek. "Because when you were a child, you learned that you were only safe if you didn't trust anybody. When you didn't let anyone know who you really were. I know more about you now than anyone you've ever met. And that's terrifying."

"I—I don't think you're going to hurt me," I said, stumbling over the words. "I'm not afraid physically. I just—you are—this is different."

He ran his finger down my jawline and back up to my temple and smiled. "I'm glad I'm different."

"I don't know if I should *be* here," I went on, speaking a little more rapidly. "I don't know if it's good for me or good for you."

"Don't worry about what's good for me," he said. "I'm doing just fine."

"I don't know what happens next. With you and me. With anything. What if things *change?* I don't like change. But what if they don't? This is all—I can't figure out what to do now," I ended unhappily.

"You don't have to figure out the next day or the next year or the rest of your life," he said. Now his hand rested on my shoulder with just enough pressure to make me think it might be a good idea to lie back down against the pillow. I resisted. "Nobody can do that. You just have to decide if you want to be here right now. I hope you do. Being with you makes me as happy as anything in the world has ever made me. I hope being with me makes you feel safe. *And* happy. But I think safe matters more to you than happy. You're so strong so much of the time. So ready to fight. I hope you can be with me and let yourself be undefended."

He was right; he understood me in ways that nobody ever had. It was too seductive—the thought that someone could read my soul and still find it beautiful, the thought that somebody else's heart could be a safe place to come to rest. I did not want to accept his invitation to be weak, but I could not pass up the opportunity to be happy. I dropped the sheet and turned toward him, giving in to the urge to run my fingers along his skin. My hands against his chest, I deftly twisted in bed, dropping one knee over his waist so I straddled him. I felt his body respond instantly to mine.

He lifted both hands to bury them in my hair. In the other beds on either side of us, I could see, I could feel, both sets of echoes replicating our every movement. "We have a half-day's journey ahead of us," he said, teasing. "We shouldn't delay."

I bent down to give him a deep and lingering kiss. I said, "This won't take long."

CHAPTER TWENTY-ONE

About two hours later, we were back in the carriage and headed toward the extensive Devenetta holdings. Dezmen and I occupied one of the benches, me across his lap and his arms loosely around my waist, while the echoes sat across from us. I found this a much more enjoyable way to travel than I ever would have anticipated. Some of the time we were silent, drowsing a little, wordlessly marveling at how good it felt to sit this close, feel this shared warmth. Some of the time we talked, telling inconsequential little stories about things we remembered from childhood, or odd people we had seen on the streets of Camarria, or meals we'd eaten that had been especially memorable. None of it was important and all of it was fascinating. The tales were like the fine background stitchery on an old tapestry; they filled in the gaps, they made the picture complete.

We stopped for a late lunch at a roadside tavern and got more explicit directions to the temple on the edge of the Devenetta land. It was close to two in the afternoon before we turned down the dusty road that the barkeeper had described. It was barely a track through the heavily forested countryside and I had to think it had been months since a vehicle as big as our coach had tried to push its way through. We could hear the constant scraping sound of low-hanging branches brushing against the sides and top of the coach; I was sure I caught more than one muffled curse from the driver.

"I know that many of the temples deliberately locate themselves in remote areas so the priestesses can pass their days in solitary meditation, but this seems extreme," Dezmen observed.

"Maybe the temple isn't even operating anymore," I suggested. "The tavern owner did seem surprised when you asked about it."

"That would be disappointing," he said. "I suppose we'll see in a few minutes."

And, indeed, not long afterward, the carriage emerged from the dense overgrowth onto a small clearing big enough to hold a few small buildings and a couple acres of well-tended gardens. The road—such as it was—appeared to end there as well, with a small circular drive just wide enough for the coachman to turn around.

Dezmen and I disembarked, followed by all our echoes, and took a moment to study our surroundings. The nearest building, a square block of gray stone, was clearly the temple; from the outside it looked to be about the size of a large bedroom suite. The clay roof, a bright terra-cotta, was a cheerful contrast to the aged and pitted stone of the walls. The whole eastern half of the building was blackened with age—mold, I thought, or maybe centuries of smoke from where the priestesses had burned off garden waste. The plain wooden door was half open in welcome, and I felt a nervous leap of my heart when I recognized the symbol painted on the front. A simple triangle accented with other small shapes. Just like the necklace around my throat.

There were two buildings behind the temple, set a little distance off the road. One, about the size of the sanctuary but even plainer-looking, I assumed to be the residence for any priestesses that served there; the other, a wooden hut, was probably used to store gardening tools and maybe house chickens. I didn't think there was room for a horse. Any priestesses who lived there either relied on parishioners to fetch them supplies and ferry them to appointments, or they were very good walkers.

"Looks like the right place," said Dezmen, sounding much calmer than I felt.

"I hope someone is here," I answered.

"One way to find out."

Dezmen and I stepped into the temple, followed by Scar, Red, and his echoes; I noticed all three of the men had to duck just a little to make it through the small door. Inside, it was as dark as dusk since there were only two small windows and neither one was well positioned to catch the afternoon sun. We stood there a moment, looking around, but there wasn't much to see. To my right was another small door, which I was guessing led to the tiny room where Nadine Burken had vomited through a wedding ceremony so many years ago. Before us were about six wooden pews, all facing a low dais. There were no statues of the triple goddess on display, as there were in so many temples, but there were three embroidered hangings on the wall behind the altar, and those depicted the goddess in her familiar poses.

A lone woman sat in the first pew, her head bent in prayer, but a moment after we entered, she rose to her feet and turned in our direction. Even in the dim light, I could see that she was very old, with sparse gray hair and seamed and wrinkled skin. Yet she was wearing the red robes of joy, and when she spoke, her voice was warm and lilting.

"A blessed afternoon to all of you," she greeted us. "Have you come to seek the goddess's benediction or merely to pray?"

Dezmen and I hadn't even discussed what to say to any priestess we found at the Devenetta temple, but I stepped forward, suddenly certain of what I ought to ask. "I'm always happy to receive a benediction, but I have come here with questions that I thought you might be able to answer," I said.

"I will tell you anything I know," she said, slowly winding past the pews in our direction. As she got close enough, I realized her large milky eyes might be partially blind, but even so she made her way to us without a misstep. "I'm Mallory."

"I'm Chessie. He's Dezmen," I said.

"And how may I help you, Chessie?" she asked.

"I was born in this region, but moved away when I was young," I said. "My mother always told me that this was the temple where I received my first benediction. Both of my parents are dead now, and I thought it would be a comfort to see my name in their handwriting. I wondered if you would let me look at the records from the year I was born?"

From the corner of my eye, I could see Dezmen nodding in approval. I must say, I was pleased with myself for having come up with the stratagem. *Something* had occurred at this temple around that time, we just had no idea what, and if I could flip through the pages of its documents, maybe that something would become clear to me.

"You may see any of the records we have, but so many of the early ones are missing," Mallory said sadly. "Imagine, this temple has been standing for three hundred years! But we only have the records for the past couple of decades."

"Why? What happened?" Dezmen asked.

"There was a fire near the altar. All the cabinets where we kept our papers went up in flames. That whole wall was burning." She waved at the eastern side of the building, where I had already noted the smoke damage. "The roof—gone! It took us two years to rebuild."

I risked a quick look at Dezmen, who was frowning. After the trail of bodies we had learned about on our quest, news of a fire seemed highly suspicious. "How awful," I said.

Mallory sighed. "Awful indeed. Worst of all was that the abbess died trying to save the records. We found her body right by the cabinets."

I was sure Dezmen was thinking what I was. *Another murder.* "That's just terrible," I said. "When did it happen?"

"Almost twenty-four years ago," she said promptly. "I remember, because it happened only a few months before dear Lady Tabitha was married to the king. Chezelle loved that girl so much. She would have been so proud to see Tabitha on the throne."

At the name, I started so violently I was sure even half-blind Mallory had to notice. I couldn't bring myself to speak, so it was Dezmen who repeated, "Chezelle?"

"The abbess. The one who died in the fire."

"Such a tragedy," Dezmen murmured. "You have all my sympathy, even so many years later."

I found my voice. "Yes, I am very sad for you—and sad for me that I will not get a chance to see my records," I said. "I don't suppose you kept copies of anything anywhere that didn't burn?"

Mallory wrinkled her forehead, as if remembering something. "No, but—there was one book, of all the ones we had, that survived the fire. Chezelle had kept it wrapped in silk under her bed, because it contained the official notice of her installation as abbess. I believe that book contains about five years' worth of records— we do not perform many ceremonies here, as you might guess, so it takes us some time to fill a volume! You are welcome to look through it if you like."

I didn't feel particularly hopeful, but I didn't see any reason to refuse. We had come all the way to Empara, all the way to this tiny temple hidden away in the great forest, looking for a clue we weren't even sure we would recognize. If there was a chance it was buried in the single saved record book, then I must try to find it.

"I think I would," I said in a hesitant voice. "Maybe—maybe there will be some other document about my parents in your book. I'd like to see it."

"It's in the house, still under her bed—Laurianne's bed now, of course. I'll just go fetch it for you."

She made her way somewhat unsteadily out the temple door while the rest of us found seats. Scar and Red and I sat in the back pew, Dezmen and his echoes in the row before us, turned to face us.

"A fire? The abbess dead? These are not coincidences," Dezmen said the minute Mallory was out of earshot.

"The abbess named *Chezelle*?" I added. "It makes no sense, and yet somehow all these pieces are connected."

"I feel sure the answers are here," he said. "I just don't know if we'll find them."

A few minutes later, Mallory returned, carrying a large and awkward volume. It appeared to be a couple of hundred pages that had been collected between two pieces of heavy pasteboard; holes had been punched in each individual page, and the whole mass tied together with thick gold ribbon. I supposed that allowed the priestesses to add more pages every time they recorded a new event.

"Here you go, my dear," she said, laying the volume in my lap. "I hope you find what you're looking for."

Dezmen and his echoes had stood up at her approach. "Perhaps you could show me around the grounds while Chessie goes through the records?" he said. "It is such a pretty place."

"It is! And with such history," Mallory answered. "Walk with me up to the altar and I will show you the stones inscribed with the names of the founding priestesses."

They strolled to the front of the church, talking softly, while I began turning the pages of the record book. Beside me, Scar and Red moved their hands as if they, too, were leafing through a volume, but I scarcely noticed. The first few documents recorded births and benedictions that had occurred nearly thirty years ago; they were followed by a cluster of death notices that had all been written in the same two-week period. Some kind of plague had visited this corner of Empara, no doubt. The following month had seen two weddings and Chezelle's ordination as abbess. The following month, one benediction and no other activity.

I didn't think I was interested in events that had occurred quite so long ago, so I gently turned a whole sheaf of pages, getting close to the back of the book. I found myself looking at dates from twenty-four years ago. The year before Tabitha married Harold. It was remotely possible that something I was interested in had happened in that time frame, so once again I began examining the documents one by one. I didn't even look up when Mallory, Dezmen, and his echoes filed past me and out the front door.

Here was news of a wedding. A birth. A benediction. Two deaths. Two more births and two more benedictions. Another wedding. Most of the documents had been signed by Mallory or another priestess whose name appeared to be Sasette (it was hard to read her cramped handwriting). But now and then Chezelle's name appeared at the bottom of a certificate in a lovely, flowing script. I assumed Mallory and Sasette were responsible for most of the day-to-day functions of the sanctuary, but that Chezelle presided over the ceremonies when one of the nobles of the region came to the temple.

And, indeed, the next page I turned to was a wedding certificate signed by Chezelle and performed for a member of the Devenetta family. I squinted at it, trying to make out the name of the bride and groom.

Tabitha Devenetta.

And Malachi Burken.

I sat there a moment, so stunned that I almost couldn't comprehend what I was reading.

The abbess of this little temple had performed a marriage ceremony for Tabitha Devenetta and Malachi Burken nearly a year before Tabitha had married King Harold. Since absolutely no one seemed to be aware of this fact, I could only assume the wedding had been conducted in stealth—a favor done by the abbess for the headstrong young noblewoman she apparently had dearly loved.

Tabitha and Malachi had married in secret! That meant she was not free to marry the king after all! Did her parents know that? Did they proceed with the negotiations anyway, knowing they were enabling bigamy, but trusting to the fanatical discretion of all the parties involved that this knowledge would never come to light?

Or—not trusting, as it turned out. Whoever tried to burn down the temple had undoubtedly also killed the abbess in the hope of eliminating all records, all witnesses, all knowledge about the clandestine ceremony.

Had that desperate act been carried out by Tabitha's parents because they were single-mindedly determined to see a Devenetta on the throne? But if they had been willing to murder a priestess to secure their daughter's future, why wouldn't they have been willing to eliminate her low noble husband as well? Or instead?

They would have been. If they were so utterly committed to seeing Tabitha become queen, they would not have let one inconvenient spouse stand in their way.

Therefore, they had not been the ones to kill the poor abbess and set fire to the temple.

It had been Malachi.

It fit, it all fit, it made so much sense that I knew without the faintest doubt that this was what had occurred. Tabitha and Malachi had wed in secret, flouting her family and indulging in some grand forbidden passion. Shortly afterward, Harold had come calling, offering his crown, promising peace in the realm, if only this one recalcitrant woman would take his hand in marriage. She tried to refuse—she delayed with every tactic she could think of except the truth—but eventually she had to give in to extreme pressure and threats of dire punishment. Although, who could say? Perhaps she was dazzled by the king's offer. Perhaps she wanted to marry him, once she'd had time to think about the life she might lead as the queen compared to the life she would lead as a low noble's wife. If she had told her parents the truth, she would have instantly scotched the deal. *She* was the one who elected to keep her marriage a secret.

I frowned. But that made no sense. If Tabitha was willing to marry Harold, if no one but Chezelle knew about the marriage—and if Chezelle was dead—why would the Devenettas keep Harold waiting for nearly a year before Tabitha accepted his suit? Why had her parents locked Tabitha in a tower room for months—"like the heroine in a children's fable," as Nadine had said—if everyone was ready to agree to the marriage?

Because she was pregnant.

My hands went so slack that the book nearly slipped from my grasp, and I had to grab for it before it went spilling to the floor. Scar and Red made scrabbling motions at the empty air.

Because she was pregnant—with me.

My breath was fast and shallow; my thoughts were in such a whirl that I thought my head might skitter off my neck.

Malachi hadn't seduced a housemaid and cast her off—oh, no. He'd sired a child in wedlock, and that child was the obstacle to the greatest honor any woman in the Seven Jewels could achieve.

Tabitha didn't tell her parents she was married, but soon enough she couldn't conceal from them the fact that she was pregnant. Together they concocted the plan—the unwilling bride, the continual delays, the long-drawn-out negotiations. Till the baby was born and bundled off with a faithful servant. Till Tabitha could emerge from confinement, wan and chastened, to accept the king's proposal.

I leaned back against the pew and shut my eyes tight, trying to work out the rest of the details. How much of the truth had Angela known? My parentage, certainly, but probably not the fact that I was actually legitimate. She must have been Tabitha's former governess, or perhaps her personal maid—someone who knew and loved Tabitha very well—to be trusted even with the fact of my existence.

Why hadn't I been killed at birth? Every other impediment had been eliminated with ruthless efficiency. It must have been Tabitha's parents who—not knowing how high the stakes were—insisted I be kept alive. Perhaps they even sent me off with Angela without Malachi's knowledge. That made sense, actually, especially if Tabitha never told them who my father was. The instant I was born and washed and clothed, they set me in Angela's arms and shoved us out the door. They had probably provided funds for my upkeep—maybe even paid for the cottage where we had lived—while insisting that Angela tell no one, not even me, the truth about my mother. But they knew where I was and Malachi didn't, which was why I had lived so long.

Now I opened my eyes and stared around the temple again. For the first time, I noticed the triangle pattern embroidered along the hem of the wall hangings, sewn into the cloth laid over the altar. Three questions still remained. Why had the Devenettas insisted that Malachi accompany Tabitha to Camarria if they didn't know of his connection to their daughter? And how had Malachi discovered where I lived? And why had he decided that—after all those years—I suddenly needed to die?

I didn't know. I couldn't guess. I could hardly think. This one simple fact had not only illuminated the dark and tortuous reasoning behind Leffert's murder, it had completely reordered everything I knew about my own life. Tabitha had been married to someone else when she married the king. And I was the legitimate daughter of a high noble—and a man who wanted me dead.

Behind me, just outside the door, I heard Mallory's voice as she and Dezmen drew closer. "Oh, no, Laurianne has gone into the village for the day. She won't be back until evening."

"It must be lonely sometimes, just the two of you out here by yourselves," Dezmen said as they stepped inside.

Mallory laughed. "But it isn't! Someone comes by at least once a week, and parishioners are always dropping off food. And, of course, there is much to keep us busy. There is always work to do in the garden, and we sew clothing for the poor, and, of course, we must feed the chickens and maintain our housekeeping."

"A very good life," he said politely.

"*I* think so."

I had closed the book and laid it on the bench, and now I was able to come to my feet, though I had to clutch the back of the pew in front of me to keep my balance. My smile was so unsuccessful that Dezmen gave me a sharp look, but Mallory didn't seem to notice.

"Did you find the records you were looking for, my dear?" she asked.

I had to think for a moment to remember what I had said I was trying to find. "My first benediction. No, I'm afraid not," I answered in a quavering voice. Dezmen narrowed his eyes at me. "But I greatly enjoyed looking through the book! I found Chezelle's ordination. And a few other interesting documents."

Mallory sighed. "Well, I'm sorry you came so far for nothing."

For a moment I locked eyes with Dezmen. Now his face brightened with excitement—he could tell I had found something—but he knew better than to ask me what. I said, "I wouldn't say it was for nothing. We enjoyed making the drive, and meeting you, and seeing the temple."

"But I think it's time for us to get going," Dezmen said smoothly. "We have a long journey back to Amilloch."

"Indeed you do! It will be past the dinner hour before you arrive. May I give you each a benediction before you go?"

I finally trusted my balance enough to loosen my grip on the pew, so I stepped over to her and bowed my head. "Please do."

She lifted her frail hand and touched my forehead, my heart, and my lips. "Blessings upon your head," she said. "May the goddess watch over you and bring you justice—mercy—and joy."

"Thank you," I whispered.

She repeated the ritual with Red and Scar, then Dezmen and each of his echoes. By this time, I had started to recover from my stupefaction, and I could feel my amazement building up so powerfully inside of me that at any minute it would spill out in the form of words. Mallory had barely touched the last echo's mouth before I gripped Dezmen's wrist and whispered, "We have to go."

We spoke a few more words of farewell and waved to Mallory as we climbed into the coach. It took off with a lurch down the narrow, rutted road.

As before, Dezmen and I had taken one of the benches, while the four echoes crowded onto the other one, but this time I wasn't lying across his lap. I sat bolt upright, turned toward him at an angle so I could stare into his face. I waited only until we were thirty yards from the temple—until we were beyond any possibility of Mallory overhearing—before baldly telling him what I had found.

"Malachi and Tabitha were married a few months before she wed the king."

He inhaled a quick burst of air and stared back at me. I could tell his mind was working feverishly. "Married," he repeated. "Was she also—was she pregnant?"

I nodded slowly. "I'm guessing she was. That's why her parents locked her in the tower while they negotiated with Harold."

"You're her daughter."

"I think I must be."

"That would explain—absolutely everything," he said. "From the murders of the servants to the existence of your echoes. What evidence did you find?"

"A marriage certificate with their names on it. Signed by Chezelle."

He took in another hard breath. "That would be enough," he said. "Enough to expose them both. No wonder they thought they had to burn the temple and kill the abbess."

"'They,'" I repeated. "Do you think anyone besides Malachi had a hand in all this?"

He nodded at the question, as if had already occurred to him. "You think the Devenettas might have been involved."

"*You* are acquainted Tabitha's parents," I said. "Are they capable of such heinous acts?"

He thought for a moment. "I would doubt it. He's a smart man who's made himself very wealthy. She's always struck me as quiet and devout. Both a little arrogant, as Nadine said, but—killers? It seems so unlikely."

I asked the next question with some difficulty. "What about Tabitha? How much do you think she knew? Did she and Malachi agree that the abbess must die? Or did he make the decision all on his own?"

Why did I care if my mother was a murderer as well as my father? Could I possibly be so naive that I still hoped—after all this time and against all evidence—that one of my parents had cared about me, had been glad that I was born? She had viewed me as an obstacle to her ambitions and at the very least had agreed to see me whisked away into hazardous anonymity. Had she also been cruel enough to plot the death of a woman who loved her?

Dezmen must have sensed some of my turmoil because he took my hands in a comforting clasp. I saw his echoes reach for Scar's and Red's hands. "I don't know," he said in a quiet voice. "I do know she appears to be a cold, unhappy woman. But she's clever. And strong. I have always thought she had an excellent ability to calculate costs and prepare for consequences. But did she sanction murder to smooth her way to the throne? I simply can't judge."

I clung to him. "She named me. After someone she cared about. Surely she wouldn't have done that if she had agreed to Chezelle's death."

"Maybe she didn't even know Chezelle was dead," Dezmen suggested. "If the temple was burned during the time she was locked away, her parents may have kept that information from her, thinking it would upset her."

That cheered me up slightly; it made sense. "If she named me, maybe she...maybe she loved me, at least a little bit," I said. I touched my finger to my chest, to feel the emerald pendant beneath my clothes. It must have been Malachi's wedding gift to Tabitha, as the ring was her gift to him. "Maybe she gave her necklace to Angela so Angela could give it to me when I was old enough. Because the necklace was the most precious thing she had, and I was precious, too."

Dezmen pulled me into his arms and rocked me against him, the motion exaggerated by the sudden jouncing of the coach over a rough patch of road. "Maybe," he said. "At the very least, she wanted you to live."

I turned my face into his jacket and tried not to cry. How could it matter, all this time later, how could I still care? I had always known I was unwanted—even worse, that I was catastrophic, that I had been the ruin of the woman I always envisioned as my mother. But in this version of the tale, my birth was even more calamitous. My existence put the very peace of the realm at risk.

"Her marriage to the king is not valid," I said into his coat. "And the princess is not a legitimate heir to the throne."

"I know," Dezmen said, stroking my hair. "But no one else knows that except Tabitha and Malachi."

That made me look up at him. "That's why," I breathed. "That's why he wanted to kill me twelve years ago. Because the princess was born."

Dezmen nodded. "That would be my guess."

"Even though I didn't know who I was. Even though I never could have unraveled this tangled story."

"You were still a complication. A liability. And it's clear he is a man who has learned to minimize liabilities."

"Did she know?"

"Did Tabitha know? Know what?"

"That he came to kill me?"

Dezmen hugged me tighter. "I can't guess."

"Because she *might* have," I said, trying to sound brave. "Once the princess was born. Once she started thinking about Annery's life, all the opportunities Annery could have—and how all that would be taken away if anyone ever discovered the truth about me."

"Maybe," Dezmen said, laying his cheek on top of my head. "But maybe not. You said that Malachi asked you your name. That means he didn't know it. That means Tabitha never told it to him. That means they never talked about you. Maybe she thought she was protecting you by never telling him you were alive. Never telling him where you were. Maybe he never bothered to look for you until Annery was born."

"I can understand why he would want to protect Tabitha, but why would he care about Annery?" I asked.

Dezmen was silent so long that I glanced up at him again. "There was always some talk," he said. "Why had it taken more than a decade for Tabitha and Harold to conceive a child?"

I pulled myself out of his arms so I could stare at him. "You think Annery is Malachi's daughter."

Dezmen shrugged. "It's a possibility."

"But surely—wouldn't Harold realize—I mean, if he and Tabitha weren't sharing a bed—"

"I think Harold knows very well whether or not the princess is his daughter. He didn't want to cause a greater rift with the western provinces by crying foul—and it didn't matter to him all that much, since he already had Cormac and Jordan as heirs."

"But if Cormac were to die before he married and produced children—"

"Then there would only be Jordan between Annery and the throne."

I shook my head in slow disbelief. "How can one man be so—so *evil?* Think of all the people he has killed! The abbess. Angela. His servants. Leffert. The two men who were hired to killed you—at least we think they're dead. Bertie. And those are just the ones we *know* of!"

"At a guess, I would say he doesn't think he's evil. I'd say that *he* thinks he's protecting Tabitha. Everything he has done has been in the cause of keeping her safe, of making sure her secrets were undiscovered. He might even consider himself heroic."

"You don't go around *killing people* just because you think they might be a danger to the ones you love!"

Dezmen gave a ghost of a laugh and pulled me close again. "No. You don't," he said into my hair. "You *do* try to protect your loved ones, of course. You build houses to keep them safe and accompany them when they head into trouble and argue with them when you think they're about to do something stupid and follow them if they go ahead and do it anyway. Maybe if some attacker has come through the window and is trying to strangle the woman you love, maybe *then* you kill on her behalf. But to commit series of—of—*preventative* murders? Just in case someone might cause you trouble in the future? That's a different kind of love altogether. A crazy kind."

My cheek pressed against his chest, I said in a low voice, "The abbess knew."

"Knew what?"

"That Malachi was dangerous. That's why she hid the book of records. She didn't care about keeping track of her certificate of ordination."

"I wonder if she would have come forward. I wonder if she would have shown the document to Tabitha's parents—or to Harold."

"I don't think so," I said, "or she would have done it the minute the negotiations started."

"Maybe she thought Tabitha would confess the truth eventually. Before things went too far. But I suppose we'll never know."

I straightened up again, but not so much that I slipped out of Dezmen's embrace. "Something else we'll never know. Why the

Devenettas insisted that Malachi accompany Tabitha to the city. If she made it a condition of accepting Harold's proposal, surely they would have realized that he was the father of her child? And if that was the case, wouldn't he have been the *last* person they would have wanted to follow her to Camarria?"

"I've been thinking about that," Dezmen said. "I'm wondering if he's the one who proposed the idea to them, pretending it had nothing to do with Tabitha. Maybe he came calling at the estate one day. Said he wanted to make his fortune in Camarria, and if the Devenettas made that possible, he would do them a favor in return. He would watch out for the young queen—be her ally in an unfamiliar city. He's certainly a bold enough man to have tried to make that bargain even under ordinary circumstances."

"Maybe," I said. "It fits what we know of him—but I don't suppose we'll ever get a chance to find out."

We both fell silent, mulling over all the things we might never know about this strange, twisted story. I couldn't help thinking that the way forward looked almost as tangled as the road behind.

"What will you tell the king?" I asked presently. "All of it?"

"I suppose I have to," Dezmen said. "If I conceal the knowledge, I am as bad as Tabitha—and Malachi. But goddess have mercy on an unjust soul! The chaos and uproar this could cause! Honestly, Chessie, if he repudiates Tabitha, the country could go to war."

"But if he doesn't contain Malachi, Cormac and Jordan could die," I said, my voice as steady as I could make it. "Is there any way to separate the two? Cast him as the villain and her as the innocent victim of a heartless schemer?"

He gave me a long, serious look. "You want to believe that," he said, "but it might not be true."

I flinched away. "I don't care about her one way or another! But if, as you say, her guilt sends the country to war—"

His hands closed more tightly on mine. "Of course you care," he said quietly. "There would be no way *not* to care in your situation. You always thought your mother was one person, and now you find she is someone else, and you can't help but wonder what she knows about you. If she thinks about you."

"If she wanted me dead," I whispered. "Or hopes that I'm still alive."

He put his hands on my cheeks, kissed me briefly, then pulled back to gaze down at me. "Let me tell Harold what we know," he said soberly. "Perhaps he will be able to determine how deeply Tabitha is mired in this plot. There might come a time you can approach your mother and tell her who you are. At the very least, you might be able to meet your grandparents. Cousins—a whole family. Your sister, Annery."

My breath caught. "I don't think I can do that. All those people—knowing about me—I don't think I can."

He kissed me again. "You don't have to. Certainly while Malachi is at large, we don't want him to know of your existence! But maybe in time. In a year or two. When you've adjusted to the idea of who you are. You might change your mind."

I pulled away from him so I could lean against the back of the bench, close enough that my shoulder rested against his. He took both my hands in his and we sat for a moment in silence.

Well, maybe. Maybe if the king arrested Malachi and I felt safe enough, I could assume my true identity. But even if I didn't go so far as to call myself a Devenetta, perhaps I could take one tiny step forward into a more elegant life. Perhaps—as Dezmen had suggested two weeks ago—I could lay my case before the king, give him an expurgated version of my story, and just tiptoe onto the edge of grand society.

I didn't want to consort with princes and high nobles. I didn't want to attend balls and vie for the king's favor and scheme for power and riches.

But perhaps I could turn myself into someone who might possibly be considered an acceptable match for Dezmen.

And even if I couldn't—oh, there was no fooling myself. It would be difficult to go back to my small apartment and my odd jobs and my nights spent serving drunks at the Packrat. It would be hard to return to being the person that I had been now that I knew the person I was supposed to be.

But that didn't make it easier to become the person I was supposed to be.

"I'll think about it," I said at last.

He lifted one of my hands to his mouth. "Good."

We didn't say much else during the long trip back to Amilloch or over our dinner in the public taproom. We scarcely said a word as all six of us trooped down the halls to Dezmen's bedroom, not even bothering to look at the door to mine. The minute the lock was set behind us, we fell into a desperate embrace, clinging to each other as if we were drowning, pressing together so tightly you would have thought we were trying to meld into one person. Six bodies and a single soul. It was, for a brief time anyway, more possible than you might have thought.

CHAPTER TWENTY-TWO

There was no reason to stay in Amilloch another day, so in the morning we began the journey back to Camarria. I settled into the carriage with Scar and Red, watching Dezmen as he consulted with a man who looked to be an ostler at the inn. I assumed Dezmen was asking for directions to the border, but when he came to the coach door and looked in at me, I was surprised to learn where he wanted to go.

"It wouldn't take us far out of our way, if you wanted to drive by Malachi's house," he said. "I know Nadine said it was closed up, but if you wanted to see it—"

My instinctive reaction was to say *no*, but I forced myself to consider the idea. If—as seemed likely—I never claimed my true identity, I would never have a reason to return to Empara. I would never have another chance to see my father's house. And I had to admit to a keen sense of curiosity, ridiculous and inconvenient though it was. *If things had been different, this place would have been yours,* Angela used to say to me. If I was ever lunatic enough to try to prove my legitimacy, I would be revealed as Malachi's heir. The house, in fact, would legally be mine.

Almost impossible to fathom.

"All right," I said, my voice subdued. "Let's do it."

He gave instructions to the driver, climbed in next to me, and took my hand. "We won't even get out of the coach," he promised. "But I want to see it, too."

We didn't talk much as we got under way. I found myself content to just lean against Dezmen's shoulder, holding his hand in both of mine and examining with fascination each joint of each finger. I loved the specific warmth of his skin against mine, the way my palm could press against his and receive pressure in return, the way he sometimes let his hand lie slack as my fingers trailed over his and sometimes curled his fingers tightly over mine. People say it as if it is a simple thing—*holding hands*—and yet it is a marvelous and unexpected and endless exploration.

We had traveled perhaps an hour when I realized that Scar and Red were exactly mimicking my behavior with Dezmen's echoes. In the past two days, I hadn't consciously gathered them up or set them free; I couldn't remember the last time I had slipped from Chessie's body into one of theirs. I thought about it a moment—it had been briefly, during the conversation with Darrily. But not once during the trip from Pandrea to Empara had I flung myself from this body to Scar's or Red's, and I had unthinkingly allowed them to behave like normal echoes ever since—

My face flamed. Ever since I had spent the first night in Dezmen's bed.

Ever since I knew what it was really like to function as an original with two echoes, and not as one person spread over three bodies.

I had always spent more time in Chessie's shape than the other two; I thought of her as my default. But now there seemed to be more weighting me in her direction, holding me inside her skin. Red and Scar seemed less substantial, less individual. I could still feel them pulling continuously on my consciousness, eternal presences as native to me as my hair or my shadow. But the *I* that was at the core of my being, the person I thought of as *me*, that seemed to be residing more permanently in the form of Chessie.

The thought gave me a sense of irrational panic. I didn't want to lose the freedom of moving between bodies; I loved being able to flit around a scene in seconds, viewing it from multiple perspectives and choosing which incarnation would react. I might be thinking of giving up my old vagabond existence for a more traditional life, but I didn't want to conform as much as *that*.

Sitting so quietly that Dezmen might think I had fallen asleep, I attempted to fling myself into Red's mind. It took a little more effort than I was accustomed to, but a moment later I was on the other side of the coach, staring through a fall of Red's auburn hair at the two people occupying the opposite bench. Another mental leap and I was in Scar's mind. I turned my head and looked out the window. Nothing to see but trees. Green leaves turning the air into a porous emerald, red and yellow leaves setting the horizon on fire. I danced back into Chessie's body and gave my shoulders a shake.

Dezmen squeezed my hand. "Were you sleeping?"

"Almost," I said. "How about you?"

"I might have dropped off for a moment. But I think we must be close. Does any of this look familiar?"

I snorted. "It's Empara. It all looks familiar. It all looks like forest."

"Right, but it's opening up a little here on this side. Take a look."

I leaned over his body to peer out the window, and he was right. The endless miles of woodland were giving way to more cultivated space; there were a couple of low hills that had been almost completely cleared of trees to make way for farmland and even a cluster of small houses. Civilization of a sort.

"Maybe—it's hard to remember—we didn't drive past his house that often. Once I see it, I think I'll know it, but—"

We drove on another mile through a stand of trees so dense you could almost believe you had dreamed the last few dwellings and that no one ever had lived here, ever *could* live here, in this overgrown jungle. Then suddenly we rounded a shady curve and the forest was stripped away. It was as if someone had taken a gigantic scythe and mowed down a patch of woodland as cleanly as he might clear a field of wheat. In its place had been planted serviceable grass, now all yellowed and brown and low to the ground, so that there was a large, bare, ugly section of flat unadorned property right in the middle of the endless landscape of trees.

Set far back from the road was a house, almost as square and serviceable as the acreage it sat on. It was a blocky three-story structure of warm red stone mortared together in a not-quite-linear pattern so that it had a sort of irregular charm. The slanted roof was tiled with terra-cotta; all the doors and shutters were deep mahogany wood. A rough track led from the road directly to the door, but it didn't look as if it had been traveled in more than a month. Maybe two.

The coachman had halted the carriage as soon as the estate came into sight, and all six of us were crammed around the window trying to get a better view.

"Dezmen, I *remember* this," I said. "This is it! This is his house! I remember how it was nothing but forest for miles and miles, and then suddenly here we were. I was always afraid he would see us from the windows, spying on him. But if he did, he never came out and demanded what we wanted."

"The house itself is lovely, but what a mess he's made of the lawn," Dezmen observed. "It's like he just pays someone to come in once a year and clear out the new growth so the forest doesn't reclaim the land. But if he planted some ornamental trees—and put in a garden or two—it could be quite picturesque."

"It's sad," I agreed. "Almost like the place itself is lonely." I pointed out the window. "And, look, every shutter is closed. There's no smoke at the chimneys. It just reeks of emptiness."

I kept staring across the lawn, but I felt Dezmen look at me. "We *could* get out and see if any of the doors are unlocked."

I shook my head. "No. It would be too strange. Even though I know Malachi is in Camarria, I'd keep thinking he might show up at the door. I'd be too afraid."

"All right. Well, let me know when you've looked your fill. Then we'll be on our way."

A few more moments I gazed at the house, wondering what it was like inside, wondering if my mother had ever come to visit him here or if they had had their secret trysts in more welcoming venues. Was there furniture inside, or had Malachi packed it up and shipped it off when he closed the house? Were there still traces of blood in the kitchen where the servants had met their brutal ends?

Did any remnants of Malachi's ambitious, malevolent spirit still linger in the corridors, echoes of a sort, drifting through the dusty rooms? Or would the whole place feel so quiet, so abandoned, that it would seem that no one had ever lived there at all?

I swallowed a hard lump in my throat and settled back against the bench. "Drive on," I managed to say, and Dezmen thumped the roof of the carriage.

We traveled a short distance in silence and then he said, "I'm sorry if that upset you. Maybe it was a bad idea to visit the place."

I shook my head. "No, it's fine. But it's strange. And to think that— But I'm glad we drove by. Now I remember it clearly again. It had started to fade from my mind."

"I wonder what he plans to do with the place. He should just sell it if he's never going to live there again."

"Maybe he thinks he'll retire there someday when he's too old to be an inquisitor."

"Maybe he'll be leaving the post a lot sooner than he thinks," Dezmen muttered.

That wrung a smile from me, though a rather small one. "So!" I said, attempting to shake off my mood. "How much do we have to backtrack to return to our route?"

"According to the groom at the inn, not at all. We have to turn down a couple of meandering lanes and pass some small market town, but we should intersect with the northwestern road within a couple of hours."

"How long till we're at the Empara border?"

"Maybe another day. Is your friend's nephew expecting you at any specific time?"

I toyed with correcting his assumption that Morrissey was my friend, but I supposed in a way he was. I knew him. I mostly liked him. We did each other favors. Were there other criteria? I had had so few friends that I hardly knew. "No," I said. "I told Morrissey I had no idea when we'd arrive."

"Once we pick the boy up, we ought to be back in Camarria in four or five days. And then—"

"And then," I repeated on a sigh. "You figure out what to tell the king, and the world spins into chaos."

"It very well could," he said, reaching over to pull me against him, my back against his chest. "These might be the last moments of calm we ever know. Better enjoy them."

I leaned against him, loving the feel of his arms around me, and idly watched what I could see of the landscape rolling by outside the window. Trees, trees, and more trees, with the occasional dent in the forest created by some small settlement. An isolated manor sitting proudly in one spot, a prosperous farming concern sprawling across another large swath of ground. Gray stone cottages, brightly painted barns, and one whimsical grain silo decorated with unnecessary turrets to resemble a castle tower.

I jerked free of Dezmen's hold and practically flung myself to the window. "Dezmen! I recognize that place! That silo! This is the road to my old house."

He leaned over my shoulder to get a glimpse of the farm as we passed. "It is? How close do you think we are?"

Now I was craning my neck, trying to see the route ahead of us, which was totally obscured by trees. "Close. Really close. We passed that little castle feature all the time. There will be a side road in a little bit, and if we turn right and go about half a mile—we'll be there."

He sat back on the bench and pulled me down next to him, his hands on my shoulders. There was no way he could miss feeling my violent shivers. "Do you *want* to see it?" he asked quietly. "Will it upset you even more than seeing Malachi's place?"

"I don't know," I admitted. "I mean—I don't know if it will upset me more. But I know I want to see it."

He watched me a moment as if giving me time to change my mind. I went on hurriedly. "I left so abruptly. That very same day. I just walked out, with all the clothes I could carry, and Scar and Red at my back. Except I didn't have names for them then. We just left, and I haven't seen it since, and—I think I'd like to."

"All right," he said, and pounded on the roof of the carriage again. When the coachman pulled over to learn what we wanted,

Dezmen poked his head out the window and shouted instructions. Then he settled beside me on the bench again. We sat in tense silence as the driver set us back in motion at a somewhat slower pace. I tried not to gasp as we made the right turn, proceeding even more cautiously on a track that was so uneven it could barely be considered a road.

A few moments later, the carriage came to a halt, and we heard the driver call, "Is this it?" I had already knelt in front of the window, and I was already staring.

It looked different—smaller than I'd thought, with blue painted shutters instead of the green ones I remembered, and the garden in front full of useless flowers instead of practical corn and beans. But at the same time, it was achingly familiar. The door wasn't a simple rectangle, as a proper door should be; the top edge was a perfect arch, fitted with a round window. The same massive oak stood guard on the eastern side of the house, spreading its branches so far they almost reached the western edge of the roof. The second-floor windows still looked out over a narrow balcony. If you were brave enough, or stupid enough, you could slip out your window, climb over the railing, dangle from the bottom edge of the balcony, and drop to the ground beneath. You never sprained your ankle, even though Angela always warned you that you could.

Behind the house I could see neatly planted rows of produce spreading out for a few acres before they abruptly stopped at the tree line. From this distance and at this time of year, it was hard to tell what they had been before they were harvested, but my guess was that whoever lived there now made at least a partial living by raising and selling crops.

I had barely registered the fact that there was smoke coming from the kitchen chimney when the front door opened and a man stepped outside. He spotted us, hesitated a moment, then walked our way.

"What do you want to do?" Dezmen asked me in a low voice. "Talk to him or simply drive off?"

"I don't—I suppose it couldn't—I don't know," I stammered.

"We'll stay then," Dezmen said.

In a few moments the man was standing just a few feet away, bending down a little to try to see inside the carriage. "You folks lost?" he asked.

Dezmen opened the door, and we all climbed out. The man stepped back a pace, clearly intimidated by the appearance of so much nobility. He added a belated, "My lord. My lady."

Dezmen glanced at me to see if I had manufactured a reason for stopping. "I used to—I used to know a woman who lived here," I said. "It was a long time ago."

The man nodded at me seriously. He was thickset and muscular, dressed in a workingman's clothes. There was a small barn in the back, big enough to hold a couple of horses, but it wasn't hard to imagine him dragging his plow through every acre by hand.

"The woman that died?" he asked.

I might have winced. I felt Dezmen move behind me, as if to catch me when I fainted, and I saw his echoes take spots behind Scar and Red. "Yes," I said as steadily as I could manage. "Her name was Angela. She used to work for my mother."

Now he shook his head. "Terrible business, that. No one knew what to make of it. All that blood—and no reason for it. Nothing stolen from the house. Nothing broken. Just the dead woman."

"No one ever knew what happened?" Dezmen asked over my head.

"Not that I ever heard."

"Who found the body?" Dezmen asked.

"Neighbor up the road. George. Came by to see if she wanted some part of the cow he was going to slaughter the next day. Said the smell was terrible, so he knew something was wrong before he even went in." He shook his head again. "All that blood," he repeated. "But George said it was even worse upstairs."

I flung my head up with a gasp and felt myself stagger back against Dezmen.

"Upstairs?" Dezmen repeated.

"The other body. The little girl."

My vision was blurring; the air around me flared too bright, then began to dim. I put a hand out, not knowing what I was reaching for, and felt Dezmen take it in a steady hold.

"I'm sorry, what?" Dezmen said. "There was a dead girl in the house along with the older woman?"

Through the buzzing in my ears, I could hear the farmer reply. "George said she was ten, maybe eleven. Throat cut just as clean as you could want."

Now I was backed up so hard against Dezmen that I could feel his buttons and buckles pressing through my clothing, leaving marks on my skin. He put his free arm around my waist, holding me to him so tightly I couldn't dream of falling. I couldn't breathe, either, but I wouldn't have been able to breathe anyway.

"Who was the girl? Do you know?"

"George said the woman had four kids who lived with her. A couple of them were simple, you know, didn't really talk or look you in the eye. I think three were girls and one was a boy, but you know how all those details get mixed up when people start telling the story. So everybody just assumed whoever killed the woman— Angela, you say?—whoever killed her killed the girl as well."

"And the other children?"

"Run off. No one ever saw them again."

I could feel Dezmen take a long, hard breath. "That's a terrible story. I'm sorry to hear it."

"It is terrible," the man agreed. "It was a couple years before anyone else would set foot in the place, but it seemed a shame to let it sit empty. No one seemed to know who owned it, either, but no one came to claim it, so about five years ago I moved in. I keep waiting for someone to come along and throw me out, but so far it hasn't happened."

"No. Well. I hope you get to stay here as long as you like," Dezmen answered.

The farmer gestured toward his front door. "Would you like to come inside? I've fixed it up pretty nice."

My whole body corded with refusal, and Dezmen squeezed me tighter. "No, I think it's stirred up more sad memories than my friend was expecting. But thank you for the invitation. And for taking the time to talk to us."

"Well, if you change your mind or come back sometime, I'll be happy to show you around," he said.

"Thank you," Dezmen said again, and urged me back toward the door of the coach.

I had lost the ability to move, so Dezmen had to push me the few steps to the carriage door and then lift me up and inside; his echoes did the same for Scar and Red. I was shaking so badly I almost slipped off the seat and onto the floor before Dezmen climbed in beside me, closed the door, and signaled to the driver to leave. I felt the coach jerk into motion as Dezmen gathered me into his arms and cradled me against his body. I was trembling too much to even cry.

"Chessie, Chessie, *Chessie*," he whispered in my ear. "What *happened* that day Malachi came to your house?"

"I—" I tried to speak but my jaw was too loose, my lips too slack. "I was—I—he—"

Dezmen's voice was so low, so soothing, he might have been speaking to a damaged child. No—he knew very well he *was* speaking to a damaged child, suddenly reliving the terrifying events from more than a decade ago. "He came to the house. You saw him kill Angela. You were afraid he was going to kill you."

I nodded as much as my tremors would allow, and he spoke even more softly against my cheek. "Chessie. Did you once have *three* echoes?"

"Yes," I managed.

"And you were able to send one of them upstairs so Malachi would chase after her while the rest of you ran out of the house?"

I wailed an inarticulate noise and buried my face against his jacket, but now, all of a sudden, the words came out in a torrent. "No," I sobbed. "*I* ran upstairs. My echoes were hiding in the parlor.

I ran into my bedroom. *I* hid in the closet. Malachi found me and he slit my throat."

No man in the Seven Jewels could ever have been so shocked. "*Chessie.* But—then—"

I scrubbed my forehead against the rough wool of his jacket. "I had never done it before. Never moved between bodies. I didn't know I could. But as the knife touched my neck I-I-I *flung* myself away from him. I don't know how else to describe it. I had this moment of terrible pain—and then suddenly I was somewhere else. In other body, in another room, crouching behind the sofa and hearing Malachi's feet stomp across the floor upstairs."

"Oh, sweet holy goddess," he breathed.

"I didn't know what had happened at first. I thought maybe I was hallucinating, or that I was really dead, and this was what it felt like to be a ghost. But I was bleeding—one small spot on my neck, where the knife had gone in—I was bleeding, and so were the echoes. So I thought I must somehow be alive."

"What happened then?"

"I was too stunned to move—too afraid. I listened as Malachi came storming down the steps and out the door. I waited for what seemed like hours to see if he would come back. When he didn't, I crawled out from behind the furniture. Me, in this body. And the two echoes I had left."

"Chessie," he said. Then, for a long time after that, nothing more. I clung to him, trying not to sob, trying to stop trembling, trying to shut down my memory of that awful day. The feel of metal against my throat, more pressure than pain, the sense of terror that consumed my whole body with such heat that I actually wondered if I was on fire.

And then the wrenching disorientation. The wild confusion of suddenly being somewhere else, *someone* else, seeing a different room from a different set of eyes. I could barely breathe; I certainly couldn't think. I just crouched there with the other echoes until Malachi left and night fell and I decided I might as well try to survive, if I hadn't actually died.

After a while I could feel my shivers ease off. Dezmen shifted his hold on me and lifted a hand to stroke my hair. "Any better?" he asked in a low voice.

"A little."

"Are you up to talking about it?"

"Maybe."

He kissed my temple. "I'm still trying to understand it all. So *this* body used to be an echo. Did it feel different when you took it over? Awkward or unfamiliar?"

"No, it was—it was me. I didn't understand what had happened and there was no one to ask—I didn't know if everyone with an echo could do such a thing—"

"No," Dezmen said wryly. "There are stories—I told you the tales of King Edwin—but as far as I know, most times when an original dies, the echoes die, too. What happened to you was extraordinary." He put a hand up, gently, to trace a track across my throat. "You said you were bleeding," he said. "But I don't see a scar."

I turned my head enough to show him the small red gash that started just under my ear. "The echoes have the same mark," I said.

"You must have left your body just in time," he said. "This body became the original, became *Chessie*, and Chessie didn't suffer the same wound as the echo."

"Or all four of us would have bled to death there in that house, even though he only murdered one of us."

"Yes."

I shook my head. "It is still as amazing to me as the day it happened."

"But, Chessie, what did you *do*? Alone and terrified at the age of, what, twelve?"

"Eleven," I said. "I walked for a couple of days, until I was far away from anyone who might know me. It was midsummer, so all the farmers in Empara were looking for workers. I hired on to pick beans and berries at one of the bigger farms I found. The echoes weren't as good as I was, or as fast, but they could copy my actions enough to pick a decent day's harvest. I told anyone who asked that they were my siblings and they were simple and I had to take care of them."

"Had you already started to dress them differently?"

"Angela's the one who started that," I said. "I just made the differences more pronounced. Let Red's hair grow, always dressed Scar as a boy. Everyone thought they were odd, but I think people mostly just felt sorry for me."

Dezmen drew a long breath. I thought he was feeling utterly wretched for me, but he was afraid he might insult me if he said so. "How long were you a farmhand?"

"I got lucky. The place I worked at in the fall hired me to stay through the winter so I could clear out old growth and put down fertilizer and help fix up some of the outbuildings. I had a bedroom up in the hayloft. I think the farmer's wife was worried about me and insisted that I be allowed to stay. I was there two years."

"That was kind."

I nodded against his coat. "One of the many examples of kindness I tried to hold on to whenever I remembered how cruel the world could be."

"How did you get to Camarria? Since I assume the story you told me last time was a lie."

My mouth shaped what might have been the ghost of a smile. "Mostly it was true. The farmer's wife had a sister in Camarria, and her sister ran a bakery. She brought me with her to the city one summer, and I decided to stay. Her sister let me work at the bakery for as long as I wanted." I tilted my head up just enough to look at him. "The rest of the story you know."

He kissed the tip of my nose then squeezed my body tighter. "The rest of the story was dreadful enough but this—! This is terrifying and impossible. I cannot believe you survived—even once you lived through Malachi's attack. An eleven-year-old child completely alone in the wilds of Empara! I would have been dead in a week."

"I'm sorry I lied to you," I said. "But I've never told anyone what really happened."

He was silent a moment. "I understand why you told the story you did. But I wish ... I wonder if ... I would like to think that someday you might have told me the truth on your own. Because you trusted me. And not because a stranger betrayed your secret."

I hid my face against his jacket again and took a deep, shuddering breath. "I don't know if I would have," I admitted. "Not because I didn't trust you. But because I didn't want it to be true. I didn't want to think he really tried to kill me."

Dezmen kissed the top of my head. "He *did* kill you," he said softly. "He believes you're dead."

I nodded. "Otherwise he never would have stopped looking for me."

"But, Chessie," he said, his voice suddenly urgent. "What if he sees you? Someday in Camarria? It could happen. What if he learns you're alive?"

"I think about that," I admitted. "Sometimes I have nightmares about it. But it's such a big city—and I'm so careful any time I'm near the palace or I see him out at a public event—"

"I'm not sure that's reassuring enough," he said. "Now I won't be able to stop thinking about what could happen to you if Malachi stumbles across you one day in the street."

I tilted my head up again. "If you tell the king everything he's done, maybe Malachi won't have that opportunity for very long."

Dezmen nodded. "Yes. It becomes more and more urgent that the king learn the truth—and imprison the inquisitor. Or put him to death for treason."

"That would make all of Sweetwater riot in celebration," I said. "I can only imagine what Jackal would do to mark such an occasion."

"He has a special reason for hating the inquisitor?"

"Malachi had his brother executed. I can't think of anything Jackal wouldn't do to harm Malachi in even the smallest fashion."

"I am starting to feel the same way myself."

I felt another almost-smile come to my lips. "Maybe we just tell ourselves 'He'll be dead soon' every time we start to feel nervous."

Dezmen leaned against the back of the bench and resettled me against him. "Then what?" he asked me. "Will you let me introduce you to Harold? Will you let me tell him at least part of your story?"

"I don't know," I said. "I can hardly imagine—the changes seem so big. Leaving behind the life I know and trying to create a wholly new one."

"You've done it before," he reminded me.

"Because someone tried to murder me!"

He laughed, but immediately grew serious again. "Well, you're going to have to accommodate *some* changes in your life," he said. "Because I'm in it now, and I'm going to stay in it. Maybe you tell the king who you are, maybe you don't, but you'll have to explain *me* away to anyone who's curious."

I probably should have been indignant at his arrogance, but instead I was flushed with pleasure at his insistence. I could think of few things I wanted more than Dezmen's continued presence in my life. Well, my survival. But after that. "I am glad to learn you don't plan to abandon me the minute we arrive back in Camarria," I said, attempting to sound jaunty. "But it will not be easy to continue on the way we are."

"*None* of this has been easy," he reminded me. "I think we can handle logistical challenges if that's all that separates us." He tightened his arms and began trailing kisses down my cheek and under my chin. "When I think of all the reasons I might never have found you," he whispered. "When I think of how perilous your life has been—how separate from mine in every way—when I marvel at the chance that brought us together. I am awed and I am humbled and I am grateful, and I am very very certain that I am never going to let you go."

I turned in his arms and kissed him frantically, feeling desire and disquiet in equal measure. Sweet goddess, we *might* never have met. Might never even have passed on the street, and glanced at each other and glanced away, not sparing even a moment to wonder what fears and knowledge and quirks and kindnesses lay behind the other person's calm expression. Surely it was the goddess's hand that had brought us together, nudged us to the same spot on the same day, brushed the afternoon with violent color and demanded of us, *See? This is a heart you should recognize. Pay attention.*

I had found him and he had recognized me, and now I wasn't going to give him up. I would die first. And I had already died.

CHAPTER TWENTY-THREE

Morrissey's nephew was tall, scrawny, awkward, and silent. I couldn't tell if he wanted to come with us to Camarria or simply felt he had no choice. He was polite, though. His farewell to his mother was quiet and unemotional, but he allowed her to kiss his cheek before he came to join us where we waited outside the coach.

"You want to sit inside with us or ride outside with the driver?" Dezmen asked him.

The boy glanced up to see the driver gazing down with a friendly expression. "With him, if that's all right."

The coachman extended a hand to help him up. "Glad for the company," he said. "You know how to handle a team?"

"Driven a gig before, but never more than two horses at a time," the boy said, easily making the climb to the top bench.

"Team's a little different. I'll show you. What's your name?"

"Orrin."

"Well, take a seat, Orrin."

As soon as we were under way again, Dezmen remarked, "There's someone whose life might have been as hard as your own."

I nodded. "I don't know the tale, but I have to think it isn't very good."

"How well do you know his uncle?"

I shrugged. "I've done some work for him. Jackal trusts him. He's never been entirely—legal—but I wouldn't think he's a hard man. I'd say he does what has to get done."

Dezmen sighed. "I guess that's the best we can hope for."

❁   ❁   ❁

The trip from the Empara border northwest to Camarria took almost four days. Inside the carriage, Dezmen and I alleviated some of the tedium of travel by sharing stories and speculations and kisses. Outside the carriage, I assumed, the coachman and Orrin entertained themselves by giving and receiving driving lessons because more than once we went lurching down the road in a haphazard fashion that made me grab for any support. We never came to grief, though, and as the days wore on, our progress became smoother. I wondered if Orrin might train to be a groom or driver once he got settled in the city. Either would be a good profession.

Dezmen and I spent the morning of the last day arguing. He didn't want to simply drop me off on a street corner in Camarria to let me make my way back home; he didn't even want me to go home.

"I can hardly return to the palace with you," I said in exasperation.

"I'll get rooms in lodgings nearby," he said. "I'll tell Cormac I need more privacy than I can find in the palace, surrounded by servants and the endless parade of guests. He'll understand."

"But you don't have those lodgings *tonight*," I pointed out.

"I think you can endure a night or two in a hotel," he said.

"Dezmen. I need to get back to my old life, at least for a few days, at least until I figure out what I want to do next. This has all been a little overwhelming for me. Pandrea—and learning about the marriage—and *you*—and seeing my old house. I need to think about it all."

"Can't you think in a hotel?"

I smiled, I kissed him, and I shook my head. "I want to go home," I answered.

In the end, we reached a compromise: I would go home, but he would take me there, the great carriage lumbering through the narrow streets of my neighborhood like some oversized sea creature tragically washed ashore. I comforted myself with the thought that the Pandrean driver had no interest in knowing where I lived, and Morrissey's nephew didn't know the city well enough to be able to find me again, even if his uncle or Jackal offered incentives to remember.

"I'm coming back tomorrow," Dezmen told me as we pulled up in front of my place late in the afternoon. I wondered how many of the neighbors were peering out their windows gawking at the sight of the fine vehicle.

"By tomorrow, Malachi's spies will be following you again," I said. "I'll meet you in Amanda Plaza and we can discuss our options then." That made me remember that—despite everything we had learned on the trip—*he* was the one whose life had most recently been in danger. I frowned at him. "In fact, you shouldn't leave the palace again until then. I'll have to let Jackal know you're back, so he can send Pippa to protect you."

"I've already taken care of that," he said a little smugly. "When I was home. I sent a couple of men from my father's estate to await me here in Camarria. They can escort me from now on."

"Good. When are you going to talk to Harold?"

"As soon as I can. Today, if he has a moment free."

"Good," I said again. "This might be almost over."

"When do you want to meet tomorrow?"

"Let's say noon. I might need that much time to organize myself."

"All right. I'll see you then."

Just in case the neighbors *were* watching from the windows, I put a little effort into differentiating my movements from Red's and Scar's as we all climbed out of the carriage. I allowed Dezmen to give me one brief kiss goodbye but didn't invite him up to my apartment. Then I waved to Orrin to climb down. "Come on," I said. "You're with me."

I made my way upstairs with a little less than my usual stealth, though I did exercise a little caution as I unlocked the door and stepped inside, glancing around quickly for any overt signs of trouble. But everything seemed ordinary and undisturbed. If anyone had been here pawing through my things, they'd left no obvious signs.

"My friends and I are just going to dump our bags in the other room, then we'll head on out to look for your uncle," I told Orrin. "If you're hungry, we can stop somewhere along the way and get food."

"I'm always hungry," he said.

The echoes and I ducked into the bedroom, washed up, and changed into clothes that we hadn't been wearing every couple of days for the past two-and-a-half weeks. Just for the practice, I skipped into Red's body so I could style her long hair and put on a little makeup. Then I bounced over to Scar's head, tugged my jacket in place, and led the way into the main room.

Orrin was standing almost exactly where I'd left him; this wasn't a kid who took liberties. Still in Scar's shape, I jerked my head toward the door and spoke in my lowest register. "Come on. Let's go."

Once we'd filed out and were hiking along the busy streets, I stayed in Scar's body to walk alongside Orrin, while Red and Chessie followed behind, apparently whispering secrets to each other. "Didn't have much chance to talk to you on the trip," I observed. "You managing all right?"

He shrugged, and then he nodded.

"You ever been out of Empara before?" I persisted.

"A few times. Never this far."

"You're going to be staying with your uncle. Do you like him?"

"Better than I like my ma's new husband."

So that was the untenable situation the boy had been living in. I could imagine all kinds of possibilities for abuse, and I thought more highly of Morrissey for removing Orrin from the household. "Your uncle's got a friend who's around a lot. JoJo. You ever meet him?"

For the first time, Orrin showed a little enthusiasm. "Oh yeah. He's even better than my uncle. He showed me how to kick a man in the kidneys so he stays down."

Well. I might have liked it better if JoJo had taught him to fish or whittle, but I suppose your gift is always whatever you have to offer.

"They've got another friend. Jackal. We're going to meet him this afternoon. He can be dangerous but—if you ever need help, Jackal's the one to go to. He's a useful man to know."

"All right."

After that, I'd pretty much exhausted the topics of conversation I had in common with Orrin. Fortunately, by this time we were in a commercial district that boasted a handful of vendors, so I could buy him an early dinner. By the time we had finished our food, we had covered another six blocks and gotten out of the habit of talking. We continued the rest of the journey in silence, except for the times I pointed out a main street, an important bridge, or some other landmark.

I was finding it an unexpected effort to maintain my presence inside Scar's head; I kept feeling my essence yearning back toward Chessie's body, a desire that I found deeply disconcerting. If I lost the ability to dance between echoes, I lost the ability to maintain the life that I had so carefully constructed. I might be contemplating changing some of the parameters of my existence, but I hadn't expected those changes to come with such drastic costs. In a quieter moment, I would have to sit down and think very hard about these possible consequences—and whether I could accept them.

It was cold and not quite dark as we finally made it to Packrat. By this time, I had given up the struggle. I had jumped into Red's body long enough to call for Scar to drop back and walk with me, then I'd hopped over to Chessie's shape and jogged up to fall in step beside Orrin. He seemed even less inclined to converse with a woman than he had with Scar, and so we'd exchanged only a few words since the transition.

As I pushed open the door to the tavern, I told him, "I'm not sure where your uncle is at the moment. He might be here. But if he's not, someone here should know where he is. It could take a little while to find him."

Orrin just shrugged. He was not the kind of boy who expected life to be convenient.

Inside the bar it was warm, full of enticing scents, and not very crowded. One swift glance around showed me that Morrissey wasn't present, but Jackal was. He was seated at his usual table, flanked by two men I didn't know; he gave me a quick nod as he saw me enter, but didn't break off his conversation. I slipped over into Red's shape long enough to blow him a kiss, but I was back in Chessie's head by the time Dallie bustled over. Moving between bodies so quickly took a great burst of energy; I felt myself sagging. Maybe I was just tired from the trip.

"And who's this fine young man?" Dallie asked with a smile.

"Morrissey's nephew, Orrin. I went to fetch him as a favor."

Her eyebrows arched up at that, but she didn't ask for the tale. "Morrissey's not here right now, but he's been coming in most every night, so he ought to be by later."

"Good. Do you think I could just leave him here if it gets too late? I've been traveling and I need to go home and get some sleep."

Dallie patted Orrin on the shoulder. "I'll take care of him if you have to leave. You don't have to worry, young man, I may look mean and ugly, but I'll only hurt you if you deserve it."

She went off into gales of laughter; I didn't think Orrin looked too reassured. Then again, he didn't look too alarmed. I figured he'd seen worse horrors than anything Dallie might dream up.

"Are you hungry?" she asked him now. "There's plenty of food in back."

He'd told me he was always hungry, so I wasn't surprised when he said, "Yes, please."

"Well, come on, then," she said, drawing him with her to the door that led to the kitchen.

I glanced over at Jackal to find that he'd gotten rid of his most recent collection of friends and was staring at me, clearly waiting for me to join him. I settled Red and Scar at an empty table, then went over to pull out a chair across from Jackal.

"How was your trip?" he asked.

The honest answer would have been *life changing*, but most of the things that had occurred weren't things I was going to share with Jackal. "Interesting," I said. "The Pandrean lord seemed to think he found some key pieces of information in this case he's investigating."

Jackal refilled his beer from a pitcher on the table and offered me a clean glass. I shook my head.

"If I have anything to drink, I'll fall asleep before I make it home," I said. "I just wanted to drop off the boy and say hello to you."

Jackal glanced at the door to the kitchen. "Morrissey's sister's kid?"

I grinned. "I told him he could turn to you if he was ever in any trouble."

Jackal made a face at that, but nodded. "They've had a bad time of it this past week. Morrissey and JoJo."

"Why? What happened?"

Jackal took a meditative swallow of his beer. "Found JoJo's brother, Trout. Dead. And—not in a pretty way. Looks like there might have been some torture before he was put to death. JoJo's taking it hard."

I couldn't say I was surprised, and I was sure JoJo wasn't, either, but I could imagine it was still a terrible blow. "Any idea who killed him?"

"The first thought that springs to mind is the city inquisitor. I'm sure he's got the facilities—and the stomach—for torture."

It was certainly the first thought that sprang to *my* mind, but there was an obvious question for someone who didn't know as much about the inquisitor as I did. "Why would he be interested in Trout?"

"Who knows why Malachi is interested in anything?" His voice dropped and he fixed his eyes on my face. "Or *anyone*."

For no reason whatsoever, I felt an uneasy chill crawl down my spine. I narrowed my eyes at him and said, "What's that supposed to mean?"

"He came by here the other day. Malachi himself."

I felt shock travel along every nerve. "*Here*? Why?" Sweet goddess, if I had been waiting tables some night when Malachi waltzed in—

"Said he was looking for someone. Didn't know her name. Described her, though, down to the two friends who usually follow her around the city."

Now I felt heat and cold chase themselves through my veins. My hands were shaking so badly I had to fold them tightly in my lap so Jackal couldn't see. "Me?" I said in a voice that sounded raw. "Why would the inquisitor be looking for me?"

Jackal shook his head. "That I don't know. My guess is that Trout was—induced—to explain what went wrong on the day he tried to murder your nice Pandrean lord. You were there, and you probably brought Red and Scar with you, and Trout described you. Maybe Trout even told him where you could be found on the days that Red is working."

"Yes, but—yes, but—that still doesn't explain why he would even care that I'm alive—" I stammered. How well had Trout described me? Could Malachi possibly have recognized, from a stupid man's confession under extreme duress, the features of the daughter he thought he had already murdered?

Jackal leaned back against the bench but never took his eyes from my face. "There is only one explanation that makes sense to me," he said. "Everyone who is connected to this case in any fashion is dead. Leffert. Bert. Trout. Maybe others. Men have *tried* to kill Lord Dezmen, and it's only by the mercy of the goddess that he's still alive. But I wouldn't be surprised if another attempt was made on his life now that he has returned to the city. Clearly whoever killed Leffert doesn't want the case to be solved. And I can think of only one person in Camarria with the power to murder so many people and cover his traces so completely."

I nodded.

Now Jackal leaned forward, his expression even more intense. "You're in danger, Chessie," he said quietly. "I know you think you can take care of yourself—I know you think you can slip through this city like a ghost, and no one will ever be able to find you—but if Malachi is hunting you, nothing will keep you safe. Someone will betray you. Someone always does." He jerked his head at the table where my echoes sat. "And if Malachi takes you out, he'll take your friends as well. Sorry as I would be to see you go, it's losing Red that would break my heart."

I tried to muster a smile at that, but it was a pretty pathetic attempt. "All right, I'm scared," I admitted. "I'm supposed to see Lord Dezmen tomorrow. I know he sent for some Pandrean soldiers who will be guarding him from now on. Maybe he'll have some thoughts about what I can do to stay safe."

I could see from Jackal's expression that he didn't put much faith in Dezmen's notions of security. "I have some thoughts," he said. "Stay at my house on Crescent Lane. There's room for all of you there. And you know the place is guarded every hour of the day or night. Someone might get to you, even so, but only after a pitched battle."

It was such a new thought that it took me a moment to examine it. I blinked at him. "Stay at *your* house?"

He put his hands up as if to show how harmless he was. "You won't have to worry that I'll try to make trouble for Red. I'll stay at one of my other properties. You'll have the run of the place."

"It's an interesting idea," I said slowly. Dezmen would hate it, which was a strong argument against the plan, but I was starting to see some advantages. Suppose someone *had* been following me during the weeks I was aiding Dezmen's investigation. Malachi might already know where I lived, or be on the verge of figuring it out. It was true Jackal's house was practically a fortress. Probably the only place in the whole city better defended was the palace itself—and that was where Malachi lived. Hardly a refuge at all.

"You could go there right now," Jackal said. "Straight from the tavern. What if someone's lying in wait for you at your apartment?"

"I was there for a few minutes this afternoon. Nothing had been disturbed."

"No, because he didn't want you to know he'd found you," Jackal retorted. "But he probably had a spy in place watching the street, and the minute you arrived, he sped off to the palace to tell

Malachi you were back. The inquisitor himself could be waiting for you when you get home tonight."

It was so easy to picture everything he said—maybe because I knew even better than Jackal what Malachi was capable of, and I had relived those memories all too recently. I was getting more and more unnerved, and I was too tired to think clearly. "Well—but—I can hardly hide out in your house for the rest of my life—"

"Just a day or two, until we can think of something more permanent." He reached his hands across the table for me like an actual supplicant. "Please, Chessie. If not for yourself, for Red. If something happened to her—" He shook his head.

Well. It wouldn't hurt to spend one night at Jackal's, I supposed. Maybe when I woke up, I'd feel less uneasy, or I'd have come up with a better plan for how to avoid the inquisitor's notice. Or maybe Dezmen would show up at Amanda Plaza with the best news of all— the king had arrested Malachi and *all* of us were safe.

"I don't have any clothes with me," I said.

He chuckled. "Trust me, the house is stocked with anything you might need, as Red would tell you." He lifted an eyebrow and said, *"Anything."*

That was meant to make me laugh, and it did. "All right, for one night, at least. But I have to go right now because I'm ready to curl up here at the table and fall asleep."

Jackal lifted a hand to signal to someone. "I'll have Pippa walk you to my place."

It seemed stupid to say I didn't need an escort, since keeping me safe was the whole point of this exercise. "And you'll take care of Orrin?"

"Who's Orrin?"

"Morrissey's nephew."

"I'll make sure Dallie takes him home if Morrissey never shows up tonight. Don't you worry about him."

I pushed myself to my feet. "All right, then. I'm ready to go to Crescent Lane."

"Send Red over to say hello first."

So I left Chessie at the table with Scar and sashayed back over to Jackal in Red's body. I was so exhausted it was hard to summon Red's usual sass. "So you've finally got me where you want me—back in your house," I said, tossing my hair.

He pulled me down to give me a lingering kiss, and kept his hand on my wrist and his eyes on my face when I finally straightened up. "I think Chessie might be mixed up in some bad business, and it's my fault for sending her down this road to begin with," he said seriously. "I can't let harm come to her because of something *I* did. And if something happened to you—"

"And people say you're so coldhearted," I marveled. "But here you are, feeling sentimental."

He smiled, but he looked a little sad. "There's something about you, Reddy-girl. Hard to get over it." He jerked his head to the table where Scar and Chessie were waiting. "I know you're all cozy with that boy these days. But if that ever changes—"

I placed my hand on his cheek, feeling the warm skin and rough stubble under my palm. "I'll let you know," I said softly. "Thanks for worrying about Chessie, though. Sometimes she needs worrying about."

He turned his head just enough to plant a kiss in the center of my hand. "Now go. Get some rest."

Pippa was already over at the table, standing with her usual feline slouch, so I cast my consciousness back into Chessie's body in case I was supposed to be having a conversation with her. Gorsey, every time I did that, I felt my bones gain another twenty pounds; pretty soon I wouldn't be able to lift my feet from the ground.

I did manage to stand up, though, and Scar beside me, as Red came over to join us. "Looks like we're ready to go," I said.

Pippa nodded and strolled through the door with negligent grace. She looked relaxed, even oblivious, but I knew that was an act. I had seen her move from slack to murderous in about a second; my sense was that she was always preternaturally alert, and cultivated an uninterested attitude to throw people off.

She was certainly uninterested in conversation as we navigated the dark streets, which was fine with me. I let Pippa take the lead and I brought up the rear, since I would be quicker to react than either of the echoes. I did shake a dagger into my fist, and I made sure Scar and Red did the same. Pippa's hands hovered by her belt; my guess was that she carried any number of weapons.

The moon was climbing and the temperature was dropping by the time we made it to Crescent Lane. Pippa exchanged a few low words with the man guarding the high metal gate, then led the three of us inside before locking the door behind us all. I must have looked surprised because she said, "I've been staying here lately. Jackal has guards that patrol all night, but it never hurts to have one more person inside."

"That makes sense."

She waved at the stairs. "Jackal says you know your way around the house?"

"Red does."

"He said you should take the blue bedroom and the green bedroom on the second floor. There's closets and dressers with clothes and everything else. When you get up in the morning, just come down to the kitchen and there will be food. Nothing fancy, but you can eat anything you find."

"Sounds good. Thanks."

"Sure."

I hauled myself up the stairs, feeling wearier with every step. The two bedrooms were across the hall from each other, and each held one bed and a few pieces of serviceable furniture. For a moment, I hesitated—I wasn't sure I wanted the echoes to sleep even that far away from me—but not sure I wanted to crowd together on a single mattress with them, either. This last week on the road, I had shared a bed with Dezmen every night, which was a whole different experience than sleeping beside two bodies that adjusted to mine automatically, even if I thrashed in my sleep. Dezmen required some negotiation, some compromising; even something as simple as turning from one side to another could upset the delicate and hard-won treaty.

It would be strange not to sleep beside him tonight. But sleeping alongside Scar and Red would only exacerbate that strangeness, I thought. Other originals slept separately from their echoes; maybe it was time I tried the same thing.

So I settled them into the green bedchamber, first making sure they were washed up and changed into cotton nightclothes. Then I made myself at home in the blue room. I was asleep almost the minute my head touched the pillow.

CHAPTER TWENTY-FOUR

When I woke in the morning, I knew exactly where I was, and why, and I didn't feel any less nervous than I had the night before. *Malachi is looking for me.* Whether he had realized who I was, or he merely wanted to tie up a loose end, the thought was still deeply unsettling. If the king didn't believe Dezmen's story—if the inquisitor wasn't arrested and locked up within a couple of days—maybe I would have to take Dezmen up on his original suggestion and go hide out in Pandrea for a while. I didn't want to, but I also didn't want to die.

I sat up in bed and, across the hallway, felt Scar and Red do the same. I stifled a groan. This was a damn inconvenient time for them to start acting like conventional echoes. I willed them to lie back down again. If I encountered anyone else while I was wandering around Jackal's house, I wanted to be able to maintain the fiction that they were completely separate individuals. *Oh, I suppose Red and Scar are still asleep. I'll go wake them up—we've got a lot to do today.*

First and foremost was meeting Dezmen at Amanda Plaza. It hadn't been a full day since we'd parted, and already I missed him. *New love,* I thought, in a tone that would have been scoffing if I'd spoken out loud. I needed to get up and dressed so I could be out the door within the hour.

I spent a few minutes rooting through the guest closet to put together a serviceable outfit of shirt and trousers and vest, all a little big for me, all meant for a man's body. But Jackal's idea of what women wore was much more suitable to Red's persona than Chessie's, and I wasn't in the mood to deal with skirts and décolletage.

As soon as I was dressed, I headed down to the kitchen. There was no such thing as a true servant at Jackal's place, though there was a thin, one-eyed man who seemed to manage the running of the house. He stocked the kitchen, brought in firewood in cold weather, and did minimal cleaning when the place got too cluttered. He never talked much, but he seemed to like Red; at any rate, he'd always greeted her with a shy smile whenever he encountered her in the hallways. But I didn't see him as I made my way downstairs—didn't see Pippa or any of the other guards, either. This was hardly a surprise. I would guess that anyone who spent much time in Jackal's employ generally tried to stay as invisible as possible.

The kitchen was a big and mostly empty room with a stove that looked as if it had never been used, a table piled with papers and a few dirty dishes, and a large shelving unit shoved against a wall. The shelves held an assortment of food—dried meat, bread that might be fresh, cans that might hold anything, and pieces of fruit that had withered to hard, dull lumps before anyone thought to eat them. Nothing too appetizing, but certainly enough to stave off hunger until I could leave to meet Dezmen.

Stuffing my mouth with a chunk of bread, I reached for one of the unlabeled cans on an upper shelf. I had my back to the door that led to the main part of the house when I heard it open behind me, and someone said my name with quiet authority.

"Chezelle."

My body flooded with hot adrenaline before I even registered the timbre of his voice, before I even remembered who might know my true name. I spun clumsily around, choking down the lump of bread, clutching the heavy can. If there were knives in the kitchen, they weren't anywhere I could see them. I had no weapon. I had no defense.

The inquisitor had come to kill me.

For a moment we stared at each other across the width of the room. Malachi looked exactly as he had the last time I'd seen him at the palace: bald, muscular, powerful, menacing. He held a blade in each hand, and I could see other weapons tucked inside his belt.

The inquisitor had come to kill me.

So many thoughts crowded into my brain at once that I could hardly sort them out through the mounting terror. First was a crushing, bitter realization that Jackal had delivered me into Malachi's hands. The man I had believed would never take Malachi's bribe— the man who had lured me here with his passionate desire to keep me safe—had arranged for the inquisitor to destroy me. *Someone will betray you. Someone always does,* he had told me. He hadn't said that *he* would be the one to do it.

Second was a silent howl of pain and despair. Dezmen! I had just found him! I had never said I loved him, but I did, I did, and he would never know that—and he would never know what had happened to me—he would wait for hours, for days, for weeks at Amanda Plaza as my body rotted under some abandoned bridge. Only Jackal would know, but Jackal would never tell him. My heart broke with pity for Dezmen even as it hammered with fear for me.

Third was a desperate, diaphanous, glimmering ribbon of hope. He had tried to kill me before, and I had survived. He didn't know about the echoes—did he?—nestled together in an upstairs bedroom. He didn't know I could fling myself into one of their bodies even as the blade came down. He didn't know that I could escape him a second time.

I should do it now. Before he even approached me, before he said another word—if, indeed, he planned to speak. I should just leave Chessie's shell behind, too frightened to fight, too stunned to flee, and let him cut her throat and watch her fall to the floor and bleed out while he waited to make sure *this* time his troublesome daughter actually died.

Could I do it? I was so afraid I felt as if my feet had been staked to the floor with giant iron spikes. I tried to gather my consciousness, tried to imagine hurling myself from this body, up a flight of stairs, into Red's dreaming mind. I felt my body flinch with the effort—but I stayed locked inside Chessie. I swallowed a whimper.

"I thought it must be you," Malachi said. "Though I didn't see how it could be."

Could I throw the can at his head? If I hit him hard enough, would he stagger backward, lose his balance, feel just enough pain that I could slip past him before he recovered? Malachi might need to be closer before I had any hope of accuracy. Just to keep him talking, I asked, "You thought who must be me? Was someone talking about me?"

"A man who was supposed to be doing a job for me at the botanical gardens," Malachi answered, gliding forward a step. "I insisted he tell me why he couldn't complete the task, and he described a woman who interfered."

It was Scar who had actually attacked Trout, but Chessie had been talking to Dezmen a good ten minutes before the fight, and Trout knew Chessie well enough to put a name to her face. And Trout had obviously been willing, at some point, to provide Malachi every small detail about that day.

I weighed the can in my hand. Such an awkward projectile, and I didn't have particularly good aim. I needed to let him get even closer. "He described a dark-haired girl in ordinary clothes?" I said, my voice incredulous. "That could have been any of a thousand people."

"I know. But I had a sense—" He shook his head. "Now and then over the past few years. In the palace courtyard. In a crowd on the street. I've caught a glimpse of a face and thought, 'That could be *her.*' But whenever I looked closer, you were gone."

"You only imagined you saw me," I answered. "Because you felt guilty about trying to murder me."

He smiled. "I am not generally subject to hallucinations," he said in a silky voice. "Or guilt."

"So Trout described me—"

"And I investigated," he said. "I saw you for myself outside a jewelry shop on Cheater's Row. The scene was quite chaotic, but I recognized you."

He must have been loitering in the neighborhood the day Dezmen and I visited Eva Candleback. Even through the mayhem and the murder, he'd given no thought to Dezmen or Bertie. He'd saved all his attention for me.

"Once I knew you were alive and working with the Pandrean lord, it wasn't difficult to find someone who knew your name—and who else you worked for—and how I could find you."

"Jackal," I said, unable to keep the bleakness from my voice.

"He was most helpful," Malachi said, inching forward. I could tell he was watching my hand, trying to gauge when I might throw the can at him, but he didn't seem too worried about it. "Eager, even, to set up this meeting. I will have to reward him handsomely."

He took one more step toward me and I heaved my sorry weapon straight at his face. He flung up his arm and dodged to one side, and the can clunked across his shoulder and crashed to the floor, rolling until it hit the wall. I choked back a sound and shoved myself even closer to the shelves. Now I was truly defenseless.

"I don't know how you managed to survive before," Malachi said. "But this time I will make certain you are truly dead."

"People know," I said, my voice so hoarse and faint he might not have been able to hear me. "About you. And me. And the queen."

He laughed. He came closer. I couldn't move. "No, they don't. Or I would already be dead."

"Don't kill me," I whispered.

"But I will."

He swept up a hand to strike and I strained against the unforgiving constraints of my own body. But before his arm could descend, before I could free myself from Chessie's form, doors slammed open from two sides. I saw four people leap forward, garbed in black like assassins. Malachi whirled around to fend off their unexpected attack. One big figure bore down on Malachi with brute force, carrying him halfway across the room and slamming him into the far wall before Malachi spun free and knocked his assailant aside.

Two more charged at the inquisitor from different directions, tearing at his arms and face, trying to drag him to the floor. I heard stomping and howling and what might have been the sound of a bone snapping. Then Malachi bucked and battled, casting off both attackers with a single ferocious roar. He whirled into a crouch, panting, both fists raised, knives in each hand, ready for the next assault.

Two people came at him from the front, blades out, and Malachi hacked viciously at their arms, forcing them to take a few steps backward. But a third person crept up from behind and seized his throat in a death grip. Malachi gasped and struggled, driving one of his knives repeatedly into the attacker's thigh, while the other two people came weaving closer, looking for a chance to strike a killing blow.

Out of nowhere, a fourth shape shot across the kitchen, diving for Malachi's ankles, and bringing the whole knot of combatants down. Somebody grabbed Malachi's head and slammed it over and over against the slate floor; somebody else drove a short blade deep into Malachi's exposed chest. There were horrific sounds of rage and agony and gurgling death—then silence, except for the continued thuds of fists and hilts landing against the crumpled form of the fallen inquisitor.

I crouched against the shelves, panting with fear, trying to sort out what had just happened. Then one of the people kneeling on the floor hauled himself to his feet and turned in my direction.

"Jackal," I whimpered.

His jacket was ripped to shreds, his hands were stained with blood, and his face wore a savage expression, but he immediately crossed the room with his arms outstretched. "Chessie."

I shrank back with a cry, making the cans on the shelves rattle together. "Get *away* from me!" I wailed. "You told Malachi—you brought me here so he could *murder* me!"

He came to a halt three feet away, staring at me soberly. Some of the wildness faded from his face. "I brought you here as bait," he corrected me. "I could tell he wanted you like he'd never wanted anything before. I thought—if I can get him here, alone, with no one knowing, I can take him out. And that's what I did. And now he's dead. I'm sorry that it had to be so frightening for you. But I'd do it again tomorrow if I could kill Malachi."

I uncoiled a little from my protective pose. I was still so afraid and confused that his words didn't make sense, and I was having difficulty standing. "I don't believe you," I said.

"I swear before the goddess it's true. I never would have let him harm you. We were here the whole time, just waiting for him to make his move."

Maybe. Maybe. But. "Why didn't you *tell* me what you were planning?"

A ghost of a smile came to his mouth. "Because you wouldn't have come then. *I* wouldn't have, if it were me."

"I hate you," I said.

"That's all right," he responded. "Because Malachi is dead."

Now I stood a little straighter, trying to peer past him. His three companions were still clustered around the corpse, holding a quiet debate. "And you'll be dead next," I said in a low voice. "When someone discovers that you murdered the inquisitor."

Jackal showed his teeth in a feral smile. "Oh, no, I won't be," he said. "Every one of us in this room has cause to hate the man even more than we love life. None of us will ever tell what happened today."

He moved aside a little, and I could finally see clearly enough to identify his fellow murderers—Morrissey, Jojo, and Pippa. Three people who had suffered deep losses at Malachi's hands. Three people who would count this day as one of the best in their lives.

"But the guards—that old man who lives here—they might tell—"

Jackal shook his head. "There's no one else in the house today. Except Scar and Red, and I've taken the precaution of locking them in their room. I wouldn't want Reddy to be upset by the sight of so much blood."

Indeed, as I saw when I took a step in that direction, the blood was pooling around Malachi's lifeless form, soaking through his black clothes, and staining the slate tiles. I stood for a moment looking down at his battered face, curiously pale and slack as the jaw hung open and the half-closed eyes looked blankly down. "What will you do with the body?" I asked.

Pippa glanced up. "Cut it to pieces and distribute them all around town. A leg here, an arm there, a nose in the ditch under some old bridge. We don't want anyone who finds a bit of Malachi to be able to figure out who he is." She sounded remarkably cheerful.

JoJo just continued studying the body, seemingly considering where it might be simplest to saw through a joint, but Morrissey heaved himself to his feet and came over to touch my arm. "Thanks for bringing Orrin back," he said. As if there wasn't a dead man at his feet! As if he hadn't just helped cause that death! "I'm so glad to get him out of that house."

I swallowed a hysterical giggle. "He seems like a good boy."

"I think so."

"Just don't—" I made a helpless gesture with my hand. "Don't let him know about this."

"No," he agreed, and turned back to join the others. I tried not to watch too closely, but it looked like they were straightening out Malachi's arms and legs so they could start chopping more cleanly.

"I think you'd best leave the kitchen," Jackal said. "Leave the house."

"I have to get Scar and Red something to eat."

"I'll come up with you," he said smoothly.

So he didn't trust me not to creep back downstairs, my companions at my back, and peek into the kitchen to watch the dissection that would shortly begin. There didn't seem to be any way to assure him that there was no single sight in all of Camarria that I would be *less* interested in seeing.

I grabbed a loaf of bread and a jug of water, while Jackal wiped his hands clean of blood. Then he scooped up a few cans and followed me out of the kitchen and up the stairs. Unlocking the door to the green bedroom, he dropped the cans over the threshold, then watched as I set my own breakfast items just inside the room.

"I'll wait right here for your friends to eat and dress," he said when I straightened up, "then I'll escort you all downstairs. No reason to take any chances."

"I agree," I said, reaching toward the door. Then I spun around and punched Jackal in the stomach as hard as I could. He *huffed* with pain and surprise, and I saw anger glitter in his eyes. "That's for scaring me half to death," I said. "And I should hit you again."

He didn't retaliate, but he radiated a distinct warning. "I would advise you not to."

I put my hands on my hips and stared him down. "So do you trust *me* not to betray *you*? All of you? Or do I still have to fear for my life?"

He put one finger against my cheek. A gesture of affection or another warning, I couldn't be sure. "Chessie-girl, you're even happier than I am that Malachi is dead."

I felt a little spurt of fear. What had Jackal figured out? "What did you hear? Before you burst in to kill him." I was trying to remember what secrets I might have given away in that last desperate conversation with Malachi. *People know. About you. And me. And the queen.* Had I even spoken the words loudly enough for anyone else to catch them?

Jackal spread his hands to indicate innocence. "Nothing useful at all! And I was listening closely."

"So you still don't know why he was trying to find me."

"No, but you do," he said. "And I'll wager my life—and Pippa's and Morrissey's and JoJo's—that the reason is good enough to keep you silent until the day you die."

I said nothing for a moment, and he let his hands fall. I sighed. "You're right," I replied at last. "But I can't tell you what it is."

"I don't care," he said.

I nodded. We stood there another moment in silence, and then he jerked his head toward the door. "Get in there and wake them up. Then get out of here as fast as you can. The rest of us have work to do."

What with the morning being so eventful, I wasn't able to make it to Amanda Plaza in advance of my noon appointment, as I normally would have tried to do. True to his word, Jackal had waited outside the door of the green bedroom until the three of us emerged, dressed and fed. With a little effort, I'd transferred myself to Red's body before we left the room, and I took his arm as he led us all down the stairs.

"Chessie tells me I should give you a good hard slap, but she won't tell me why," I said provocatively.

Jackal laughed. "Chessie shouldn't be telling other people to do things that will get them in trouble," he responded.

I squeezed his arm. "A lot of Chessie's ideas are pretty dumb," I whispered, loudly enough for the echoes to overhear.

Jackal glanced back at Chessie in amusement then whispered back, "I've noticed."

He walked us to the wrought-iron gate, shut it behind us, and watched us till we were out of view. I wondered if I would ever be back inside that house again. At the moment, I was hoping the answer was no.

We'd only gone a few blocks before I paused to cast my consciousness back into Chessie's body. It was hard to believe that I used to be able to make the switch instantaneously, almost without thought, in the middle of some complex action—in the middle of a *conversation*. Someday, when I had a little time to sit and think, I was going to decide how I felt about this change.

Then I hurried on toward Amanda Plaza, my speed increasing as I got closer. Scar and Red jogged along close behind me. I had to make a tremendous effort to keep them from copying my movements so exactly that the people we passed would start to notice. I made sure the rhythm of their footfalls was a little different from mine, that Scar swung his arms and Red kept one hand closed around her long hair to prevent it from tangling as we ran. But I had to think about it the whole way.

It was a few minutes past noon before we crossed onto the red brick of the plaza. It was crowded as always, and I had to push my way past the clerks and gawkers and young lovers and rambunctious families to finally make it to the circle of statues at the center of the square. I could see Dezmen standing there, anxiously scanning the crowd. I wondered if I was even later than I'd thought.

When I was close enough for him to hear me, I called his name and saw his face light up with relief. I flung myself into his arms and had to fight to keep Scar and Red from repeating my action with his echoes. Surely it was my imagination that all four of them seemed disappointed.

"Chessie, I've been so worried!" Dezmen murmured in my ear as he held me close. "You're always here before I am, so I arrived about an hour ago, but you were nowhere in sight. I didn't know what to do—whether to go to your apartment—when I should panic and try to find Jackal—"

"Jackal. Right," I said, reluctantly pulling free of his embrace. I did hold on to his hand, though, lacing my pale fingers through his dark ones and pausing as always to admire the contrast. "That would have been an interesting search."

His grip tightened. "Did something happen?"

I nodded. "Yes. We need to talk. But not here. Did you see the king?"

"Not till this morning. Right before I came here, in fact."

"What did he think?"

"He believed me. Every word. He said he would have Ma—" At my look of warning, he glanced around the plaza and obviously changed what he was going to say. "He would make some arrests before the day was over."

"That's also going to be interesting," I said.

"Chessie, what *happened*?"

I tugged on his hand to lead him from the plaza. "Let's go somewhere we can talk."

We followed progressively quieter streets until we made it to the semi-abandoned commercial district we had visited once before, on the day we met with Ronin. The six of us were followed by two Pandrean guards who stuck closer than Bertie and Pippa ever had; they were big enough, and menacing enough, that people moved out of our way with alacrity. I reflected wryly that today of all days we were safe to walk the city without any protectors at our back, but I couldn't say that I minded knowing they were there.

Leaving the guards a good twenty yards away so they couldn't overhear our conversation, we clattered up the metal bridge that arched over this dispirited neighborhood. By this time, I had stopped trying to keep the echoes' movements distinct from my own, so when I fell back into Dezmen's arms, they melted into their own embraces. It felt utterly right.

"Malachi is dead," I whispered to Dezmen. "Jackal killed him this morning."

His hold tightened so abruptly that I was crushed to his chest. "What? *How?* What happened?"

Still whispering, I told the tale as concisely as I could. He uttered low exclamations of astonishment at the appropriate moments, and gasped with anger more than once. "So now he's dead," I finished up, "and pretty soon parts of his body will be scattered all over the city. And we can't tell anyone, ever, not even the king. I want this to be a mystery that's never solved."

"I agree," Dezmen said at once. "The fact that Malachi is dead is more important than anyone *knowing* he's dead. But it will cause mayhem for the inquisitor's staff as everyone tries to figure out what happened to him."

"That's not really my concern."

"No. Well! This is splendid news! I think I feel carefree for the first time since the day I met you in the gardens!" He paused and shook his head. "But I might never forgive Jackal for putting you at risk like that. Malachi could have *killed* you before Jackal and his friends broke into the room."

"Believe me, I thought he was going to. I was prepared to fling myself into one of my echoes to save myself, like I did the *last* time he tried to kill me … except … Dezmen … it's so odd." I tilted my head up, and he drew back just enough to look down at me. "Ever since you and I spent that first night together, I don't feel as connected to the echoes as I used to. Or maybe I feel *more* connected. I can't explain. I feel more and more like Chessie is the original and the other two are just shadows. I can still move between bodies, but it's harder. Do you think I'm going to lose that ability?"

He lifted a hand to stroke my hair. "I don't know. Maybe that—that—fluidity was a way your body came up with just to make sure you stayed alive. And as long as you needed to be three different people in order to survive, your body knew it had to retain that power. But if you truly start thinking of yourself as an original with echoes, that power will fade." He considered me a moment. "How do you *want* to see yourself? How do you *want* to live?"

I stared up at him. "I don't know. I like being one person who can dance between three bodies. I like the thought that I am never *trapped*. I can always get away. But I also like being..." I couldn't figure out how to express it. "I like being *me*. Chessie. All the time." I leaned in to kiss him. "I especially like it when I'm with you."

His face gathered in a slight frown of worry. "I don't want you to change on my behalf," he said seriously. "I don't want you to give up your mobility because you think it will please *me*. I love that you're so different. I love that you've created this incredible life, this marvelous charade, and lived inside it with such cleverness and grace. I think I would recognize *you* in any incarnation you chose. So only change if it pleases *you*."

"I'm not sure it pleases me, but I'm not sure I can control the change," I responded with a sigh. Then I caught my breath and added, "You said it."

"Said what?" But he was smiling.

"That you love me. Or, well, that you love things about me."

"I do love you," he said, and dropped a kiss on my mouth. "But don't we have some other very important things to talk about?"

"I can't imagine what," I said. "Oh, and I love you, too."

"Well, I love you, but we probably ought to discuss the conversation I had with Harold this morning."

"I don't love Harold—I love you—but I suppose we ought to talk about it," I agreed. "What did you tell him?"

"Everything. That we'd found the emeralds in the envoy pin, that we'd tracked the pattern down to a little temple in Empara, that we found the record of Tabitha's marriage to Malachi. And that everyone who seemed to know about the wedding—or about Leffert's attempt to assassinate the prince—has wound up dead."

"What did he say?"

"It was a lot to take in, as you might expect. He was enraged when he realized that Malachi was behind the attempt to kill Cormac—but I don't think he was surprised. I think it has been some time since he trusted the inquisitor. When I was done, he said, 'So Malachi tried to murder my son. There are guards in the palace who answer to no one but me. They will arrest him before the day is out. We will see a public execution within a week.' That sounded good to me," Dezmen added, "but I confess I was a little worried that Malachi might escape the net. He's so cunning and so ruthless."

I clung to Dezmen a little more tightly. "I agree. I think Harold might have found it difficult to arrest—or contain—Malachi. This way is more horrible, maybe, but better."

"Did Jackal realize *why* Malachi was so interested in finding you?"

I stood for a moment with my forehead pressed against Dezmen's chest. "I don't know," I said at last. "He said he didn't know and he didn't care. He said he locked Scar and Red in their room so they wouldn't be witnesses. He doesn't seem to have realized that they're my echoes, and he doesn't seem to have realized who I am." I lifted my head to give him a sober look. "But Jackal trades in information. And he's a smart man. So I wouldn't be surprised if he's figured it out."

Dezmen kissed my nose. "I love you," he said, probably thinking I might have forgotten. "Do you care if he knows? We don't want anyone to learn that Tabitha is your mother, obviously, but will it matter if Jackal finds out you're a noblewoman with echoes?"

I hesitated. "I'm not sure I'm going to be able to keep it a secret from anyone for much longer," I said at last. "I can't see my way clear yet, but I don't think I'm going to be able to go back to my old life." I thought that over a moment, trying to imagine how I would explain my situation to Dallie, to my landlady, to Nico and Brianna. "Maybe

I just disappear from that life without letting anyone know what's happened to me. Doesn't that sound easier?"

He watched me steadily. "You've done it before."

I nodded.

"But you might find it harder this time," he added. "I think there might be too many people in your life right now for you to just walk away from it."

I gave a faint laugh. He was right. It seemed too cruel to make people who cared about me wonder and worry what disaster might have come my way. All these years of trying to keep myself solitary, secretive, separate, and I had still managed to accrue a small band of friends. I had to confess I was surprised. "Did you tell the king about me?" I asked.

"I wanted to, but I promised you I wouldn't, so I didn't," he said. "Besides, I had given him so many other things to think about!"

"So he doesn't know Tabitha and Malachi had a child."

"No. Just that they were married."

"Of course, that's bad enough," I said. "His own marriage is a sham, and his daughter illegitimate—if she *is* his daughter."

"We didn't even get into that," Dezmen said. "I'm sure he'll start thinking through all the implications once he can focus on anything except Malachi. I do not envy anyone in the royal household the week they are about to have."

"No," I said with a sigh. "But since I've had a bad week myself, I can't feel too sorry for them."

Dezmen drew me closer and kissed the top of my head. "No more bad weeks for you," he whispered. "No more bad days. No more bad minutes. Nothing ahead but safety and security and laughter and love."

Impossible, of course—no one went through life without tribulations and setbacks and sudden, heart-stopping bouts of pain. But for the first time in my life I was prepared to believe that better options lay ahead—that I could welcome the advent of each new day instead of wondering what terrors it might hold. For the first time, I was willing to hope.

CHAPTER TWENTY-FIVE

Three days later I met King Harold for the first time.

I had, as much as possible, resumed my ordinary existence for those three days, mostly because I had the sense that this was my last chance—that I would soon be bidding goodbye to these people, these places, and these routines. I struggled a bit to keep in Red's shape the one night that I worked at the tavern, but I blamed my absentmindedness on a headache and no one seemed to find my behavior peculiar.

Malachi's disappearance was the talk of Camarria, from the drawing rooms at the palace to the loading docks on the southern edge of town. In polite society, Dezmen told me, the speculation was all about whether he had come to financial ruin through poor investments or hurriedly decamped after an affair with some high noblewoman whose husband threatened exposure. But in Sweetwater, the conversations were full of vindictiveness and glee.

"You mark my words, he'll turn up dead," I heard more than one half-drunk patron say with conviction. "A man like that doesn't give up his place just because he's afraid of a little scandal. He didn't run away. He's not in hiding. He's dead. And that calls for another beer."

"What does the king think happened to him?" I asked my cousin Nico when I had dinner with him and Brianna on the second night.

"He's baffled. And angry," Nico said. "I gather he learned something damning about my uncle a few days ago and was preparing to bring him to justice—and let me tell you, that would have been a public exhibition like nothing this city has ever seen before! So many people hate Malachi that there would have been riots in the street as people lobbied for his execution."

I leaned my elbows on the table and regarded him. "You don't sound overly sad," I remarked. "Are you worried about him?"

Brianna gave him a wry look. "Yes, Nico, how do you feel about your uncle?"

He made a face. "He was always good to me. I owe my position to him—everything I have achieved in this life. And yet he is a hard man who can be frighteningly brutal. I have tried to respect him, but I've never been able to love him. I find myself more shocked at his disappearance than grieving."

"What do *you* think happened to him?" I asked.

He shook his head. "I can't imagine he had any secret so terrible that he would fear it coming to light," he said. "I think he must be dead. And I think we'll never know how or why."

"So what happens to all the inquisitors who worked for him?" I said. "Hey, maybe you'll be promoted to his position."

Brianna rolled her eyes and Nico laughed.

"Not a chance," he said cheerfully. "Whatever distrust the king had for Malachi seems to have extended to me. I was never my uncle's confidante, but Harold doesn't know that, and I can't blame him for looking at me with suspicion." He shook his head. "I've been thinking about leaving the life. Maybe now is the right time."

Brianna toasted me with her glass of water. "Yet another good thing to come out of Malachi's disappearance," she said.

I didn't say so out loud, but I agreed with her. There didn't seem to be a single reason to mourn his passing. I returned her toast with one of my own.

Dezmen had refused to spend another night apart from me—saying, "Who knows what new scheme Jackal might cook up to put you in danger?"—and my apartment wasn't big enough for all six of us to sleep comfortably. So we spent the next few nights at one of the luxurious hotels clustered near the palace. It was an establishment that catered to high nobles, so a good number of the rooms were outfitted with multiple beds designed to accommodate echoes. The beds were so comfortable, in fact, that I had a hard time forcing myself to climb out of mine every morning—although perhaps that was because I was so reluctant to leave Dezmen's side. Indeed, the first two days, it was close to noon before either of us managed to be dressed and out the door, and the only reason we beat that deadline on the third day was because the king was expecting us that morning. I had agreed to let Dezmen tell him my story, and he wanted to meet me.

I'd had the foresight to bring some of my Counting Day outfits with me from the apartment, so this morning I dressed Scar and Red and myself in matching ensembles and tried to style our hair exactly the same. The lengths were still all so different that I wasn't entirely successful, but we certainly looked a great deal alike when I finally surveyed us in the mirror.

"Do you think Harold will believe I am who I say I am?" I asked Dezmen, who murmured his approval of my appearance.

"Looking at you, I don't think he'll have a choice."

I was nervous as we crossed the three streets that separated our hotel from the palace and nervous as we arrived in the grand echoing foyer and explained to Lourdes that we were there to the see the king. She gave me such a thorough inspection that I wondered if she would recognize Chessie-the-messenger in her new guise as a noblewoman with two echoes. She was, like Jackal, highly intelligent and habitually observant, and I would never be surprised at what she was able to piece together. But this morning, at least, she didn't seem to draw any inconvenient conclusions.

"I will take you up to see the king," she said.

I was too edgy to pay much attention to my surroundings except to be overwhelmed by the sheer size and opulence of the hallways as we passed through them. Paintings, statuary, tapestries, rugs, decorative pieces of silver, suits of armor—the palace was stuffed with lavish details. I couldn't take them all in.

By contrast, the room that we eventually entered was simple, restful, and spare. The furnishings were all gray and muted maroon;

the only embellishment was the sunlight pouring through two tall windows. This was a place where a person living in this overcrowded palace might come to think in silence.

Harold was standing in the center of the room, flanked by his three echoes. All of them wore expressions that were part serious, part curious, and I thought all of them looked wearier than they had the last time I had caught sight of the royal family almost five weeks ago. A lifetime ago.

"Lord Dezmen and Lady Chezelle," Lourdes announced us.

It was the first time someone had added a title to my name, and I almost corrected her. But she had dropped a curtsey and left the room, closing the door behind her, before I could figure out what to say.

"Majesty," Dezmen intoned, performing a deep and graceful bow. I hurriedly offered my own curtsey, though graceful wouldn't have been the word to describe it. When I straightened, I found Harold's intent gaze fixed on my face.

For a long moment, there was only silence in the room.

"So you are Malachi's daughter. Or so you say," the king greeted me.

"I believe I am," I said in a low voice. "But I have very little evidence to support my claim. The woman who raised me wholeheartedly believed Malachi was my father. A woman who was married to Malachi's brother says I look like their sister."

"And don't forget Malachi tried to kill you, on more than one occasion," Dezmen added.

"Yes," I answered, "but apparently Malachi has tried to kill many people, and none of the others were his children, so that doesn't seem like proof." I pulled out the emerald necklace that lay hidden under the neckline of my dress. "I also have this. I have been told that Malachi has a ring that features the same design."

Harold nodded. "Such a ring has been found among his belongings, though no one remembers ever seeing him wear it." He tipped his chin at Dezmen. "He tells me that the same symbol can be found inside a small temple near Devenetta land."

"Yes."

"Where there is a document recording the marriage of Tabitha Devenetta to Malachi Burken twenty-four years ago."

I had to take a deep breath. "Yes."

"And you believe you are the child of that union?"

I lifted my hands in an uncertain gesture. "Only because I believe Malachi is my father—and because I know the circumstances surrounding Tabitha during the time when I was born."

Harold nodded and spoke deliberately. "She was confined to a small, solitary property where no one was allowed to see her for several months. All while I was negotiating with her parents for the opportunity to marry her."

"Yes," I said again, keeping my voice steady with an effort. "It seems like she could have borne and disposed of a baby during that period of time."

"Again, that is hardly proof," the king said. "In fact, it would appear that the only people who would know with certainty whether you are their child would be the queen and the inquisitor."

He didn't have to say it, but it was obvious what he was thinking: *And neither of them would confirm the story.* Well, Malachi wouldn't be able to, of course, but I couldn't see any reason why Tabitha would be willing to.

Dezmen spoke up. "Excuse me, majesty, but my guess is that Tabitha's parents also know the truth. Whether or not they would acknowledge it is another question."

"Like the queen herself, they have every incentive to lie," Harold said. I thought I heard an old fury threaded through his voice.

Now I held my hands palm-up, almost a gesture of surrender. "It doesn't matter to me if you believe I'm Malachi's child. Or the queen's. I haven't come here to ask you to recognize me. I'm here because Lord Dezmen thinks you should know I exist, since that might affect how you view your queen—and your daughter. But *my* life does not change whether you believe me or not."

That made him smile, though the expression was small and sad. I wondered how often he had cause to smile these days. "As it happens, I think you're telling the truth," he said. "But maybe only because I am willing to believe any despicable behavior on the part of my queen."

There didn't seem to be anything useful to say in reply to that, so Dezmen and I were both silent. Harold's attention briefly went past me, and I knew what he was looking at. "And because you have two echoes," he added, "which would indicate at least one of your parents is a high noble."

"So I understand."

He returned his gaze to my face. "And yet, I am not as convinced by echoes as I might once have been. Just this summer, in fact, a lady's maid played the part of her mistress's echo for several weeks and fooled everyone in the palace."

"Did she? That's impressive," I murmured.

"Of course, we were not watching her closely, or we might have noticed mistakes," the king added. "Perhaps you would be willing to make a demonstration for me? Something simple. Place them somewhere in the room where they would not be able to see you, and then go through a series of complicated motions."

"Certainly," I said.

It was a matter of a few moments for me to step toward the back of the room while Scar and Red stepped forward. Somewhat ostentatiously, we all closed our eyes. Then I went through the three poses assumed by the triple goddess, holding my hands out to either side for justice, before me for mercy, and above me for joy. Just in case the king thought that might have been choreographed, I then swayed back and forth, stood for a moment on one foot, then offered a low bow. I couldn't see them, of course, but I knew the echoes copied me exactly, every movement timed perfectly to coincide with mine.

"Enough," Harold said after a couple of minutes. I opened my eyes and watched him gravely. He went on, "I cannot see any way you could fake such a performance. As I say, the presence of echoes indicates that, at the very least, you were born to a member of the nobility. I am inclined to accept that the rest of your story is true as well. But even if it is, I must think very carefully about how I am to proceed."

Dezmen held his hand out to me, and I slowly made my way to the front of the room, while Scar and Red stepped back until they were behind me once more.

"I will assist you in any way I can," I said, though I certainly hadn't intended to make that offer when I came into the room. "If you think it would be helpful for me to meet the queen ... for her to be confronted with the fact of my existence ... " I couldn't get out the rest of the words. I could hardly believe I had spoken any of them. What was I expecting? Did I believe my mother would see my face and dissolve in tears of tenderness and remorse? Did I think she would murmur my name, then cover her eyes, so overcome with emotion that she wouldn't be able to look at me?

Or would she be shocked—furious—that I had managed to escape Malachi's violent attention? Would she see me as the great, explosive hazard that I really was, the embodiment of her destruction—the face and hands and living spirit that made every second of her life a traitorous lie?

Would she want to love me or would she already hate me? Could I bear to find out?

Some of my agitation must have showed on my face because Dezmen tightened his grip in a comforting way, and the king regarded me with something that might have been sympathy. "Do not cherish any romantic illusions about your mother's heart," Harold said softly. "If I had to guess, I would say Malachi did not act against you without her knowledge or without her consent."

I nodded and looked down at my feet. "I see. I'm sure you're right. I just thought if it would help *you*—"

Dezmen spoke up. "My preference would be to *not* tell the queen of Chessie's existence," he said. "Just in case that puts her life in danger again. If Malachi has disappeared and Tabitha believes Chessie is dead—then Chessie has nothing left to fear. *Chezelle*, I mean."

"I would tell my sons the story. They will advise me on this matter in the coming days," Harold said. "But otherwise, I am happy to keep the secret." He nodded at me. "But perhaps Chezelle feels differently. If she wants to try to secure her father's inheritance, claim a place for herself in society—"

"I don't," I said quickly.

Harold regarded me. "Well, we must construct *some* identity for you," he said. "Unless you mean to entirely disappear again."

I risked a glance at Dezmen. "I don't," I repeated.

Dezmen squeezed my hand. "I was thinking perhaps some variation of the story you always believed," he said to me. "Your father was a noble who seduced and abandoned a servant girl. She found herself raising a child with echoes, and made her way to Pandrea, where I found all of you. I brought you to the king's attention, and he made some slight monetary reparation." He finished up on an interrogative note, glancing at Harold.

The king nodded. "The crown will be seizing all of Malachi's assets. There should be enough there to provide you a modest dowry. No one needs to know how you were funded."

"Yes, but I—I don't need funding. I don't have plans to—attend balls at the palace or—or—visit the ladies of Banchura…" I couldn't even think of what activities to say I was spurning since I had no idea how high nobles passed their time.

"You may live as quietly as you like," the king said. "But you do deserve some compensation for the life you have endured so far, and I am happy to provide it to you. What you choose to do going forward is up to you."

Dezmen squeezed my hand again and grinned at me. "I'll help you come up with ideas," he promised.

I smiled back somewhat tremulously, before turning to drop a small curtsey in Harold's direction. "Thank you, sire."

Dezmen's attention was back on the king. "If I may ask, what do *you* plan to do going forward?"

"I don't see my way clear," the king admitted. "I could retrieve the record book from the Empara temple and confront Tabitha with it. The document is evidence enough for me to arrest her and nullify our own marriage. I could arrest her parents as well, and confiscate all the Devenetta lands. I would be within my rights to do so."

"That way lies war," Dezmen said softly.

The king nodded. "Orenza is still smarting from the death of Lady Marguerite. I assume you heard about the grievous acts of violence that occurred along the Charamon Road shortly after she was executed. We have managed to smooth things over with Empara and Alberta, and I am willing to see my son Jordan married to a woman of Alberta if that will ease tensions even more. But Orenza is still simmering. If I cast off the queen, Empara will surely rise in rebellion, and Orenza will gladly join the fight. At that point, I can't imagine Alberta will hold back, even if a marriage has been consummated. If everything you say is true—and I believe it is—my queen has committed treason and might even now be plotting against me. But to denounce her might be more of a danger than to keep her close. I must tread very carefully."

He was silent a moment before he added, "And then there is my daughter. To treat Tabitha as she deserves would be to brand the princess a bastard and subject her to great humiliation."

I spared a moment to think how odd it was that a street girl like me was the legitimate child while the pampered princess was the one who had been born out of wedlock. What a reversal of roles! How little the marriage certificate mattered to me, but how greatly it would change Annery's life! If it were revealed …

Dezmen raised another point in a careful voice. "If people learn of the connection between Malachi and Tabitha, there might also be uncomfortable questions about the princess's parentage."

Harold offered us another grim smile. "Oh, Annery is my daughter, I am quite certain of it. Some years ago, my advisors met with me to insist I needed another heir and that I must at least try to produce one with my wife. You do not need to know the details of my arrangements with Tabitha, but it was clear to me early on that fidelity would not be one of her virtues. Thirteen years ago we made a deal—in return for some concessions from me, Tabitha would bear my child—and she would agree to be attended night and day by women of my choosing until such time as she conceived. We were both relieved at how quickly she became pregnant so we no longer had to continue the attempts to procreate."

It was embarrassing enough to hear the situation described; it must have been agonizing to live through. I looked down at the floor, and Dezmen just said, "Ah."

"So I must consider the cost to Annery before I brand her mother a bigamist," Harold said. "I am fond of her, I must admit, and I do not want to see her hurt."

"I do not envy you any of the choices you have to make," Dezmen said.

Harold's cold smile returned. "No. For the most part, I do not believe my life has been an enviable one. Though there are many who would be astonished to hear it."

Dezmen bowed. "As always, Pandrea stands ready to aid you in any way it can."

"It's a great comfort to know," Harold said. "Your support has been invaluable—bitter though your news has sometimes been."

What Dezmen might have answered I couldn't guess, but he didn't have a chance to speak. There was a slight commotion in the hallway and a woman's imperious voice declaring, "I *will* see him, and I will see him now," before the door slammed open and Queen Tabitha strode in. She looked furious and magnificent, all flashing eyes and glittering jewels and fiery colors—deep red for her, a slightly paler crimson for her echoes.

"I am convinced you know something you're not telling me," she exclaimed, stalking past Dezmen and me as if she didn't even see us.

By contrast, I could look at nothing and no one else. *The queen. My mother.*

The queen.

My mother.

"The inquisitor has been missing for three days, and you act as if it is a matter of no concern," she went on heedlessly. "Should I hire my *own* soldiers and send them out looking for Malachi? Do you not care at all about the whereabouts of the man who keeps order in your kingdom?"

"I am very eager to find Malachi, and I have men scouring the city," Harold replied evenly. "You shall be among the first to know when he's returned to us."

She appeared dissatisfied with this calm answer. "I wish I could believe you."

"Perhaps we can discuss it later when my guests are gone," the king said in a steely voice. "Tabitha, you remember Lord Dezmen, of course? And this is his friend—ah, Chessie."

Tabitha shifted impatiently in our direction, clearly uninterested in social niceties at the moment. She glanced at Dezmen and murmured, "Very good to see you again," before turning to look at me.

For an instant our gazes locked. My skin ran with heat, then cooled to the bone. This close, I could see the color of her eyes, a complicated green speckled with gold. Her mouth was a petulant twist; her auburn hair framed her face with dramatic color. Twenty-four years ago, she would have been just this spirited, just this defiant, and even more beautiful. She looked like a woman capable of doing almost anything if it meant she could get what she wanted. She could marry a man. Abandon a man. Bear a child in secret.

Throw the child away.

No hint of recognition flickered across her face. She held the gaze barely a moment before looking back at Harold. "I won't keep you," she said in a quieter tone. "But I am glad to know you are searching for Malachi. I feel uneasy when he is away from the palace. Sometimes I think his vigilance is the only thing that keeps any of us safe."

"Yes, his devotion has been impossible to overlook," Harold said dryly. I wondered if that was a faint flush that crossed Tabitha's cheeks. "I will keep you informed."

Tabitha nodded at the king, nodded at Dezmen, and ignored me completely as she and her echoes swept from the room. The three of us were silent for a moment before the king said, "Well. I believe we have covered everything for the day. If you learn anything about Malachi, I trust you will let me know."

Dezmen bowed again and I followed the pressure of his hand to offer yet another curtsey. "Of course, majesty. You can count on Pandrea."

"Thank you. You both may go."

I couldn't wait to get out of the palace with all its opulence, intrigue, heartache, and heaviness. I practically towed Dezmen down the elaborate hallways and through the echoing foyer. Finally we were outside in the chaotic courtyard amid the vendors and visitors and workers and gawkers. The sun was high but ineffective; the air had a cold and mealy feel, as if studded with particles of ice. I came to a halt so I could fall into Dezmen's arms and burrow into his warmth. Around us, my echoes and his echoes similarly sought comfort from each other.

"Well, that was horrible," I said, my voice muffled against his jacket.

"Which part of it?"

"All of it. He's so sad and she's so terrible! And the princess's life might be ruined, and the provinces could go to war. All in all, I think it was better when I was living my own obscure life and nobody knew who I was."

Dezmen lifted my chin up. "I love you," he reminded me. "And none of this is your fault."

"I love you, too, but it *feels* like it's my fault."

"You're the most innocent player in the whole game. Even Harold is partially to blame for courting a girl who didn't want to marry him. But all you did was arrive in the world because two people loved each other when they shouldn't have."

I tilted my head as I considered what he'd said. "It doesn't sound so bad when you put it like that," I said. "Although, then I remember how awful those two people were, and I feel dreadful again."

He kissed the top of my head and then turned me forward again, urging me to start walking. "Well, I certainly don't want you to feel dreadful," he said. "What can I do to cheer you up? Should we go to your apartment and start packing your possessions? Should we look for rooms to rent so we can move in together? Should we find a place to eat lunch? You're dressed up so fine we could go to the fanciest place in the city. We could sit there and discuss your future, since I think we've finally put your past to rest."

There was so much to talk about, so much to do, but the conference at the palace had left me so drained I didn't have the strength to start planning my new life or dismantling my old one. I just wanted to be someplace quiet, someplace beautiful, someplace where I could think about how strange and marvelous it was that Dezmen was now a part of my life. All the turmoil had been worth it if it brought me this single gift, I thought. I knew it was a complex treasure that came with its own tears and sorrows; I didn't know much about love, but I was pretty certain it required as much hard work as basic survival. Maybe more, because its returns were so much greater. I was willing to do the work—even looking forward to investing the effort—but right now I just wanted to exist.

"I know it's cold out, but let's go to the gardens," I said in a low voice. "Let's remember the beginning."

"What, the assassination attempt and almost drowning in the pool?"

That made me laugh, and that made me stop in the middle of the street and throw my arms around him again. "No," I said. "The true beginning. When I caught my very first glimpse of *you.*"

Be sure to read the third Uncommon Echoes book, *Echo in Amethyst*.

An Echo and an Original

Lady Elyssa despises her echoes—the creatures who look just like her and copy her every move. But it's only the echoes that mark her as a high noble, someone elite enough to marry the king's youngest son, Jordan. She can't get rid of the echoes, so instead she amuses herself by torturing them when no one is looking.

But there's something Elyssa doesn't know: Her casual cruelty has brought one of the echoes to life. And this echo, Hope, is learning to think and speak and act on her own.

And there's something else Elyssa doesn't know: Hope has witnessed her secret meetings with revolutionaries bent on starting a war and overthrowing the king. And Hope has made friends in high places—very high places.

ABOUT THE AUTHOR

Photo by Todd Kneib

Sharon Shinn has been part of the science fiction and fantasy world since 1995, when she published her first novel, *The Shape-Changer's Wife,* which won the Crawford Award. In 2010, the *Romantic Times Magazine* gave Shinn the Career Achievement Award in the Science Fiction/Fantasy category, and in 2012, *Publisher's Weekly* magazine named *The Shape of Desire* one of the best science fiction/fantasy books of the year. Three of her novels have been named to the ALA's lists of Best Books for Young Adults (now Best Fiction for Young Adults). She has had books translated into Polish, German, Spanish, and Japanese. She can be found at sharonshinn.net and facebook.com/sharonshinnbooks.

ABOUT THE PUBLISHER

This book is published on behalf of the author by the Ethan Ellenberg Literary Agency.
https://ethanellenberg.com
Email: agent@ethanellenberg.com